ST. MARTIN'S

W9-DIY-759

MINOTAUR
MYSTERIES

GET A CLUE!

Be the first to hear the latest mystery book news…

With the St. Martin's Minotaur monthly newsletter,
you'll learn about the hottest new Minotaur books,
receive advance excerpts from newly published works,
read exclusive original material from featured mystery
writers, and be able to enter to win free books!

Sign up on the Minotaur Web site at:
www.minotaurbooks.com

Mansions of the Dead

"Sarah Stewart Taylor has written an exciting mystery featuring characters that are so easy to like . . . The heroine . . . is spunky, sweet, and sparkling, and readers will want to read more books featuring this dynamic character."

—*Midwest Book Review*

"An intelligent tale, leaving readers begging to know more."

—*Booklist*

"This moody, atmospheric novel will appeal to fans of darker cozies."

—*Publishers Weekly*

O' Artful Death

"Taylor does a lovely job of setting an atmospheric scene and luring us inside."

—Marilyn Stasio, *The New York Times Book Review*

"[*O' Artful Death*] rings subtle—and enormously satisfying —changes on the venerable tried-and-true."

—*Newsday*

"A strikingly atmospheric debut. The writing is crisp and the characters all quite forcefully alive, especially Sweeney."

—*Denver Post*

"An elegantly wrought first mystery with layers within layers like carved ivory balls . . . Rich and rewarding reading."

—*Booklist*

"A nicely puzzled plot, a closely confined rural setting, remarkable characterizations, and eminently readable prose."

—*Library Journal*

Also by Sarah Stewart Taylor

O' ARTFUL DEATH

Available from St. Martin's/Minotaur Paperbacks

MANSIONS
OF THE DEAD

Sarah Stewart Taylor

St. Martin's Paperbacks

MANSIONS OF THE DEAD

Copyright © 2004 by Sarah Stewart Taylor.
Excerpt from *Judgment of the Grave* © 2005 by Sarah Stewart Taylor.

Cover photo © Dennis Deganan/Corbis.

Library of Congress Catalog Card Number: 2003070718

ISBN: 0-312-98595-9
EAN: 9780312-98595-0

Printed in the United States of America

St. Martin's Press hardcover edition / July 2004
St. Martin's Paperbacks edition / June 2005

St. Martin's Paperbacks are published by St. Martin's Press, 175 Fifth Avenue, New York, NY 10010.

10 9 8 7 6 5 4 3 2 1

For Matt,
for everything

PROLOGUE

❧

1863

It was Belinda's favorite time of year, the three or four weeks of early spring when winter was transformed into something else, some halfway season that smelled of percolating earth and trickling streams. The grass was still brown and sickly-looking from the long winter, but when she bent her head to inhale the wet scent of the ground, she could see a fur of pale green growth below that promised a stronger green, could feel the hesitant sun that whispered its promise in the cool air.

She was on her way to her family grave plot on Asphodel Path, in one of the newest sections of Mount Auburn Cemetery. They were expanding the cemetery and she was aware of the movements of the workers as they carted soil to build more new roads. On the weekend there had been visitors thronging the little avenues—it was the custom now to come for a stroll among the headstones, seeking respite from the busy city, from news of sons and brothers and sweethearts killed by the Confederates—but today the grounds were silent. While she'd heard the workers laughing together as she'd arrived the first day, they seemed to be trying to respect her privacy now.

She had come nearly every day since he had died. And she had found that she had begun to look forward to her trips to Mount Auburn, the only time of day when she was really alone. She liked wandering along the little lanes and reading the stones. There was one that she found herself walking by nearly every time she went, a simple white marble likeness of an angel with the words, "My wife and child."

The ground had not thawed sufficiently for burial and it would be months before Charles's monument would be ready, but she had been trying to tend to the plot with a dull little pair of sewing scissors, eventually giving up and using her fingers to pull up the dead weeds and grass by their barren roots.

Belinda smoothed the necklace that she wore at her throat, made of hair carefully braided into a chain. Charles had possessed such dark hair, a rich brown lit with auburn, and it hadn't grayed much at all, even during his long illness. It had grown out in those last months—he had had a strange superstition about cutting it—and by working the locks of hair around a mold to make twenty intricately netted balls and then stringing them together, she had been able to make a necklace that reached the third button of her dress. After preparing the locks of hair with soda water according to the instructions in *Godey's Lady's Book*, she had sat alone in the parlor night after night with the strange little hairwork table that the gardener had made for her. When she was finished, she had taken the necklace to her father's jeweler, who had put on the clasp.

The pursuit had pleased her; it had been something to do during those strange evenings when if she didn't miss him exactly, she missed the bulk of him across the dinner table or in the parlor, where he had always sat with the paper, drinking port while she read or worked at her embroidery.

She shook her head to clear away the image of his sickbed, the stained rags littering the floor, the housemaid scurrying around nervously, crossing herself as his time neared. It was funny how she had become attuned to his condition in those last few days, and she had known he was going to die before the doctor knew. His color, and the way the room smelled, had told her that she would soon be a widow.

"I'm sorry, ma'am, I have to bring a load of earth by and I wouldn't want to be disturbing you, ma'am." She started and turned to find one of the laborers behind her, standing with a cart. Irish. She stepped back.

"That's all right. Go ahead. It won't bother me," she said, looking into a pair of blue eyes, a boyish face. He wasn't very old. Not much older than she was. Twenty-three, she said to herself. I am only twenty-three and already I am a widow.

It was her own fault, what had happened. She had married a man as old as her father because she had wanted an easy life. She had been just a girl, prone to daydreaming. She had liked to sketch. That was how she had known he had an interest in her. They had met in Newport, at the Ocean House, where her father liked to go for the sea air. She had been sketching in the music room of the hotel one evening and he had wandered in. Her father knew him through business and they had spoken the evening before. When he came in, holding a newspaper and looking uncomfortable, she had had the idea to sketch him in his discomfort and had asked his permission. He had smiled as though it surprised him and agreed, and it wasn't until later that she had looked at the sketch and seen something in his face that made her stomach knot.

That night she had played cards with him and chatted flirtatiously. She felt somehow that she was acting out a script and when she examined her own actions she was ashamed. The next day she had agreed to stroll along the cliffs with him.

When they were back in Boston, her father had asked her to come into the library and he had told her about the proposal. "He is aware that the age difference is a problem," he told her, stammering a little. "It is up to you. I admit that I always thought of you marrying for love, someone who could match your high spirits. I wish that your mother were still alive to talk to you about the demands of marriage, about the difficulties in living with another person. But he is a good man and I don't have to tell you that we have been hard hit in the markets. It won't be many months before we have to sell this house. It's up to you to decide how you want to live."

She had told him she would think about it, but she had known, even as she left the room, what her answer would be.

It was her own fault. God would punish her. She knew this now. God would punish her for her thoughts and . . . for her actions. She had not been a good Christian wife to him.

She sat down on the grass, feeling the dampness soaking through the wool of her dress. The cold shocked her skin. But the dress was dark and the stain would not show. She smiled a little at this. No, she had not been a good Christian wife to him at all. Still . . . if she was truthful with herself, she had never felt so free.

ONE

The first thing Becca Dearborne noticed was Brad's angelfish.

It had flipped onto its side, its eyes staring into the bubbling water, its catlike whiskers trailing. The other fish—a few more angels, a swarm of tiny, flashing tetras, a grumpy catfish—swam around nervously, as though they knew something was wrong. She extracted a little green net from the jumble of supplies next to the tank, bottles of chemicals and fish food, thermometers, a pair of rubber gloves, then scooped out the dead fish and took it through to the bathroom, where she flushed it down the toilet and rinsed out the net.

"It must have died in the night," she said softly to Jaybee. "Otherwise, he'd never have left it there." She put a finger to the glass and felt something in her stomach, a pang, of sadness perhaps, for the fish.

"Yeah. He'd probably have taken it to the hospital." Jaybee, who had been Brad's friend since ninth grade and his roommate since their freshman year of college, liked to make fun of Brad's obsession with the aquarium. He spent a fortune buying special plants and various concoctions that were supposed to kill bad bacteria or add good bacteria, or change the pH of the water. And he spent hours testing the water and taking notes on how various changes affected the health of the fish. Becca, who had known Brad even longer than Jaybee had, thought she understood. She could stare into the depths of the aquarium for minutes on end, mesmerized by the movements of the fish in the water, lazy one moment, quick the next.

"I'm taking a shower," she said. Jaybee reached for her arm and pulled her toward him, kissing her long and hard. Dizzy, she pulled away and escaped into the bathroom.

Under the hot spray of water she arched her neck, soaping her hair and body and feeling the tightly knotted muscles along her shoulders give way. It felt so good that she turned the tap toward hot until she could feel her nerves scream and stood under the scalding spray for a few seconds before twisting the handle to off. Drip, drop, came the final water from the tap.

Becca wrapped herself in a bath towel, and wiped a little window in the steam on the mirror. Her face seemed blurry to her, her eyes too big, the whites cloudy, the color of weak tea. She squeezed her eyes shut, then opened them again, but she looked the same and she turned away from the mirror, going out into the living room where Jaybee was standing in the middle of the area rug—a castoff from his older brother's apartment—looking perplexed.

"What's the matter?" she whispered, coming up behind him and pressing her body against his. Jaybee—his long back, his grin, his soft, auburny hair, his right index finger, bent from a childhood accident with a car door—made her feel somehow at a loss. She felt displaced, almost sick when she was with him, a completely new experience. The three other sexual relationships she'd had in her twenty years—with her boarding school boyfriend and two casual college flings—had seemed a sort of kindly, benign prostitution. By sleeping with those boys, for they were boys, she had secured companionship, affection, dates for important events, and presents on her birthday. It had seemed, in each case, a worthwhile exchange. But this was something else. She had woken up the night before to find him missing—he'd gone outside for some air, he told her when he came back to bed—and she had experienced the most profound panic she had ever experienced. She had felt that she would do anything to feel his back against her arms again as she did now.

"I don't know," Jaybee said, looking around the room. "The apartment looks different. Weird." Becca looked around too. Due to Jaybee's influence, the apartment was usually messy. There were books piled on every surface, dirty dishes in the sink, bikes and helmets tumbled on the floor behind the black couch. But he was right: there was something different about the room. All of the kitchen cabinets were open, as were the doors of the entertainment center in the living room. There was a jumbled pile of tools and videotapes and odds and ends on the floor beneath the television stand. The room smelled of vomit.

Becca felt cold all of a sudden. "He was really drunk, and really out of it. Maybe he just . . ."

"Yeah." Jaybee tried to smile. "That's right. He was pretty trashed, wasn't he?"

"I'm going to get dressed." She walked past Brad's closed door and into Jaybee's room, where she hurriedly put on her clothes, toweling her hair for a second and then going back out into the living room. Jaybee was standing in front of Brad's door.

"You going to check on him?" She was making a conscious effort to stay calm, though she knew something was wrong. Later, she would wonder if it was Jaybee's pale, terrified face or something less tangible that had made her so afraid.

Jaybee didn't say anything. He just put a hand on Brad's doorknob and turned it, hesitating a few minutes before pushing the door open. "Brad?" Over his shoulder, she saw the gravestone photographs that Brad had all over his walls. The black-and-white images seemed to crowd the room.

And then she heard nothing but the waterfall rush in her own head as she followed Jaybee in and saw Brad, lying there on the bed.

"Jesus!" Jaybee whispered. "Jesus!"

TWO

꩜

Detective Timothy Quinn stood in the doorway, preparing himself, as he had only done a couple of times in the year he'd been working homicide, for his first sight of an unnaturally deceased human body.

This one was male, young, lying facedown on a large double bed pushed against one wall. The body was naked except for a pair of boxer shorts. The shorts, which Quinn fixated on for a moment in order to avoid looking at the rest of the body, were blue madras, well made. A working-class, Hanes-briefs-wearing boy from Somerville, where people didn't shop at Brooks Brothers, Quinn thought back to college and knew this was high-quality stuff. Though he was later ashamed to recognize it, they made him sit up and take notice.

The boy was thin but muscular, a tennis player or a runner perhaps, his back still dark with last summer's tan. Because his arms were tied to the bedposts—with bright, striped neckties, Quinn saw—the lean muscles across his back stood out in stark relief. His arms looked oddly stiff. Rigor setting in, Quinn thought, checking his watch. It was now 2 P.M. That meant he'd been dead for around twelve hours. Early this morning. He'd taken his last breath sometime before the sun came up.

Beneath the clear plastic bag that covered his head and was secured around his neck with another tie, a jaunty red-and-blue-striped one, the boy's longish hair was a dark shadow. His face, pressed into the bedspread, could not be seen.

But Quinn could see the jewelry the kid was wearing. Around his neck, trailing down to the middle of his back like a snake, was a long, dark chain, made of twenty or so beads. Pinned to his boxer shorts, just over his left hip, were two brooches. One was white and had a drawing of a woman sitting in a graveyard, her head in her hands. The other was smaller and darker and had a crisscrossed design on the front. He suddenly remembered buying a shamrock brooch for his mother the Christmas he went away to college. "What a nice brooch," she'd exclaimed, pronouncing the double o.

"No, Ma, it's 'broach,'" he'd corrected her, pronouncing it like the clerk in the store in Amherst. She'd shot back that now he was a college boy he thought he knew everything. He almost smiled, thinking of the way she liked to take her American son down a peg in her Dublin brogue.

Someone had tried to put the last piece of jewelry, a gold locket on a chain, around the boy's neck, but the chain had caught on the plastic and was kind of half slung around the back of his head.

"You got any idea what this stuff is, Quinn?" Marino asked, a small smile on his lips. He was testing him. Quinn had already heard the kids who had found the body telling Marino what it was. They were sitting out in the living room now, the girl crying, the boy looking terrified. Quinn had made a note of how terrified the boy looked. The roommate, he'd told them. He was the dead boy's roommate. The girl was a friend of both of theirs, the dead boy and the roommate, though from the way the two of them were locked together on the couch, Quinn decided that they were a little more than friends. They'd come back because the shower in the girl's apartment wasn't working.

But Marino didn't know that. He just wanted to make Quinn look stupid. They had been working together for a year, ever since Quinn had been moved over to homicide after Marino's partner was stabbed by his wife during what the Cambridge police dispatcher would have referred to as a "domestic" and what Quinn had heard was a knockdown wife-beating session.

Quinn had been hoping for the transfer to homicide for four years, and he'd been—he realized now—a little eager probably. Marino was a compact, barrel-chested guy with a salt-and-pepper crew cut, a cauliflower ear from high school wrestling, and eyebrows that peaked in the centers. He loved paperback westerns and he always had five or six piled up on his desk, a couple tossed into the back of his car in case he got stuck somewhere without something to read. He didn't seem to read anything else and Quinn had always liked the idea that Marino got off on cowboys and ranchers' daughters and desert sunsets.

Marino resented the death of his partner, resented it because the way the guy had died, he was prevented from talking about him with the reverence that his colleagues used in talking about their own dead partners, killed heroically in the line of duty. And he resented his own place in the department, which Quinn had soon realized was somewhat insecure. Marino and Quinn got pulled off cases by the lieutenant in charge of the homicide division when they got thorny and Quinn knew that they weren't the first choice for anything, that they'd been put on this one because it it had happened on Sunday morning.

He also knew that Marino disliked him. Quinn's second week on the job, he'd come back from a coffee break and overheard Marino referring to him as "college boy" and he'd been careful around him ever since. But Marino knew the job and he had good instincts. Quinn could learn from him.

He inspected the brooch for a moment, trying to look thoughtful, then said, "I took this class once about English history and I remember this whole thing about mourning jewelry. It wasn't quite like this, but I think that's what it is."

"Okay," Marino said. "Now tell me what else you see."

Quinn took his time, studying the boy's back and the ties before speaking. "Well, the obvious cause of death is suffocation, but we'll have to wait for the postmortem to be sure."

"Good," Marino said. "Anything else?"

Quinn sniffed the air. "Well, I'd do a tox screen. He reeks of booze. Tequila."

"Sure does. What else?"

Focusing on the details of the room and letting the noise in the apartment fade away, Quinn turned his gaze around the bedroom. He squatted down and looked at everything from waist level. "Well, there's the source of the tequila," he said, pointing to the half-empty bottle pushed under the bed. He dipped his head and surveyed the floor. There were a couple of dusty, but neatly labeled boxes—"BOOKS," "SWEATERS," and "MISC."—a pair of dress shoes with dust kitties in them, and a small notebook. "And there's a notebook under there," he said. "Check it out. It looks less dusty than the rest of the stuff. It may have been pushed under there more recently."

"What? Shit! You're right. Good one, Quinn." Marino was grinning and Quinn felt inordinately satisfied.

"What about suicide? You think he did this himself?"

Quinn went to the bed and stood next to it with his feet wide apart. He leaned over the body and put a hand just over each of the low bedposts, taking care not to touch the posts, the hands, or the ties holding them there. "I don't know," he said. "It would have been tricky. I think he had help getting tied up. And someone put the jewelry on after the bag was already over his head. This might be sex-related. He got drunk, invited someone back here, asked them to tie him up."

"Yeah," Marino said. "I think you're right. We better check for signs of sexual contact—heterosexual and homosexual. In the meantime, it's a good bet the jewelry was just some weirdo thing he liked to do while he got off, but I want you to check up on it, in case it points to a ritual murder. Try someone at the university or the museum. We'll ask the family about it but I want to get an expert's opinion first."

Marino waved him out into the hallway, dismissing him.

The phone calls didn't take long, though since it was Sunday, it took some doing to get the home number for the chair of the art history department. But the switchboard operator gave it up when Quinn explained that he was from Cambridge P.D. A few minutes later he was talking to the chairman's wife, who said that he was out but gave him the number of the department secretary. Once he had the secretary on the phone, he asked if there was anyone who specialized in mourning jewelry, if that's what it was called.

"Oh, that's Professor St. George you want. Professor St. George knows about death. Give me your name and number and I'll call her and tell her to get right back to you. I'll have to go into the office to get it, though. She might even be there. She's in the office a lot on the weekends." Quinn heard a note of disapproval in her voice.

He gave her his number at the station and was just hanging up the phone when one of the uniformed cops came back into the room. "They're talking to the kid that found him, the roommate. He told us the kid's name when he called but no one put it together until now. The kid's a Putnam."

"As in . . . ?"

"As in."

The cop was almost grinning.

THREE

Sweeney St. George was having her lunch on Cuphea Path in Mount Auburn Cemetery, leaning up against a monument carved to look like an elaborately draped coffin, when her cell phone rang.

It was Sunday and she had meant to turn off the phone—which she hated, but had come to depend upon—but she had forgotten and now it trilled harshly at her.

She checked the display, and seeing it was the number of the department secretary, leaned back against the stone and let it ring. It was Sunday, for God's sake. If it was important, they'd leave a message.

As a small breeze came up in the trees, Sweeney closed her eyes and breathed deeply the wet, cool air. It was late April; after a long, unusually frigid winter nature hovered at the edge of spring. The snow had melted, but the ground was soaked and cold, not yet fertile. The tree branches above her were a lime green pointillist haze and the bright sun felt different, stronger, than it had only a few weeks ago. A friend's art opening she'd attended the night before had gone too late—the artist hadn't even welcomed everybody until almost midnight and she'd stayed an hour or so after that, having too much of the good wine. She leaned into the stone, sinking into the sharpness, and she felt the fresh air cleanse away the last vestiges of her hangover.

The phone had stopped ringing and she opened her eyes, enjoying the relative silence again. Somewhere out there she could hear cars and trucks rushing by on Mount Auburn

Street. But in here she could almost believe that she was in the country. She turned around and pressed her face against the moist stone, breathing in its gray, outdoor odor.

Set on a small rise on the Cambridge/Watertown border, a stepped series of sloping hills with the family plots of some of Boston's most important families decorating the hillsides, Mount Auburn Cemetery had been founded in 1831 as one of America's first garden cemeteries and had marked a shift in the way Americans thought about death, a change from the festering, overcrowded churchyards and catacombs of the city to the pastoral quiet of the hills outside. The graves, marked with markers and monuments large and small, were placed along little roads with names like Tulip Path and Fir Avenue, nodding to the trees and flowers that were carefully cultivated around the cemetery.

The cemetery had gotten its name from the university students who, in the early nineteenth century, had liked to hike on the plot of land and called it "Sweet Auburn," after the Oliver Goldsmith poem "The Deserted Village."

Sweeney had always liked the idea of those early students, obsessed with Goldsmith's ideal of a pastoral country village. Later, when those very same students were running the city, they called on those old memories of youthful contemplation of mortality when faced with the problem of overcrowded and unsanitary churchyard cemeteries and charnel houses, and the question of where Boston's dead should be laid to rest.

She finished her egg salad sandwich and got up to go. There was work to do in the office, tomorrow's lecture on mourning and the decorative arts to prepare for her senior seminar, and a pile of seminar papers to read so she could get them back to the class tomorrow.

As she slipped through the gate, she listened to her cell phone message, from the department secretary. "Sweeney?" Mrs. Pitman's hesitant voice came over the phone. "This is kind of strange, but the Cambridge police just called. A Detective Quinn. They need to talk to someone who knows about mourning jewelry. I thought of you of course and they said they want to talk to you as soon as possible. Even though it's

Sunday. I . . . here's the number they left." Sweeney listened and her good memory immediately had it. The phone had barely rung when she heard a youngish male voice answer "Quinn. 6345."

"Yes, my name's Sweeney St. George. I got a message that someone there wanted to talk to me about mourning jewelry." In the background she could hear phones ringing and a low hum of activity.

"Hey, I got her. The professor," Quinn called out to someone. "Thanks for calling back, Ms. St. George. I'm wondering if you could come down to the station. We have what I think is some mourning jewelry down here. It's been, well . . . uh, connected with a crime. And we're just looking for any information you can give us about it." He had a classic Boston accent, his R's disappearing into the ether. Quinn. A good Irish boy from Dorchester or Revere, Sweeney said to herself. Everybody was proud when he became a cop.

"Okay. When should I . . . ?"

"I'm here now, so whenever it's good for you." When-evah. "If there's a problem . . . Do you know where the station is?"

"Yeah. The Central Square one, right?"

"That's right."

"Can you tell me some more about the jewelry? Should I bring anything with me?"

He hesitated. "I'd think we'd prefer that you just come down and take a look. If there's anything you need, you can get it later." He hesitated again and then said, "I'll see you soon."

FOUR

The Cambridge police department headquarters were located on Western Avenue, just off Central Square, almost directly across from Cambridge City Hall. The building was decrepit-looking from the outside, faced with beige bricks, and suggesting a Victorian prison or reform school. As she walked from her car to the front entrance, Sweeney passed two men about her age, dressed in jeans and leather jackets, conferring secretively next to a car. They stopped talking as she walked by.

The lobby, up a short staircase from street level, smelled of creosote and after announcing herself to a young female police officer through a glass window, she wandered over to look at a series of photographs mounted on a far wall. At a distance, she thought they must be honored policemen, but when she stepped closer, she saw the pictures were of missing children, row upon row of them, the jaunty school portraits and family pictures revealing nothing of warring parents or unhappy homes. She stared into the eyes of a ten-year-old girl named Soriah Diaz, missing for six years now and believed to be kidnapped by her stepfather, and then stepped away from the wall.

There was nothing to read, so she took a pamphlet from a plastic holder on the wall.

Personal Safety Plan, it read. *You Have a Right to Be Safe.* Inside were a list of do's and don'ts for victims of domestic violence: *Safety During an Explosive Incident.* "If an argument seems unavoidable, try to have it in a room or area where you have access to an exit. Try to stay away from the bathroom, kitchen, bedroom, or anywhere else where weapons might be available."

She was reading about how to stay safe after taking out a protective order when a voice said, "Ms. St. George?" and she looked up to find a good-looking guy wearing a crisp blue plaid cotton shirt and khakis and looking very, very surprised to see her.

His crispness made her suddenly conscious of her wildly curly red hair, her ratty pair of overalls and sweatshirt Jackson-Pollocked with the side effects of painting her living room walls.

"I'm Detective Quinn," he said. "Thanks for coming."

Detective Tim Quinn was as young-looking as he'd sounded on the phone, hardly more than a teenager, but when he looked up at Sweeney, the harsh overhead lighting illuminating lines around his eyes and circles beneath them, she saw that he was probably closer to her age than she'd thought. He had dirty blond hair, cut short, thinning a little on top, and blue eyes set in a conventionally handsome face. And she noticed he was wearing a wedding ring. His good looks were those she associated with frat houses and beach parties, a blond girl-friend in a bikini. The wedding ring seemed incongruous.

"Thanks for coming down here on such short notice," he said. Once again, she heard the broad Boston in his voice—"he-ah" for "here," "sho-ut" for "short." "If you'll just follow me . . ." They went through a set of doors, out into a hallway. Another set of doors led into a small empty room furnished with filing cabinets, a low table, and a couple of chairs.

"Sorry about the room. It's just that I wanted you to have a quiet place to look at the . . . at the objects." He shut the door behind them and gestured for her to sit down at the table. "Can I get you a cup of coffee or anything?" he asked. "It's from one of those machines. Frankly I wouldn't recommend it, but if you really need the caffeine . . ."

"No thanks. I'm fine."

"I called the MFA after I got back here," he said, unsmil-ing. "Just to see if there was anyone else they would recom-mend to look at this stuff. They said I should call you. Spoke very highly of your work."

"Oh . . . Thanks."

He opened up a manila envelope that had been sitting on the table and took out a plastic bag. Inside were four pieces of mourning jewelry, each in its own smaller Ziploc bag, each dangling a little white tag with a number on it. Sweeney did a quick inventory—a hair-work necklace, a locket, and two brooches.

"The jewelry was connected with a crime scene we responded to this morning," Quinn said. "It's mourning jewelry, isn't it?"

Sweeney took the bag from him and turned it over in her hands. "Yup. This is an interesting little collection. Especially that one brooch. Earlier than a lot of the stuff you see outside of Britain. Can I . . ."

He nodded and she took the individual pieces out to look at them, carefully examining them through the plastic. "If you had a magnifying glass—oh, and some paper and a pencil—that would be helpful," she said. Quinn punched a number into the phone on the table and passed on the request.

"Okay, so this is a classic hair-work necklace," she said, showing him the first piece, which was made of twenty intricate balls of woven dark brown hair, threaded together with a piece of cord and fastened with a distinctive three-part clasp. "When I get the magnifying glass, I can tell you some more about how old it is, although you may need to ask a jeweler who specializes in antique pieces for details. But from the style of the clasp and the pattern of the braiding, my guess would be mid-1800s. That's just a guess, though."

"I'm sorry, did you say *hair*?" She looked up to find Detective Quinn looking slightly pale under his tan. "I assumed it was some type of cloth or fiber."

"Oh no. It's made of human hair. Hair-work jewelry was popular in the late eighteenth and early nineteenth centuries. People would save the hair of a loved one who had died and have it made into these braided necklaces and bracelets. Or they'd do it themselves. It became a popular pastime for well-bred ladies. This one would have been made by weaving the hair around a little wooden mold to form the balls, and then sewing them together and stringing them on the cord so the necklace wouldn't stretch too much."

He still looked a little stunned, so she went on. "I know it sounds kind of weird to us. We don't have as much intimate and regular contact with death anymore, but back then it was very much a part of life. Children died all the time, people lost their spouses at much younger ages. Mourning was an important part of subscribed social etiquette. There were rules about what you could wear and when you could wear it.

"Anyway, the idea was that hair is the part of the human body that doesn't decay, so it became a lasting reminder of the person you'd lost." Sweeney examined the necklace again as a young woman in a uniform brought in a magnifying glass and a notebook and pencil. Sweeney swiveled the glass over the necklace's large, three-part clasp. "There we go. There's a little inscription. 'Beloved Husband. January 3, 1809—April 2, 1863.' So this would have belonged to a woman whose husband died on April 2, 1863. She would have saved his hair and braided it or had it braided. It makes sense that she chose the pattern she did. Most men wouldn't have had hair long enough to make a single coil. Then she would have worn it to keep a piece of her husband close to her and present a proper face of mourning to the world."

Sweeney picked up one of the brooches and looked at it carefully under the magnifying glass. Then she held it out so Quinn could do the same.

"Now this piece is a little more unusual. It's also Victorian, but about twenty years later than the necklace." The brooch was milk glass with a gold frame and painted on the milk glass was an intricately detailed scene of a woman standing over an urn in a graveyard with a weeping willow in the background. The weeping willow and the woman's hair and dress were constructed of light brown hair, knotted and scrolled, and painted delicately below the scene were the words "Beloved Son, Edmund."

"It's a pretty common mourning scene. See, it's painted on milk glass and then the hairwork was added as embellishment."

Quinn looked at the brooch. " 'Beloved Son, Edmund,' " he read aloud. "So it belonged to this Edmund's mother?"

"Probably."

"Would this and the necklace have belonged to the same person? To a woman who lost her husband and then her son?" Quinn handed the brooch back to Sweeney.

"I don't know. It depends on where the collection came from. If you knew its provenance, you could figure out who Edmund was and probably the woman too." She turned the brooch over and placed it on the table. "Now this is the really interesting thing. The dates of this Edmund's life are on the back of the brooch, see? Inscribed on the gold backing. 'March 4, 1864–June 23, 1888.' "

She pointed to the lettering so Quinn could see it.

"It's interesting to compare this brooch with the other one, which is earlier, probably 1850 or so." She looked at it for a few minutes, carefully inspecting the engraving and the initials. It was a small window of blond hair arranged in a basketweave and on the frame it was inscribed "B.C. R.I.P."

"Same collection?"

"No way of knowing. But it was common for members of the upper classes to have mourning jewelry commemorating the lives of more than one family member, so that's what this could be, I suppose."

Quinn didn't say anything and Sweeney went on. "The history of mourning or *memento mori* jewelry is really interesting. In Europe, since medieval times, wars and plagues had made death very much a part of life, and people wore *memento mori*—which means 'Remember death' or 'Remember that you must die'—jewelry, pieces like rings with skull's heads on them. The idea was that you had to remember death was always near in order to be prepared.

"Anyway, in the seventeenth century, Europeans started wearing jewelry made of hair. Frequently a piece of the deceased's hair would be woven and placed on a panel. It might be decorated with initials or a little gold design and covered with glass. The designs were usually something specifically representing death—a skeleton, an hourglass. But as time went on, the iconography of death changed. We start to see symbols such as urns or willow trees, or sheaves of wheat."

"So are you saying that this stuff is from Europe?"

"No, not at all. In fact, I would say all this was made right in Boston. Jewelers here, and in Philadelphia and New York, started making hair-work jewelry in the late 1700s and early 1800s. There are people who could tell you exactly where this was made. I could take it to a woman I know, if you want."

"Maybe." He was about to say something when a cell phone rang and he reached for his pocket. He looked at the phone, glanced at Sweeney, and answered it as he crossed to the other side of the room, turning his back to her. "Yeah? What? Is she okay?" she heard him ask in a whisper.

Sweeney picked up the other brooch and looked at it again through the plastic, tracing a finger over the intricately etched willow tree.

"No, I can't really talk now," she heard him whisper. "Just see if she wants to . . . okay, yeah, call the doctor. Let me know. Okay, bye."

He sat down across from her again and said, "Sorry about that," laying the phone down on the table and reaching up to rub his eyes with his fingertips. "Okay, so what about the locket?"

Sweeney picked it up. "It doesn't have any markings, so I can't date it with any confidence, but it looks like some Civil War–era ones I've seen. Have you opened it up?"

He shook his head.

"There may be something inside that would give you a clue to who owned it. I could do it through the plastic, I think." She fiddled with the clasp for a moment, then the locket clicked open. "Oh, there's a lock of hair in here. It's about the same color as the necklace, so it could be that it was a lock of hair left over. The dates are right." The small brown lock of hair was tied with a red ribbon and nestled comfortably in the bowl of the locket. Sweeney clicked it closed again.

Quinn thought for a moment, as though he was choosing words. "Would this . . . this jewelry have any kind of a sexual significance?"

Sweeney looked up at him. "Well, we could get into a discussion about sex and death and sexual climax as a kind of death. The Victorians were quite—"

He blushed, and she felt guilty for having embarrassed him. "No, no . . . what I mean is . . . what would you say if I told you that this jewelry was involved in a crime with uh . . . possibly . . . sexual, uh, aspects to it."

Sweeney's eyes widened. "I don't know. It seems unlikely that it would have significance, but you never know." Quinn blushed again. "Can you tell me some more about it, I mean, what kind of a crime?"

"I can tell you what the press will get," he said. "But you have to promise you won't talk about the jewelry." She nodded and he went on. "It was found on a guy who was murdered sometime last night or early this morning. There was nothing to indicate why it was there or whether or not it belonged to the dead man. He was found in a . . . in a position that leads us to believe there may have been a sexual element to the crime, or at least some kind of dominance. That's all I can tell you. Obviously we want to keep the information about the jewelry secret. It could point to . . ."

But Sweeney was leaning forward, staring at him. "You think that this is some kind of ritual killer, don't you?" The idea was strangely fascinating. A murderer who left mourning jewelry as his signature?

"Not necessarily. But we want to explore all the possibilities, you know? What's your feeling on that? Is there something about the jewelry that could mean something for someone? I'm not even sure what I'm asking here. If there is a chance that this was some kind of ritual crime, we would want to start looking for likely people right away. And in any case, we're going to want your help tracking down the jewelry. If we can figure out where it came from, it may lead us to a suspect."

"I would have to know more about the victim, more about the crime," she said. "I mean, it would be hard to say without knowing who he was. Can you tell me a little bit more?"

Before Quinn could answer, there was a knock on the door

and a heavyset guy came in and waved at Quinn over Sweeney's head. "You got the stuff from the Brad Putnam case?" he asked. "They're asking down in the lab."

"Can't they hang on two seconds? This is important. We're—"

Sweeney gasped. "Brad Putnam?" The room felt very stuffy all of a sudden. "Brad Putnam?" she asked again, interrupting him.

Quinn ignored her. "Two seconds. We're looking at it right now."

The guy shut the door.

"Did he just say Brad Putnam? As in *the* Putnams?"

Quinn looked surprised. "Yeah. We weren't going to release the name yet, but the family's been notified, so I guess the press will get it soon enough."

No," she said again, tears rushing to her eyes. "You don't understand. I know him. He's one of my students. We were studying mourning jewelry in my seminar."

Quinn nodded slowly. "I'm sorry you had to find out this way. I didn't realize you knew him. He was studying this stuff in your class?"

"Yes. I . . ." She was suddenly horrified. "Do you think that's why he had it?"

Quinn didn't say anything.

"Look, I can look into it for you. I know some people who . . ."

"No," Quinn said sharply. "We don't want you to talk to anyone about this until we contact you. Okay?"

Sweeney nodded.

And then she began to cry.

FIVE

He had blue eyes, the kind of blue eyes that revealed themselves in degrees, greenish blue in one kind of light, turquoisey as a vacation sea when he shifted his head slightly. You *learned* about his eyes, something new each time you looked into them.

Sweeney had been sitting on the floor of her office, talking to him about death, when she had noticed this.

She had met Brad Putnam the previous fall, when as a junior he'd enrolled in an intermediate-level art history course she was teaching entitled Looking at Culture; Art and Social History. She hadn't particularly wanted to teach the class and therefore, she realized now, had focused it around her own interests, talking to them about gravestone art and mourning jewelry, drawing connections between world events and attitudes toward death. It hadn't been an illegitimate approach to the subject exactly, just a narrow one.

But for six of the kids in the course, including Brad, it had been a revelation. They had all done well and, she had noticed, begun to hang around together. Sometimes, after class, she'd watch them out the window of her office, meeting up on the sidewalk and chatting for a few minutes before moving away en masse. At the end of the semester, the six of them had presented her with a photograph of a mid-eighteenth-century headstone featuring a skeletal Death holding an hourglass. They had taken it in a cemetery near Lexington, they told her, and she had been surprised and touched that they had made the effort.

She hadn't been surprised when all six signed up for her Mourning Objects seminar that spring.

Brad, she had sensed from the beginning, was the one most seriously interested. He would read widely outside the assigned reading, bringing in photographs he'd taken of gravestones that exemplified a particular style, an unusual iconography. Sweeney had been a little surprised by all the extra effort at first and had wondered if it was personal, if perhaps he had a crush on her. But it hadn't been anything like that, she'd soon realized. It was just that, like Sweeney, he was really passionate about death. When he had asked her about graduate schools where he could pursue his interest in mourning objects and the decorative arts, she had felt unexpectedly proud.

And then there had been that strange day in early March when it had warmed unseasonably. All day, there was a strange heaviness in the air. Sweeney had pulled her car around and parked illegally in the lot behind the museum where she had her office, leaving the engine running and the hazards blinking madly to scare away the campus cops. She was carrying a box of books, as well as the backpack for her laptop and teaching materials, and she had put a foot up on the car and balanced the box on her knee so she could open the driver's side door of her ancient Rabbit. But she must have had slushy snow on the bottom of her shoe because she slipped, sending the box of books tumbling into a snowbank. At that moment, the elastic band holding back her hair broke, shooting off into a puddle in the parking lot, and as she had bent to retrieve the now sodden books, she'd slipped on a patch of ice and fallen. Her nearly six-foot frame did not topple easily and she banged her knee on the sidewalk as she fell.

"Um.... do you need any help, Sweeney?" She had felt him standing there on the sidewalk and had looked up to find Brad trying not to smile.

There had been nothing for it but to burst out laughing. He had laughed too and helped her pick up the books, put them back in the box, and load it into the back of the Rabbit.

"Do you want a ride somewhere?" she'd asked, after thanking him for his help.

"I don't have far to go," he'd said. "I can walk."

"No. Get in. It looks like it's going to rain."

Well mannered, he had accepted gracefully and slid into the passenger seat, looking around at her messy car as though it were an interesting museum exhibit.

"Don't tell me you have a really neat car," she'd said.

"Yeah, I'm a little anal actually. But I respect people who are messy. It probably means you're creative. Something like that." He'd grinned and she remembered being surprised at how natural he was with her.

They had been almost to his apartment—on Harvard Street, he'd told her—when Sweeney had remembered she'd been planning to go back and pick up a second box of books from her office. In the confusion of her fall, and then running into Brad, she'd completely forgotten that she'd left her office door open, the box of books still on the floor. "Shit." She slammed her hand against the steering wheel.

What?" He'd looked startled.

"I was going to get another box of books. I left my office door open and I just completely forgot. That's all right. I'll drop you off and then go back for them."

"But if you drop me, it's one way, and you'll have to go all the way around again. If you take a right up here you can just swing back to the museum and I can help you carry the box out," he'd said sensibly.

"You sure? You don't have to be anywhere?"

"Nope."

The skies had opened just as she'd pulled up in the lot again, and they'd run cursing from the car to the back door of the museum, then stood for a minute in the stairwell to the upper-floor offices.

"I'm so sorry," Sweeney said. "Jeez, we're soaked."

Upstairs she had found everyone gone and her office door still open. She looked out the window and saw that the rain was coming down in planes, violently pounding the pavement. "I think we should just wait a minute, see if it slows down. I don't want these books to get wet too. Oh God, I'm soaked. And you're leaking." He was standing in the hallway and a puddle was forming beneath him. "Here, you want a cup of coffee or something? I have an electric kettle and a French press in my file cabinet, the sign of a true addict."

"I thought professors were supposed to have bottles of bourbon in their file cabinets."

"Well, I've got one of those too, but I think the administration might frown on me offering it to you."

She'd made coffee and they had sat on the floor of her office, so they wouldn't drip on the chairs, and talked about the class.

"You did a really good job on those samplers," she'd told him. His first paper for the seminar had been on mourning samplers and he'd drawn some interesting conclusions about how the process of cross-stitching a sampler helped girls—for it was girls who sewed the interesting little mourning items, complete with epitaphs and the name and date of the deceased—come to terms with death at a time when their own chances of eventually dying in childbirth were pretty high.

"Thanks," he'd said, embarrassed.

"How's the mourning jewelry one going?" He'd been working on Civil War–era mourning jewelry for his final paper and Sweeney had been looking forward to reading it.

"Okay. There are a couple of things I'm trying to figure out, but . . ." He'd stopped as though he was deciding whether or not to tell her something.

"Let me know if you want to hash anything out before you start writing."

"Yeah, sure. Thanks." He'd looked around at her walls—the office was so small that there wasn't room for much. But she had posters from a few exhibits and photographs of gravestones and cemeteries. She'd typed a fragment of poetry from Robert Blair's "The Grave" and pasted it onto a moody black-and-white photo of an English churchyard.

Brad read aloud.

"Well do I know thee by thy trusty Yew,/ Cheerless, unofficial Plant! that loves to dwell/'Midst sculls and coffins, Epitaphs and Worms: Where light-heel'd Ghosts, and visionary Shades,/ Beneath the wan cold Moon (as Fame reports)/Embody'd, thick, perform their mystick Rounds./No other merriment, Dull Tree! is thine."

"Wow," he said. "That's pretty grim."

"Didn't I have you guys read some of the Graveyard Poets?" He'd shaken his head. "Hmmm. I'm falling behind. Next week. Anyway, that's Robert Blair. He's pretty interesting."

He read it again, thoughtfully, then he'd asked, "What do you think death is like?"

"I don't think it's like anything," Sweeney had said. "It's unconsciousness."

"So you don't believe in heaven or Judgment Day or anything like that? I thought that . . ."

"That because I spend so much time studying religious responses to Death, I must believe in the premises on which all that art is based? Nope. I'm a good old atheist. I think heaven is for children's bedtime prayers. What I'm interested in, though, is why human beings need a heaven."

"I think we need it because when someone you love dies, it's just hard to believe that they're not *somewhere*. You know?" He'd looked almost wistful.

"I think you're right." Suddenly she'd panicked. "I'm not offending you, am I?"

"No. My dad always says we're Episcopatheists."

"Ha." She'd laughed. "I like that. Episcopatheists. I come from a long line of Episcopatheists myself."

"But I believe in heaven," he'd said. "Or something anyway. I believe that there's something else, after."

Sweeney had felt she'd been cruel and she'd blushed before saying, "You're lucky, then."

He had been quiet for a moment, then he'd said, "Can I ask you something?"

"Sure."

"I heard from some of the other kids about what happened in London. About your husband."

They had gotten that part of it wrong.

"He wasn't my husband. We were engaged."

"Oh. I'm sorry." He'd hesitated, then he'd stammered on. "I heard about how it happened, about how it was an explosion and they never caught the person or people or whatever who did it and I was just wondering . . ." He'd stopped there, as though he was trying to figure out what to say. "Have you ever, when you were doing research or something, have you ever found out something about somebody, something that would change everything, change the way people looked at things?"

Sweeney had been confused. "Do you mean about a gravestone?"

"Maybe, or about . . . I mean, have you ever come across information that could maybe hurt someone, but that could be important? I mean . . ." He'd struggled. "If someone had a piece of information that was . . . something else about a person, some important *thing* that you didn't know before, and they could tell you—would you want to know?"

"I'm not sure I know what you're asking," she'd said. "It would depend on what the information was. Do you want to tell me anything more?"

She'd had the sense that her answer was very important to him and had felt somehow that she had let him down by not figuring out what he wanted. She had watched as he'd wrestled with something, staring at her with his strange, changing blue eyes. But in the end, he had just shaken his head.

They had sat there on the floor of her office, staring at each other awkwardly, and she had felt an urge to embrace him.

So she had gotten up, a little too quickly, and had said that they should get downstairs before someone towed the car. The next day, in class, she had been concerned about how he would act. Would he assume an intimacy that would make things awkward? But no, he had behaved perfectly, giving her a conspiratorial grin when he came into the lecture room, but treating her exactly as before.

And now he was dead. It had seemed impossible, when Quinn had told her, to believe that he was no longer alive. It was just as Brad had said—she couldn't accept that he wasn't *somewhere*.

Quinn had been embarrassed by her tears, handing her a tissue from a box on a side table. He hadn't given her any more details about how Brad had died, and he'd reminded her not to talk about the jewelry to anyone and had said that they would be in touch tomorrow. "We may need your help in talking to the family about where the jewelry came from," he'd said. As she'd gone, he'd said kindly, "I'm sorry you had to find out about it this way. If we had known you knew him, we wouldn't have let it happen like this."

She took Mass. Ave. toward Somerville and Davis Square. It was almost six when she pulled onto Russell Street, the Victorians lining the street shadowy and spooky in the low light, the dusk descending in a cloud of spring-scented mist.

Toby, wearing a raincoat, the hood pulled over his head, was waiting for her on the sidewalk. She had called him from her cell phone to tell him about Brad and he had promised company and dinner—Chinese she saw from the logo on the bag he carried.

The gods smiled and she found parking right out front and in a few seconds she was enfolded in a hug and the scent of *kung pao* chicken and dumplings. "You okay?" Toby asked, watching her face. He had been her best friend since college, had been with her through three deaths—no, four, she realized—in a little more than a year. This was the fifth.

Sweeney led him upstairs.

"Jesus," she said, collapsing onto the couch and leaning back against the cushions. The moist blur of the headlights on the way home had given her a headache and now her head was pounding. "I feel like someone mugged me." The apartment, clean and freshly painted, the walls covered with photographs of gravestones and monuments, the black-and-cream color scheme pleasingly simple, usually made her feel better.

"I did some asking around after you called," Toby said. "Want to hear what I found out?"

"Yeah, hold on a second." She got up to pour them both a scotch—neat for her, on the rocks for him—took off her coat and lay back on the couch again. Toby's hair had gotten mashed down by the hood of his jacket and he looked slightly mad, his black eyes wide behind his glasses, his curly dark hair pressed into an odd sort of cap. They had known each other for ten years now and the sight of him still filled her with pleasure.

"Well, I called a couple of kids in Brad's class who I knew from that play I directed last year."

Toby, who had been a thespian during his undergraduate years, had directed a student production of *Macbeth* the year before. His interpretation had been set in a 1980s New York crack house. Privately Sweeney believed it not to have been a success. She recalled with a cringe the opening scene—three homeless addicts mumbling "Double, double, toil and trouble" around a grate fire. But Brad had done sets and Toby had gotten to know him a little.

"You know Jaybee Mitchell and Becca Dearborne, right?"

Sweeney nodded. They were both in her seminar, Jaybee—a long-go approximation of J.B.—a smart but somewhat lazy kid who, she suspected, had chosen Sweeney's classes because his friends had, and Becca, a more motivated scholar, who had often worked with Brad on group projects. She had even wondered once if Brad and Becca were dating, but their casual way with each other had offered her no clues.

"Well, Jaybee lives . . . lived with Brad. They've been friends since they were kids and went to prep school together and I think Becca's family knew Brad's from Newport. Apparently he and Becca found him when they came home this morning. They slept at Becca's and came back to the apartment because the shower at Becca's dorm wasn't working. Anyway, they came in and found him. The police told them not to say anything about how he looked when he was found, but Becca called a bunch of people before the police got there and it seems like everyone knows at this point. When they came in, he was wearing only his underwear and his arms were tied to the bed with neckties. He had a bag over his head and he was wearing the jewelry. Well, you know that part of it."

Sweeney felt guilty all of a sudden for telling Toby about her conversation with Quinn. Quinn had asked her not to say anything, but she had been so shaken when she left the station that she'd called Toby and blurted out the whole thing.

"Yeah, you know what? Don't tell anyone about the jewelry. I was supposed to . . ." She closed her eyes for a moment, her head pounding. "Toby, what do you think happened to him?"

"I don't know. It seems like it must have been someone he knew, to let them tie him up like that. Maybe he met somebody and brought them home and they killed him."

"Was he gay? I don't think he was gay. That's silly, I guess, but it's just hard to imagine a woman tying him up like that. He was pretty tall."

"I don't know." Toby was preoccupied with the dumplings.

"And putting a bag over his head? Why wouldn't they use a knife or a gun or something. It seems weird."

"Apparently, Jaybee and Becca had come home earlier that night and found him really drunk. Maybe someone came along, found him passed out, and tied him up and put the bag over his head so they could rob the apartment."

"But that doesn't explain the jewelry," Sweeney said, sitting up on the couch. "I think the police believe he was killed by some kind of ritual killer who uses the jewelry as a calling card or whatever you call it. They were trying to find out from me whether the jewelry had significance. When I told them that he'd been working on a project on mourning jewelry for my class, they almost seemed disappointed."

"Had you seen it before?"

"No. And I can't figure out where he would have gotten it. I told the class to go out to museums and antique stores and see if they could find examples of mourning jewelry. I didn't mean for them to go out and buy it." Sweeney took a bowl of rice and chicken from him.

"God, that poor family. You knew his younger brother died a few years ago, right?"

"What? I didn't know that."

"You knew who he was, though?"

"Yeah, I mean when I heard the last name I wondered and then I think one of the other kids in the class asked me if I knew that he was a Putnam, of *the* Putnams."

There were a handful of families who were synonymous with the history of Brahmin Boston and the Putnams were one of them. An early ancestor had come over from England to make his fortune, and that fortune had been made a generation or two later in overseas shipping, then multiplied through savvy real estate deals and influence wielding. Putnams had served in almost every political office in the Commonwealth, and Brad's grandfather, John Putnam, had been an influential U.S. senator when moderate Republicans could still get elected in Massachusetts. His career had crossed paths with a far more famous Boston pol, Senator Patrick "Paddy" Sheehan, whose family name had become synonymous with politics in the city.

Sheehan came from a family of Irish immigrants who had risen to prominence in the city, and it was when his youngest daughter, Kitty, had fallen in love with Andrew Putnam, the youngest son of his Republican rival, that the two families were forever melded. Andrew and Kitty Putnam had gone on to have five children. Brad was the second to youngest.

Now that Toby said it, Sweeney did vaguely remember a tragic death. "I think I remember something," she said. "What was it?"

"Five years ago, Brad went to college, I think. They were down at the family house in Newport and there was a car accident. Brad's younger brother Petey died in the crash. All of the Putnam kids were in the car but they never told anybody who had been driving. The police up in Newport tried for months to get them to talk, but they all claimed that they'd been knocked out and couldn't remember anything. The assumption was that whoever had been driving was drunk and they were covering it up, but the Putnams threw their weight around and the case was closed eventually."

Sweeney ate her chicken slowly, thinking.

"So what do the police want from you?" Toby asked.

"I don't know. They said they might call me to help with the jewelry some more. I think they have this theory about a ritual killer."

He was quiet for a few minutes.

"What?" Sweeney asked him.

"I don't know. I was just thinking about Brad."

"What about him?" The images flashed up before Sweeney again. Those eyes.

"Just that I thought once he seemed like the kind of person who I could imagine getting himself killed. Do you know what I mean?"

"Yeah. It was like he'd given up. Not on the things he did every day, but on the big stuff."

"He was what, sixteen, when his brother died? That must have been pretty traumatic. Maybe that's what it was."

"Yeah," Sweeney said. But she didn't feel convinced.

While Toby did the dishes, Sweeney pressed play on her answering machine and heard the voice of Katie Swift, a friend from college. Katie hadn't received Sweeney's RSVP card . . . maybe it had gotten lost in the mail . . . she just wanted to check . . . she was so hoping that Sweeney would be coming.

RSVP card?

"Did you forget to RSVP?" Toby called from the kitchen. "That's so rude. You're going, right?"

"Shit!" Sweeney brushed past him and started searching through the mess of stuff on her refrigerator.

It was covered with pieces of paper—parking tickets, invitations, and other assorted summonses—and, behind a picture of another college friend's new baby, a surprised-looking, very new baby girl named Hester, Sweeney found the tasteful ecru card informing her that Mr. and Mrs. Donald Swift requested the honor of her company at the wedding of Katherine Marie Swift and Milan Simic in Newport in two weeks' time.

"I completely forgot," she said.

"You're going, though, aren't you?"

"I don't know. It's Newport . . ."

He turned to look at her. "When was the last time you were down there?"

"Five years ago. My grandmother's funeral. Before I left for Oxford."

"Really, you haven't been down since then?"

"No. And I don't really want to go now." She took a plate from him and dried it with the hem of her sweatshirt, then put it away.

"But it's Katie."

"I know, I should go, shouldn't I? If I do, can I be your date? I hate going to those things alone. They always stick you at a table with the teenage cousins or something."

"Of course. But don't wear something weird."

"What do you mean?"

Toby disapproved of Sweeney's affinity for vintage clothes. "Just what I said. Don't wear something weird. It's a wedding. It's supposed to be a happy occasion."

"All right. But I'll only promise if you promise not to hit on teenagers." The last time they'd gone to a wedding together, Toby had ended up going home with the bride's nineteen-year-old sister.

"Ha," he said, flicking a palmful of soap bubbles at her. "Ha, ha, ha."

When Toby had gone, Sweeney looked up at the antique mantel clock on her bookshelf. It was only eight. Not too late for reporters' deadlines. She found the phone book and dialed the main number for the *Boston Globe*.

"Paul Blum, please." The secretary put her through. Paul was a friend of Sweeney's from college and had recently come back to Boston after a stint in Little Rock, Arkansas. He was covering the cops beat now and Sweeney was betting that he'd been put on the Brad Putnam story.

"Hi, Sweeney," he said distractedly. "It's not a great time. I'm on deadline. I'm sure you heard about this thing with the Putnam kid."

"I know. I know. Look, he was one of my students and I was thinking I could give you a quote about him. I knew him pretty well. He was a nice kid."

"Great. Let me bring up the . . . okay. Go ahead." Sweeney gave him some very nice words about Brad, about his talents as a scholar and her regard for him. When she was done, Paul said, "Listen, thanks a lot. I've been having trouble getting anything like that. That family has a pretty formidable PR operation. I owe you one."

"Actually," Sweeney said, "I was going to see if you could do me a favor. After you've filed your story, fax or e-mail me whatever you've got on the Putnams. Stuff about the accident, about the family business. Anything recent. I'm just kind of curious, since I knew him and all."

"Okay, great. I've got it all right here. You can look it up on the archives online if you want, but there's a charge and it'll take a lot of searching to find all of it. I'll fax it. But it'll be a couple of hours or so. That all right?"

"Yeah. Thanks."

She tried halfheartedly to clean up a bit around the apartment and to not stare at the fax machine. It was just after ten when the fax line rang and the machine began to spit out paper. She poured herself another scotch, and when the machine was finished, took the stack into bed with her and began to read.

From the printed sheets Paul had sent her, Sweeney surmised that the *Globe* archive only went back to 1979. There were a couple of pieces about the death of Senator John Putnam, a formal obituary and a long story about the star-studded funeral. Sweeney noted that there weren't any stories about the death of Paddy Sheehan. She had assumed he was dead too but apparently not. He must be at least eighty by now.

And then there was a piece from five years ago, when Brad was sixteen, about the accident near the family's Bellevue Avenue home in Newport.

"Celebration turned to tragedy last night for one of Newport's most well-known families," the article started off. As far as she could tell, Brad and his younger brother Peter, fifteen, their older brother Drew, twenty-nine at the time, another older brother named Jack, who had been twenty-five, and their sister Camille, twenty-eight, had been driving home from a Newport bar called Full Fathom Five when the family's Jeep Wagoneer went off the road and into a ditch. Peter had been thrown out and had been killed instantly. When the police arrived on the scene, the Putnam siblings were trying to resuscitate him. When questioned by police, the Putnam children had all said that they were knocked out directly after the accident and couldn't remember who was driving.

The reporter had written a snide little paragraph about how police were unable to determine the cause of the accident because the Putnams had "tampered with the evidence." The police had requested that the siblings all submit to blood alcohol tests, but a lawyer had been called and by the time he had spoken to everyone, it was too late.

There were a few more articles about the police investigation, with a final one about a press conference in which Newport police announced they were closing the case due to the impossibility of determining what had happened.

Then, about eight months after the accident, there was a small piece about Kitty and Andrew Putnam's separating and saying that Kitty was living in the family's Newport house. It mentioned that their son Peter had died in a car accident the previous summer and listed the names of their surviving children.

Some earlier articles told Sweeney about Brad's siblings. A few years before the accident, Drew had been made partner at the family law firm. Camille had decided on public service, and at only twenty-five, had been elected to the state assembly. A more recent piece announced that she was running for Congress. Jack Putnam, Sweeney saw from a series of arts section articles about him, was a sculptor.

She poured herself another drink and went to sit by her window, which looked toward Davis Square. Every summer of her childhood, she had gone alone to spend five or six weeks with her paternal grandparents in Newport. Their house was an old Victorian, right in town on Narragansett Avenue. It had a back garden, which Sweeney's grandmother had planted with formal English perennial beds, and from the upper floors you could see the water.

When she visited her grandparents, Sweeney had always stayed in the room that had been her aunt Anna's. It was overbearingly feminine, but she had loved it just the same, the pink- and red-rose pattern on the walls, the chenille bed-spread, and the canopy bed. The shelves had been filled with books about adventurous girls of the twenties and thirties, with names like Madge and Nan. She remembered lying in Anna's bed, which always smelled of rose petals, moonlight filtering through the windows. She had looked forward to those summers all year, looked forward to waking up that first morning to the sound of her grandparents moving about downstairs, to the distant sound of classical music on the radio. No other part of her life had that sense of timelessness, of permanence. There was nowhere else she felt as safe.

Until her mother had fallen out with her grandparents the summer she was sixteen and she hadn't gone to Newport anymore. After she was in college, she had gotten back in touch with her grandparents, even went down to visit them one summer for a couple of days. But Newport had never again had the same magic for her; it never again looked as beautiful as she remembered it from her childhood.

She remembered the thick, salty air, the constant rush of the sea. What had it been like for them, the sudden crash, then silence, being out there all alone with their dead brother and one of them—who was it?—responsible for that death.

Before she got into bed, Sweeney made some quick sketches of the jewelry. Her photographic memory made it easy and she was pleased when they were done, though not quite sure why she'd done them. As she drifted off to sleep, she thought again of Newport, of the night air, and of the Wagoneer, hurtling through the night toward death.

SIX

It was nearly eleven by the time Quinn left the station. He was tired, but his brain was moving fast, churning and sifting images and information. It was why so many cops had trouble at home, he'd decided. You couldn't just turn off your brain at the end of the day, couldn't just go home and talk about the fact that the furnace needed to be serviced or that your wife needed a new car. He pushed down a wave of guilt. He'd forgotten about Maura. For most of the day, while he'd focused on the murder case, he'd forgotten about what was waiting for him at home. He took a deep breath. He had to give himself a break. The doctor had said that he needed to leave her alone sometimes.

As he drove through Davis Square, he hesitated for a minute, then pulled over and parked across from Easter 1916, one of the best Irish pubs in the neighborhood, locking the car and leaving his jacket behind. The inside of the pub was warm and close, with the usual Sunday-night crowd—neighborhood couples, kids on dates, a few old men scowling into their Guinnesses—ensconced in the front bar. From the back room, Quinn could hear the strains of the session, the clean dance of a fiddle bow on strings, the whine of the elbow pipes, the low thrum of the bodhran. He ordered a Guinness from the girl behind the bar and made his way to the back, waving at the few people he knew along the way.

As a kid, he'd often come along when his father played sessions—not at this pub, but at ones like it all over the city. He found an empty chair in the corner and settled in. His father had closed his eyes while he played, holding the bodhran like a baby, the playing stick moving over the skin in figure eights and stars. Quinn remembered feeling disturbed sometimes, watching his father surrender to the collective effort of the music. It was as though he'd lost him to drink for those hours while he was playing. Quinn had always felt relieved when his father had stood up and stumbled outside, ready to go home, still intoxicated with the music.

They were just fooling around tonight, a couple of fiddlers and flute players, the bodhran player not keeping the beat very well. Quinn listened for a half hour and then, feeling guilty, got up and took his empty glass into the bar.

The little house off Holland Street was dark and quiet. The day they'd gone to look at it, he remembered Maura saying that it reminded her of a cottage out of a fairy tale. It was a double-decker with a robin's egg blue front door. The white vinyl siding was stained in places and the lawn needed a trim, but he was pleased overall by its appearance.

They had planted bulbs along the little stone path the past fall, when they were full of hope and happiness, waiting for the baby, and in the streetlight he could just see the beginnings of the bright green stalks trying to catch up after the long winter. He had forgotten about them until that moment and they seemed somehow cruel, reminding him of their innocence, of their life before, of all their expectations.

He hesitated for a moment outside the front door and listened. He turned his key in the lock and stepped inside, the stifling atmosphere of the house contrasting with the fresh, cool air outdoors.

In the dim light from the kitchen, he could see Maura sleeping on the couch, the television muted and flashing the bright lights of a late night talk show. The room smelled stale, rodenty. He needed to do some laundry, but there had just been too much going on.

He climbed halfway up the stairs to the second floor and listened. Everything was quiet, except for Maura's sister Debbie snoring loudly in the guest bedroom at the top of the stairs. In the living room again, he tiptoed quietly over to the couch and looked down at his wife's sleeping face. He knew he should wake her and convince her to go upstairs, but she looked so peaceful he couldn't bring himself to do it. He turned off the TV and covered her with the afghan draped over the back of the couch. She stretched in her sleep and for a moment she looked almost happy. He stared down at her, trying to recall the person she had been. But it wasn't that he couldn't remember—their smiling faces in their wedding picture on the fireplace mantel provided a cruel point of comparison. It was just that it was a kind of torture to think of how she used to be.

That morning as he'd left for work she had spoken to him softly. "I sometimes feel as though I'm nothing more than a creation of your mind, that all of the things you used to like about me were things that you made in me, that I'm nothing more than a shell that you filled with your expectations."

It struck him as strange that it was only in this crisis that they should be having the kinds of conversations he had always wanted to have with her, the kinds of conversations he imagined people like Sweeney St. George had all the time, profound, intellectual conversations that mattered. The times he'd tried to start those kinds of conversations with her she had looked at him strangely and said, "You okay, hon? Why do you want to talk about all this heavy stuff?"

He flipped through the mail, made sure she was warm on the couch, and went upstairs to bed, stopping to look in on Megan. She was sleeping, on her back as the doctor had told them she should sleep, and her tiny fists were curled up against her face as though she were protecting herself from some dreamworld demon. He wanted to pick her up, wake her, and look into her eyes, to make her feel safe again, but he knew that there'd be hell to pay if Debbie had to get out of bed because she heard the baby crying. Instead, he put a hand on her head, still dented, the soft, wispy hair so pale it could barely be seen, and felt himself start to choke up, then turned away and closed the door.

Their bedroom was a mess, clothes draped over the end of the bed and the bureaus. He started to separate the clean

things from the dirty, but got frustrated and dumped everything into the basket they used as a hamper. Then he stripped
down and took a quick shower before getting into bed alone.

He lay there in the dark and thought about the Putnam kid.
Quinn and Maura's bed was a low four-poster, about the same
height as the bed the kid had died on. He flipped over onto his
stomach and stretched his arms out, grasping each post. How
long would it take to secure one of his hands? A minute at
least, to make sure it was really tight. But it hadn't been that
tight. In fact, if Brad Putnam had really tried, Quinn thought
he could have gotten his hands untied. So why hadn't he
tried? Why, while his assailant was tying the other hand,
hadn't he slipped his other hand free and tried to escape?

There were two possibilities. One was that he had wanted
to be tied up and the other was that he had been unconscious.
Quinn remembered the reek of tequila. Perhaps it was both.
Perhaps he had invited someone back for a little S&M and
then gotten so drunk he'd passed out. They had asked the
roommate if he knew of anyone Brad was seeing who might
have done this to him and the roommate had just looked horrified and said that he knew all of Brad's friends.

As he drifted off to sleep he started awake, sure he had
heard Megan crying. But when he sat up in bed, he realized it
was only the wind.

SEVEN

———✦———

The warbler didn't know she was there. The small form sat atop the branch, the head perfectly still. His feathers were very slightly blurry through her binoculars and she adjusted the focus before they came into crystal-clear view. She watched him for a few minutes, delighting—for a single, miraculous instant—in the way he bobbed on his branch before she lowered the binoculars and turned to check on the dogs.

She had trained them to wait at the top of the cliff for her so they wouldn't disturb the birds. They were quite good at it now—only Bella sometimes broke the stay, though it was usually just to nose around in the bushes and then lie down again next to Rufus and Ollie.

Now she looked up and saw the three golden heads, watching her, waiting for the release. She climbed back up the path a ways in the early morning light and called, "Okay," and they came running toward her.

Suddenly, Kitty remembered Brad running toward her down the very same hill. It was as though she'd found a picture, so clear was the memory in her mind. It had been summer and she had been watching birds along the Cliff Walk and had walked back to the house. She'd been coming back up the path when he'd come running with the dogs—they'd had four goldens then, Rufus and the ones who were dead now, Molly, Sally, and Polly.

Brad was dead now too! It seemed impossible. She decided that if someone had asked her three days ago how she would react if one of her other children were to die, she would have said that she knew what it was like, that she knew exactly how she would feel. But it was not like that at all. This was different, this was Brad. But of course she had felt that way about Petey too. She felt the tears begin to fall again and she stood there stupidly, looking out over the ocean.

"Dogs?" she said, choking on a sob. "Come here, Rufus, Ollie, Bella." Where were they? She felt suddenly that she needed them, needed the weight of them leaning against her knees. She needed to stroke their silky heads.

She wiped her eyes and looked back up toward the house for them.

Andrew was standing at the top of the path, the dogs leaping delightedly, happy to see him.

"Hello," he called. "I thought I'd find you here."

She just stared at him, seeing Brad in his face, and turned away.

She sobbed quietly while he scrambled down to her. He was wearing perfectly pressed trousers and a new pair of loafers, and he slipped a little on the loose earth of the path.

When he reached her, he touched her arm and flinched when she turned away. He put his arms out and pleaded with her, "Kitty, please . . . our son."

She sobbed once and turned to him, letting him hold her for a minute. When she pulled away, she saw that there were some tourists on the Cliff Walk, looking up at the house. "Let's go up. I'll make you a cup of tea or something."

"Okay," he said, taking a deep breath and following her up the path. "This is one of those times I wish I was still drinking, you know?"

She didn't smile.

It was odd having him in the house again, after four years. It was her house—she felt this with an intensity that surprised her sometimes, considering she had only begun spending time in it in her adulthood. In the years of their marriage, the house, in the Putnam family for one hundred years, had grown to be hers, gradually shed its formal wallpaper and carpets and objets d'art and taken on her more relaxed style. But he moved around it assuredly, remembering where everything was, and it made Kitty feel strange and somehow violated, as though the years of freedom had been turned back in the instant he'd entered Cliff House. When the water had boiled, she filled a pot with loose Earl Grey and the hot water, and set it on a tray. She carried everything into the den.

"How are Camille and Jack and Drew?" he asked. "They said they were coming up last night."

She didn't say anything, just looked over his shoulder and out the window, where the sea was. He let her be silent for a moment. Through the glass, she could just hear the waves.

"Did they tell you? Did the police tell you? About how he was found?"

He didn't say anything for a few minutes. Then he looked at her and nodded. "A bit, the basics. They seemed nervous about telling me too much."

"What does it mean, Andrew? What does it mean? It can't have been . . . They wouldn't."

"I know, I know. No . . . they wouldn't. Of course not. It must be something else."

She stared over his shoulder for a few long moments. "You know how I've always hated the way the Putnams sweep in when something goes wrong, how they try to *control* everything?"

He nodded.

"Well, I want someone to control this. I have a bad feeling about what may come out of it. I mean we don't even know if . . ."

"I'll call someone," he said.

"But, how . . . ?"

"Kitty, don't worry. I'll call someone."

She choked back a sob then and turned away from him, wrapping herself into a ball on the couch. He got up and went to sit next to her, and she turned away, her sobs coming out in little gasps. The dogs had come in and stretched out on the floor, looking up at her mournfully, confused.

Finally, she turned toward him and let him hold her again, then pulled away after a few minutes, not wanting to let it go too far. She remembered the night Petey had died, how she had been unable to do anything but scream when they told her. They had made love that night—it had surprised her that she would be capable of such a thing—angry, violent love. She had bit his shoulder during the act, drawing blood, and she remembered that he had slapped her as he finished. She hadn't cared. It hadn't been enough to make her feel alive. She had screamed when they finished, trying to wear out her voice, wear out her feelings.

Now, she didn't have the energy to scream, but she kept crying until she was so tired that she couldn't cry anymore.

EIGHT

❦

Brad Putnam's death was above-the-fold news in the *Globe* Monday morning and as she drank her coffee, Sweeney read the story slowly, looking for subtext.

"Bradley D. Putnam, the grandson of the late Senator John Putnam and Senator Patrick 'Paddy' Sheehan, was found dead in his Cambridge apartment yesterday morning under what police have called suspicious circumstances." It went on to mention that he had been a history of art major and that he had enjoyed tennis, painting, and hiking, and it quoted Sweeney as well as a number of other students and professors and left the reader with the impression that Brad had been an exceptional scholar. The story didn't say anything about the way he had been found and, Sweeney was interested to note, didn't mention the jewelry. The Cambridge police had managed to keep at least that part of the story out of the papers.

There was a sidebar by Paul, sensationally titled TRIUMPH AND TRAGEDY, and detailing the Putnam family's successes and failures over the years.

The story led with an anecdote from Andrew Putnam and Kitty Sheehan's wedding. Paul quoted an account by a guest who said the wedding was a sort of living embodiment of the city's political history, the colonial-era patriarchy on one side of the aisle and the new power elite on the other.

"The children of Andrew Putnam and Kitty Sheehan seemed to thrive on the combination of histories and attributes their parents bequeathed them," Paul had written.

Then it went on to describe the accident on Ocean Drive. "The ensuing police investigation took on much of the atmosphere of other celebrity scandals, with a well-heeled family putting up roadblocks for the police, though this time there was no determined public demanding justice for the victim. The case was eventually closed and the Newport police were open about the Putnam family's hostility.

"The remaining Putnam siblings seemed to have moved on from the tragedies of the past. Drew Putnam is a mainstay of the family firm, specializing in real estate law and spearheading a number of development projects. Jack Putnam, a sculptor whose work the *Globe*'s own Jennifer Termino has described as 'Tragic and lyrical . . . a study in human suffering and human joy,' is one of ten or twenty artists regularly mentioned as the new generation of young, up-and-coming American painters and sculptors. And Camille Putnam, who made what can only be described as a meteoric rise through the ranks of the state assembly to the Democratic leadership of the state senate, is currently seeking to unseat incumbent Republican Congressman Gerry DiFloria in the Eighth Congressional District. DiFloria won a surprise upset in the heavily Democratic district almost two years ago after Democratic front-runner Hal McCarty was forced to drop out of the race when allegations of his involvement in a murder twenty-five years earlier while he was in college, surfaced two weeks before the election. Putnam is vying to upset DiFloria, who has turned out to be a popular congressman in the Democratic district.

"But now tragedy has struck again. And once again the Putnam family is under the microscope."

There was a picture of Camille, giving a speech. She looked outdoorsy and kind, with short dark hair and large, intelligent eyes in a plain face. And there was a picture of Brad on the inside page that made Sweeney's chest contract. He was sitting on the edge of a porch or deck railing, and below him was a wide expanse of ocean. He was grinning—she had never seen him grin that way in life—and he looked tanned and happy and brave.

She ran a fingertip across the photo. When she looked

more closely she saw that he was gripping the railing so tightly that the small bones in his hands nearly shone white in the bright sun.

Until she walked into the seminar room later that morning, she hadn't thought about what she would say to her students. Actively in denial, she had gone over her lecture notes and had planned to swallow her own unease and lecture on mourning objects and the Civil War. She had the slide carousel in her bag and photocopies of instruction on making hair-work jewelry from *Godey's Lady's Book*. She had even been looking forward to losing herself in her lecture.

But when she got there and saw the three of them—Jaybee and Becca hadn't come—sitting around the seminar table, their faces horrified, she knew that it would be impossible to teach the class as though nothing had happened.

"Hi, everyone," she said, taking off her raincoat. "I know how hard this is for me and I know it must be really awful for you too."

They stared at her, shocked, and she decided, afraid. She sat down and looked around at what was left of her Mourning Objects class.

Rajiv Patel was a tall, good-looking kid who had grown up outside of Detroit and was apparently quite a good fiction writer. He dressed like a literary wunderkind, in tweed jackets and horn-rimmed glasses, and Sweeney had always suspected that his interest in funerary art belied a stronger, more literary interest in death. He had one of the quickest minds she'd ever encountered; it instantly owned new concepts, leaping through contradictions, making connections, resolving outstanding questions. It was a pleasure to watch him think.

The other members of the little group were Ashley Jones and Jennifer Jones.

Ashley was about as improbably an Ashley as Sweeney could imagine. She had a severe bowl cut and dyed her hair a dark, inky black. She liked to wear baggy black trousers and torn black T-shirts with band names scrawled on them in red or pink. She was much pierced, some of the piercings having been abandoned and allowed to scab over, so that her ears and nose seemed gaily chicken-pocked. She was very bright and had an oddly formal writing style that Sweeney enjoyed reading. She also talked openly and loudly about heterosexism—though she was apparently herself heterosexual—and liked to instigate arguments about the morality of marriage.

Jennifer Jones was the daughter of a wealthy international businessman and had grown up all over the world, attending American and British schools in far-flung places that she would bring into their classroom conversation in her careful, slightly accented American English, as in "That's interesting, because in Indonesia there's this thing they do where they dig up the bones of the dead and rebury them." Jennifer had an exotic beauty that belied her English/Welsh roots; it was as though she'd picked up a little something from each country she'd lived in, and she wore expensive, designer clothes that Sweeney coveted. She had a bored, unimpressed way about her that seemed to make people nervous.

Sweeney had assumed that all of the men in the class would be half in love with Jennifer, but she turned out to be wrong. It was Becca who seemed the feminine center of the class, Becca who, with her sunny shoulder-length blond hair and small, muscular body clad in fleece jackets and sweatpants, was the one who had flirted and been flirted with. At various times, Sweeney had caught Brad, Jaybee, and Raj all staring at her across the seminar table. Becca was a good student, though Sweeney had decided early on that her intelligence was a result of a lifetime of expensive schools rather than any innate brilliance. When Sweeney had wondered about what Brad and Becca's relationship was, she had felt a little prick of resentment, that he was much smarter than she was and that he deserved better.

Jaybee was undeniably good-looking, with a roguish flop of dark auburn hair and dark eyes that always seemed to be flirting. He was lazy, the only member of the seminar class whom Sweeney had ever had to talk to about late papers, but he was so charming that she found herself letting him get away with things that she'd never allow from someone like

Ashley. This embarrassed her when she recognized it, and she tried not to think about it too much.

They were an odd little group, and while she knew that they socialized sometimes as a class, Sweeney suspected that with the exception of Brad, Becca, and Jaybee, they actually had other friends whom they lived with or went out with on weekends. The fact that they had become friends at all was just one of those strange accidents of college.

"So, how are you all doing?" she asked them.

No one said anything. Rajiv looked tired, his usually dapper getup downgraded to jeans and a Dartmouth sweatshirt.

Ashley looked up as though she were about to say something, but thought better of it. Her eyes were red and a bout of crying had eroded the banks of heavy mascara and eyeliner so that you could actually see her light amber eyes. In her grief she seemed younger and prettier.

Jennifer had decided to keep her emotions to herself. She looked up and met Sweeney's eyes, then looked away, revealing nothing.

"Up until the minute I walked in, I was thinking I'd have class as usual," Sweeney told them. "But I don't feel like it and I don't think you do either. Is there anything you want to talk about?"

No one said anything. When she looked around, she had the sense that they were afraid of her. Even Raj, who could usually be counted on for a smile in her direction, was stony, frozen in a kind of half-slouch, his head bent over his notebook, on which he was doodling small, seashell-shaped designs.

"It's just kind of strange, with Brad and all," Jennifer Jones said quietly.

"Have you ever had someone you knew well die before?" Sweeney asked, feeling like a shrink.

There was a long silence and then Jennifer said, "My grandmother. Oh, and this girl I went to boarding school with who slashed her wrists in the locker room."

Sweeney flinched.

"My grandfather died when I was six, but I didn't really know him," Ashley added. "And my twin sister died. In the womb. I was in there with her for two months. People say I didn't really know her, but I can remember her. I remember trying to get her to wake up and she wouldn't and she just kept staring at me with her cold, dead little eyes."

Sweeney was struck dumb and Jennifer and Raj looked horrified. There was a long uncomfortable silence after which Ashley said, "Well, it's true."

Sweeney cleared her throat. "Okay, if you need to talk to anyone, if you're feeling afraid or depressed or anything, you have my home number and I want you to feel free to call anytime. And don't forget there are a ton of counselors who are ready to talk to you too. Okay?"

Afraid, they all nodded and she let them go.

NINE

❧

Drew Putnam had been dreading seeing Pam all morning, and when he finally came out of the elevator and encountered her sitting at her desk, looking perky and for all the world like an exotic butterfly surrounded by the jungle of floral arrangements, he felt a flash of panic, an urge to do physical violence to the framed picture of her husband and son, the neat surface of her desk.

"Good morning, Pam," he murmured, looking down at the ground as he passed by her desk on the way to his office. It seemed strange that everything should look exactly the way it had only three days before. But the office was as coolly elegant as ever, thanks to the $400 an hour decorator who'd done the place over last year. He had to admit that she'd known what she was doing. The offices of Putnam and Wisecraft—on the fourth floor of a financial district office building—called up an English lord's personal library, all mahogany and richly upholstered furniture. The suite had been recarpeted in an elegant gray carpet that was the next best thing to hardwood floors and the walls were covered with original art, much of it from the family's personal collection. Many of these paintings had been hanging on the walls of the law firm since the 1800s, and though the venue was entirely modern, part of why they'd chosen it, he had the sense that he always did of going back into history. It was exactly what he hoped clients felt when they walked into the offices, a sense that Putnam and Wisecraft would always be there, would always be able to help. It was what he had told the interior decorator and he had to admit she'd gotten it just about right.

"Mr. Putnam." Pam stared at him in openmouthed shock. "We didn't think you'd be coming in . . ."

"Could you hold all my calls, please," he said, slipping out of his jacket and hanging it in the mahogany wardrobe just outside his office. "My brother and sister will be here a little bit later. Please show them in. And I'd like some coffee, please."

She had half stood behind her desk and he felt a flash of annoyance at her colorful getup—a pink-patterned miniskirt and a too-tight lime green sweater. In the old days, when his grandfather had been in charge, the secretaries would have all worn somber black for a month or so. He noticed that her eye makeup was the exact same green as her top.

"Mr. Putnam," she said. "I just wanted to say how sorry we all are. Everyone, we . . ."

"Thank you, Pam." Her sympathy was too much. He felt something loosening in him and he cut her off with his eyes, stepping into his office and shutting the door with a final "click."

His office was immaculate, the desk a perfect geometric pattern of leather blotter, leather pen cup, and two leather-framed photographs, one of Melissa and one of the whole family a couple of years before Petey's death. He put both photos facedown on the desk. He wanted to think and he felt as though he needed to be alone to do it.

A few minutes later there was a tentative knock, like a bird tapping against a tree. When he called out, "Come in," Pam opened the door and made her way over to the desk with a tray containing a French press coffeemaker filled with steaming coffee, a mug, and a little pitcher of milk. She reminded him of a crab, walking sideways in her too-high heels while trying to stay out of his line of sight.

"Thank you, Pam," he said, taking the tray from her and placing it on the coffee table. She looked as though she was going to say something else, but he silenced her with his body language, turning his back to her and busying himself with the tray. A few seconds later he heard the soft click of the door.

When she was gone, he poured the coffee and leaned back into the couch, trying to lower his heart rate by counting down from ten the way the doctors had taught him.

"You're thirty-four years old, Drew, and you're twenty-five pounds overweight and about two years away from a heart attack if you don't learn to relax a little. You've got to pinpoint where the stress is coming from in your life, perhaps through therapy or stress management classes, and work on eliminating it."

"I don't believe in therapy," he'd said. "I'll start jogging."

He still remembered the cardiologist's raised eyebrows as he'd written out a prescription for the heart meds.

"Six, five, four, three, two, one, calm," he whispered quietly, then took a deep breath. His heart was still going like a rabbit's.

Pam had put his mail in a white plastic postal service box on the floor beneath his desk, the way he liked it. He flipped quickly through the pile, but the only thing that interested him was the white cardboard tube. He pried off the plastic cap and extracted the tightly rolled design drawings for the Back Bay project. He had been waiting for them for weeks and he felt the little charge that he always did when looking at building plans for the first time. Everything looked in order. He'd show them to his contractor and then they'd get started on the inspections as soon as possible.

There was another knock on the door and without waiting for him to say anything, his sister came in.

"Jesus," she said, picking up his mug of coffee and taking a swig. "That's about the ugliest floral display I've seen since Grandfather's funeral." She was dressed in what seemed to be her uniform these days, a dark skirt and jacket combination with a plain silk blouse underneath. He wondered if she had gone out and bought twelve of them in different colors when she'd decided to run for office. Not enough to ask her, though. He only had the energy to say words that absolutely had to be said.

"Cam," he said, looking right at her. "We need to talk."

She glanced at him quickly and he saw she was afraid. "I know," she said. She looked toward the door. "Is it . . ."

"It's fine. I had it soundproofed when they did it over."

They were both silent for a moment, listening to the hollow, soundproofed air.

"Has the press been all over you?"

"Not really," she said. "We got a couple of calls about how it would affect my schedule. If there's been anything else, they haven't told me."

"Good." He hesitated, then said, "I went by your place last night. Where were you?"

Again, she looked afraid. "Oh, talking strategy with Lawrence."

"It was midnight." He raised his eyebrows and gave her a little grin, giving her a chance to make a joke out of it, admit she'd been out with someone. But instead she blushed.

"I must have been asleep and didn't hear the door," she said. "I was wiped."

But your car was gone, he wanted to say. Your car wasn't in front of the house. Instead he shrugged.

She paced to the other side of the room and he saw how unsettled she was. "Drew, what are we going to—?"

She was interrupted by another knock on the door and then Jack's dark head peeking around it. He came in, carrying a huge bottle of noxious-looking green iced tea. He was wearing jeans and tan suede Birkenstocks and he had on a ripped T-shirt covered with red paint. He looked effortlessly handsome, the dark circles under his eyes adding to his bedroom-eyed appeal. Drew felt a pang of the jealousy he'd felt as a younger man when he'd bring women home and know that they'd rather be with Jack, know they were goners the second they saw him and picked up on his tortured artist vulnerability. To Jack's credit, he had rarely taken the women up on what Drew was sure were explicit come-ons. But it hadn't mattered. Once they'd met Jack, Drew could predict with unerring accuracy the end of his own chances.

Melissa had been the first one who had seemed unimpressed with Jack's good looks. But then by the time he met Melissa, Drew was starting to realize that looks really weren't everything, that there was a certain aura that money and power conveyed as well.

"Hey," Jack said, kissing Cammie on the cheek and nodding at Drew before going to sit down on the couch and taking a long drink from his iced tea. He'd been drinking the night before. Drew recognized the signs, his bloodshot eyes, the way he leaned carefully back on the couch as though he was afraid of bruising his skin.

"How's Dad?" Jack asked.

"Okay, I guess," Cammie said. "I offered to stay with him, but he said no." She turned and went over to the window. "I don't think we should leave him alone, but he wouldn't let me stay. If you guys could just kind of check in a couple of times, see if he's okay."

"I'll go by tonight," Jack said.

"Good. Thanks." She picked up the architectural drawings and looked at the black lines as though they were a map she needed to read, then put them down again on Drew's desk.

"How's Melissa handling all this?" she asked him.

"Fine, fine." He didn't want to talk about Melissa.

"You sure about that? This must be pretty awful for her."

"I know that."

"Drew, she's fragile about this kind of stuff. I'm just saying." She reached up to scratch her head, messing up her hair. Somehow, Cammie always managed to get bad haircuts.

"I know," he snapped, then looked around at them, not sure what to say now.

They all spoke at once, then laughed nervously.

"Did either of you . . . ?"

"Did you . . . ?"

"What . . . ?"

"All right," Drew said. "We need to talk."

TEN

After returning some e-mails in her office and reading a memo from the Dean of Students about how to handle students' reactions to Brad Putnam's death (*Do* let students talk about their feelings. *Do* be alert for signs of depression or talk of suicide), Sweeney got out the sketches of the jewelry she'd made the night before, then took a couple of reference works down from her bookshelf.

In a few minutes she'd found a number of examples very similar to the hair-work necklace and decided that it had probably been made from a pattern in *Godey's Lady's Book*. That well-distributed magazine had introduced American women to the art of making hair-work jewelry in the early 1850s.

Women had little round tables, specially made for the purpose, with holes in the middle. The individual strands of hair were weighted with bobbins and the women would place little paper patterns on the top of the tables and wind locks of hair around a wire according to the instructions on the paper. When the coil was finished, the hair was boiled, baked in an oven, and the wire removed. To make balls like the one in the necklace Brad had been wearing, you had to weave the hair around little wooden forms. Sweeney looked through a dealer's catalog and discovered that the necklace would be worth anywhere from $400 to $600.

The two brooches were a little more interesting. The earlier brooch with the basketweave design was very similar to one from the late 1850s in the catalog. The later one was quite typical of the 1880s, and she had been right that the locket was also Civil War–era—there were a couple of examples in her reference book that were almost identical. Altogether, the collection was worth a couple of thousand dollars.

Where had Brad gotten it? When they'd started talking about mourning jewelry a couple of weeks before, Sweeney had told the class that there were dealers in the Boston area who carried the jewelry and in whose shops they could find examples. The logical thing was to go to some of the stores and see if Brad had bought the jewelry there. That would be useful information.

The police hadn't asked her to look into it, of course—in fact, Quinn had told her not to discuss it with anyone—but he had said they might be contacting her for further help. If she found out something more about where the jewelry came from, the police would surely be grateful, she reasoned.

"Hey, Sweeney." Sweeney's colleague Fiona Mathewson rolled past, her motorized wheelchair humming. "Are you doing okay?"

"Hey, Fiona. I'm hanging in there."

"I'm so sorry about Brad Putnam. I know he was one of your favorites."

Sweeney thanked her. "Hey," she said as Fiona headed toward the end of the hallway. "Have you heard anything about the tenure track job?"

Fiona, whose specialty was modern sculpture, was Sweeney's contact with the political inner workings of the history of art and architecture department, and with the mind of Ernest Bovato, the department chair. She was something of a gossip, but she could always be counted on for the latest news.

"Yeah, word on the street is that Bovato is talking to someone from the University of Michigan."

"Darn."

"Sorry. I know he's got it in for you. Have you talked to him about it?"

"Not lately. The last time we talked, he said he wanted someone who 'added to the international reputation of the department.' Implying of course that I don't."

Fiona smiled. "It's a ruthless world, this career we've chosen. What are you up to this afternoon?"

"Nothing," Sweeney said. "Just a little research."

Dannika's Fine Vintage, just off Newbury Street, was Sweeney's favorite of the three or four concerns in the city that dealt in vintage mourning jewelry, and she decided to start there. In the course of her trips to the shop over the years, she had developed a fondness for Dannika Montrose and her wares. She often found herself stopping in on a Saturday afternoon or a Sunday morning just to browse. Usually, when Dannika caught sight of Sweeney's bright head bent over the display cabinets, she would invite her back into the stockroom to look at a new jet pin or a particularly well-preserved hairwork necklace.

Their companionability was in their shared enjoyment of objects that many people found macabre. The shop was a small, dark building with wide glass windows in the front and a selection of vintage jewelry laid out among antique clocks and silver cutlery. Dannika changed it with each season, sometimes suspending items of jewelry from a sparkling Christmas tree or arranging them with potted spring bulbs, the old rubies and emeralds and pearls setting off shining white narcissus or pink angelique tulips. Today, it was springy daffodils planted in tubs and wearing bracelets around their stems. From the top of the window, Dannika had suspended a banner made of old parchment on which she had calligraphed, "Fluttering and Waving in the Breeze, a Host of Golden Daffodils."

Sweeney pushed through the door, and was greeted by the peculiar smell she'd come to associate with vintage jewelry stores. It was, she'd decided, an old metally kind of smell, mixed with must and the sharp tang of window cleaner.

"Hi, Sweeney," said Dannika from behind the counter. She was a thin, Dickensian figure, her gray hair in a severe bun at the top of her skull, her clothes tending toward lamb's wool cardigans, tweed skirts, and thick, flesh-colored pantyhose. Her appearance argued with her cheerful personality, though.

She had four grown children, all boys, and a fat, kindly husband, who sometimes helped out in the store. "I was wondering when you'd stop in. I haven't seen you for a while and I've got something I think you'll be interested in. Come on over here."

The inside of the store was crammed with every variety of display case—tall ones, short ones, modern chrome and glass ones, and antique ones made of old dark wood scrolled at the top. They went over to one of the older cabinets, where Dannika displayed her extensive collection of mourning jewelry, and she used one of the small keys hanging around her neck to open the latch and raise the top wide. She reached inside and pulled out a large brooch, handing it to Sweeney to inspect.

The center was an intricate web of hairwork, the blond strands braided so that they looked like a net of gold. The hair was framed by a small rectangle of diamonds and outside of that was an elaborate band of gold, scrolled intricately into leaves, fruits, and flowers.

"It's English," Dannika told her. "Got it for a song at an estate sale."

Sweeney turned it over in her hands. "It's gorgeous. How can you bear to sell it?" Sweeney knew Dannika to display items she had no intention of selling, or to refuse to part with an item at the last minute because she disliked the buyer.

"I might not," she said, smiling wickedly. "Want a cup of tea? I have the feeling you're not here to browse."

"Why would you say that?"

"Because it's Monday. You never stop by to browse during the week. And because you've got a very determined look on your face."

Sweeney laughed. "All right. I do have something to ask you about. And tea would be great."

Once Dannika had made the tea and they were seated across from each other in chairs behind the counter, Sweeney took out the sketches of the jewelry she'd made the night before and handed them over. "Do these look at all familiar? Do you think they might have passed through here in the last few months?"

Dannika took the sketches and flipped through them, staring at each for twenty seconds or so before moving on. "I don't think so. But you know, the necklace and locket are pretty typical. I see a lot of similar ones. Nice drawing of the clasps. I can't say for sure about those, but no to the brooches. What's going on anyway?"

"A bit of detective work," Sweeney said. "But I can't tell you what it's about."

"Hmmmm. You're a dark horse, aren't you?"

"I know you're the only mourning and memorial jewelry dealer worth anything around here." She winked. "But is there anyone else who might know about this stuff?"

Dannika grinned. "I don't know what you're up to, but you could try Bob Philips at the Blue Carbuncle in Concord. Him or Jeanne Manders at Beacon Antiques."

Sweeney thanked her and said she wanted to browse a little. She spent a happy ten minutes looking at the jet jewelry. Jet, the black carbonized wood that had long been associated with death and dying, had been embraced by Queen Victoria as proper mourning jewelry for its dull sheen and modest appearance. It had always held a special fascination for Sweeney, and this seemed as good a time as any to add to her collection.

She picked out a brooch in the shape of a rose and a string of jet beads, their matte facets barely reflecting the overhead light. Flushed with the pleasure of acquisition, she paid Dannika and watched her wrap the pieces up in black tissue paper and slip them into a little white paper shopping bag.

She decided to try Beacon Antiques first, finding surprisingly easy parking on Walnut Street and pushing through the door into the luxe space, inhaling the scent of potpourri and the expensive wood oils Jeanne Manders used on her wares. Sweeney always felt as though she were a guest in a very expensive and perfectly appointed home when she walked in the door, hyperconscious of her body, feeling all dangerous knees and elbows. Unlike Dannika's shop, Beacon Antiques featured furniture and decorative arts as well as a small collection of vintage and estate jewelry. Jeanne usually had a few pieces of mourning jewelry, but it wasn't her first love. Sweeney looked at the pieces she had—ones she'd seen before—and showed Jeanne the sketches.

"As you can see, I haven't had anything new here in months. It's funny, I've been going to sales, but I just haven't seen any mourning stuff recently. Sorry, wish I could help you. You tried Dannika already?"

Sweeney nodded. "Yeah, she hadn't seen it."

"I don't know what to tell you. Maybe the Blue Carbuncle?"

"Yeah, that's where I'm going next. Thanks, Jeanne. I always love coming in here."

It was still early afternoon and the traffic out to Concord wasn't too bad. Sweeney always liked going out that way. There was something about Concord that made her feel she'd traveled much farther from the city than she actually had. The stately homes that led the way into the town and the compact little commercial district took her back in time; the South Burying Ground—one of her favorite cemeteries in the Boston area—occupied her interest for a half hour before she headed over to the Blue Carbuncle.

The antique jewelry and decorative arts shop was in a blue colonial building next to a toy shop and Sweeney pushed the front door open and spent a few minutes browsing among the estate jewelry and old silver before approaching the counter and asking for Bob Philips. When the middle-aged man behind the counter said that he was Bob Philips, Sweeney explained what she wanted. He took the sketches and looked at them briefly before saying, "I didn't sell this jewelry, but a young man came in a month or so ago asking me about it. It's the earlier brooch that makes me remember him. He had all these pieces with him and he wanted to know about them, when they were made, how much they were worth, all that kind of thing."

"What did you tell him?"

"Just told him a little bit about hairwork, you know, and mourning jewelry in general. He seemed to already know a lot about it. I wasn't sure exactly what he wanted, to tell you the truth. He seemed to have some concern about the jewelry, I think. Perhaps about its value or its authenticity. He asked me if it was possible that the pieces had been tampered with, or changed. I had a quick look and they all looked authentic, but I told him I couldn't do a proper appraisal unless he left them with me. He didn't want to do that, though. I'm not sure I was able to offer him information that could ease his mind."

Carefully, Sweeney asked "Do you remember what he looked like?"

He looked suspicious at that. "I don't know that I should tell you," he said. "It seems . . . dishonest somehow. Who did you say you were?"

"I'm sorry," Sweeney said, introducing herself. "I'm just trying to track down the jewelry. My interest is scholarly. Was he fairly tall, dark hair, blue eyes? Good-looking?"

"That's him," Bob Philips said, still looking suspicious.

Sweeney was back in her Somerville apartment by five o'-clock. After sorting through bills and making a to-do list for the next day, she listened to her sole message, from her father's old friend and lawyer Bill Landseer. Sweeney's father, a well-known painter who had committed suicide when she was thirteen, had left behind a couple hundred canvases that were technically her responsibility. Bill had been nagging her about them.

"Hey, Sweeney," Bill's voice said. "I was just thinking about you and wondering how you're doing. Martha and I want to have you over for dinner and there are a couple of business things I need to discuss with you. We've had some more calls about your dad's work and I want to talk about the possibility of maybe selling a few pieces. Anyway, give a call sometime and we'll get together. Love from Martha."

Sweeney saved the message and made a note to call him back.

The rest of the mail was unpromising, credit card come-ons and advertising flyers and Sweeney was about to chuck it all into her mail basket when a slim blue envelope with a London postmark slid out onto the table. Her heart sped up and she stared at it for a few minutes, then propped it up against a vase full of daffodils from the supermarket. The crisp blue paper was richly textured, the black ink a sharp contrast to the pale background. The envelope seemed somehow fraught with danger. She knew who it was from and she knew she couldn't open it. She'd open it tomorrow. Tomorrow, she thought, with a little charge of excitement and fear.

She left it propped up against the daffodils, then got up to pour herself another drink, and took out the sketches of the jewelry again.

With Brad's interest in mourning jewelry, it didn't surprise her that he had gone out and acquired some for the seminar project. After all, he had the money and he certainly had the interest. Why wouldn't he go out and buy a few pieces? She remembered now that she had told the class about sites on the Internet where you could purchase mourning jewelry. Brad might have bought some jewelry online and then gone to the Blue Carbuncle to make sure it was authentic.

But why had he been wearing it at the time of his death?

It was when she caught sight of the student essays piled on her desk that she remembered Brad's presentation. Her senior seminar students had been working on semester-long papers. Sweeney liked to have them present their work to the rest of the class during the week they were to turn in their papers. She found her syllabus and saw that Brad had signed up to present his work on mourning jewelry in a couple of weeks. Knowing him, he'd already started writing. Surely his early draft of the paper would offer some clues to the possible significance of the jewelry, or at least what his concerns had been. So how could she get hold of it? It was something to think about.

She had found out something today, she told herself. She had found out that Brad had acquired the jewelry before his death and that he was concerned about it for some reason.

Should she call Quinn? This new bit of information meant that the police would likely be wasting their time trying to trace the jewelry to a third party. But Quinn had told her not to talk to anyone about it. If she went to him and told him what she now knew, he would be very angry. What could she do? Who would know what Brad's concerns about the jewelry were? Brad might have told Becca and Jaybee, but it would be awkward to ask them. What about his family? She had no idea if he was close to his family. Would he have talked to them about it? How could she talk to his family about the jewelry?

She decided that the key was finding Brad's paper. Then she'd have an excuse to call Quinn.

ELEVEN

❦

But as it turned out, Quinn called her first.

She was busy most of the next day and didn't get his message until she had finished her last class and checked her mailbox in the third-floor department office. Mrs. Pitman had written the message on a pink "While You Were Out" form. They had voice mail in the department, but it was impossible to convince Mrs. Pitman that it was more convenient to be able to listen to the message oneself than to scramble around for the slip of paper.

She dialed the number and when she heard Quinn's voice, she had a moment of panic. Had he found out somehow that she had gone to the antique stores? Had someone been following her?

But no. He was wondering if she would be willing to come along when he questioned the family about the jewelry that afternoon. The police were going to ask the family if they'd seen the jewelry before and they wanted to have someone present who knew about it, in order to figure out where it might have come from, on the off-chance that it had been known to Brad's parents or siblings.

"We'll ask you to keep the details of the conversation confidential," he said sternly.

Trying to keep the satisfaction out of her voice, she told Quinn that she'd be happy to help out.

She was antsy, so she locked her office door and headed for Mount Auburn Cemetery. The trees were just budding—in a week they'd be covered with blossoms. She'd brought her

well-worn map of the cemetery and she perused it as she
walked, locating the Putnam family plot on the list of prominent Bostonians buried within Mount Auburn's walls, and
finding it on the map. It was one of the older plots, on Asphodel Path, not far from the main road, but private because it was
at the end of the little path.

The plot was surrounded by a low, granite fence that had a
finial at each corner and read "Putnam" on either side of the
low gates. Sweeney stepped between them into the plot to
look around.

The highlight of the plot was the large marble monument
that sat in the very center, with the rounded heads of the
twenty or so other family stones surrounding it. The monument was in the shape of a tall church tower, with intricately
carved columns twined with ivy and roses, and exacting architectural detail. At the bottom were the words, "Charles
Danforth Putnam. January 3, 1809, to April 2, 1863. Here he
lays his quiet head; Amid the mansions of the dead."

It was a fairly common epitaph, though you usually saw it
on earlier stones. It wasn't that uncommon, though, for people
to choose an epitaph they'd seen on a parent's stone and use it
for themselves or for a family member. The reference was an
old one. It appeared in the Greek—Sophocles, Sweeney
thought she remembered—and then again and again throughout history. There were a couple of hymns that used the phrase
as well.

And she remembered with a start, it appeared in the Robert
Blair poem she'd been discussing with Brad.

"And tatter'd coats of arms, send back the sound/Laden
with heavier airs, from the low vaults,/The mansions of the
dead," she whispered to herself. "Rous'd from their slumbers,/
in grim array the grizzly spectres rise, Grin horrible, and, ob-
stinately sullen,/Pass and repass, hush'd as the foot of night."

She looked over her shoulder, feeling cold all of a sudden
in the uncertain spring air, and got out her notebook, going to
work charting the Putnam family tree from the dates on the
stones. The earliest stone marked the graves of Charles Putnam's parents, who had died in 1845 and 1852. Charles Put-

nam's stone was the second oldest and it was surrounded by stones she assumed marked the graves of a brother and sister-in-law, Joshua Putnam and Hannah Danville Putnam. They had died not long after Charles Putnam and their daughter and son-in-law were buried next to them. Sweeney always found it interesting to wonder about how certain family members were invited to be buried in the family plot and others were not.

Then there were a number of later Putnam stones, from the late 1800s and early and mid-1900s, and a series of stones with interesting floral iconography, lilies on one, ivy on another, and ferns on a third. It was common to use a broken-off rosebud as a symbol for a child who had died too young, and lilies were also relatively common, but it was interesting to see the three together. As she walked around the perimeter of the plot, she found Peter Putnam's stone, a simple black granite rectangle with his name and the dates of life and death: "Peter Sheehan Putnam. August 10, 1983–July 20, 1998." Sweeney stood before it for a few minutes, then moved on.

She walked toward the back of the plot and was looking for more synchronous dates when she caught sight of a large marble stone, its top carved to resemble a shroud. Below the folds of thick, rich cloth rendered in marble, the stone read, "Edmund Danforth Putnam. December 4, 1863–June 23, 1888. All Is Bright."

Edmund! Could it be the Edmund from the brooch?

She went around to the back of the stone but didn't find any more information. Wait, what was the date of his death? June 23, 1888. It was the same as the one on the brooch. So it had to be the same Edmund. It must be.

Sweeney grinned. That explained how Brad had gotten hold of the jewelry—it was a family heirloom. She felt a little surge of satisfaction at having figured it out ahead of Quinn. She kneeled down and cleared away some dead grass from the base, reading the epitaph again, then copied the dates and the epitaph into her notebook.

She went through all of the stones again, trying to figure out who Edmund's mother was. But there wasn't anyone with the appropriate birth and death dates.

As she was leaving, she noticed the small bouquet of wilted daisies someone had left on the grass to one side, against the fence. And when she went over to look more closely, she noticed that there was a small, white marble statuette of an angel. There were no words or dates of any kind and though the historian in her was bothered by this, she also saw the appeal of the simple anonymous angel. Whose grave marker could it be? Angels often marked the graves of children. But it wasn't Peter Putnam's stone, and she didn't think the Putnams had any other children who had died. And who had put the daisies there?

As she walked back toward campus, she tried to imagine the circumstances under which Brad had acquired the jewelry. Had he had it for a long time? Was that where his interest in mourning objects came from? But if he had had it in his possession for a while, why hadn't he ever shown it to her? It would have been the natural thing for him to bring the jewelry into class to show everyone. But for some reason, he hadn't. Why?

TWELVE

Sweeney sat in the hallway outside Andrew Putnam's library, looking up at a very modern wood and metal sculpture of a man reading a book, and listening to the murmur of voices from inside the room.

She would not have thought she'd find a piece of decidedly modern sculpture anywhere in this house. From the outside, it looked like a classic Beacon Hill residence—all brick and imposing angles, a tiny neatly landscaped garden in front planted with a few different varieties of hostas, the shiny leaves shimmering with droplets of water from the spring rain that had fallen during the night. Sweeney had expected to find a formal entryway, lots of oriental carpets and dark wood furniture. But when she'd been shown in by a middle-aged woman with a German accent and told that Detective Quinn would come and get her when he was ready, she had looked around in amazement at an airy, modern foyer, the walls painted a pale blue, a silver-and-blue geometric carpet covering the floor. The walls had simple chrome light fixtures and a few modern paintings in shades of blue and green. Through doorways leading off to other sections of the house, Sweeney could see airy rooms, the walls all cool blues and greens. Wet, spring light ran into the foyer through a skylight over her head, giving her the feeling of being underwater.

She had been told to sit on a blue silk upholstered love seat in the hallway and so she sat, feeling the lack of a magazine.

Instead, she looked up at the sculpture. She didn't recognize the artist, but there was something about it that she liked.

The human form reminded her of a little wooden artist's model, and the sculptor had managed to capture the relaxed pose of someone enjoying a good book.

The German woman came out of the room and nodded at Sweeney as she pulled the door closed behind her. It didn't quite catch and the door swung open very slightly, allowing the voices inside to carry out into the hall.

". . . need a list of his friends," a male voice was saying. "Anyone who might have been with him that night, might know what happened."

"He didn't have that many friends, actually," another male voice said. "Jaybee and Becca. The three of them hung around together a lot. There were probably others, but you know how college is. You get to be friends with people, but your family doesn't necessarily know about it."

"Jaybee and Becca are who I would say," a female voice— young, Sweeney thought—said. "They were always hanging around together. There was a girl he dated his freshman year, an Australian girl, I think. Danielle or something like that."

"Danielle Weedbottom." A different male voice this time.

"Jack!" The young woman's voice was exasperated. "It was Weedman. That's it. Danielle Weedman. Remember, Mom, he brought her for Easter or something?"

Sweeney rose to shut the door, but as she stood she discovered that she could see into the room from the love seat, that in fact she had quite a good view of a large desk and a half-moon grouping of chairs around it. The library, like the rest of the house, was a clean modern room with pale blue walls, white leather furniture, and slim glass bookshelves, suspended from the ceiling with wires. It was coolly retro, a tall, summer drink for the soul. Quinn was standing, his arms folded in front of him and his jacket hiked up at the back so she could see the holster on his belt and the silvery gun. Behind the desk was a slim, silver-haired man who she knew must be Andrew Putnam. He had his hands folded on the desk and seemed to be consciously trying to keep his posture in check.

There were eight adults in the room. The small middle-aged woman with short blond hair sitting on the opposite side of the desk had to be Kitty Putnam, and from the newspaper photos, she knew that the tall young woman—whose face she could not see—wearing a not particularly stylish dark-colored jacket and skirt that almost matched her short hair would be Camille Putnam.

The other woman in the room was far more glamorous than either her mother-in-law or sister-in-law. Melissa Putnam struck Sweeney as being very tall, though she was sitting in a chair to the side of the desk. She had a long, equine nose, high cheekbones, and impossibly blond hair. Her long legs were crossed and Sweeney could see that she was wearing high-heeled sandals with her dark trousers. Her toes were a perfectly pedicured scarlet and Sweeney found herself wondering if she'd had them done before Brad's death or after.

She could only guess about the remaining two men in the room, but she thought that the older and heavier of the two must be Drew Putnam. She could see three-quarters of his beefy, bland face, the rather thickly formed neck that rose out of a white dress shirt, the collar girded by a blue-and-red rep tie. His face was pink and Sweeney couldn't help but think of a boar. The younger man in the room was sitting with his back to Sweeney, and she saw only a pair of broad shoulders under a black leather jacket, long legs crossed, a head of longish, slightly wavy dark hair. Jack.

"Well, we'd appreciate it if you could put a list together," Quinn said. "Anyone you can think of. It may not seem important to you, but put it down anyway. Any girlfriends, even someone he may have dated very briefly, may have . . . spent time with." Quinn cleared his throat.

"I don't know what your relationship with your family is like, Detective Quinn," said the man Sweeney guessed was Jack Putnam. "But I doubt you told them about everyone you've ever dated or"—he paused and gave the words the sexual innuendo that Quinn had intended but not expressed—"*spent time with.*"

"Well," Quinn said, embarrassed. "Anything you can think of." He cleared his throat again and said, "Now I'm going to

bring in Ms. St. George. She was, as you know, your son's—
Brad's—art history professor. We . . . the police, I mean, have
asked her to help us track down where the jewelry that was
found at the crime scene might have come from and whether
it might tell us who killed him. She can answer any questions
you might have about it, but we mostly just want to know
whether Brad owned it before his death and where it might
have come from."

He came over to the door, opened it all the way, and stuck
his head out. Sweeney was looking up at the sculpture again,
as though she hadn't heard a word.

"Hi, thanks for coming," he said. "You can come on in."

He held the door for her and she stepped into the room just
as the three Putnam men stood up politely to greet her. Quinn
introduced her to his partner, Detective Marino, a middle-
aged guy who reminded Sweeney of the football coach at a
high school she'd gone to in Michigan. When he sat down, his
jacket gaped open and she caught the title of the paperback he
had tucked into his waistband, *The Rancher's Daughter*.
Sweeney had been right about Jack Putnam and as she shook
his hand, she felt a little lurch; her stomach knew that he was
good-looking before her brain did.

"It's nice to meet you," Andrew Putnam said kindly. "Brad
loved your classes and he thought a lot of you. And thank you
for the very kind things you said in the paper."

Jack caught her eye and smiled, making her flush. He had
darker hair than Brad and his facial features were similarly
angular, only on him they had been arranged more precisely,
more perfectly. But the eyes were the same.

Sweeney awkwardly murmured her sympathy and then
Quinn told everyone to sit down before taking out a large
photograph of the four pieces of jewelry laid out on a white
background.

He nodded at Sweeney and she leaned forward to take the
photograph from him.

"The first question, I suppose, is have you ever seen these
pieces of jewelry before?" Sweeney asked them nervously,

feeling that she was performing. "Are they something that Brad had ever shown you or told you about?"

She walked slowly around the room, showing the picture to each of them.

"What are they?" asked Melissa when Sweeney showed it to her. "It's so strange." She looked almost childishly curious and Sweeney was struck by her childlike beauty, her large blue eyes and straight, pale hair.

Jack looked up at Sweeney and she felt herself looking back into those familiar chameleon-blue eyes, fringed with thick lashes. "It's mourning jewelry, isn't it?" he asked. She nodded. "It looks kind of familiar. Is it . . . Mom?" He motioned for Kitty to come over and she leaned over the photograph.

"Oh my God," she said.

"What? Have you seen any of these pieces before?" Sweeney tried to affect a note of total surprise.

"Yes, of course," Kitty Putnam said. "They belonged to Andrew's mother."

Andrew Putnam came over and looked down at the photograph too. "Oh yes," he said. "I haven't seen these in ages. But I think you're right. I think they were my mother's."

"That's right. You used to have them in your jewelry box, Mom," Camille said. "Drew and Jack would try to scare me with the necklace, tell me it was the hair of dead people."

"It *is* the hair of dead people," Jack pointed out, glancing at Sweeney.

"Had you given the jewelry to Brad?" Sweeney asked Kitty.

"No . . . at least I don't think so. They must have been in some boxes of stuff up in the attic at the Newport house. Brad was down for the weekend a month or so ago and he asked if he could look around up there. He must have taken them."

"But he didn't tell you he'd taken it?" Quinn asked her. "Would that have been strange? For him to just take something that belonged to you and not say anything?"

Kitty looked up at him, impatient. "It wasn't like that. It was just, you know, old stuff up in the attic. He said he was working on a project for school or something and could he look around up there and see what he could find. I said that of course he was welcome to anything he found up there. It was mostly things belonging to Andrew's family, anyway."

"What is it?" Melissa asked again. "Is it really made from hair?"

"Yes," Sweeney said. "It was very common, particularly in Victorian times, to have jewelry made from the hair of the deceased. It was a way of keeping the person with you always, even after death."

Melissa's eyes grew wide.

Sweeney looked around at the rest of the family. "Now that you know where it came from, does it ring any bells? Do you ever remember Brad talking about the jewelry?"

"I don't think so," Drew said. He looked around at his siblings and they all shook their heads.

"He was interested in that kind of stuff, though," Camille said quietly. "He liked graveyards."

"He did," Kitty said. "He liked graveyards. When he was little he liked to sit in them. He wasn't scared at all." She almost started crying again, and when she looked up at Andrew, Sweeney saw that his eyes brimmed too.

Her eye was caught by a framed family photo on Andrew's desk and partly because she was interested and partly because she wanted to give him something to do, she said, "What a great picture."

"Thanks. That was Jack's opening at the Davis Gallery a couple of months ago."

Quinn cleared his throat. "Okay, we'll leave you folks for now. Thank you for your help." He put the photograph away.

Sweeney looked up quickly at him. "But there are a lot more—"

"I'll walk you out," he said firmly. Jack looked up at Sweeney and raised his eyebrows.

Camille said quickly, "It was nice to finally meet you. Brad loved your class, you know."

Sweeney, confused, looked around at them. "It was nice to meet you too," she said. "And again, I'm so sorry."

Out in the hallway, Quinn said, "Thanks so much. You were a big help. And we found out where it came from anyway. So we don't have to go looking for a third party." His accent seemed stronger to Sweeney—he said "thuud" for "third." "That's great—"

"But there are a lot more questions I'd like to ask them," Sweeney cut in. "We need to know what he was interested in about the jewelry, how long he'd had it." Why he'd been asking Bob Philips at the Blue Carbuncle about it, she almost said, and then caught herself.

"Yes, we'll take care of that," he said distractedly. He looked very tired, his blue eyes bloodshot and shadowed.

"But you can't just let it go! You said you wanted to know about the jewelry. There are so many more questions."

"Ms. St. George, you helped us determine that the jewelry wasn't brought into the apartment from the outside, that it was in fact in Mr. Putnam's possession before he was killed. That's what we were trying to figure out. So again, thank you." He leaned over slightly, trying to emphasize his height advantage. But he only had an inch on her and she leaned forward too, forcing him to step back.

"But . . . I think he was suspicious about it for some reason. There are a number of really interesting possibilities for why he might have been."

"Ms. St. George, we can take it from here. I've got to go back in now."

"I don't think you understand what this could mean for—"

"Good-bye." He went back into the room and shut the door behind him.

Still furious by the time she got home, she stripped off her clothes, throwing them against her bedroom wall, and padded through to the bathroom to start a bath.

One of Sweeney's favorite features in her apartment was the old, claw-footed tub in the otherwise unremarkable bathroom. She did some of her best thinking lying in a tubful of slightly too-hot water. She sprinted naked—having forgotten to close the drapes in the living room—through to the kitchen to pour herself a scotch, and just as she was preparing her dash back to the bathroom, saw the thin, blue letter propped against the now tired-looking daffodils. On impulse, she took it too.

The tub was almost full and she lowered herself into the scalding water gratefully, then sipped her scotch and sank down into the water with a long sigh.

She lay there for a good ten minutes, letting her anger seep out of her into the water before she reached over to pick up the envelope she'd left on the window ledge. She turned it over in her hands. It had been a long time since she had received a letter, a real letter—she had often thought of future scholars looking for the epistolary remnants of the late twentieth and early twenty-first centuries. What would they find? Files on computer hard drives?

She used a nail file to slit the top and pulled out the sheet of thick, expensive blue paper. As she stared at the careful handwriting, her eyes dropped to the signature, "Yours, Ian," written in a slightly more flamboyant version of the writing that spelled out, at the top of the letter, "Dear Sweeney." The writing reminded her of him, careful, neat, but with more of an edge to him than it had seemed at first. Ian! She had managed to put him mostly out of her mind since that strange and horrible Christmas in Vermont. Except for a few guilty flashbacks—half-dreamed memories of how her body had felt pressed against his—she had tried to forget about Vermont, about the murders, about the way they had revealed Toby's family's secrets, about the way they had driven her into the arms of an enigmatic Englishman, divorced, with a small daughter. Someone entirely unsuitable for her. Too far away, too encumbered.

Still, she read on. "I have resisted writing for weeks now. But this morning I woke up and no longer felt like resisting. It was hugely relieving, as you can imagine, to shrug off this great weight and to sit down to, finally, write you a letter. It is only a letter, I told myself. I will be chatty and tell her of the things that I am doing at work, about Eloise and about my life.

"Work has been fine. We've taken on three new people at

the auction house and while I suspect one of them of being peripherally involved in an international drug ring, he has quite a good eye. Well, well, as long as he doesn't bring it to work . . ." Sweeney could almost see his wry smile, the dark eyebrows rising ironically.

"Eloise is well. She has taken up writing, it seems, and sends me letters from school with long stories in French that seem to be more clearly written versions of her favorite fairy tales, Cinderella down to the basics. As for myself, I've been working on cataloging the contents of a country house in Devon. I stayed at the local inn and went for long brisk walks each morning out to the house, where I spent my days with various family members, all suspicious of one another and all watching me like proverbial hawks. There was a bit of a mystery while I was there— about a Chinese vase; I can't really do it justice here—and I thought of you and how you would have enjoyed sleuthing around and finding out the truth about it. But that brings us back to you, doesn't it, and to me wishing that you were here. So you see, I have tried to write a letter that did not once mention that fact that I wish you were here, but I have failed.

"I returned to London in early January thinking that I would wait for you to contact me. You have been through so much and I didn't want to complicate things for you. But then I remembered you standing there in that awful, cold snow, that snow that seemed to compound the losses we had all suffered during those weeks. As we stood there together in the falling snow you said, 'Maybe I'll come visit, in the spring.'

"At lunchtime today, I went for a walk in Hyde Park. The grass is newly green and everywhere there was a sense of life trickling back into things, of that sweet syrup that runs through all living beings. There were daffodils everywhere I looked, daffodils that not so much fluttered and waved at me as bowed. The fruit trees were in full flower, the branches of the cherry trees like lamb's tails with their heavy flowers."

There was a word crossed out and then, in slightly darker ink, "It is spring, decidedly so. It is spring."

And as though the beautiful words had given him courage, he had signed his name with a bit of a flourish. "Yours, Ian."

THIRTEEN

The bride stood for a moment under the arched door at the end of the aisle. It may have been the way the spring light had gathered up behind her in the open church door, but she seemed, Sweeney thought, to be hovering in space, her father beside her, the strains of the Wagner wedding march rising up around the congregation. Her dress was blinding white and the voluminous veil, studded with pearls, shrouded her in mist.

They rose. When Katie and her father appeared at the end of the aisle, Sweeney couldn't help but turn to look at her groom. He stood next to the minister, his face turned toward the sun in expectation. When he saw his bride, he smiled broadly and didn't stop smiling.

The guests watched as Katie and her father walked slowly, arm in arm. When they reached Milan, Katie's father lifted her veil, kissed her on the cheek, and let it fall again. She turned to her bridegroom, bravely, confidently, and stepped forward into a small pool of light on the red runner. The music stopped and they all sat down. It was very silent in the church. The minister began to speak.

Katie had met Milan in London. He was from Croatia, and his family's home had been destroyed in the early days of the wars in the former Yugoslavia. A neighbor had died in his arms, and he had joined the army and been responsible for more deaths. When it was all over, he had gotten a scholarship to the London School of Economics and met this American princess, working for an investment bank in London.

Sweeney wondered suddenly how they'd come across each other. They seemed so entirely different that she had trouble imagining how that first spark had been fanned. But they were good together. She had been invited for dinner at their apartment in the Back Bay a few months ago and had liked their rapport—Katie a soothing, almost maternal presence, calmer and happier than Sweeney remembered her from college, making dinner and refilling their wineglasses. Milan, in his perfect but heavily accented English, had asked Sweeney about her work, talked about his wine collection, and closed his eyes when a favorite passage of classical music had come on the stereo.

Sweeney watched his face. A cloud must have crossed the path of the sun through the stained glass windows, because the shaft of light that had been illuminating the couple disappeared, leaving them standing there on the shabby carpet.

"Marriage is a leap of faith," the minister was saying. "We go forward out of giddy love, not knowing what the road ahead holds for us. But we promise, and in promising we make real. Katie and Milan are promising themselves to each other today, not for the foreseeable future or until it's no longer fun, but forever after, for the rest of their lives, and it is that promise that will hold them together when things get difficult, when sadness comes into their lives, as it surely will, when they are fighting, when they can no longer remember the emotions that bring them here today."

Sweeney found herself remembering one of her parents' almost-constant fights in the year before she and her mother had moved out. Her mother had been appearing as Lady Macbeth and she and her father had gone to the dressing room before the show. Sweeney's parents had started to argue about something—Sweeney couldn't remember what it was, though she remembered their words. Ivy had been wearing bloodred robes, her long, ramrod-straight reddish hair piled in elaborate braids on her head, her face pancaked and rouged.

"You're so bloody selfish!" she'd screamed. "You don't care about anyone but yourself! I can't believe you would do this to me now!" Sweeney had huddled in a corner and watched her mother, a petite, red fury, storming around the dressing room. Her father had done what her father always did, gone stony silent, staring at Ivy, egging her on.

Ivy had given one of the best performances of her life that night. She had inhabited her rage, explored it on stage in front of the audience, plumbed its depths. Six months later, she and Sweeney had left.

But then they had never gotten married. Her father had thought it bourgeois and unnecessary. Would these simple words have saved them? Would the fact of the ceremony have given her mother a reason to stay? Sweeney didn't think so.

"I, Katherine Marie Swift, take you, Milan Simic, to be my husband," Katie was saying, pronouncing his name lovingly the way he pronounced it, "Mee-lawn Sim-ich."

As she spoke, the light returned. The voices went on and Sweeney found that tears were streaming down her cheeks. Toby looked at her curiously and took her hand, rubbing the top of her thumb in a comforting way.

"What God has tied together," the minister said in a booming voice, "let no man put asunder."

When the ceremony was over, Sweeney and Toby drove through Newport, along Bellevue Avenue toward Ocean Drive, Toby holding their gift—an ice cream maker from the gift registry that was the only one of the possible gifts that had attracted Sweeney when they'd gone shopping.

The tree-lined sidewalks passed discreetly by the big houses, the "cottages," offering glimpses of high third-story windows. She had spent more time here than she'd spent almost anywhere else, but the sheer opulence of Newport always surprised her. It seemed incredible that there should ever have been enough money to have built The Breakers or Marble House or Rosecliff.

Or for that matter, Cliff House.

It was just as she remembered it, behind high gates toward the end of Bellevue Avenue, almost at the point where the road turned sharply.

"That's the Putnams' house, right?" Toby asked as they

passed. Sweeney nodded, slowing the car so they could look through the black iron gates, the high turrets of the gray stone house. The sign on the gates read CLIFF HOUSE. PRIVATE. They could just see the sweeping grounds leading down to a high hedge over the ocean. The upstairs windows reflected the pinkish sky. Sweeney sped up as they passed and the house dissolved into pieces, flashing through the bars of the fence like the images in a child's flip book.

"I always feel weird here," Sweeney said after a few minutes. They had turned onto Ocean Drive and were passing Bailey's Beach.

"Why?"

She glanced at the beach again. "You know, because of the way everyone treated us. My parents not being married and all that."

"It seems hard to believe that it would have been that big a deal." Toby, who had spent much of his childhood living on a Berkeley commune, was always surprised by Easterners and their strange sense of propriety.

"Well, it was. There were kids who weren't allowed to play with me because of it. It always mortified my poor grandmother."

They drove past the houses built by the more recently affluent, huge modern structures made of glass, with too-symmetrical stone walls and stark landscaping surrounding them. "Okay, this is it. Number 496, on the left," Toby said. She slowed and turned into a long drive. At the top, near another huge, stone house, half a dozen teenage boys in tuxedos were parking cars. Sweeney surveyed the detritus of her life that had washed up on the floors and seats of the Rabbit—papers, books, a pair of black socks, candy bar wrappers, and empty coffee cups. Well, she supposed they'd seen everything.

The parking attendant directed them toward the white tent that sat in the middle of the sweeping lawn. The entrance to the tent had been decorated with huge pots filled with spring bulbs in shades of pink and white and violet—tulips and grape hyacinths and pale white narcissi. They put their box on the gift table and accepted glasses of champagne from the tuxedoed waiter who greeted them.

"Toby!" A group of women who looked vaguely familiar to Sweeney set upon them, hugging Toby and looking curiously at her.

"You remember Sweeney, don't you?" he was saying, and the women were being kind and saying that they did, though Sweeney didn't believe them. And for her part, she had only a vague sense that she remembered them, from freshman year, she thought, before everyone had gone off into their own little groups, groups they wouldn't emerge from until senior year, in a fit of fellowship. Yes, of course, freshman year. They had been on her hall, as had Katie. Toby had been on the boys' hall at the other end of the dorm and they had all kind of leaned on one another that first year.

She listened to Toby's introductions and her good memory matched the faces with the names. Lily Nakamura, from New Orleans, Sweeney had always liked. She had been a biology major, Sweeney thought, and won some kind of prestigious prize their senior year. Hallie Tyler, who had joined the Peace Corps and been taken hostage in Tanzania. Something like that, though in her robin's egg blue strapless dress and shawl, her blond hair in a chignon, a tall, happy date on her arm, she looked none the worse for wear. And finally—the fourth woman had wandered off to greet someone else—there was a woman named Hannah Allbright, who Sweeney remembered was from Boston. From a newspaper family, she thought she recalled.

They caught up for a few minutes, discovered they were all at the same table, and then Sweeney and Toby set off to find the bar. The tent had been opened at one end to afford a view of the water and it sparkled beneath them, pure and perfect.

"You doing okay?" Toby asked as they waited for their champagne. A passing waiter offered them blinis with caviar.

"Fine. Why?" Sweeney said through a mouthful of sour cream and fish eggs.

"I don't know. You just get weird at these things. I always

feel like I have to check up on you. And you wore that weird jewelry."

Angry, she looked down at the jet pin and beads, hardly noticeable against her black cocktail dress. "Well, as a matter of fact, I'm fine. And you don't have to check up on me. I know people here too. Why don't you go back and talk to your girlfriends and I'll find someone to talk to on my own."

She took a champagne flute from the bartender and left him.

"Christ," she heard Toby say behind her.

It would be all right. She'd find him for dinner and things would be fine. They fought like siblings most of the time, and if in the past it had masked a more complicated relationship, she felt confident that they'd resolve this one without any of the past angst.

A little over a year ago, when Colm had died in London, Toby had dropped everything to come and care for her.

And then at the end of the year, she had been able to return the favor. After what had happened in Vermont, after all those deaths and the wounds that had been inflicted on his family, they had spent most of January acting as though Toby were terminally ill. Every night, Sweeney had brought him takeout or made him elaborate and expensive dishes from recipe books she rarely used. They had watched movies and they'd drunk too much. Then, one night in late February, Toby had called her and said that he was going out with some friends and did she want to join them. Slowly, he began to seem more like himself.

On the first anniversary of Colm's death, Sweeney had gone to Mount Auburn by herself and found one of her favorite graves, belonging to a sailor who had died at twenty-seven. Colm's real one was in Ireland, of course. She hadn't ever seen it. His parents had invited her to come for the wake, but she hadn't felt she could. She had let Toby pack up her stuff and take her home. He had even made the phone call to the department, asking if she could teach.

But on that cold January day, she had mourned in front of that substitute grave.

And now after the long winter, it was finally spring. Two weeks had passed since Brad's death and the sun had grown stronger, the days longer. Sweeney wandered over to the edge of the tent and looked out over the water, inhaling the wet, new scent of it. Below, the lawn was a fresh green and the flower beds were full of spring bulbs. The tulips had been planted in a progression of color, pink fading to white, then to palest peach and then to yellow as they swept across the beds. Overhead, the trees that shaded the lawn were leafing enthusiastically.

She was looking for someone she knew when she caught sight of Jack Putnam across the crowd, in mid-conversation with a middle-aged man. When he saw her he gave a little wave, gestured in her direction to the man, and made his way across the grass to her.

"Hi, I thought that was you," he said.

He looked—really looked—at her, studying her eyes, and she recognized the little flutter of something in her stomach that she'd felt the first time she'd met him. He was wearing black tie, like all the other men at the wedding, but his suit looked somehow more modern than everyone else's, and rumpled, as though he'd slept in it. His hair looked slept in too, but his eyes—*exactly* like Brad's, it struck her again—were alert and interested.

She hadn't said anything yet and he looked worried. "I'm not taking you away from anything, am I?"

"No, no. Hey. I was just going to have a scotch. Want one?" She raised her eyebrows in expectation.

He grinned. "Sure," he said, and she ordered and handed him his highball.

There was an awkward silence and then Sweeney said, "So, how are you all doing?"

"Not great," he said honestly, but his emotions were under control. There was nothing raw about him. "I thought that coming out to this"—he gestured around him at the party—"would be healthy, but I don't know . . ." He nervously patted the pocket of his tuxedo jacket, then looked out across the lawn beyond the tent. "I really need a smoke. Do you . . . ?"

Sweeney shook her head. "But feel free to . . ."

"Come out with me. I don't feel like being reminded of my leperlike status as one of the last smokers in the free world."

Sweeney laughed. "All right, since you put it like that. I wouldn't want to contribute to the further social isolation of a promising young artist."

He winked at her. "Yes. Who knows what could happen? Giant sculptures of cigarette packs. It would be all your fault."

They laughed, and she followed him out of the side of the tent. It had grown dark suddenly while they'd been inside and it seemed to Sweeney as though she was stepping off the edge of the earth. She stumbled a little in her heels as they came out onto the grass and Jack reached to steady her. He was taller than Sweeney. His hand quite naturally clasped her upper arm.

"Thanks." She took off her shoes, the feel of wet grass on her bare feet waking her up, sending blood clanging through her veins, and she looked for him, searching the darkness for his features. They walked down the sloping lawn to a wide stone bench set at the top of the hill and sat down. Jack took a cigarette pack out of his pocket and tapped one out. He put it in his mouth and lit it, then leaned back against the bench with relief and inhaled deeply.

"So how do you know Katie?"

"College. She was on my freshman hall. We were friends, though not really close ones. I was actually surprised I was invited."

"I think Katie's one of those people who you think would have a lot of friends, but in fact doesn't. Not that that's why you were invited. I mean, I think people are more important to her than they think they are."

They were silent for a few minutes as he smoked and Sweeney listened to the ocean, crashing far below them.

When he was finished he stood up and tossed his cigarette over the edge. Sweeney stood up too. "I guess we should get back. Toby will be looking for me."

"Your date?"

"Best friend. He was on our freshman hall too. Actually he and Katie dated briefly, but of course they've stayed good friends. Toby has an amazing ability to stay friends with his exes. Not me. I'm usually lucky if they don't hate me." They started walking back up the hill.

"Me too," he said. "I think there are clubs devoted to hating me, peopled by my exes." When they got to the tent, he said, "Thanks. Maybe I'll find you for a dance later."

Sweeney looked up at him and felt her stomach pitch again. He smiled.

"I really am sorry about your brother. I liked him. He was . . . well, he was . . . special. More so than the other kids I taught. I'll really miss him."

"He liked you too. I think he had a crush on you, in fact. Now I can see why." He studied her for a moment. "Hey, you know what? It would mean a lot to all of us if you could come to the memorial service tomorrow. We can't bury him yet because of the police, but . . . we thought it would be good for everyone. And then we'd love to have you come back to the house afterward."

"I'd like that," Sweeney said.

"Good." He smiled and headed off just as the music stopped and the band leader announced that it was time for everyone to take their seats.

Toby and Sweeney were at a table with Lily, Hallie and her date, and Hannah Allbright and her husband. Hannah and her husband both worked for the *L.A. Times* and, blaming their interest on their occupations, they were asking Toby about Brad Putnam when Sweeney joined them. "It's big news everywhere," Hannah was saying. "It's these kinds of stories that make you search your soul. You know, why is Brad Putnam's death big news when the five black kids who got killed in Washington, D.C., last week don't even make the *Post*. Hi, Sweeney."

Toby gave her a look to make sure she wasn't still mad, and Sweeney crossed her eyes at him to show she wasn't.

"So," Hannah said in a conspiratorial voice. "I saw you talking to Jack Putnam. How do you know him?"

"I don't, really. Just through this whole thing with Brad Putnam."

"He was one of her students," Toby explained to them.

"I grew up with Brad and Jack and the other kids," Hannah said. "You can't imagine what a crush I had on Jack when I was ten. He was always kind of *bad*. You know what I mean?" She rubbed her husband's arm reassuringly. He shrugged in a funny what-am-I-chopped-liver? kind of way that made Sweeney like him.

Since she was sitting next to Lily, Sweeney turned and asked her what she was doing these days.

"I work for a private lab," Lily said. "It's interesting work, although I feel like a bit of a sellout. But they're letting me head up my own division. I do mitochondrial DNA research and it's a good opportunity. I hope I'll get back to MIT at some point, though."

"Mitochondrial DNA?" Sweeney asked, genuinely interested.

"Yeah, there are two kinds of DNA, nuclear and mitochondrial. Nuclear DNA is found in the nucleus, the center, of the cell, and it contains genetic material from both parents. When someone's raped, or when you've got a lot of blood, that's what they use to identify the person who the material came from.

"Then there's mitochondrial DNA. That's what I'm specializing in. Mitochondrial DNA is, in many ways, more promising because it stands up over time better than nuclear DNA. It only links to the mother's side of the family though, which limits the applications somewhat. But you can find it in more parts of the body. Hair strands with no skin attached for example. I'm working on improving our methods so that we can extract usable samples more easily."

"What kinds of stuff does the lab do?"

"Oh, these days, half of our work is paternity suits. I swear. You wouldn't believe the things that people do. There was a case I was working on where this woman didn't know who the father of her son was. There were a bunch of likely candidates, but two guys she liked more than the others, and she had decided that if one of them was the father, she would marry whichever guy it was. So she had to get DNA samples from the two men, but without them knowing. She ended up waiting until they were asleep and yanking a handful of hair out of each of their heads. She said they thought she was crazy. But she got it and we figured out who the father was. She even sent me an invitation to the wedding!"

Sweeney laughed.

After the waiters came around with the first course and poured the wine, everyone stopped talking for a while as they watched Katie and Milan dance their first dance. And then there was dinner—filet mignon—and toasts and dancing, and it wasn't until Katie and Milan had cut the cake that the conversation turned back to the Putnams.

"I just feel so sorry for them," Hannah was saying. "Losing Petey, and now this."

"Were you around when Petey died?" Sweeney asked her.

"Yeah. It was the summer, of course. So everyone was around. My parents were pretty good friends with Kitty and Andrew when they were together and they and the Dearbornes and some other friends spent a lot of time up at the house, trying to help them. The police were just awful. They wouldn't let them alone."

"What did everyone think about it at the time?" Sweeney asked her. "Did people believe the story about none of the kids remembering anything?"

"I don't think anybody did. But you know we all felt that there wasn't any point in trying to figure out who did it. Whoever it was—and I always thought for some reason it must have been Drew, I guess because he was the oldest—but if it was, I kind of felt like it didn't matter. He must be living with it and he didn't mean to do it, obviously."

Sweeney looked up to see who else was listening. Toby was engrossed in a tête-à-tête with Lily and everyone else had gotten up to get cake.

"Anyway," Hannah said. "I think everyone felt sorry for them, because of the way they'd grown up."

"What do you mean?" Sweeney asked.

"Well . . ." Hannah looked down at the table, then back up at Sweeney. "Andrew Putnam was . . . let's just say he liked to drink. And apparently Kitty had completely stopped dealing with it at some point. And the kids were the ones who had to handle it. All of us who were friends with the Putnams knew about it. At some point you'd be sleeping over and one of the kids would have to take the bottle away from him. Camille was always having to go down and pick him up at some bar or another when they were in Newport. And when he came home, they would have to undress him and put him to bed."

She looked around, watching the dance floor, where Jack Putnam was dancing with Katie's mother, who looked pleased and girlish.

"The ironic thing, of course, is that he quit after the accident. Never took a drink again. My parents always thought it was so odd, because that had been the big problem with the marriage. And then he stopped and they split up anyway. I always wondered why she left him then, after everything else that she'd put up with. But of course, there are statistics about that, aren't there? When a child dies. Most people split up, I think."

"It's that people grieve differently. It's alienating, it makes you feel this chasm between you and the other person, because your experience of grief isn't the same," Sweeney said.

"It's interesting, though, because with Drew and Melissa the accident brought them closer together," Hannah went on. "They had been kind of off and on and then after the accident they got married right away."

She changed the subject and was going on about something else, but Sweeney had stopped paying attention. "Hannah," she said. "I just remembered something I have to do. I'm sorry. It was really good to see you."

Hannah looked confused. "Are you all right?"

"Yes. I just . . . I have to go."

She looked around the tent for Jack Putnam. He wasn't on the dance floor, and when she walked around the perimeter of the tent, checking the tables and the small groups of people smoking outside, she couldn't find him either. Maybe he'd gone home already. She found Toby and Lily talking—and leaning dangerously close to each other—in a corner of the tent.

"If I leave now, do you think you can get a ride back?"

Toby looked up at her, bewildered. "What . . . ? You can't leave now. The dancing's just started. Are you okay?"

"I'm fine. I just realized something is all. And I need to go talk to the person who it concerns. I . . . it's too complicated to explain. But I'll call you tomorrow, okay?"

"I guess. Are you sure you don't want me to come with you?"

"Yes," she said. "Nice to see you again, Lily. See you soon."

"You too," Lily said. She and Toby exchanged a glance.

It was almost eleven. One of the teenage valets got the Rabbit and looked disdainfully at the dollar Sweeney gave him when he opened the door for her.

Sweeney opened the windows to feel the night air on her face. She'd had a couple of glasses of champagne, as well as the whiskey. Not enough for her to be drunk, but she felt a little foggy, a little buzzed. She was pretty sure she'd be able to remember where the Putnams' house was. At night, Ocean Drive was inky, the big houses barely visible high on their bluffs. The air smelled thickly of salt and seawater, the wind was strong, and it seemed to Sweeney as though it blew through to every part of her through the open windows. It was cold and jarring, but it kept her going, kept her awake. She stopped for a moment and got out of the car, turning her face toward the churning surf.

She headed down to Bellevue Avenue and a few minutes later, she pulled into the driveway of Cliff House, relieved that the gate was open and that there wasn't anyone on duty at the little gatehouse that waited just inside like a squat, stone sentry.

The driveway curved around a flat, green lawn, shadowy and dappled by moonlight. The house was mostly dark—the only lights were on the first floor, and as she pulled up alongside a station wagon parked at the edge of the circular drive, she was suddenly nervous. From Bellevue Avenue, you had the sense that the house was not that far away, but here, behind the iron gates, it seemed a silent island of privilege.

The dark windows were a cypher. If someone was watching her from inside, she didn't want to appear furtive. So she strode right up to the front door, knocked loudly, and listened to the frantic barking of dogs from inside. She was expecting the door to be answered by a housekeeper or a butler, but it was Kitty Putnam herself who opened the door.

"I'm sorry, I didn't want to scare you, but I need to talk to you about something. Is Jack home yet?"

"No, he's at a wedding. What is it?" Kitty's eyes stared and Sweeney had the awful sense that she was reenacting something for this woman. A strange figure coming up the steps at night, disturbing her grief. Of course! She thought Sweeney had come to tell her that someone else had died.

"Everything's fine," Sweeney said hurriedly. "I mean . . . I just came to talk to you." The dogs, three golden retrievers with silky, luxuriantly groomed auburn coats, had stopped barking and now they pushed out the door, trying to nuzzle the visitor.

"I realized something tonight, about Brad," Sweeney said quickly. She knew she didn't have much time. "I think that the way he was tied up, well, I think it was familiar to you and I think that you . . . all of you . . . think it was someone in the family, that someone in the family must have done it. Because it was something you used to do, wasn't it? When your . . . when Mr. Putnam had been drinking, you and the children used to tie his arms loosely to the bed, so that he couldn't turn over on his back and drown in his own vomit."

Kitty stared at her and then nodded very slowly. "How did you know?"

"Because I used to do it myself. I used to do it to my mother when I was a child."

FOURTEEN

❧

"I know that the memorial service is tomorrow," Sweeney said. "And I'm willing to let you go to the police yourselves, when it's over. If you don't say anything, though, I'll have to tell them. Because of the way he was tied up, they think they're looking for some kind of ritual killer."

Kitty Putnam had let her into a big mudroom, painted a pretty yellow, and told her to sit on a wide wooden bench against one wall. Sweeney was conscious that she had not been invited into the house, but rather into this in-between room, which nevertheless revealed much about the house's inhabitant. A pair of rubber Wellington boots, caked with mud, was leaning against the bench, and a muddy pair of overalls hung on a hook on the wall. The tiled floor beneath a high workbench was covered with potting soil. A tray of seedlings, green and spoon-leafed, sat in a window. Next to the door leading on to a long hallway was a bag of recycling that hadn't quite made it outside.

"Why are you telling me this at all?"

In khakis and a rose-colored T-shirt, Kitty could have been one of the models for a gardening catalog. Her hair was messy and didn't appear to have been washed in a few days.

"Look, the police have to know about this if they're going to figure out who killed Brad. But I'm willing to wait and let you talk to the rest of the family and then go to the police yourselves. I liked Brad a lot and I didn't want to go to the police and have them kind of, I don't know, swoop down on you, without making sure I was right."

Kitty thought about that for a moment.

"Thank you," she said. "I don't know what . . . I'll talk to them. I don't know what it could be." She was genuinely bewildered and Sweeney realized that from the moment she had heard about her son's death a week ago, she had been holding in her fears over how he had been found.

And then, to Sweeney's horror, tears began to run from Kitty's eyes. She wasn't crying exactly. Instead it was as though something inside her, something that wasn't grief but rather all the stuff left over from grief, was finding its way out. The tears streamed and she just stood there, as though she were confused by this too.

Embarrassed, Sweeney got up and said, "I was at the wedding too. I saw Jack there and he invited me to the memorial service tomorrow. But if you don't want me to come, I won't."

Kitty ran the sleeve of her T-shirt across her face. "No, no. We'd like you to be there," she said, nodding. "You were Brad's favorite professor. You should be there."

Sweeney wanted to ask about the jewelry, but it seemed so inappropriate all of a sudden that she just let Kitty walk her to the door.

"Well, I'll see you tomorrow then," she said as Sweeney stepped out into the cool night. She could smell the sea again.

"Wait, Sweeney." Kitty's voice came hesitantly when Sweeney was halfway down the walkway. Sweeney turned around and faced the figure standing in the door.

"Yes?"

Kitty absentmindedly plucked at one of the dogs' ears, staring out into the darkness.

"Nothing," she said. "I'm sorry."

When Sweeney had pulled away from the house, she drove slowly along Bellevue Avenue, vacillating up to the moment she actually jerked the wheel over and turned right onto Narragansett. The Rabbit crawled down the street. It was after midnight, but the house was illuminated from within. An old Volvo—the same one she remembered her aunt Anna having—was the only car in the drive. It was clear she was home and

Sweeney turned into the circular driveway, hidden behind a tall hedge.

Her grandparents' house was a medium-sized—by Newport standards—Victorian only steps from the Cliff Walk and the Bellevue Avenue mansions. It had a small yard and perennial gardens lovingly tended by her grandmother over the years, and a certain homey, well-cared-for feeling inside that Sweeney had identified in other houses, but never quite to the same extent it existed in this one.

It had been a little more than five years since she'd been here. Her grandfather's funeral, three months after her grandmother's, had been the last time. The house seemed as she remembered it, though she realized that she had tended to come in the summer during her childhood and remembered the flower beds in full ripeness, the air warm and salty, the streets crowded with tourists. This was a different house, a different time.

She rang the doorbell and listened as footsteps inside padded toward her, as the owner of the footsteps unlocked a series of bolts and swung the big front door open and then stared at her, surprised, for a few long moments before she managed to get out, "Sweeney! What . . . ?"

"I was here for a wedding and I'm too tired to drive back. Is it okay to stay here for the night?"

They didn't hug, didn't even touch. Anna didn't ask any questions, just stepped aside to let Sweeney enter. The house had not been changed except that it seemed emptier, but Sweeney wasn't sure if that was just the absence of her grandmother or if some of the furniture was in fact gone. It smelled exactly as she remembered it.

"Well, God, come in and sit down."

The television was on in the little sitting room next to the kitchen. It had been a rather cold, pointless room when Sweeney's grandparents had lived here. But it was different now, cluttered and warm, but somehow lonely.

The room had been arranged for one person, a person who did not often receive visitors, and Sweeney thought about a nesting animal pulling cloth and hay around itself. The couch was drawn up close to the fireplace and the two wing chairs that had always sat against one wall were now near the couch—one a footrest for a human, one a bed for the big Maine coon cat who was stretched out there on his back. The cat looked up at Sweeney disinterestedly.

"Sit down, sit down," Anna said, switching off the television. She had put on weight and she was wearing jeans and a sweatshirt, her steel gray hair cut short, spiky, and boyish. "Do you want something to eat?"

"No, I just ate at this wedding."

"Whose wedding?"

"Katie Swift."

"Oh, yeah. The huge place up on Ocean Drive. Computers or something, right?"

"I guess. I went to college with her."

"What can I get you? I have a bottle of wine open in the kitchen. White."

"Scotch?"

Anna hesitated. "Sure." She went through to the kitchen and Sweeney heard her moving around in there, opening and closing cupboards. She looked around the room, trying to remember what had been on the walls when her grandparents lived here. Nothing very interesting—fruits and flowers, she thought. It had always bothered her father that his parents didn't think more about what they put on their walls. "It's *art*," he'd tell them. "Not interior decorating, for God's sake!"

But the fruits and flowers had been removed and Anna had put up framed watercolors of fairy-tale scenes, one a tableau of Little Red Riding Hood tripping through the forest, a wolf—a real wolf, not the anthropomorphized one Sweeney remembered from her own childhood fairy-tale books—peeking out from behind a tree. The painting was both whimsical and dark. The trees seemed sinister and alive. Red Riding Hood looked almost ridiculously naive, her legs in mid-skip, her eyes lifted to the sky. The other paintings in the room were also fairy-tale scenes: Sleeping Beauty stretched out on an opulent bed, one eye cocked open while a prince climbed through the window; a wicked-looking dwarf watching Snow White from a window.

"Are these yours?" Sweeney asked as Anna came back into the room carrying their drinks.

"Oh . . . Yes. I've been doing some children's book illustrations lately."

"They're fantastic. I didn't know . . ." There was an awkward silence. Sweeney didn't know anything about Anna's life.

Sweeney sipped her scotch and stared into the fireplace. Finally she said, "Well, that's a first. I never thought Ivy would help me with anything." It was more sarcastic than she'd meant it.

Anna was baffled. "What?"

"It's funny. Remember how I used to have to tie her to the bed when she'd been drinking?" Sweeney was conscious that with Anna, she took on a kind of swaggering, challenging aggressiveness. "Well, it may help the police solve a murder." Anna, who had a quality of not seeming surprised by anything, did not look surprised.

"It's good to see you, Sweeney," she said after a minute. "Are you tired? The bed's made up in my old room. That's where you used to stay, isn't it?"

Sweeney nodded. But Anna didn't get up. She just sat there and stared at Sweeney, as though she knew there was more to be said.

Finally Sweeney said, "Brad Putnam was one of my students."

"I wondered about that, when they said he was studying art history. Did you know him very well?"

"Pretty well. He was a nice kid, smart, and he liked the class."

"I'm really sorry."

"Me too."

"That poor family." Anna sighed and leaned back in her chair.

"I know." Sweeney took a long sip of her drink.

"Why does it seem like some families just have bad luck?" Anna asked. "You know what I mean?"

"But they've actually had quite good luck, haven't they? I mean being so rich and all. Maybe they're being paid back for something, maybe all their good fortune was ill-gotten in some way and the fates are evening the score."

Anna stared at her for a moment, then grinned. "For someone who proclaims herself an atheist, you have about the most Old Testament sense of justice I've ever heard of."

"That's not true," Sweeney said. But it was.

"Have you talked to Ivy lately?" Anna asked innocently. "It was her birthday the other day and for some reason I remembered. It's funny how those things stick in your mind."

"No," Sweeney said. "Not in a year or so."

The reason hung between them in the air. "I should have come over, back when it happened," Anna said. "I was so sorry and it was so hard for me to . . . well, you know. I figured that Ivy would be there and I thought you wouldn't have wanted me. I called a few times and Toby made it sound like everything was under control. But I should have known that Ivy wouldn't be able to do it. What happened?"

Sweeney took another long drink of her scotch. "I was in the hospital, after . . . after it happened. My back and my arm were burned a little, nothing serious, and I had some cuts on my face. But I was a mess. I kept hearing the nurses whispering about me. 'Her fiancé,' they kept saying. 'The bombing on the tube. She saw it.' And I lay there in the bed, feeling sorry for this poor girl who had watched her fiancé get blown up on the tube.

"Anyway, Toby came and he was handling things and then he called Ivy. I'd seen her a few times since I'd been in Oxford—she was living down at Summerlands, in a guest cottage or something—and she'd managed to keep it together. But then Toby got her to come up and when she came into the hospital room, I just knew. She was completely trashed. I don't know how she even got there. Toby tried to get her sobered up before letting her in to see me because he knew I'd go ballistic, but there wasn't anything he could do. She came into the room and fell over some piece of machinery at the end of the bed. I told her to get out. I haven't talked to her since."

"You've always been so *sure* about everybody, Sweeney. When you were a child, you would take against people. Do you remember the man who did gardening? I forget his name. You didn't like him, refused to be in the same room with him. Do you remember that?"

"Yeah, and later we found out he'd molested that kid down the street." Her own voice sounded young to her, whiny and smug.

"Yes. I guess that's right. But Ivy's your mother. How can you just write her off?" The words sounded hollow even as she said them. Anna had written off more things and people in her life than Sweeney thought she cared to remember.

"I'm fine as far as Ivy is concerned," Sweeney said stiffly. "I don't need any advice on that front."

Anna watched her for a moment. "Oh, Sweeney," she said. "I haven't been much of an aunt to you, have I?"

There was a long silence. Sweeney was the first to look away.

Anna took a deep breath. "Why don't I show you where everything is upstairs." They rose and Sweeney waited in the hall while she locked the front door and went around turning off lights.

"Why does the house smell the same way it always did?" Sweeney asked, sniffing the air as they climbed the stairs.

"Smell the . . . Oh. It must be the stuff Carla uses to clean." At the top of the stairs, Anna turned on the lights and opened the door to the bathroom. "It will be cold in there for a bit, but we'll leave the door open and hopefully it will warm up soon."

She pushed open the door to the bedroom at the back of the house and Sweeney was overwhelmed by memory. It was the room that her grandmother had always called the girls' room. It had been Anna's, and then, once Anna had married and gone to live in New York, it had been Sweeney's in the summers. It was aggressively feminine, with faded wallpaper patterned with pink and red roses, a tall canopy bed with a white chenille bedspread, and a sheer white canopy that hung delicately over the pencil posts. It struck Sweeney suddenly how uncomfortable Anna must have been in that room. For Sweeney it had been different. It had only been the summers. In September she had always gone back to wherever she and her mother were living and slept in rooms that were largely generic, shabby, decorated with her own books and posters and whimsical, impractical payday gifts from Ivy. The Newport room had always seemed like a glorious holiday room, available only during those warm, airy summers or at Christmastime.

But all the time, for Anna . . . She was about to ask about it when Anna said gruffly, "I've set up a studio in the nursery. If you'd like to see . . ." and Sweeney looked up to find her smiling shyly and pointing toward the door to the room that had always been known as the "nursery" but in her time had been used for boxes and suitcases.

Anna turned on the light and led the way inside. Sweeney felt she had walked into a room filled with people. Anna's drawings and watercolors covered the walls, the familiar fairy-tale characters seeming to watch them from their posts above.

"They're beautiful, Anna," Sweeney said sincerely, wandering around. "Are you showing them anywhere?"

"I just finished a book and I gave some of the extras to a gallery downtown. They sold pretty quickly so they want some more. I don't know . . . I don't want to *have* to produce them, you know." Sweeney suddenly remembered her father, angrily fielding a call from his agent, who wanted him to send five paintings to a gallery in Los Angeles. "I can't just go into my studio and find five paintings for you," he'd yelled.

Anna seemed somehow younger and Sweeney, on impulse, kissed her cheek.

"Why did you do that?"

"I don't know. Sleep tight."

Sweeney closed the door to the bedroom and wandered around looking at the familiar photos and knickknacks. There was a collection of teacups on a shelf above the bed. And on the dressing table were the two photos that Sweeney had always thought of as Anna's, one of Sweeney's father, taken when he was in college, and one of Julian, Anna's husband, who had left her nearly fifteen years ago now.

Why would Anna still have a picture of Julian? The last time Sweeney had seen him had been just before he moved out of the New York apartment and in with the daughter of a good friend of his, another painter. Sweeney remembered his gray beard, his intense gaze. She looked at his picture one more time, then turned out the light.

FIFTEEN

When Sweeney came downstairs the next morning, Anna had made coffee and the kitchen smelled of toast and butter. They sat in companionable silence, reading the papers, and then Sweeney said her good-byes and told Anna she was going to go for a walk around town before driving home.

"Don't be a stranger," Anna said, and winked.

It was a sunny, moist morning and the sidewalks along Bellevue Avenue were full of people, out early for the papers or breakfast. Sweeney walked down toward Touro Street and Touro Synagogue, then stopped at the Colonial Jewish Cemetery of New England. Founded by settlers fleeing religious oppression, Newport had been uncommonly accepting in its early days and had attracted Jews, Quakers, Seventh Day Baptists, and others unwelcome wherever they had come from.

In the little Trinity Church cemetery, she wandered around reading the old stones, many of which had toppled and lay flat against the ground.

One in particular caught her eye. It belonged to Mary Cranston Gidley, who had died in 1737 at the age of twenty-four:

> *Great were her ornaments because divine*
> *And in all other virtues she did shine*
> *From hence she's gone until the Judgement Day*
> *And then her Blessed soul will joine her Clay*
> *To be forever with the Glorious Three*
> *And live with God to all eternity.*

As with most cemeteries from the period, a number of the headstones were half sunk in the ground and many were illegible because of the effects of acid rain and/or time. Sweeney, who had always made gravestone rubbings, now took only photographs because of the deleterious effects of rubbing, especially in well-traveled cemeteries.

She saved the best for last. As a child, she had loved trolling Newport for graveyards and she still remembered when she had discovered St. Joseph's, popularly known as the Barney Street cemetery. It was a small yard of graves, fenced in with black iron. At the front was a beautiful Celtic cross that had been placed there to honor the early Irish who had settled in Newport. Now it was surrounded by daylilies and other perennials. There had once been a schoolhouse on the site, but it was now a grassy plot with trees shading the little burial ground. Sweeney stood and took in the peaceful atmosphere of the cemetery and then headed for the Cliff Walk.

The walking path that hugged the coastline and passed by most of the Newport mansions as it wound its way around the blunt shape of the coast was empty in the late morning light, a last week or so of peace before the tourists started coming. Sweeney picked it up on Narragansett and walked briskly south, passing Salve Regina and The Breakers, the home of Cornelius Vanderbilt, the magnificent Rosecliff, and the Marble House, which had belonged to Alva Vanderbilt Belmont.

Sweeney smiled as she walked, remembering many other walks along the Cliff Walk. Her grandmother had been a believer in daily exercise and every morning she had taken her Scottish terriers and gone for her "constitutional" before picking up the newspaper and the doughnuts that Sweeney's grandfather liked on her way home.

Sweeney walked into the wind, enjoying the salty chill of it washing over her face. She was still weary and the cold air woke her up, woke up her brain, woke up her reasoning abilities. She had been so tired last night that she hadn't really processed her conversation with Kitty Putnam. What did it mean that Kitty knew one of her family members had likely tied Brad up the night he'd been killed? And for that matter, what did it mean that Brad had been concerned about the jewelry in the weeks before he'd died? And that he'd been wearing the jewelry when he was murdered?

He'd talked about the jewelry that day in her office. She had asked him how his project was going. What had he said? That it was coming along okay, she remembered. She had offered to go over it with him, if that would help. He had thanked her, but then he had asked her that strange question, about whether he should reveal a piece of information.

She struggled to remember something more about what he'd said—I was wondering if you ever, when you're doing research on a gravestone or something, if you ever come across information that could maybe hurt someone, but that could be important. That was it; he'd wanted to know if he should reveal a piece of information that could hurt someone.

He'd said, "Maybe" when she'd asked if it had to do with gravestone research, so perhaps it was something that had come up in his research into the jewelry.

Had he been trying to tell her something? And had she let him down by not figuring out what it was that he wanted?

She was approaching the Tea House, on the grounds of Alva Vanderbilt Belmont's Marble House. The Chinese pagoda had been built for tea parties and receptions, including meetings of Alva Vanderbilt's suffragist societies, and it had always been one of Sweeney's favorite parts of the Cliff Walk. Just below the pagoda was the spot in the Cliff Walk where the first of two tunnels cut through the rock. Inside the first, which was stone lined with aluminum, the sunlight was almost completely blocked out. She shivered in the cold air.

Sweeney was almost through when she heard something behind her, footsteps on the gravel. She wheeled to confront whoever or whatever it was. But there was no one there. She was alone in the tunnel. It had just been her own footfalls echoing on the walls.

But she was spooked. Trying to keep calm, she walked very quickly toward the sunlight and back into the bright day. The ocean was blue and cheery-looking once again and she could see people walking up ahead of her on the path. The Cliff

Walk was just the Cliff Walk again, nothing sinister or scary about it at all.

So why had she gotten so nervous?

It was because of Brad. It was because she had realized that Brad could have been killed because he knew something about the jewelry, that he had scared someone, whoever it was, enough to kill.

Perhaps she should leave it alone. She had a sudden flashback to Vermont, the cold blanket of the river rising up to meet her, the thin shape of a rifle coming out of the fog, the certainty that she was going to die there. She knew better than most the lengths to which determined people were willing to go in order to keep their secrets.

But then she saw Brad's eyes and she knew she had to figure out what it was that he had wanted from her. She owed him that much at least.

SIXTEEN

Becca lay in a small pool of light coming through the window of her bedroom and looked at Jaybee's back. He still had the vestiges of a farmer's tan, left over from a summer of landscaping on the Cape. With her index finger, she traced the melting line at the top of his back and the matching ones on the backs of his arms. There were old acne scars set across his back like lace, the darker splotches a kind of map for her to follow with her fingers. He didn't stir.

He was a hard sleeper, she'd discovered. The morning after that first night she had rolled over and rearranged her body next to his and she had been afraid for an irrational moment that he was dead. That was how still he was, his body unmoving in unconsciousness.

It was hard to believe it had only been a month since that first night. They had been out with a group of classmates, people from the Mourning Objects class and some others, and had ended up back at Jaybee and Brad's apartment. They all sat around drinking and she had fallen asleep on the couch. Much later she had awakened to darkness and disorientation, and it had taken her a few minutes to remember where she was.

She had become slowly aware that someone was watching her and as her eyes adjusted to the light, she realized it was Jaybee. He was sitting in the leather armchair across from the couch, wrapped in a blanket.

"Is everything okay?" she'd asked him. He had given her the feeling that something was wrong, staring at her like that, as though he were willing her to wake up.

"Yeah," he whispered. "I guess it is."

She sat up on the couch. "What?"

He had gotten up from the chair and come over to sit next to her on the couch. She had been so sleepy that it had taken her a moment to tune in to the panic in his eyes. He turned to face her and he said, "Bec, I . . . for the last couple of weeks, I've been thinking about things and I think I . . ."

She'd been suddenly awake, looking into his eyes, knowing what he was going to say. She'd felt it too, the last few weeks, something different in their relationship, an edge to their friendly banter. She'd caught him watching her once in class and when she had looked at him quizzically, he'd blushed, something she'd never seen him do.

She hadn't said a word. So how had it happened, how had they silently agreed on the kiss, each of them leaning forward, then coming together in the middle of the couch, breathing hard, overwhelmed by feeling? Jaybee had held her face for a moment after the kiss, then said quietly, "We can't tell Brad."

"No." They both knew how Brad felt about Becca. It hadn't been something they'd needed to discuss. Though later, she'd realized that it was Brad's feelings for Jaybee that needed to be spared too. She had never quite understood their friendship, secretive and long-standing as it was. Once, she had walked into the apartment and found them lying on the couch together watching TV, their limbs entwined, Brad's hand resting on Jaybee's head. She had wondered about that, continued wondering after that night, after they had begun to lie to Brad about where they were and what they were doing.

They had kept everything a secret from Brad. Until that night . . . She pushed the memory away. They just had to get through the memorial service tomorrow . . . or today, she realized. Then they could go back to the way it had been.

She stroked his arm, felt him shift slightly in response to the touch. Since they'd been sleeping together, Jaybee had seemed somehow older to her. Before, she had thought of him the way she thought of her brothers, someone whose sexuality was theoretical, but beyond understanding; now she gazed at him and was overwhelmed at his *manliness*, his long back and the short hair that grew at the base of his neck. She felt suddenly that she had discovered something about the universe, that she understood something of what made people do the things they did.

Was it possible that other people had felt this, this *pull*? Surely, Becca's parents hadn't felt it. Whatever it was that had kept them together for twenty-seven years, it couldn't be this melding of bodies, this *wanting*.

For some reason, she thought about Sweeney. Everyone knew that Sweeney's husband had died and Becca wondered, Had Sweeney felt *this* for her fiancé? How was it possible for her to go on. How could she? How could she?

She stroked his back again. "Jaybee?" she whispered. "Jaybee?"

He stirred a little.

"Jaybee?" she whispered again. But he was snoring, his back rising and falling with his breath.

SEVENTEEN

❧

Water. He was drowning. He could feel the cold water closing over his head, the ache in his lungs as he struggled not to breathe, struggled for air. The water was dark, strangely gelatinous. He tried to summon enough strength in his limbs to propel himself forward, but it was futile and he began to sink.

Quinn's head jerked up; it had been about to hit the passenger side window of Marino's Chevy. He had been dreaming. Trees and buildings whizzed by outside. The sunlight was bright through the glass. He blinked.

"You okay there, Quinny?" Marino asked. The lieutenant had told them to get out and talk to Brad Putnam's roommate and his girlfriend. Marino was pissed they had to do it on Sunday and he was taking it out on Quinn.

"Yeah. Sorry. Just didn't get a lot of sleep last night."

Marino looked over at him. "Everything okay at home? How's the baby?"

"Yeah, yeah, fine. Sorry about that."

"Okay." He managed to imbue the two syllables with a paragraph's worth of condescension. "If you're sure." He drove through a yellow light on Mass. Ave. "Tell me about those interviews."

"Okay, great." Quinn sat up and struggled to clear his head. "Well, I talked to the family again." He got his little notebook out of his pocket. "Here's what they were all doing Saturday night. Andrew Putnam had been at a benefit dinner. Youth Arts Society of Boston. Something like that. He got home at ten, took care of some paperwork, went to bed. His housekeeper,

Greta Bergheim, was out for the evening, but when she came home around midnight, his car was in the garage. That's what she says anyway."

Marino raised his eyebrows. "You got any reason to think she's lying? There anything between them?"

"Probably not. She's kind of . . . I don't know. Doesn't seem like Andrew Putnam's type."

"What about the mother?"

"Kitty Putnam? She was down in Newport. No alibi, except for her father, who lives in the house. But he's pretty old, seems pretty out of it. I don't think he'd know if she'd gone out and come in again in the middle of the night. The house is so big, you wouldn't even hear.

"Then there's Jack Putnam. He was at some kind of art opening that night. Doesn't remember what time he got home. I checked with some of the names the gallery gave me and they all remembered seeing him there, though no one could remember when. As far as Drew Putnam goes, he and his wife were at a dinner party Saturday. That checks out." Quinn flipped the page in his notebook. "Everyone says they seemed fine, nothing out of the ordinary. They got home about ten-thirty and Melissa Putnam went straight to bed, says she took a sleeping pill. Drew Putnam says he got some paperwork done and went to bed himself around twelve-thirty." Quinn anticipated Marino's next question and cut in before he could ask it. "No housekeeper or anything like that. No way of confirming it. I asked some of the neighbors, but it's one of these neighborhoods where you wouldn't know what anybody's up to. Long driveways. Lots of bushes and trees."

"And what about the sister?"

"Camille Putnam. She attended a fund-raising dinner and says her campaign manager dropped her off at her home around nine. Here's the thing, though. One of her neighbors looked out her window around eleven and says she didn't see the car. It's pretty distinctive. Black Jeep with state senate plates."

"That right? What does she say?"

"She says the neighbor must have been mistaken. She was home all night."

"Hmmm. So anyway, whaddya think, Quinny? Who's the favorite?"

Quinn forced himself to focus. "Well, according to the postmortem, there wasn't any sexual contact, but that doesn't rule out that it was why he asked this person back. Say he got off on wearing the jewelry and being tied up. So he invited someone back and the guy . . . or the woman, I guess . . ."

"Woman?"

"Well, assuming the bondage was consensual, this wasn't a crime that took a lot of strength, right? Anyway, so this person ties him up and puts the jewelry on and puts the bag over his head and maybe something goes wrong. We know he was all full of liquor when he died. He's drunk, the bag's too tight or whatever, and he dies. Then the person doesn't know what to do and he leaves and doesn't say anything."

"That's good. What about the stranger scenario?"

"Well, maybe the guy—in this case I think it had to be a guy—was planning on assaulting him and got it all set up, you know tied him up, put the bag on his head, found the jewelry somewhere in the apartment and put it on him, then before he could uh . . . you know, do whatever he was going to do, maybe someone was outside and he was nervous, or he lost his nerve. So he left the kid there and the kid suffocated."

"Pretty good. So what kinds of stuff do we want to ask?"

"I'd say whether he was gay, whether he was known to have hired prostitutes."

"Prostitutes . . . that's a good idea. He could have hired someone to tie him up like that and then . . ."

"And then something went wrong and he died and the girl got out of there."

"Yeah," Marino said. "Hey, maybe you should go talk to some of the girls who help us out from time to time."

"Okay. I'll do it tomorrow."

"What about drugs?"

"He didn't have any in him when he died, right?"

"Not as far as we know," Marino said exasperatedly, "but what about the rest of the time. These rich kids get mixed up in some nasty stuff. Remember that kid from the university last year?"

"Okay, I'll find out."

"The other thing I want to know is why there weren't any fingerprints on that bag or on the jewelry."

"The killer had gloves?" Quinn let just a little too much sarcasm creep into his voice.

"I know the killer had gloves, but what kind of gloves? Were they leather gloves or fucking ski gloves?"

Quinn decided to keep quiet until they reached campus.

"So what are we asking these kids?" Marino asked, glaring at him.

"Anything they know about his friends, whether he was dating anyone. That kind of stuff."

Marino pulled up in front of the dorm and waited for a group of kids to cross the driveway before parking right in front of the entrance. It was an old brick building, with dull green vines twining along the sides and over the windows and doors.

"Guess that's why they call it the Ivy League, huh?" Marino said.

Quinn looked around the yard. It was a warm day, and the bulbs planted in the low beds in front of the dorm were just coming open. He bent to sniff a cluster of hyacinths planted in one of the flower beds.

The summer after his senior year of high school, he'd worked for a landscaping company. They'd been on a job in Cambridge, and on his lunch hour he'd come across to the yard and sat on a bench while he ate his sandwich. Someone had left a folded-up piece of paper wedged between two slats of the bench, a photocopy of a poem, John Keats's "Ode to a Nightingale," and he remembered thinking of Florence Nightingale. He didn't know Florence Nightingale from Adam, but still he'd had this picture of a beautiful woman, dressed in white. He had read the poem in a junior high English class, he thought, but he couldn't recall anything about it. It had just been one of any number of bewildering things that adults had asked him to do.

But sitting there in the yard that summer afternoon, he had read the poem to himself and suddenly—and it had been sudden, one moment clearly delineated from all the moments after it—he had understood, understood that the poet was listening to a bird singing, and he had understood what the bird's song meant to the poet. He remembered breathing in the air around him, air that seemed suddenly different, rarefied and rich.

Quinn had been about to head off to UMass that summer. He hadn't applied anywhere else, hadn't even thought about it. The fact that he was going to college at all was such a big deal to his mother that he hadn't been able to get past the basic fact of it. But sometime that spring, his English teacher had said to him, "Timmy, have you thought at all about majoring in English when you get to college? You've done so well this year and I would hate to see you stop your work with literature."

"I was thinking Criminal Justice," he said. "Maybe be a cop or something."

The teacher, Mrs. Lieber, he remembered, had taken a deep breath, as though she were afraid of offending him. "I know you'll do well and I know that the criminal justice field needs more smart, sensitive people like you, but I just hope that you won't close yourself off to anything."

He hadn't been sure what she was talking about then. But that summer he had sat on the bench and read those mysterious words and suddenly he had felt a rushing of his hopes and dreams, a kind of intense feeling of *being*. He had the feeling, which he had experienced only a few times before, of understanding something about the world, something of what every human being experienced when they lived in the world. He hadn't been able to discuss it with anyone. He hadn't known anyone who he could say it to without sounding crazy.

He was almost dizzy and he closed his eyes for a moment to ground himself. When he opened them again, Marino was looking at him oddly, but he felt steadier, better.

They pressed the buzzer next to "R. Dearborne" on the panel next to the door.

"Have to talk to her about letting people up without checking first," Marino said as the door buzzed open and they started up the staircase. "What do you think about this kid anyway, Quinny. I mean, you've been asking around for a few days now. What was he like?"

Quinn thought carefully for a few seconds. The inside of the dorm smelled of new carpet and puke.

"I think he was sad," he said. "I think he felt as though life had gotten out of his hands, that it was something happening to him that he couldn't turn around or change."

EIGHTEEN

It was raining and after stepping in a puddle next to her car and going back for another pair of shoes, Sweeney had arrived late and slipped into the back of the Bigelow Chapel at Mount Auburn, passing a knot of reporters who had been relegated to the steps outside. As she walked by, a guy in a tweed jacket and glasses tried to ask her a question, but she brushed him aside. Seeing the pews were full inside, she joined about twenty other mourners on fold-out chairs lined up against a back wall.

"We feel sometimes that God is unfair when He takes our young from us," the minister was saying as she took her seat. "We feel angry at Him, we feel that He has betrayed a promise to us. But God makes no promise but to love us, and love us He does. He exacts His plan in mysterious ways. We do not know until the end what He has planned for us and we do not know until the end what our true purpose is."

Sweeney found that she was weeping for the second time in twenty-four hours. She did not believe that there was any plan. She did not believe that there would be any meaning and purpose in this death—there was not in any other death.

And yet, she cried. She cried for Brad's unlived life, and for all the other unlived lives. She cried because she thought that he might have asked her for something and she hadn't understood and she was afraid that she had let him down.

The Putnams were sitting in the front rows, and she had a good view of them across the pews. Jack was at one end of the front row, next to an elderly man who Sweeney assumed was

Paddy Sheehan. He was in a wheelchair, his thin frame slumped forward, his pale hair almost gone. He raised a hand to scratch his cheek and Sweeney saw it tremor violently.

Next to him was Kitty, and then Camille, unadorned and somber in another dark suit. In contrast, Melissa Putnam was quite heavily made up, her long legs in sheer, dark hose and stiletto-heeled shoes. Next to her were her husband and father-in-law.

All of them were dressed in dark funereal colors except for Kitty, who was wearing yellow—the bright, Easter egg suit was a kind of protest, Sweeney decided, and she liked Kitty for making it.

None of the family members got up to make speeches or eulogies. It was a staid, formal kind of memorial service but when the family stood to the organ strains of "Morning Has Broken," she saw that Jack was gripping his mother's arm, his face streaked with tears.

As the song ended, Sweeney heard a high keening coming from the front of the church. Someone was sobbing, and she craned her neck to look through the rows of people. It was Melissa Putnam. Drew had put an arm around her and was trying to quiet her, but she would not be quieted, and finally an older woman helped her down the aisle.

The minister announced that guests were invited back to the family home for refreshments and that burial would take place privately at a later date. The reason seemed to hover in the air above the minister's head.

The family stood in a line in the entryway and as the mourners filed out of the church, they stopped to say a few words, their voices low and polite. Thirty or forty men and women in dark suits, talking seriously among themselves, approached the family as a group and Sweeney heard someone in line behind her say, "See all those state legislators? They love these things."

Jack saw her before she reached him and gave her a sedate smile and wave. She wondered if he knew yet about her conversation with his mother last night. Perhaps not.

"Jack told us that he saw you last night at Katie's wedding,"

Andrew Putnam said. With his silver hair and perfectly cut dark suit, he reminded Sweeney of the older Cary Grant. "We really appreciate your being with us today."

As she moved down the line, she shook hands with Drew and Melissa and murmured her apologies. Melissa seemed better, though when she lifted her face to accept Sweeney's expression of sympathy, a tear squeezed out of the corner of one eye and rolled down her cheek. Sweeney had to resist the urge to wipe it away.

Camille Putnam was another story. A politician through and through, she pasted on a serious smile as Sweeney shook her hand and said it was good to see her again. Sweeney searched her face for signs of grief and found only a sense of quiet, as though the tragedy had happened to someone else and she was trying to be respectful.

Sweeney smiled nervously at Kitty and was turning to go when Jack ducked out of the line and caught up with her in the doorway.

"There's something I want to talk to you about. You're coming back to the house, right?"

"I was going to, but . . ." Sweeney glanced over at Kitty, who was accepting an embrace from an elderly woman. "Are you sure it's not just for close friends? I feel like I fall more into the acquaintance category."

Jack grinned at her, a small, sad turn of his mouth. "You haven't figured us out yet, have you? The Putnams only have acquaintances."

People seemed to be parking all along the street without worrying about incurring the wrath of the Beacon Hill parking Gestapo, so Sweeney pulled up behind a BMW with a "Putnam for Congress" sticker on it. Her black suit, bought three or four years ago for another funereal occasion, did little to shield her from the chilled May morning, and she wrapped her arms around herself and massaged her shoulders. She'd chosen sensible shoes, at least, rubber-soled black leather Mary Janes that would shrug off the mud lining the sidewalk.

She followed the crowd up to the house and waited while they slowly filed in.

A young woman in a black-and-white uniform took her coat and the German woman whom Sweeney remembered from her first visit asked her to sign a leather-bound guest book. She wrote her name and the date and then went through into a large living room, where a bar was set up against one wall. Sweeney got herself a scotch and wandered around looking at paintings and photographs set on low tables. There was one of Senator John Putnam speaking from the floor of the Senate, and another of Andrew as a much younger man, leaning against the mast of a sailboat. On one low bookshelf was a beautiful bridal portrait of Melissa Putnam; she was wearing a veil and staring off into the distance.

Sweeney staked out a vantage point in the living room and pretended to be absorbed in the Putnam's art collection while she observed the family. Kitty, Drew, and Melissa were standing at one side of the living room receiving visitors and Paddy Sheehan was next to them in his wheelchair. At the other end of the room, Andrew and Camille were doing the same. Sweeney wondered if the arrangement had been agreed upon beforehand or if they had just naturally gone to stand on different sides of the room. Jack was nowhere to be seen.

She watched them in action. Kitty seemed to have her emotions in check as she comforted a weeping middle-aged woman. Melissa kept dabbing at her eyes with a handkerchief as she shook hands. Drew was smiling in an appropriately somber way and shaking hands, but he looked exhausted, Sweeney decided, his eyes underlined with bruised circles and his skin pale. Next to Drew, Paddy Sheehan sat in his chair, offering a shaking hand to the mourners. Sweeney was wondering whether he had an actual physical infirmity or if it was just age when he stood to embrace an elderly woman. His hands shook as he spoke, but he stood on strong legs.

She shifted her gaze to Camille and Andrew. Like her brother, and as she had in the church, Camille had perfected a sort of regretful smile. Andrew seemed the least together. He kept staring off into space and running a hand through his silvery hair.

She was beginning to feel awkward when Jack waved at her from across the room and came over, holding a highball glass. "Are you doing okay?" he asked. "Do you need anything?" He smelled of soap or perhaps cologne. Something clean and nautical.

"No, I'm fine."

"Good. Let's go find somewhere quiet to talk. I really appreciate your coming back."

"No problem." She smiled up at him. His cheeks were flushed and there was a fine mist of perspiration on his upper lip and forehead. His eyes bored into hers and she stepped back, glancing away.

He steered her toward a doorway and then stood aside to let her climb the wide staircase in the hall in front of him. The walls along the staircase were adorned with huge metal disks that looked like circular-saw blades. Upstairs, he led her down a long hall, their shoes clacking on the hardwood floors, and into a small bedroom she assumed was a guest room. The walls were a tomato red, and the bed had a black upholstered headboard that matched an armchair next to the window.

"Sorry about this," he said, closing the door. "It's just that the rest of the house is so full of people. Anyway, I wanted to talk to you because my mother told me about your visit last night. I just wanted to say that we've called the police and we're going to tell them what happened."

Sweeney wasn't sure what to do. The room felt small all of a sudden and he was standing very close to her, so she sat on the edge of the bed and looked up at him. "Good. I'm sorry about all of that. I wouldn't have said anything if I didn't think it was important, for Brad's sake, to find whoever did this."

"No, no. I'm glad you did." He looked embarrassed for a moment. "Anyway, the truth is that I was the one who tied Brad up. He called me that night, very drunk, asking me to come over. When I got to the apartment, I found him passed out on the floor. I was worried about him throwing up and choking, so I did exactly what you figured out that I did."

Sweeney watched him for a moment, trying to decide if he was telling the whole truth.

"I didn't say anything because I thought that if I did, it would just obscure the issue of who really did this to him." He tapped his fingers against the desk. "God, I want a cigarette."

Sweeney looked up at him again. Was he really that naive? "Didn't you worry about them finding your finger-prints, footprints, other evidence that you'd been in the apartment?"

His eyes widened and he reached up to wipe a hand across his forehead. "Well, I'd been there before. We were always going over there to feed his fish or whatever. I don't know, I guess I didn't think much about it. It's how . . . it's how lying happens, quickly. People don't usually plan ahead when they're going to tell a lie."

"Unless they've planned a murder," Sweeney said.

"Well . . . yes. But I didn't." He sat down in the armchair by the window and leaned over the side to look at her directly.

Sweeney looked past him out the window. A sparrow was pecking at something on the windowsill. Tap. Tap. Tap. "Was he wearing the jewelry when you left him?" she asked.

"No. I would have remembered that."

"But you'd seen the jewelry before?"

"Yeah, once you and Detective Quinn showed me the pic-ture that day I remembered it—it was always in my mother's jewelry box."

"Did you know that Brad was interested in the jewelry? Did he tell you that he was working on a project on mourning jewelry?"

Jack picked up a red and black Venetian glass paperweight on the desk and turned it over in his hands. "I think I asked him how the class was going and he said that he was doing his final project on some mourning items. He didn't go into it too much, though."

Sweeney wanted to ask him more about the jewelry, but he was starting to look bewildered and she didn't want to set off any alarms.

"I wanted to say thanks for going to my mom about it first.

It was really nice of you. I appreciate it." He got up and came over to sit next to her on the bed.

"That's okay." Sweeney took a deep breath. "I should probably let you get back to things downstairs."

Jack smiled at her. "Probably," he said. "Anyway, I wanted to tell you first and to tell you that I've asked Detective Quinn to let you be there while we tell him about it. It was my mother who asked for it. She said that you understand, that she would feel better if you were there."

"He's going to love that," she said, leaning back on the bed so that she wasn't quite so close to him. "He thinks I'm much too involved already."

Jack leaned back too. They were eye to eye. "Are you?"

"What?"

"Are you involved?" He was staring right at her, his blue eyes steady.

"Well, I liked Brad. I cared about him. In their minds I guess that puts me a little too close for comfort to . . . to everything." She had been about to say "To you" and she blushed.

He was still staring at her and as Sweeney stood up suddenly, her back to the window, she was sure he had leaned in closer, that he had been about to kiss her or take her hand. But by the time she looked back at him, he had stood up too.

"Thanks for talking to me," he said formally. He glanced away when her eyes found his. "You've been really nice about all of this."

"No, no. I wanted to. As I said, I cared about Brad." She let him hold the door for her and they walked silently back down the stairs. The crowd had thinned out a bit, and when they reached the living room, she saw Jaybee, Becca, and Jennifer standing with a girl she didn't know in a little huddle and she said, too quickly, "There are some of my students. I think I'll go say hi."

"I'll see you," he said. She watched him make his way to Camille's side and whisper something in her ear. She looked up, her eyes rushing to Sweeney across the room, and Sweeney turned away.

Becca was wearing a black-and-green-plaid miniskirt and black tights and looked cold. She and Jaybee, Sweeney noticed, were holding hands.

"Hey, guys, it's good to see you."

Jaybee and Becca looked up and in the instant before Becca recomposed her face and gave Sweeney an entirely appropriate smile, Sweeney saw something else there: wide-eyed, startled fear. Jennifer smiled.

"Oh, hey," Jaybee said. "We just got here." He introduced her to the girl standing with them, a tall, blonde named Alison. She was pretty in a Barbie-doll sort of way and looked vaguely excited, Sweeney thought, her cheeks flushed, her eyes bright.

They all stared at her dumbly for a moment until Jennifer, ever gracious, said, "We were just talking about the house. Isn't it beautiful?"

"Yeah, it is." She turned to Becca and Jaybee. "I just wanted to tell you how sorry I am. And that you shouldn't worry about class. If you want notes or anything, e-mail me and I'll be glad to send them along. And take as long as you need to get back to things. I know this must be an awful time for you."

"Thanks," Jaybee said. There was another awkward silence. A phone rang from somewhere in the house, but stopped after two rings. Sweeney looked up and scanned the room. Jack was now standing with Drew and Melissa, his slim figure a counterpoint to Drew's heftier one.

"Well, I've got to get going," the blond girl said. "I'll see you guys later."

"Yeah, bye," Becca said, in a falsely cheery voice.

They all watched her head for the front door and Sweeney was about to tell them she wanted to get home when Jaybee said, "That bitch. I can't believe she came."

"She wasn't even friends with Brad," Becca explained to Sweeney. "She just wanted to come and see the house."

"I heard her tell Brad's mom that she and Brad had been friends since freshman year," Jaybee said.

There was a long silence as they all looked around the room.

"Well, people have their own reasons for doing things," Sweeney tried to say soothingly. "Death brings out strange behavior. A lot of people feel they want to be part of the mourning, it makes them feel like they belong."

"No offense, Sweeney, but that's bullshit," Jaybee said. She had never seen him this angry. His usually easygoing demeanor had morphed into raw rage. "She just wanted to get inside the house."

For the first time, Sweeney had a sense of what it must be like to be a Putnam.

The coats had been hung in the closet of the downstairs reception room, she was told when she was ready to go. The uniformed young woman who had taken her coat was nowhere to be seen, but Sweeney followed another guest's directions and found the little room off a small hallway near the front door. There were two armchairs and a huge closet that ran the length of one wall. The opposite wall was covered with mirrors in various shapes and sizes and Sweeney found herself staring at her refracted face, her green eyes oddly bright. She looked flushed and excited in the glass. Is that what Jack Putnam had seen when he had stared at her upstairs? And had he leaned forward to kiss her before she stood up? It seemed strange that he would kiss her after his brother's memorial service, but as Sweeney had told Becca and Jaybee, death brought out strange things in people. Jack Putnam wouldn't have been the first person to look for a little affirmation of his status as a living breathing lusting human being in the face of his mortality.

Her coat was easy to find and she was slipping it on when she heard Jack's voice out in the hallway.

"Cammie, stop it, just stop it."

In the mirrors on the opposite wall, she could see them, Jack and Camille and Drew, standing together in the hallway. She stepped back, pressing herself against the opposite wall until she could no longer see herself in the mirrors.

There was a short silence and then Sweeney heard Camille's voice.

"But it's dishonest. I'm running for office, for Christ's sake."

"Cammie, he's right. It's simple. Just leave it the way we discussed." Drew's voice was hoarse and definite.

"I don't know. Is it worse if it comes out now or if it comes out later?" Camille's words ended in a gasp. "Oh God! Why is it coming down to this? I've worked so hard."

"You have. And that's why we have to do it like this. Okay?" Drew's voice was older-brother-sure.

"Fine with me," Jack said.

Camille didn't say anything. In the mirror, Sweeney watched Drew put an arm around her and whisper something in her ear. The three of them walked out of the hallway and Sweeney counted to fifty before she slipped out of the coatroom and out the front door.

On her way home, Sweeney got Indian takeout and stopped at the video store. It was so cold and damp and she was so drained from the weekend that all she wanted to do was curl up on the couch with *North by Northwest* and feed herself soupy, spicy, comforting food.

But when she got home, she paced restlessly around the apartment and finally went to get the notes she'd taken about the Putnam family plot.

The problem was Edmund's missing mother. Without her stone, it was impossible to put together a family tree. Sweeney brought her laptop into the living room and signed on while she dumped her chicken korma onto a plate and dipped the nan bread into the sauce. Then she went to one of her favorite genealogy Web sites and started looking for Putnams.

There were a lot of references to the Putnams of Boston and it didn't take long to put together a rudimentary family tree.

Edmund, she saw from the family tree, was the son of Charles and Belinda Cogswell Putnam. Charles Putnam had died in April 1863, eight months before his son was born. Belinda, who had been born in 1840, had lived to the ripe old age of eighty-five. But she had lost her son in 1888, when he was only twenty-four, newly married and with a son of his own. That was Joshua Putnam, Brad's great-grandfather.

The mourning jewelry, Sweeney realized with a sense of satisfaction, could have belonged to Belinda Putnam. Assuming it was all part of the same collection, the first brooch probably commemorated the death of one of her parents, or perhaps a sibling. The hairwork necklace and locket must have been made when Charles died, the dark hair—almost exactly the color of Brad's and Jack's—from Charles's head. And the second brooch must have been made when Edmund died.

Belinda Putnam. It was an evocative name. Sweeney had a sudden image of a Victorian lady in dark mourning dress, her hair piled high on her head, the mourning brooch pinned to her bosom.

While she ate, she read over the notes she'd made in the cemetery. Some of the stones had included months and years, and some had just listed the years of the person's life. Sweeney had always disapproved of the incomplete ones. It was partly her role as historian and it was partly that she always felt as though it mattered whether someone had died in January or October. Surely they ought to get credit for those last few months. She started comparing her notes with the dates on the family tree to make sure that the genealogy site had gotten them right.

The phone rang. "Hey," Toby said. In the background she could hear music and people talking.

"Are you on your cell phone?"

"Yeah. Lily and I are at that bar on Mass. Ave. that you hate."

"Lily and I?"

"Mmmmm." He sounded embarrassed.

"So, I take it that my presence wasn't missed last night?"

"I'll tell you later," he said quietly. "Anyway, I just wanted to make sure you were okay. You took off so quickly."

"I know. I'm sorry about that. I'm fine, although I went to Brad's memorial service today. It was kind of awful. But I got Indian and Hitchcock."

"Ah. Better than Vicodan. So you're okay? Where did you stay last night?"

She hesitated. "At Anna's."

"Really? That's great. Was it good to see her?"

"I don't know. I guess. Anyway, Cary and Eva Marie are waiting, so I'll let you go."

"But you're okay?"

"Yeah. Have fun."

After she hung up, she stood up and went over to the window. The apartment felt cold and empty and she put on another sweater before getting out her sketches of the mourning jewelry and comparing them with the dates in her notebook that she'd copied down the last time she'd gone to Mount Auburn.

But something was bothering her. She wasn't sure what it was until she got out her notes on the mourning jewelry. The date of birth given for Edmund Putnam on his gravestone was December 4, 1863. But the brooch listed it as March 4, 1864—three months later.

It must have bothered Brad too, she realized now, because surely it was why he had gone to see John Philips at the Blue Carbuncle and asked him if the jewelry had been changed or tampered with.

But she supposed that there were all kinds of discrepancies when it came to one-hundred-year-old lives. There were lots of possibilities. The jeweler who had inscribed the back of the brooch may have read Edmund's birth date incorrectly. She served up the rest of the korma and put *North by Northwest* on the VCR.

By the time Cary Grant and Eva Marie Saint were tumbling around in their train compartment, she was fast asleep on the couch.

NINETEEN

❧

Becca and Jaybee were back in class the next day.

Sweeney had wondered whether they would come. But when she walked into the seminar room, there they were in their regular places, Becca looking miraculously well rested and happy and Jaybee his usual, charming self. He grinned at her and then went back to a conversation with Rajiv.

"Hi, everyone," she said. "How are we all doing?"

They seemed more relaxed today than they had last week. This was better, this felt more like before. Jennifer, dressed today in a pair of flowing silk pants and a pale blue embroidered sweater that had probably cost as much as Sweeney's monthly rent, had done them all the favor of sitting in Brad's regular chair, so that they wouldn't have to stare at it.

Sweeney dropped the slide carousel into the machine and shrugged out of her raincoat. She waited until she had their attention and then started, "So I think we were saying during our last class that mourning jewelry was somewhat popular in the new American nation prior to the Civil War, but that we see a real surge in popularity after 1861. Let's talk a little bit about that. What are the two events that we see in 1861? Do you remember from your reading?"

"The start of the Civil War and, in England, the death of Queen Victoria's mother and then of Albert, the prince consort," Rajiv said.

"Good. Remember that the time before the start of the Civil War had been one of relative peace and prosperity. The horrible deaths that attended that war—remember everything you know about battlefield medicine in those days, the amputations without benefit of anesthesia, the infections that would get started in wounds and move slowly up the body, remember the letters home that those soldiers wrote—America had to figure out a way of dealing with death, a way of dealing with numerous deaths and the sense that those deaths might not end anytime soon.

"At almost that exact moment," Sweeney went on, "England, which had always dictated the fashion to her former colonies, experienced the two deaths to which Raj referred.

"After her mother's death, Queen Victoria suffered greatly and went into a deep mourning which was only made worse when her beloved Albert died of typhoid on December 14, 1861.

"She responded to the death by doing everything she could to memorialize him, in short, not to move on from it, but to remain in a state of perpetual mourning. She built an elaborate sarcophagus for his body, with a marble effigy on top that she could visit. She surrounded herself with pictures and busts of him, and her dress reflected this state of mourning.

"Albert's room was kept exactly as he had left it and the queen forced all of her courtiers and family to remain in strict mourning for three years. In sympathy with the queen, her subjects took to wearing jet and other mourning objects.

"In America, the new fashion for mourning dress and jewelry coincided with the sudden need for a publicly acceptable way of handling the raw emotions that these years of death brought on.

"Just as England had joined this cult of mourning, so did America. Hair-work jewelry became an important part of the mourning ritual. Before someone left for war, he would leave behind a lock of hair that could be a remembrance and—if the soldier died—a piece of mourning jewelry."

She turned the lights down and showed them thirty slides of typical Civil War–era jewelry.

"Now I want to show you some portraits of women from the 1860s and 1870s wearing mourning jewelry." She clicked ahead to a photo of a proper-looking matron wearing a high-necked dress and a mourning brooch.

They talked about mourning jewelry for a while longer and then Sweeney showed them a slide picturing the participants in an 1872 séance.

"In addition to finding ways of coping with grief over the death of a loved one, the Victorians also fell prey to a new brand of hucksterism. Spiritualists claimed to be able to contact the dearly departed so that they could communicate with their loved ones.

"There are well-known stories of spiritualists being locked in cabinets during séances to prevent them from interfering with the so-called visitation. But they had elaborate ways of getting around this and often the ghostly figure who appeared in the spiritualist's drawing room was nothing more than the spiritualist herself in disguise.

"But spiritualists were increasing in popularity. Those who could afford it went to séances where they were told they could speak with the dearly departed. Of course the spiritualists charged exorbitant fees, but perhaps worse was the emotional price they exacted from their victims."

She was getting ready to move to the next slide when Ashley said, "How do you know that it wasn't real? Who are you to say there's no such thing as spirits?"

Sweeney looked sharply at her. "Come on, Ashley," she said. "From an academic perspective this stuff is really interesting. But it's very well documented that these so-called mediums were scam artists and that the spiritualists used a series of highly sophisticated instruments to achieve their effect. They preyed on the grieving."

"But how do you *know*? How do you *know* that people who have died don't come back to visit us? How do you *know* that people who are murdered don't come back to tell on their killers?"

Sweeney didn't know what to say. She looked around at the rest of the class, but they just looked uncomfortable, staring nervously down at the table. Before she could think of anything, Ashley went on.

"People think they know," she said angrily. "But they don't. They don't know anything. There's a whole world out there that we don't know anything about. Anyone could come back, anyone could try to contact us, even . . ."

But Jennifer cut her off. "Calm down, Ashley, she's not attacking you personally. She's just saying that this is how we have to study this."

"But, what about—"

Now it was Raj who cut her off with a warning, "Ashley . . ."

There was a tense moment of silence, and then Ashley, surprisingly, sat back in her chair and let it go.

"Anyway," Sweeney went on, a little tentatively, "what people were seeking when they went to spiritualists wasn't so much the actual contact with the departed as the comfort of knowing that the contact was possible. People sought to relieve guilt, to resolve unresolved emotions. The spiritualists became an important part of the American response to widespread death. Mourning jewelry—whether it was hair-work jewelry or a mourning scene—became the outward manifestation of these responses. The jewelry was as much about societal roles as it was about emotional response to death. Any questions?"

Usually, the class spent the last half hour or so of their time discussing Sweeney's lecture, but today they didn't have a lot to say, so Sweeney let them go early.

And as she walked back to her office, she wondered about Belinda Putnam and what her mourning jewelry had meant to her.

TWENTY

❦

"It was the wedding of the century," Henrietta Hall was saying. "Really, it was. It was old Boston on one side and new Boston on the other. You can't imagine how excited everyone was about it. You would have thought Kitty was Princess Grace or something. And the rumors about the Putnams being against it just made it that much more fun. Everybody was watching Senator Putnam's face during the ceremony."

The historian's bluish-gray hair was pulled back and fixed in a French twist at the back of her skull, her elegant dancer's neck twisting as she told the story. Sweeney was mesmerized by her thin, gesturing hands, both ring fingers encircled by three or four diamond and sapphire bands.

Henrietta Hall was legendary around the university. She had won a Pulitzer in the 1980s for her biography of Paul Revere. Earlier in her career she had written a definitive history of Boston. But it was her biography of the Putnam/Sheehan family that Sweeney was interested in, and it was to learn more about them that Sweeney had come to the spacious office and sat in a comfortable chair next to a wide picture window, all of which made her painfully aware of her own lowly status and tiny office.

"What's your interest in the Putnams anyway?"

"Brad was one of my students."

"Yes. So sad. It's funny when you've written about a family. You almost feel like you're one of them. I spent five years doing nothing but talking to Putnams, reading Putnam letters, trying to imagine, for purposes of my narrative, what various

Putnams were thinking at various times. I was heartbroken when the other son died a few years ago, and when I heard about Brad I felt again as though I'd lost a member of my family."

Sweeney took a deep breath. "He was working on a project in my class about his family, particularly during the 1800s. He had started to do some very interesting work and I was . . . Well, I was thinking that it would be a way to honor him . . . to finish his work and then have it published under his name somewhere. He was an accomplished scholar."

"The first Putnam came over on the boat after the *Mayflower*," Henrietta Hall continued. "He wasn't anybody very special. He had a farm in Braintree and a whole bunch of children. One of his sons took over the family farm. He had something like ten girls and then, finally, the boy. That was Elijah Putnam. This was after the Revolutionary War of course, and suddenly there were all these opportunities in shipping. Elijah made a fortune trading with Asia and bought up land on Beacon Hill, which was what all of the successful families were doing. The house that Andrew Putnam lives in now was built on that land. They held on to a dozen or so more lots and sold them off. Made a killing."

"What about the connection to the Back Bay?" Sweeney remembered reading that the Putnams had also bought up a lot of land in the Back Bay.

"Well, Elijah Putnam's grandson, Charles Putnam, started buying up large tracts of land in the Back Bay in the 1850s, just as urban planners started filling it in. It was all swampy nothingness at that point, but someone had a vision and they just kept bringing in loads of gravel. A lot of the work was done by the new immigrants, Irish mostly. Anyway, over the years, they've made a couple of fortunes selling those houses that Charles Putnam built. I believe that they still own at least a few of them. It'll be interesting to see what the Back Bay Tunnel project does to their real estate values."

The hulking cranes and snarled traffic had been a part of Back Bay residents' lives for so long that Sweeney wondered whether people would actually miss them once the construction crews packed up and went away. But no, the easier access to Cambridge and points north would probably make up for it.

"What about the house in Newport?" Sweeney asked. "When did they build that?"

"Oh, Cliff House was built around the turn of the century, I think. That was Joshua Putnam, Brad's great-grandfather. His son was Senator John Putnam. He was elected to the U.S. Congress in the early sixties, and then to the Senate in 1972. You probably know all this. He was kind of at the center of a coalition of moderate Republicans from New England but he got voted out of office in the eighties."

"And Paddy Sheehan?" Sweeney asked. "How does he fit into things?"

She knew that John Putnam's career had coincided with that of Paddy Sheehan, who had first run for the Senate in the mid-sixties. It had been commented upon many times that the two men represented the past and present of Boston—the original Brahmin ruling elite and the more recently arrived Irish, who would become the public face of the city.

"The original Sheehan—I forget his name—arrived in Boston in 1848," Henrietta Hall said. "Potato famine probably, or just poverty. He married a girl he'd met on the boat and they settled quietly and uneventfully into a city split in two— the Brahmins and the Irish. The native-born leaders and those who, buoyed in their efforts by the huge new voting bloc they had brought with them from Kerry and Cork, would become the new leadership of the city.

"As a young man, Paddy Sheehan gained fame and notoriety as a city councilor about whom it was said that that he skirted the law but never broke it, and he was elected to the Senate as a relatively young man. There, he became a powerful Democrat, wielding influence when his party was in power and finding leverage when it was not.

"Of course it's the point at which John Putnam's son, Andrew, and Paddy Sheehan's daughter, Kitty, fell in love that everybody really got interested."

"How did they meet?"

"Oh, in college I think. As I was saying before, the wedding was kind of the event of the year. Everyone knew that both fathers were fairly well displeased. But it was a beautiful wedding and whatever else you might say about the Putnams, Andrew and Kitty were deeply in love that day. There was no mistaking it."

"What do people say?" Sweeney asked slyly.

"Oh, you know. That Paddy Sheehan had a voracious sexual appetite. That he had been drunk at the wedding and had tripped as he'd walked Kitty down the aisle. That Andrew Putnam was believed by his father to be something of a dolt, and though he had gotten through law school, had never lived up to the promise of the family name. That he's an alcoholic. But that's all gossip. Most of it anyway."

"I'm wondering if you know anything about a Putnam ancestor named Edmund Putnam. He was born around 1863 and I'm trying to see what I can discover about him."

"Edmund, Edmund. Let's see. It doesn't ring a bell, but let me check my index." She took a copy of her book down from the shelf and turned to the back.

"He died very young," she said. "Only twenty-four, but he had a son before he died. Joshua Putnam. That would be Brad's great-grandfather."

"And Edmund was Charles and Belinda Putnam's son. What do you know about Belinda?"

"Belinda Putnam I remember. She was a very interesting woman, you know. She was widowed young. Only twenty-three. And she was left with a baby to raise and her husband's law firm. The natural thing, of course, would have been to turn the firm over to one of the partners, but she retained her husband's stake in it, maintained control over the family's extensive properties around the city, including all those Back Bay properties. The Putnams really were instrumental in creating the Back Bay as it is today."

"Or instrumental in paying Irish laborers almost nothing to do it," Sweeney said grouchily. She'd read accounts of Irish immigrants doing backbreaking work hauling fill to make the Back Bay neighborhood.

"Yes," Henrietta said. "But history never remembers those

who toil, does it? I read a wonderful book recently about the men who built the White House. Fascinating. Anyway, there was quite a lot of Putnam money and Belinda lived alone for the rest of her life. There were marriage proposals of course, but she chose not to accept. She became an important benefactor in the city, you know. Gave to all kinds of charities and started her own, a home for unwed mothers. And something for African-American women in Newport, if I remember correctly. An education fund. Everything I read about her led me to believe that she was a remarkable woman."

"I haven't been able to find her gravestone," Sweeney said. "Do you know where it is?"

"The family has a plot at Mount Auburn, I think."

"Yes, and I found Charles's grave, and Edmund's, but not Belinda's. Can you think of any reason why she might have been buried somewhere other than the Putnam family plot?"

"I suppose it's possible she was buried in her own family's plot somewhere. Her maiden name was Cogswell, if I remember correctly. Her father was in shipping, I think. Very wealthy at one point and then lost everything. It always seemed to me that she must have married Charles Putnam for his money. He was so much older and he didn't live long after the marriage."

"And do you have any idea where the Cogswells might have had their cemetery plot?"

"I'm sorry. I don't."

Sweeney got up to go. "Thanks so much for your help," she said and wrote her e-mail and phone number down on a slip of paper. "If you think of anything else, let me know."

"Of course. Now can I ask why Brad was writing about her in your class?"

"Sorry," Sweeney said. "He had gotten interested in a collection of mourning jewelry that had been owned by her." She felt suddenly nervous. The police could only keep that aspect of the murder quiet for so long.

"Oh yes. I've always liked mourning jewelry. There's a portrait of her, you know. At the MFA. By Sargent."

"Really? I can't believe I've never seen it."

"It was recently donated. By the family, I think."

"I'll head over this afternoon," Sweeney said, thanking her. "And let me know if you remember anything else about her."

The day had started out bright and sunny and by noon it was seventy degrees. Sweeney, who didn't like the heat, found that she was relieved to step into the marble foyer of the Museum of Fine Arts. The gray and palest pink floors seemed to draw the heat away and she surreptitiously slipped a foot out of her sandals and pressed it to the cool stone.

Sweeney had spent so much time at the MFA over the years that she always felt as though she were visiting a friend's house. She said hello to the bronze replica of Frederick William MacMonnies's *Bacchante and Infant Faun* in the entryway, recalling the uproar that the original of the sculpture had caused when it was donated to the Boston Public Library in 1896. The skipping, nude woman, clutching a bunch of grapes in one careless hand and a nude infant in the other, had divided the city, with some leaders calling it a glorification of vice and harlotry and others hailing it as a great work of art.

On her way up to the rotunda, she stopped to greet Bela Lyon Pratt's *Water Lily Girl* and Hiram Powers's bust of *Eve Disconsolate*. She stood for a moment looking up at the Sargent murals painted and sculpted in relief on the concave dome. Whenever she brought people to the MFA and told them that the murals had been painted by Singer Sargent, he of the society portraits of bored women staring off into the distance, she was always met with disbelief.

She had always loved coming to the MFA and looking at the Sargents, especially the women. And she had always thought that his portraits of Boston's elite, with their combination of well-heeled circumspection and caged intelligence—said more about the experience of being female than did a whole library of feminist texts.

Wanting to prolong the anticipation of seeing Belinda Putnam's portrait, Sweeney wandered downstairs and out into the Garden Court. It was almost empty, most of the visitors having fled the heat for the cooler halls of the museum, but

Sweeney strolled the perimeter, letting the sound of splashing water in the fountains surround her.

She sat down on one of the stone benches and found herself wondering if Ian had ever been to the MFA. He probably had, he was an art dealer after all, but she found herself wishing that she could bring him here for the first time, see his face as she led him up into the rotunda and showed him the murals, as she took him out into the Garden Court.

What did that mean? She wasn't sure and she realized she was going to have to decide what to do about the letter. It had been sitting on her kitchen table and she hadn't read it again since the first time.

When she thought of Ian, she thought of her confusion during those weeks in Vermont. It was as though all of their blindness as to what had really happened had seeped into her feelings about him.

She had been attracted to him—or had she? Had that just been the murders too? She was discovering that crisis set up its own universe. You couldn't trust the way you responded to someone in a crisis, could you? She couldn't honestly say what she was feeling for him. She didn't know. And until she knew, she couldn't do anything.

He was so different from Colm. That was part of what was throwing her, she realized. She had loved Colm because he was loud and raucous and hard-drinking and hard-living. Ian was . . . different.

And then there were her slightly confused feelings for Jack Putnam. She'd realized, when she saw him at the house after the memorial service, that she had been looking forward to seeing him. She was attracted to him; in fact it was hard to imagine anyone whose tastes ran to men not being attracted to him, but there was something else there too, a sense of recognition. Talking to him at Katie's wedding, she had felt instantly comfortable with him, instantly at ease.

They'd had a drink and laughed about their exes hating them. They had stood out on the lawn while he smoked and she had felt more alive than she had in months. Shocked, she realized that he reminded her of Colm. He had the same energy, the same intense creativity, the same directness.

She took a deep breath. It was all too much to think about, and she decided to focus on the Putnam family instead.

She made her way back into the museum and to the ground-floor room that held the Sargents. Sweeney searched the room quickly for the Belinda Putnam portrait. It was the only one she hadn't seen before and she spotted it right away. From across the room, it gave the impression of being very dark, the background of brown wallpaper and furniture blending with the woman's dark dress. But as Sweeney got closer, she saw the subtle lighting of the woman's hair and clothes.

In the portrait, Belinda Putnam was a woman of about sixty, with brown hair lit with gray. She was sitting on a low sofa, her back ramrod straight, her hands folded in her lap, and she was looking straight out from the painting, her eyes direct and almost challenging.

Sweeney, when she viewed portraits of women, especially upper-crust women, was often struck by the way in which you felt the absence of the woman's husband. It was a kind of subtle sexism that painters incorporated into their work, Sweeney had always thought. But she had no sense of this looking at Belinda Putnam's portrait. Instead, she seemed a whole subject in and of herself.

But to Sweeney's mind, the most remarkable thing about the portrait was the piece of jewelry that Belinda Putnam wore on the bodice of her dress.

It was the mourning brooch.

Sweeney recognized it right away, though in the portrait it was rendered impressionistically, the little mourning scene blurred and indistinct. She couldn't read the words "Beloved Son, Edmund," but Sweeney recognized the shape, as she imagined Brad had if he had ever seen this portrait. Had he? What had Brad found out about the jewelry before his death?

She took some notes on the portrait and made a final stop at the two gravestones on display in the American decorative arts section of the museum. The stones were excellent exam-

ples of eighteenth-century American carving and there was a
nice little display explaining about the hourglass symbology
on one of the stones. All along the walls of the hallway next
door were wonderful photographs of stones from the Old Gra-
nary and King's.

But they were doing renovations on the museum and the
hallway where the photographs were displayed was dark and
lonely, on the edge of the construction site. The room seemed
filled with dust, and while the upstairs galleries were filled
with people, Sweeney was all alone down here looking at the
gravestones.

Typical, Sweeney thought, and sneezed.

TWENTY-ONE

Melissa Putnam sat at her dressing table, rubbing night cream into her neck and décolletage. Drew was sitting up in bed, pretending to read the *Globe,* but really watching her in the dressing table mirror, and when she met his eyes, he looked away, embarrassed.

She stood up and slid out of her dressing gown, folding it carefully over the chair and going over to the bed, knowing he was watching her, watching the way her breasts moved against the inside of her silk gown.

"Hi," she whispered, sliding into bed.

He didn't say anything, just turned out his bedside light and rolled away from her, making a noisy show of plumping his pillow and finding the right position. She turned off her own light and rolled over, touching his shoulder.

"What's wrong? What's wrong, Drew?"

She heard him say, "Just go to sleep, Melissa."

She made a conscious effort to keep her tears in check, counting to ten before she spoke.

"I was thinking . . ." She stopped, afraid to say it, afraid of his reaction, then went ahead anyway. "I was thinking we could start trying again. The doctor said it was okay. It's been three months now."

He started to say something, but the words came out sounding strangled and unintelligible.

"Drew?"

"I don't think this is the time, Melissa."

"But I don't understand. After the last miscarriage we said we were going to keep trying. We . . ."

"I just lost my brother. I don't want to . . . Just go to sleep, okay?"

In the dark, she could hear his breathing coming fast, could feel his energy.

"No. You promised we could. Why are you changing your mind?" She could feel the tears start, the hot pressure at the base of her throat building. "It's the same . . . it's the same as before. We have to!" She clutched at him, feeling him shrink away from her.

"It's not the same as before." He nearly whispered it, the words almost lost in the bedclothes. "My brother's dead."

"But it didn't . . ." She had been about to say that it hadn't mattered before, when it had been Petey who was dead, and she knew he knew she'd been about to say it.

In an instant, he was out of bed.

"Where are you going?" She sat up and turned on her light, watching him struggle into a pair of pants and shirt he'd hung over the end of the bed only fifteen minutes ago.

"Nowhere. Go to sleep, Melissa."

"Drew!" She felt herself losing control, felt something slide inside her. "Don't go! Come back here! I'll stop asking, I promise!"

He was hunched over, putting on his shoes.

"Don't leave," she screamed at him. "Where are you going? Who are you going to see?"

But he was gone. She heard his footsteps clattering on the stairs.

Sobbing, she got up and went into the bathroom, sitting on the edge of the Jacuzzi and cradling her abdomen as though care could fix what was wrong in there.

She'd had the last miscarriage—her seventh—in January. Just after Christmas. She'd only been a month in, but it had felt different somehow than the other times. Or maybe, it occurred to her, it was exactly the same. Maybe she had been that hopeful every time. She couldn't remember now, couldn't see anything beyond the awful endings, the familiar hand that seized her belly, squeezing so hard she could barely breathe.

What had she done, what had they done, to deserve this horrible penance? Four years had passed in an endless pattern of hope and despair. It had gotten to the point where she saw teenage girls with babies on the street and screamed inwardly, "Idiots! Idiots! Why can't I have a baby when any idiot can!"

She took a deep breath. The doctor had said that he couldn't find any reason for the miscarriages, that they should just keep trying. Drew hadn't meant that he didn't want to try at all anymore, just not now. And it was understandable. Brad had . . . it had only been a little over a week. She swallowed hard. They were all still grieving. She had to remember that.

She took the bottle of sleeping pills out of the cupboard, popped one into her mouth, and swallowed it with a handful of water from the faucet.

She had to try not to make Drew mad. She had to try to keep things together for him, for the whole family. That was the only way it was going to happen. That was the only way she was going to have her baby.

She lay in bed, saying the words over and over to herself, can't make Drew mad, can't make Drew mad. As she drifted off, she heard the front door, and then the low grumbling of a car starting in the driveway.

TWENTY-TWO

❧

Sweeney was checking her mail in the department office the next day when she caught sight of Jaybee coming out of a colleague's office.

"Jaybee," she called out, a bit too enthusiastically, so that Mrs. Pitman looked up and Jaybee himself started.

"Sorry . . . Would you mind just coming into my office for a second? I have something I want to ask you." He followed her in his good-natured way and she shut the door behind him.

She swallowed hard. "This is . . . so embarrassing. I feel terrible asking you about this, Jaybee. A couple of weeks ago, I lent Brad a couple of library books, taken out on my card. The library's been calling and I've got to get them back, but I don't want the family to have to worry about it."

The muscles next to his eyes quivered. "I don't think I could . . ."

"I know, I know. I wouldn't ask you to go back or anything. Look, I was thinking I could just borrow your key. I already asked the police and they said it's okay, it's just that they're always too busy to go over there with me and . . . I know it sounds crazy, worrying about books, but I have to take some other things out and they won't let me until I return these."

Jaybee looked as though he was trying to decide what to do. "I don't have a key, I gave it to the police. But there's one in a plant next to the door, under the rock. That's where we kept it, so you could always get in, you know . . . You can just use that if you want." He looked suspicious, though, and Sweeney searched for something to reassure him.

"Thanks, I really appreciate this. I'll put it right back. And we can kind of keep it between us, can't we? Brad's family might think it was a little, I don't know, heartless or something."

"Okay," he said, still looking at her strangely. "I won't say a word."

"No," Toby said when she dropped by.

"Come on. If there was anyone else I could ask, I would. Please. It'll take fifteen minutes."

"No." He was picking up his apartment, something he frequently did when Sweeney was visiting. Toby wasn't much of a housekeeper and he only liked to engage in cleaning when he had someone to talk to. He lived in a cluttered, book-filled apartment in an old Victorian a couple of blocks from campus.

"Please."

"Sweeney, I, of all people, know where your sleuthing can lead. Why would I want to help you?"

She looked up at him, hurt.

"All right. I'm sorry. That wasn't fair."

"Please. I'm not even interested in it as a mystery—not a murder one anyway. It's the mourning jewelry and the gravestones. It could be an interesting academic problem. See, if the mourning jewelry is correct and the gravestone isn't, it sets up this interesting thing of the stone as the public face of the death and the jewelry as the private face. You know, it . . ."

Toby straightened a pile of *New Yorker*s on his coffee table. "I don't have to go in with you?"

"No, I would never ask you to do that. I just want you to stand out in the hall and let me know if someone's coming."

"Do I get to do a birdcall or something?"

"You may use whatever method you choose."

Toby smiled. "Okay," he said. "But only because of the birdcall. I've always wanted to do that. Shall we say the phoebe? Or the humble chickadee?" He tried both, as Sweeney impatiently got his coat for him.

Brad's apartment was in a building on Harvard Street that had once been a single-family Victorian home, but had been converted to student apartments sometime in the seventies, to judge by the splashy avocado and sunshine wallpaper that climbed the walls of the dingy stairway. It was a shabby-looking place, but Sweeney, who had tried to find an apartment closer to campus and failed, knew that the rent was probably upward of $1,500 a month.

Brad and Jaybee had lived in number 5, one of two doors on the second floor. Sweeney made Toby wait just outside the door—which was barred with police tape, but not so efficiently that she wouldn't be able to duck under it. Just as Jaybee had said, there was a big ficus plant in a green plastic planter next to the door. It looked dried out and dying, as though it hadn't been watered in weeks, but there was a rock half buried in the dry soil and she found the key beneath it. She slipped the key into the lock. It turned easily. Keeping her hand on the doorknob, she replaced the key in the planter, and said to Toby, "Okay, you wait here. If someone comes in and it looks like they're heading upstairs, just whistle and I'll come out. We can pretend that we're going to that other apartment."

Toby nodded.

Sweeney pulled the door shut behind her and looked around. The apartment reminded her of numerous student accommodations she'd lived in. There was a cramped, uncared-for feeling about it that seemed familiar. The walls were off-white, long unpainted to judge by the streaks of light brown that decorated the walls here and there and cracks had come up at the point where wall and ceiling met. The floors were covered with industrial carpet in an unattractive shade of gray, but there was a very nice black leather couch and an expensive stereo set. The place looked emptied out, sterile. Sweeney assumed that Jaybee had gotten all of his stuff out as soon as the body had been removed. She wondered to whom it would fall to come and pack up Brad's belongings.

On an elaborate stand in the living room was an empty aquarium and inside were a filter, a net, a pair of rubber gloves, various bottles that seemed to contain chemicals to fix the aquarium's pH, and some other aquarium paraphernalia, including a fake plant and a gaudily colored pirate's ship.

The tiny kitchen looked as though it was rarely used—the refrigerator was empty save for an unopened bottle of champagne and a jar of kosher dill pickles, and the cupboards, when Sweeney opened them, held a few plates and mugs, a pile of mismatched stainless steel silverware, some Tupperware, and about twenty boxes of Kraft macaroni and cheese.

Two closed doors flanked the small bathroom, and she was able to tell which one was Brad's bedroom from the police tape across the door. She pushed it open, ducking under the tape, then shut the door behind her, just in case someone came in.

She had been nervous about seeing the place where Brad had died, but the bedroom was innocuous in the bright sunlight coming in the unshaded window. These walls were freshly painted a pleasing pale blue and it was where Brad had clearly focused his decorating energy. The bed was oak, with four low posts at each corner—Sweeney shuddered, thinking of his thin arms tied to those—and covered now with a blue sheet. Presumably the police had taken all of the bedclothes that had been there.

Sweeney smiled when she saw that he had covered his walls with framed photographs of gravestones.

She recognized many of the stones from Boston and Cambridge graveyards, including a couple from Mount Auburn. Brad had obviously been there, seen his family's stones. Had he wondered about the same things she had?

He had possessed a good eye. The stones he'd chosen all had unusual features or rare iconography. One in particular caught her attention. It had been taken at night and it showed a group of people sitting in a cemetery and holding candles. It was quite beautiful, the light from the candles showing up a few of the stones in relief.

She looked more carefully. She couldn't distinguish all of the people, but one face jumped out at her.

It was Raj.

That was strange. She had known that Brad and Raj were friends, but this suggested a much closer relationship, didn't it? Confused, she turned to Brad's work space.

His desk was Mission style, with an ergonomic chair that must have cost a couple thousand dollars. There was a brand-new Mac on the desk, but little clutter, and while she turned it on and waited for it to boot up, she went through the rolling, wooden file cabinets on the floor next to the desk. Brad had labeled everything neatly—Sweeney felt a small glow of pride at his developing skills as a scholar.

She found a file labeled "Seminar/Professor St. George—final project" and took it out, laying it on the floor and going through the papers. There were a few notes on early mourning objects in general that Sweeney recognized from a class a month or so ago, but not much else.

She flipped through the rest of the files, finding research related to other classes and a few fat file folders filled with financial documents and records. She looked through them quickly. He seemed to have a trust fund that paid out about $4,000 a month, along with a number of inherited IRA's and a few other accounts from which he had interest and income. There were itemized statements from a couple of different trust funds with names like the "John C. Putnam Trust" and the "Andrew B. Putnam Living Trust." She flipped through the lists. "Payout from sale of IBM stock, Proceeds—sale of property in Cambridge, Massachusetts Home and Life payout." Brad had a pretty complicated financial life for a twenty-one-year-old.

The computer was warmed up and ready to go. Sweeney, wanting to save time, tried to look at the files on his hard drive by date, so she could see the ones most recently viewed. But everything on the computer had been opened the day after Brad's death—the police, she decided.

So she searched for key words like "mourning jewelry" and "hairwork" to see if there was anything that might relate to the jewelry. There were a couple of files—one was a paper Brad had already handed in and the other was the beginning of his paper for his final project. Sweeney read the first few pages. It was good, very good, but there wasn't anything in there that she didn't know about the jewelry.

She had just shut the computer down when she heard the

door open. She jumped and held her breath until Toby's head appeared over the police tape. "Are you almost done? People keep coming in and out and I'm starting to feel really nervous about this," he whispered. "Can you hurry up?"

"Yeah, yeah. Let me just look through one more file cabinet."

She was opening it when they heard footsteps in the hall and then someone fumbling at the door.

Toby raised his eyebrows in alarm and Sweeney motioned for him to come into the bedroom. He shut the door and she saw the closet just as they heard a key turn in the lock. It was a small closet, but someone had taken the clothes out and there was just room for the two of them to crowd in and pull the door closed behind them. They had to embrace in order to fit and as she mashed her face against Toby's neck, Sweeney could smell soap—Irish Spring—and cigarettes. He'd been smoking again. The only place to put her arm was around his neck and she could feel blood pumping through his veins.

The bedroom door opened and they heard footsteps, then the door shutting again. Sweeney's heart sped up and she buried her face in Toby's shoulder. Whoever it was stood silently for a few long minutes before walking across the floor—away from the closet, it sounded like, and toward the bed—and stopping there for a few minutes. She tried to decipher the footfalls. Couldn't blind people tell who was approaching just by the footsteps of that person? Something to do with the fact that everyone had a unique weight, a unique way of walking. But they just sounded like any other footsteps to Sweeney—she could tell the person wasn't wearing high heels, for example, or rubber boots. But beyond that, she couldn't tell much from the "flunk, flunk" of his or her footwear on the carpet.

Toby's breathing seemed awfully loud to her and she had a sudden urge to kiss his neck.

Whoever it was didn't spend long in the room. In a few minutes, she heard the footsteps go out into the hall and into the other bedroom. It wasn't more than twenty seconds before she heard footsteps in the living room again and then the door to the apartment open and shut.

Toby shifted his body and Sweeney whispered, "Stay there." She slipped out of the closet and over to the window. At first she didn't see anyone on the street, but after a couple of seconds the front door of the building opened and a man in a tweed jacket came out, looked in either direction down the sidewalk, and crossed the street. He looked up at the windows of the apartment and Sweeney stepped away from the glass and tried to memorize his plain face, his close-cropped beard, and little round glasses. When she looked again, he was disappearing down Harvard Street toward the square.

"Who was it?" Toby whispered.

"I don't know. A guy. It wasn't anyone I know. Damn. If only he'd gotten into a car, I could have gotten the license plate."

"What do you think he was doing?"

"Didn't it seem like he was looking for something?"

"Yeah. Do you think he found it?"

"I don't know . . . He wasn't in here very long."

As they were leaving the bedroom, she bent down and opened the last file cabinet. The white label on the front read "Personal."

"What are you doing?" Toby asked nervously.

"Hold on . . . transcripts, correspondence, tax . . ." She read the titles on the folders aloud. "Yes! 'Putnam Family History.'" She took it, and for good measure, the rest of the files in the drawer.

"Sweeney! Won't they notice they're gone?"

"Yeah, but they'll think the police took them. Don't worry, I'll bring them back."

She was on her way out of the room when she saw again the photograph on the wall of Raj and decided to take that too. Then she followed Toby out of the apartment, locking the door carefully behind her.

"I'm sorry about that," she said, once they were out on the sidewalk.

Toby just rolled his eyes.

The whole way home, Sweeney was antsy. "Tell me not to pull over and look at them right now."

"Don't pull over and look at them right now."

"Okay, okay." She found parking on Russell Street, and as she and Toby were walking toward her building, she said, "Let me just see it."

"No," Toby said maddeningly. "You're always going on and on about the sanctity of research materials. You can wait." He held the files close to his chest.

Once inside her apartment, Toby handed them to her and she sat down at the kitchen table and started reading. Toby started a pot of coffee, and by the time it was ready, she was pretty sure that Brad had had some of the same realizations she had. He had drawn a crude family tree that looked almost exactly like hers.

And he had circled his ancestor Edmund Putnam and written the two birth dates—the one on his gravestone and the one on the mourning brooch.

"Toby, do you see what this means? Brad had the same questions that I did about the jewelry. He realized that there was a discrepancy."

"I don't understand. What is it that you think is so scandalous about this mourning jewelry? What was it Brad was hiding?"

"Toby! Don't you see? Look." She got out her drawings of the mourning jewelry and spread them out on the kitchen table. "This mourning brooch was owned by Belinda Putnam. She would have gotten it when her son Edmund died in 1888.

"The brooch lists the date of his birth as March 4, 1864. But when I went to Mount Auburn, I saw his gravestone and it lists his birth date as December 4, 1863."

"Yeah?"

"Toby! Charles Putnam died in April 1863. April, May, June, July, August, September, October, November, December, January, February, March." She counted on her fingers. "If the date on the mourning brooch is correct, there's no way that Charles Putnam was Edmund's father. He had to be illegitimate."

"And you think Brad figured this out?"

"He must have. Because he was asking about the jewelry.

He knew there was something wrong with it. Or that there was something wrong with the dates."

"But even if he did know about it, what could it possibly have to do with his murder?" Toby sat back in his chair. "You think someone was so scandalized by an illegitimate birth a gazillion years ago that they couldn't bear the idea of it getting out? That's crazy."

"When you say it like that, it does sound kind of ridiculous."

"Although . . ."

"Although what?"

"Although that guy did break into the apartment earlier. Maybe he was looking for proof of all this, or . . ."

"Toby, you said I was being crazy."

"Yeah, but . . . what if Edmund Putnam *were* illegitimate? What would it mean?"

"Well, maybe that the family's whole claim to its wealth is in doubt. Right?"

"But it would depend on a lot of things, wouldn't it? Besides, if someone killed Brad to stop the truth about the mourning jewelry from getting out, why would they leave the jewelry on him? Wouldn't that be the first thing you'd hide?"

He had a point. Sweeney went over to the couch and stretched out, hoping that Toby would come over and, without being asked, give her a back rub. But he sat at the table and fiddled around with her mail. He picked up the envelope from Ian and turned it over in his hands. "What's this? A UK postmark, the elegantly embossed return address of one I. V. Ball. Who could it be?" He made as if to open it and Sweeney jumped up and took it from him. He looked as though he were thinking about wrestling her for it, but settled for crossing his arms. "Why didn't you tell me you heard from Ian? What's the letter say?"

"It's really nice," she said, blushing. "And I didn't tell you because I don't know what I'm going to do about it."

"What do you mean? You write him back. Pen, paper. You know the routine. It's a very old tradition. You could even call him if you were feeling crazy."

"No. I mean, I don't think I should write him back unless I'm really serious about it."

"Sweeney, I presume he didn't ask you to marry him. Maybe he just wants to be your pen pal for a while, get to know you better."

She crossed her eyes at him. "What about you and Lily? Are you going to see her again?"

"I think so. I kind of like her."

"That's great." She was quiet for a moment.

"What are you thinking about?"

"Nothing."

"What?"

"Just that, since the wedding, I've been thinking about marriage. Have you ever thought about getting married? In an abstract sense, I mean?"

"Other than to you?" There was a time when he wouldn't have been able to look at her while saying it, but now his eyes were steady.

She blushed.

"Not really. I figure we've got lots of time," he said.

"Maybe we don't. I mean, we're almost thirty. If you want to have kids, you have to start thinking about it pretty soon. At least I do."

"I thought you didn't want to have kids."

"I don't know. I thought I didn't. But maybe that was just because Colm didn't." Sweeney remembered Colm—who had been one of twelve—ranting on the subject. "Children are an instrument of female oppression. As long as you're a mother, you can't ever be equal in this society."

"You've got lots of time," Toby said, looking at her strangely.

She watched him. "But haven't you ever felt like you *wanted* a child? Do men feel that? When you see a baby on the street? I mean, you're the one who's always been so gung-ho about having kids."

"Yeah, but I think it's more theoretical. I want to have kids someday, but I don't think of it as something I have to do right away. And it changes your life a lot. I haven't thought a whole lot about that."

"Arggh. That's exactly the thing!" Sweeney flashed him a glare. "If I want to have kids I have to plan ahead so I'm not too old, and I have to think about how I'm going to rearrange my life and everything. And you can just say 'Oh yeah, it would be cool to have kids someday.' Maybe Colm was right. Maybe women can never be truly free as long as they fulfill their biological imperative."

Toby just looked perplexed, as though he was trying to figure out where the conversation had gotten away from him.

"I have to tell you something," Sweeney said after a minute. "When we were in the closet, I wanted to kiss your neck."

Toby laughed. "That's because I'm irresistible," he said. "But I'll admit something. I was pretty turned on too."

"It was because we were in danger," Sweeney said.

"Yeah. Danger's kind of a big turn on."

Sweeney, thinking of Jack Putnam, told herself to remember that.

TWENTY-THREE

Sweeney was in her office reading up on mourning jewelry from the 1860s to try to identify the jeweler who had made the brooch when Quinn called.

He was angry. "I had a call from Kitty Putnam yesterday," he said, his voice grim and tight. "She told me something kinda interesting."

"Oh, yeah?"

"She told me that you visited her Saturday night in Newport and you convinced her to tell me that there was something about Brad's death the family hadn't been totally honest about. And she said the family wants to talk to me, but that they want you to be there. Because you understand, she said."

"Oh. Yes, well. I told her that if she didn't call you, I was going to," Sweeney told him. "I thought that was the right thing to do. It's kind of a personal thing. A family thing I don't think they wanted to reveal. Since I kind of forced them into revealing it, I thought it was fair to let them tell you in their own way."

There was a long silence, and then he exploded. "Do you think we're doing some kind of family therapy here? This is a murder investigation."

"I know it is and I know you wouldn't know about this if I hadn't figured it out."

There was a long silence. Finally he said, "Look, I'll pick you up at two o'clock this afternoon by your office—come out and stand in front of the museum, and we'll go to the Putnams and talk to them about this thing, whatever it is. Okay?"

At two, she was standing on Quincy Street waiting for Quinn. It had grown breezy, the wind picking up pieces of paper here and there on the sidewalk and whipping them around. She wondered suddenly how he had known where her office was, but when she looked up, there he was, driving a battered Toyota Celica. She got into the car wordlessly, afraid of antagonizing him. The car smelled strange, feminine, like talcum powder.

He still seemed angry; he pulled away from the curb so quickly that her head snapped back. She put on her seat belt and gripped the door handle.

They were completely silent for ten minutes or so, listening to top forty on the radio, and then he said, "Anytime you're ready."

"What?"

"You can start telling me what this is about anytime you're ready." His hands gripped the steering wheel hard.

"Oh . . . well, I was talking to someone, over the weekend, and I found out something I didn't know about the Putnams, which was that Andrew Putnam was an alcoholic. Before the other son died. And when the kids were younger, he would come home so drunk that he'd pass out. The kind of passing out where you worry about someone choking on their vomit."

Quinn glanced over at her.

"So anyway, I realized that it was possible that in that family, it was kind of a habit, to tie someone's hands to the bed, so they couldn't roll over and choke. Jack Putnam told me that his brother called him, that he was very drunk. Jack was worried and he went over to the apartment and did in fact tie Brad's arms to the bed."

Quinn hesitated for a moment, but then he saw that she could help him.

"We got the cell phone records a couple of days ago. Brad called four people that night. All three of his siblings and the roommate's girlfriend."

"Becca Dearborne," Sweeney said.

"Yeah. Anyway, the first call was to Jack Putnam's cell phone. That must be the one he told you about. Then there was one to Camille Putnam, and another one to Drew Putnam, also at home. Then finally he called Rebecca Dearborne."

"And they didn't volunteer this?"

"Nope. Well, Becca Dearborne did. When we talked to her a couple of days ago. That's what helped us pin down the time of death. He called her at eleven. She said he was just drunk, babbling on and on about stuff, nothing of significance. But the family didn't say a word."

Sweeney didn't say anything at first. Then she said, "It seems kind of stupid. I mean, wouldn't they assume you'd get the phone records?"

"Yeah, but with the kind of influence that family . . . Anyway . . . we're meeting them out at Drew Putnam's house in Weston."

He looked exhausted, his eyes lined with lack of sleep and his clothes rumpled. She wondered why.

Drew and Melissa Putnam's house was at the end of a long driveway off the Concord Road. The neighborhood, and Weston itself, was undergoing the same transformation that so many suburban Boston towns had experienced. A few modest ranch houses on large lots remained, but most of the homes were newish, overlarge McMansions built to look like stately Colonial or Federal residences. There was a uniformity to these houses, the proliferation of bay windows and skylights, the landscaping precise and marked by young lilac bushes and perennials planted in neat circles and surrounded by cedar wood chips. As Quinn pulled into the Putnams' circular driveway, though, Sweeney saw a big old Colonial, flanked by a carriage house and a barn, both painted a bright white and trimmed with blue.

Melissa answered the door and showed them into a wide foyer, papered in a royal-blue-and-gold pattern; Sweeney looked over to find Quinn slack-jawed at the opulence of the house. It had been done up in a kind of French Baroque madness, gold and blue everywhere in the entryway, rich-looking rugs on the hardwood floors. She quietly checked out an ornate, gilded side table against one wall and decided it was the real thing. It was not at all to Sweeney's taste, but it must have cost a lot of money, and it couldn't have been more different from either of the houses that Drew had grown up in, so Sweeney guessed that the house had been Melissa's project.

Sweeney had been assuming that Drew would take the lead in explaining the situation, and she was surprised to walk into a dark, wood-paneled library and have Jack stand up to greet her and Quinn.

"Please sit down, wherever you want," he said. But there were only two empty chairs and Sweeney realized that the room had been carefully composed in order to maximize the family's advantage. They were seated in armchairs grouped on one side of the room. Quinn's and Sweeney's chairs were—subtly so—on the side of the room near the door. Sweeney felt stage-managed.

"I'd like to apologize for all of us, Detective Quinn," Jack said. "As you now know, we kept an important piece of information from you and I ask your forgiveness. I can only say that we never would have done it if we thought it was important. I think you'll understand when we explain."

As though they had rehearsed it, Jack sat down and his father stood up. "I am an alcoholic," he said. "I'm not proud of it and I've been sober now for five years, but when my children were younger I was in pretty bad shape most of the time. There were nights when I would get so drunk that I would pass out and the kids would have to put me to bed. My wife had begun the practice of tying my arms—gently, mind you—to the headboard of the bed so that there was no danger of my turning over in my sleep and choking on my vomit. It's not a nice story and I'm embarrassed to have to tell it to you. But my children adopted this . . . um, technique . . ."

Jack stood up again. "The night that Brad died, he called me. He was very drunk and I was concerned. So I went to his apartment—he was alone—and by the time I got there, he had passed out. I could see that he'd been throwing up and so I dragged him to his bed, turned him over onto his stomach, put a wastepaper basket next to him and tied his arms loosely to the bed. If he had been sober enough or had had to go to the bathroom, he could have untied them himself. Again, I'm very, very sorry that we weren't totally candid. As I said, it didn't seem that it mattered very much. I mean, we expected that you would find the person who did this quite quickly and . . ." It was a shot at Quinn and Sweeney could see that it was meant to keep him in his place.

Quinn didn't say anything.

"What did he say to you?" Sweeney asked quietly. She hadn't checked with Quinn to see if it was okay for her to ask questions and she didn't look over at him in case he was glaring at her. "When he called?"

Jack gave her a small smile. "Oh, nothing in particular. He was just very, very drunk. You know, babbling on and on." He fiddled with a paperweight on the desk and said quickly. "Anyway, if we can help you at all, please let us know. Again we're sorry that we weren't immediately honest about this. As you know, I'm an artist and I recently found out that I'm going to be in a show at a prominent gallery. And I was concerned about the press." He started forward as though he were about to show them the door.

But Quinn jumped in. "How tightly did you tie his arms?"

"What? Oh . . . not that tight. Just kind of so he couldn't pull out of them. But as I said, if he'd sobered up, he probably could have gotten up to go to the bathroom or whatever."

"And how was he dressed when you left him?"

"Um . . . in his underwear. I took off his clothes so he'd be more comfortable. I hope you won't make too much of that, detective. I'm sure you've tended drunks before."

Quinn said, "And the jewelry?"

"He wasn't wearing it when I left."

"Did you see it anywhere in the apartment?"

"No, but it could have been there. I wasn't looking for it."

"And what time was it when he called you?"

Sweeney had the feeling that Quinn was more interested in how Jack answered his questions than in the answers themselves.

Jack hesitated for a moment. "A little before eleven, I think."

"So you went right to his apartment and you say that you found your brother drunk and tied his arms to the bed so that he wouldn't turn over and choke on his vomit. Why didn't you stay with him if you were so concerned?"

Jack looked down at the floor. "Well, of course now I wish that I had," he said. "I don't know if you can imagine quite how much I wish I had." Sweeney heard his voice catch on the words and she wanted to tell Quinn to stop.

"I think that was my fault," Andrew said, breaking in. "Because of my alcoholism, my children have all come to accept a certain amount of abnormal things as being perfectly normal. They learned to handle the results of my drinking in a particular way and when they saw it in their brother, it wouldn't have occurred to them to do anything else."

He was right of course. Sweeney hoped Quinn saw it.

"The phone records said that Brad made a seven-minute call to you the night of his murder. What did you talk about?" Quinn asked, looking at Drew.

Drew looked a bit flustered. "He was very drunk. Just like Jack said. I told him to go to bed and that I'd call him in the morning."

"Why did he call you?"

"I don't know. I'm his brother. People make phone calls when they're drunk. It's quite a common thing to do, I think."

"Where were you, Mrs. Putnam?" Quinn looked at Melissa.

"I think I must have been upstairs. We'd been out to dinner and when we came home I went right up to get ready for bed. I took a sleeping pill and went to sleep right away. I don't really know what time it was."

Quinn nodded and looked back at Drew. "But you didn't think it was worth going to see your brother? Was this a usual occurrence?"

"No, but he was a college student. I mean, let's be honest, this isn't the strangest thing for a college student to do."

"Did you leave anything in the apartment when you were there, by accident?" Quinn asked Jack.

Jack looked back and forth between Quinn and Sweeney.

"I . . . no, I don't think so. It's possible, but . . . what did you find?"

Quinn didn't answer. "I have one more question." He looked over at Camille. "What did you and Brad talk about that night?"

Camille's eyes widened. "What do you mean? It was Jack that . . ."

"According to phone records, your brother also called you that night. I'd like to know when he called you."

"Oh. Yes, of course. He left me a message. He just said hi and that he hoped my speech had gone well that day and then, I don't know, he was drunk. He babbled a bit. That was it." Her eyes filled with tears.

"Did you save the message?"

"No." She looked right at Quinn, daring him with her eyes. "I listened to it the next morning before I heard about . . . about what had happened, and then I erased it. I wish I had saved it. Then I would be able to listen to his voice. But I didn't."

Quinn looked around at them. "Did Brad call either of you that night, Mr. and Mrs. Putnam?"

"You seem to know already that he didn't," Andrew Putnam said.

Quinn looked back at Drew. "Why didn't you tell us about these calls immediately?"

"Because they don't have anything to do with how he died. It was our business."

"Detective Quinn," Kitty said. It was the first time she had spoken since they'd been there. "I don't understand what this is all about. Why are you questioning us when there's someone out there who . . ." She caught her breath, but then continued, almost screaming. "Someone who put a bag over my son's head! Someone who left him there to die! Why don't you find that person and leave us alone." Camille put an arm around her and glared at Quinn.

"I guess that's it," Quinn said, getting to his feet. "I don't need to tell you that if there's anything else you haven't told us, you need to let us know right away. This kind of stuff is usually thought of as impeding a police investigation, you know."

Camille, angry now, said, "I think that if you use some imagination you can figure out why we didn't say anything. And this has nothing to do with the investigation. Someone, some crazy maniac, came into Brad's apartment and saw him . . . like that. And this person must have killed him."

Quinn was standing and he loomed over her, furious now. "We have spent the last week following up leads related to the way he was found. This is all wasted time now. I'm sure you've heard that the first couple of days are the most important in a murder investigation? Well thanks to your brother's little white lie, we've lost that window of opportunity. If we don't find Brad's killer, it will be your fault. We'll be in touch."

Sweeney was shocked by how cruel his words were. She got up and was almost out of the room when she turned around and asked them, "Did you think of Brad as having a drinking problem?"

Jack and Drew looked at each other, and Drew said hurriedly, "No. But as I said, he's in college. It wouldn't be the most surprising thing in the world."

"Okay," Quinn said, sounding calmer now. "Thank you."

Drew and Melissa walked them to the door. Sweeney watched Melissa put a hand on his back, rubbing small circles with her index finger. Drew stepped away neatly, and a hurt look flashed across Melissa's face.

"Would it be all right to use the bathroom before I go?" Sweeney asked.

"Of course," Melissa said. "The one down here is being renovated, but I'll show you up to the guest bath."

They climbed the elegant staircase and Melissa led Sweeney through a pristine guest bedroom papered with a black-and-white toile pattern. The bed was made up in black-and-white satin and covered with a huge array of black and white pillows.

"Here it is," Melissa said.

"Great, thanks." Sweeney smiled at her and awkwardly closed the door. Was Melissa going to wait out there for her?

The bathroom matched the guest room—the same black-and-white wallpaper, black towels monogrammed with elaborately scrolled P's and little black-and-white soaps in the shape of swans. Afraid to ruin one of the birds, she rinsed her hands with plain water. When she came out again, Melissa was nowhere to be seen, so she took her time going back downstairs, looking into a few of the bedrooms along the hall. Two were clearly guest rooms, sterile and empty. The third was the master bedroom. It was completely overdone to Sweeney's mind, lots of pink and gold, and so many pillows on the bed that it must have taken ten minutes to remove them all before going to sleep.

She listened to make sure there was no one coming up the stairs and ducked into the bedroom. It smelled of expensive perfume and clean laundry. There were two matching bureaus, ornate and scrolled. One was clearly Melissa's and on its polished surface, there was a wedding photograph, Drew looking serious and Melissa grinning as they exited a church. On a low dressing table, there were a couple of bottles of expensive perfume; Sweeney picked each up and sniffed the caps.

Listening again to make sure that there was no one in the hall, she moved over to Drew's bureau. It was very neat. There was a photograph of a young woman in a wedding dress—Kitty, Sweeney could see when she looked closer—and a family photograph taken sometime in the late eighties or early nineties, from the look of the clothes. Kitty and Andrew sat in Adirondack chairs on the lawn in front of the Newport house, the children standing around them. Sweeney felt her heart constrict a bit at the sight of Brad, a skinny nine- or ten-year-old with sun-burnished hair and a goofy grin. Petey was a year or so younger, with reddish hair and freckles. Camille and Drew, already adults, looked basically the same, but Jack, a teenager in the picture, looked much younger. He had a pseudo punk haircut and was wearing a leather jacket.

There was another photograph on the bureau too, a more recent one, of the whole family in formal dress, and she recognized it as the same family photo that had been on Andrew Putnam's desk. Other formally dressed people milled around in the background of the photo looking at a series of huge statues, vaguely human forms with loose, moving limbs. The window behind them in the picture read—in backward letters—"The Davis Gallery." Jack was grinning broadly. Andrew and Kitty were on either side of their children, grinning too. Andrew had on a bright blue tie and Sweeney was again struck by how handsome he was, and how much he looked like Jack and Brad.

"Did you get lost?" Melissa asked from behind her. Sweeney turned around, still holding the photograph.

"I'm sorry, I must have taken a wrong turn and then I saw your photos."

"That's okay," Melissa said. "Isn't that a nice one? That was Jack's opening a couple of months ago."

Sweeney, still humiliated at having been caught, put the photo down and said, "It's great," in a falsely cheery voice. "I guess I should get going."

Melissa didn't say anything. Together they walked silently back downstairs.

Quinn was quiet until they got out to the car, but once he was safely behind the steering wheel and Sweeney had shut the passenger's side door, he slammed his hand on the dashboard. "Those people, screwing around with me like they don't even know what they're doing. They know exactly what they're doing."

"They did come clean, though."

"But only because you confronted them about it. And that's *if* they're telling the truth," Quinn said, glancing quickly at her.

"I think they are," she said. "I don't know why. I just do. Why did you ask Jack if he'd left something behind?"

Quinn looked straight ahead, thinking. "We found something, near the bed. A steno pad with some writing on it. It wasn't in Brad's handwriting and it didn't belong to the roommate."

"What did the writing say?"

He looked over at her again, considering.

"Something about the Back Bay Tunnel project. There were a couple of notes about when the construction started and some general history of the project. Whoever it was jotted down a question about who benefits from the development project. Does that ring a bell for you?"

Sweeney shook her head. "The Putnams own some buildings in the Back Bay, I think. But I doubt they're benefiting from it very much right now."

"I don't think anyone's benefiting much from the tunnel project right now except for those guys who try to sell flowers to you when you're stuck in the traffic for twelve hours."

Sweeney laughed.

The Back Bay Tunnel project was one of those endless urban renewal projects that had been going on for what seemed like twenty years. Actually, it probably had been going on for twenty years, Sweeney realized. The project—which would offer easier access via a tunnel from downtown to Cambridge and points north of Boston—had been approved by Congress nearly two decades ago and was just now nearing completion. It had snarled traffic, torn up neighborhoods, gone wildly over budget, and considerably added to the stress levels of Bostonians.

"Anyway," Quinn said. "If you hear anything about who the notebook might have belonged to, I hope you'll let me know."

"Yeah, of course."

It struck her that he had only told her because he thought she might be able to help him.

TWENTY-FOUR

The figure lay prostrate, arms stretched out over its head, its back arched as though in agony. The slim hips and narrow shoulders gave it a boyish quality. It had no face to speak of, just a blank plane of wood. Yet you could almost imagine the figure screaming out in pain.

Jack Putnam took a sip of his coffee and went back to work. He had carved the figure's body and limbs from red cherry and it gave the figure an oddly lifelike look, as though blood were pumping through its veins. He had sanded it only roughly, so that the surface was grained and textured, as scratchy as a cat's tongue.

He turned away from the sculpture and went to pour himself another cup of coffee. He had been working almost nonstop for twenty-four hours now, driven by the kind of inspiration he hadn't felt in months. The idea had come to him at Brad's memorial service, a man, bent in supplication before God. It would be nearly life-sized. He had attached the limbs with bolts and nuts that he had painted black and he liked the play of the dark metal against the auburn-hued wood.

But the coffeepot, when he lifted it, was filled only with the burnt remnants of the last pot. Shit. He kept forgetting to turn it off. Now he'd have to go up to the kitchen to wash it out. He had an extra-deep utility sink in his first-floor studio, but it was filled with paintbrushes soaking in turpentine, so he took the coffeepot and climbed the stairs to the main part of the house on the second floor.

It was a gorgeous spring day, the sky a cloudless blue, the

sun enthusiastic and unhesitant through the wide windows in his living room. He left the coffeepot to soak in the sink and went upstairs to the roof deck. He was barechested—it was how he liked to work, no matter how cold the day—and he stood with his back to the sun, his eyes closed, enjoying the feeling of warmth on his back.

It was the first sensual pleasure he'd allowed himself since the night Brad had died. Well, perhaps the second. He had, after all, let himself enjoy talking to Sweeney St. George, to enjoy the feel of taking her arm to lead her upstairs at the house after the memorial service. He had allowed himself a quick erotic fantasy as they'd walked downstairs, then shut it off, feeling guilty. But those few moments of the fantasy stayed with him, teasing him with their vividness. He was holding her arms above her head, pressing them against the headboard of his bed. Under him, she could barely move her legs and she struggled playfully as he kissed her neck . . . The fantasy unspooled for another couple of seconds before he forced himself to stop thinking about it.

He had been thinking of calling her. He liked the idea of an evening with her, drinking and talking, and if she was willing, a few moments of physical escape. Again he stamped down the image of her arms stretched above her head. It would feel good. It would make him feel alive. But he wasn't sure if she would welcome any kind of an advance from him.

She was an odd person. There was something wild about her, which he'd picked up on right away, but there was something else too, something that made him suspicious. Why was she so interested in Brad anyway? He remembered Brad talking about her, about her class, and blushing when he said her name. Jack had kidded him about it. "You hot for teacher, Bradley?" he'd teased. Brad had gotten pissed off and punched him in the arm. Was it possible she'd been interested in Brad too? Was that why she seemed so intent on finding out who had killed him?

Anyway, maybe he would call her. He'd had the strangest feeling, right after meeting her, that they knew something of each other, that they could skip over much of the initial small talk and move on to the part of relationships he liked, the companionship, the easy physical knowingness, the anticipation of desire.

Warm now from the sun, he opened his eyes and went back downstairs to the kitchen where he rinsed out the pot and headed back down to the studio.

As he came down the circular staircase, he saw the figure for what it was.

It was Brad, lying on the bed, his arms fixed, his back arched.

"Oh God!" he screamed, rushing to it as though it was a person he could save if he could only get there in time. But instead he took a handsaw from the workbench and went to work destroying it, rasping the saw across the figure's limbs. He hacked and pulled at the wood, splintering it, cutting his hand when the saw caught on a bolt. The blood poured down over the red wood and still he worked, making the figure unrecognizable.

And then he went to the file cabinet in one corner of the studio, his hands shaking. He never allowed himself a drink until four, when he had stopped working for the day. It was his own private rule and he had never broken it, not once.

But now he took out a bottle of vodka that he kept there. It was Stoli, half empty, the liquid glistening beneath the glass as he struggled to unscrew the cap. He lifted it to his lips and drank straight from the bottle, ignoring the protestations of his stomach. He drank and drank, past the gagging, past the burning down his throat. He drank until he shuddered, and lay down amid the wreckage of the sculpture.

TWENTY-FIVE

"Okay, Cammie, try it again from the top."

Someone flicked on the stage lights and Camille Putnam stepped up to the podium. They were practicing for the debate in the gym of a suburban high school that someone had secured because it was about the size of the stage they'd be using for the real debate. She pressed her palms to the tops of her thighs to calm herself. It was a trick she'd learned long ago to get her hands to stop shaking.

"Who's DiFloria this time?" she asked.

"I'll do it," called out Lawrence Freeburn, her campaign manager. "And Roberta will be the moderator."

"Okay. Got it. Let's go." She took a deep breath and raised her hands to rest them on the podium. After the last run through they'd gotten after her for keeping her hands folded throughout the practice debate.

"Use them for emphasis," Roberta had said. "Use them to punctuate. Gestures are the icing on the cake of your speech." Camille had resisted the urge to roll her eyes at Lawrence. Roberta was a debate coach someone had brought in from D.C. She was a small, heavily made-up woman who had obviously had her colors done at some point and took her palette with her every time she went shopping. Camille still had the little plastic "Winter" envelope that she'd gotten when she was elected to her house seat. "It'll make dressing easier," the woman who'd done her colors had told her. The experience had left Camille with a few unflattering jewel-toned silk blouses hanging in her closet and a new dedication to her plain black or navy blue suits and cotton broadcloth shirts from Brooks Brothers or Land's End.

But it seemed to have stayed with Roberta, who wore identically made suits in various pastel shades all firmly within the "Spring" palette, and accessorized with nearly identical scarves to coordinate with the suits. Today it was a lavender skirt and jacket, with a yellow scarf at her neck.

Camille found her incredibly annoying. But everybody said she knew what she was doing. She'd last worked with a successful U.S. Senate candidate in California, and she'd made Camille watch a video of his last debate. Camille remembered lots of gesturing. The guy had practically decapitated his opponent, chopping his hands through the air when he got to an important point.

"We must bring fiscal responsibility back to the federal government," Camille muttered under her breath, chopping the air at "must." She'd give 'em some gestures.

"Okay, we're just about ready to go. We're taping this one," Roberta was saying. "So we're not going to stop for anything. I want you to pretend that this is the real thing. If you screw up, we're going to keep going, so you better think of some creative ways of dealing with screw-ups. Then we'll watch and see how it worked. Got it?"

She nodded.

Lawrence, looking nervous, stepped forward. "Oh, one more thing, Cammie. I just wanted to let you know that I've thrown in a question about your brother's death. We want to be prepared in case DiFloria . . ."

"What do you mean?" She felt fear wash over her all of a sudden.

"I mean DiFloria likes to hit below the belt. He's running scared right now. You're up in the polls and he may take desperate measures. Mentioning Brad might be his way of referencing your family's history. He's already been referring to you as 'Paddy Sheehan's granddaughter' to try to bring up all the baggage about Paddy's drinking and womanizing. He may try to do the same thing here."

"You've got to be fucking kidding me."

"Look, I doubt he'll do it. It would make him look like a jerk. But the last thing I want is for you to get up there and be surprised if he does bring it up, okay? All you have to do is say that your family is mourning your brother and that you're certain the police are doing all they can to find out who killed him and that you're grateful for the prayers of the people of Massachusetts at this difficult time. Got it?"

Camille grabbed the podium to steady herself. Then she leaned forward, willing herself to stay calm, though she could feel the fear and anger bubbling up inside, looking for a place to escape.

"If he so much as says my brother's name," she shouted at Lawrence, "I will personally walk over to his podium and take off his fucking head. Got it?" She chopped the air so hard with her hand that she thought she heard it whistle through the air.

Lawrence looked shocked, but Roberta broke out in a wide grin.

"Hey, Cammie," she called out. "Great hand gestures."

TWENTY-SIX

The next morning, Sweeney took her coffee out on the balcony and watched one of her neighbors hanging laundry in her little backyard. It was early still and the sun hung low on the horizon over a foreground of rooflines. The air was wet and chilled and there was something soothing about the repetitive task, the way the woman bent and straightened, bent and straightened, the sheets and nightgowns and blouses colorful banners on the line.

In the early, rising light she had been staring at the photograph she'd taken from Brad's room, but it hadn't offered up any more clues. It had clearly been taken in a cemetery at night and while Raj's face was the only one she could see, she could sense the presence of other beings in the patterns of light and dark outlined on the print. Peering into the darkness of the photograph, she thought she could make out a shadowy profile here, the outline of a leg or an arm there.

She remembered a class a few weeks ago. She had been running late and coming in she had said, "Hey, everyone, how was your weekend?"

No one had said anything and, trying to buy herself a few minutes to collect her thoughts, she'd persisted. "Come on. Let me live vicariously through you for once. What do you do on the weekend anyway? Parties? Or do you stay in the library and study?"

When she'd looked around at them, she'd sensed an undercurrent of something, sensed that they'd all been thinking about the exact same thing at that moment.

"We went to—" Brad started to say, but Rajiv broke in.

"If we told you," he'd said, looking up at Sweeney with an ironic smile, "we'd have to kill you."

She'd laughed, and the exchange had given her the couple of minutes she needed to arrange her notes. She'd let it go and hadn't thought about it until just now.

But it presented some interesting possibilities.

Sweeney took her coffee cup inside and found her class rosters. She always asked students to write down their phone numbers and addresses on the first day of class, in case she needed to contact them, and she was grateful for the practice as she scanned down the list for her Mourning Objects class and found Rajiv's dorm and room number. She had classes all morning, but she'd get him later that afternoon.

Raj lived in one of the older dorms on campus, one she'd lived in her sophomore year. She remembered a lot of concrete and orange shag, but when she looked in the glass window next to the front door, she saw that it had been renovated in pale wood and a more subtle gray all-weather carpeting. She lurked around the entrance for a few minutes before two girls came out, engrossed in a conversation about a friend who seemed to be dating one of her professors. Sweeney pushed aside the urge to follow them to continue eavesdropping and caught the door. Raj's room was on the fourth floor, so she took the elevator up and found room number 423.

She knocked a few times, and when she got no answer, she settled down on the floor to wait. She was reading the *Globe* when he came around the corner a half hour later, carrying his own newspaper, rolled under his arm.

"Sweeney! What are you doing here?" She searched his face. Was he nervous? She couldn't tell. But he was back to his usual dapper mode of dress and he looked cool and elegant in khakis and a French blue shirt.

"I wanted to ask you about something. Something about Brad."

Now he was nervous. "Well, okay. Do you want to come in? I've got class at four, but that's not for an hour and a half."

She nodded and he unlocked the door and stepped aside to let her enter the room first. It was one of the more pleasant dorm rooms she'd ever been in, she decided. It had a sort of English country house feel, with decent furniture and books on the walls. He even had, she saw, a little rolling bar, with a bottle of sherry and a couple of bottles of scotch.

"Nice place."

"Thanks. I find living in a dorm room very distasteful, but I figure I can at least change my environment."

She took the picture out of her bag and handed it to him. For a few moments, he just looked at it and then he handed it back. "Brad took it."

"Where?"

"Concord."

"When?"

"A month or so ago."

"Do you want to tell me about it?"

"What's there to tell? We went out to Concord one night and hung out in the cemetery and I guess Brad took some pictures."

"Who's 'we'?"

"You know, the class."

"The class? But why?"

He cleared his throat. "To study the stones. You should be proud of your didactic abilities. We got interested enough to go do some extracurricular study." He gave her a disarming smile.

"Raj, I spend a lot of time in graveyards, but even I don't hang out in them at night. It makes it kind of hard to study the iconography."

He went over to a little table next to his bar and found a cannister of coffee. "Would you like some coffee?" he asked.

"Raj."

"I'm going to tell you. I'd just like a cup of coffee first."

"All right. Fine."

"Milk and sugar?"

"Just milk please."

While he made coffee, Sweeney picked up a copy of the *Atlantic Monthly* on his coffee table and leafed through it. Raj fiddled around with a stove-top espresso maker and then poured it out into matching blue china cups.

"Okay," he said, handing her one of the steaming cups. "We went to cemeteries at night sometimes. To, you know, kind of hang out with the dead or whatever. Brad was really into it."

"What do you mean, 'hang out with the dead'?"

"I mean we had séances and things. I didn't really believe in it. I don't think Becca or Jaybee or Jennifer did either, but I was interested in why Brad and Ashley were so into it."

"Is that why Ashley got so mad at me the other day?"

Raj nodded.

"How did it start?"

"You had us do that cemetery cataloging project for class last semester and we all decided to go together. It was kind of fun, so we did it again and then Ashley got kind of obsessed. She'd been doing all this reading about pagan holidays and last fall there was one where the boundaries between the living and the dead were supposed to be broken down or whatever so she got us to go that night."

"Samhain," Sweeney said.

"That's right," Raj said, pronouncing it carefully. "Sowwen. That's what it was. Anyway, we went, and we had this sort of weird experience. I can't describe it, but it did feel like there were some people there with us. Ashley claimed that she was communicating with them telepathically."

"You guys just scared yourselves," Sweeney said. "The imagination is an amazing thing. What about Brad? What was the attraction for him, do you think?"

Raj hesitated and when Sweeney looked up at him, his brown eyes were direct and serious. "It was his brother, I think. He wanted to talk to his brother."

Sweeney stared at him. "What do you mean he wanted to talk to his brother?"

"His brother died. Like five years ago or something."

"I know that, but what do you mean he wanted to talk to him?"

Raj got up to pour himself another cup of coffee. He was

defensive now. "Look, I told you that I didn't believe in this stuff, but we were doing the Ouija board in a Concord cemetery a couple of months ago and this guy came on and said that his name was Pete."

Sweeney was looking dumbfounded and Raj said, "Haven't you ever done the Ouija board?"

"Yeah, of course. It's just been a while."

The last time Sweeney had played with a Ouija board had been in college. She'd stuck around campus over the Thanksgiving break and one night, on her way home from a solitary movie, she'd run into a couple of girls from a group she and Toby had always referred to as the Euro Kids, the wealthy, fish-out-of-water children of Saudi sheiks, English lords, or upper-caste Indian or Pakistani lawyers. These two, an Englishwoman named Violet and a beautiful Spanish girl, whose name Sweeney couldn't remember, had told her they'd just bought a Ouija board and asked her to come up to play it with them.

Lonely and bored—Toby was in California visiting his mom—she had agreed and they had drunk wine coolers and talked to "spirits." Sweeney remembered that they had conversed for a long time with someone who said she was a Scottish witch who had been burned at the stake in the eleventh century and urged them to go out and kill a heifer for her. It had been eerie at the time—she remembered feeling deeply shaken and sleeping with the light on for days—but later she was embarrassed to realize how much her subconscious had been directing the whole thing. She had been reading something about the Salem witch trials for a class and learned how livestock deaths in medieval Europe were blamed on witches. Obviously her brain had mixed it all together and directed her hands. Afterward, someone had explained to her that there was a psychological explanation for the phenomenon of spiritual appearances on Ouija boards: when one person moved their hands on the marker very slightly, toward a particular letter, the others followed suit. The Ouija board created a kind of collective subconscious action.

Raj was saying, "Well, you know, you all put your hands on

the thing in the middle and it moves around and spells out words. So it had kind of been all about Ashley. She's so obsessed with her dead twin—Victoria, her name was—and Victoria kept turning up on the Ouija board and telling Ashley she loved her and all this stuff. Ashley was asking her if she was in a nice place and Victoria was saying it was beautiful and she was so peaceful and everything. Blah, blah, blah. The rest of us were getting a little bored with the whole thing. But then all of a sudden, the Ouija board shifted—I mean, it just kind of jumped—and we said 'Who's there?' the way you're supposed to, and it started spelling, really fast—it freaked me out, if you want to know the truth—it started spelling out 'Peter.'

"We all knew about Brad's brother, so we looked over at him, and he was really scared. He'd taken his hands off the board and he looked like he was about to jump up and run away.

"But we convinced him to put his hands back on it and the thing started spelling out really quickly, 'You must tell them. You must tell them.' Over and over again. Brad was almost crying." Raj, reliving the memory, looked pale and disturbed.

"Did he think that his brother was saying he should tell who had been driving in the accident?" Sweeney almost whispered. She felt suddenly afraid too.

"No, that was the thing. That's what we all thought," Raj said. "But then Pete—or whatever it was—started saying 'Tell about Edmund. Tell about Edmund.' And Brad literally picked the board up and threw it across the grass. He was so freaked out that he couldn't talk for a couple of minutes, couldn't talk at all, and then he said he was going home."

"Edmund?"

"Yeah."

"Did you ask him who he thought Edmund was?"

"No, he didn't want to talk about it. He took off. Just got up and ran out of the cemetery and drove his car home. We'd brought two cars and we all had to cram into Ashley's Honda. I saw him the next day and he seemed okay, but none of us had the nerve to ask him."

"When did you say this was, Raj?"

He thought for a minute, then got up and found his Filofax. "Like two months ago. It was the weekend of my birthday," he said, paging back in the calendar. "So it was Saturday the fourth." Sweeney consulted the calendar too. It had warmed up that next week. She remembered because it had been the week before St. Patrick's Day.

So only a couple of days after his experience in the Concord cemetery, Brad had sat on the floor of her office and they had talked about the afterlife and whether he should reveal an important piece of information.

Raj replaced the calendar and came back to sit down across from her. "Raj," she said, "did Brad ever talk to you about his final project for the class?"

"He was doing mourning jewelry, right? Yeah, I think he said it was coming along pretty well. I ran into him in the library and he had a big stack of books about Rhode Island history or something. Maybe it wasn't for your class. But other than that, we didn't really talk about it."

He still looked nervous, so she said, "Did you see Brad the night he died?"

She wasn't sure if it was surprise or hesitation, but he waited a beat and then said, "No. No. I was at the library."

"What about everyone else in the class? They didn't make a cemetery visit that night, did they?"

Again, he hesitated, then looked down at the ground. "No. I don't think so. They would have told me."

She didn't pursue it further. She wasn't positive he was lying and she didn't see how she was going to get him to tell the truth if he didn't want to.

"Okay," she said, handing him the picture. "You can do whatever you want with it. Thanks for being honest."

He got up and walked to the door with her.

She was already in the hallway when she thought of something else. "Hey, Raj?"

"Yeah?"

"What did you think about Brad? You were friends with him."

Raj was thoughtful. "I don't know if anyone was really

friends with him. He didn't let you, really. It was like he was always afraid he was going to let go and tell you something he didn't want to tell you. Ever since I knew him, that's how he was."

TWENTY-SEVEN

❧

Sweeney had agreed to meet Toby and Lily at a new tapas place on Newbury Street at seven, but by the time she got home from Raj's, it was already six-thirty. After a quick shower, she took the T to the Back Bay, so she wouldn't have to worry about parking.

"I'm sorry, I'm sorry," she called out as she got to the restaurant thirty minutes late.

But they didn't seem to mind. Toby was looking vaguely starry-eyed, and Sweeney noticed that his hand was on Lily's knee under the table.

"We were just talking about Brad Putnam," Toby said after Sweeney had kissed Lily on the cheek and sat down at the oddly low table.

"Ow. What's the story with this table? It's just the right height for banging my knees."

"That's because you're a giantess."

Sweeney stuck out her tongue at him.

"I'm completely fixated on the murder investigation," Lily was saying. "I read the updates every day, even though there isn't anything new. Why do you think the police are having such a hard time figuring out who killed him?"

"I don't know," Sweeney said. "I guess there isn't any obvious suspect. And a family like that is probably putting up a whole bunch of roadblocks."

"You don't think it's someone in the family?" Lily looked horrified.

"No." Sweeney realized she had to be careful here. "It's

just that the police are probably having a hard time getting basic information about who Brad was friends with, stuff like that."

"I wonder how the Putnams are doing?" Lily asked. "You know them, don't you, Sweeney?"

"A little. I don't know how they're really doing, though. I think with a family like that it's hard to know what they're thinking about anything. They've lived in the public eye for so long."

"I was thinking that when you told me about the funeral," Toby said. "How awful to have *reporters* there."

Toby and Lily had already ordered and when the waiter brought over little plates of tapas, they all fell to eating. Sweeney was munching on pickled white asparagus when she thought of something.

"Lily, remember how you were telling me about your work with DNA? Well, can I ask you something?"

"Sure."

"Have you ever tested anything really old? Say, a piece of hair from someone who's been dead for a while? Is that possible, hypothetically speaking?"

"What's a while?"

"I'd say 150 years or so."

"I've worked with a few samples that old. It's kind of iffy, though. Would you have the root of the hair, hypothetically speaking?" Lily gave her a sly little smile.

"I don't know," Sweeney said.

"Well, if you don't have the root, we could try mitochondrial DNA testing. But it's only good for tracing the maternal line."

"What if I'm trying to establish a link through the father's side of the family?"

"Well, then you'd have to have the root and it has to have been stored under pretty good conditions. Even then, it's a question of the integrity of the material. I'd probably give you fifty-fifty odds."

"What would affect the integrity of a hair sample?"

"Heat, moisture, that kind of thing. It's hard to know."

Toby looked at Sweeney suspiciously. "You're not thinking of . . ."

"No. I'm just curious," Sweeney said as a second round of sangrias came and they talked about other things.

Toby and Lily were going to a movie and though they invited Sweeney to come along, she wasn't in the mood to be the third wheel. As she strolled back to the T station, she mingled with the crowds enjoying the balmy evening and thought about the jewelry. She now knew that it was possible there was a way of finding out whether Charles Putnam was Edmund Putnam's father. But what were the chances that the hair in either the necklace or the locket had been pulled out by the root? Probably pretty slim. And even slimmer were the chances that it had been kept under the right conditions all these years. It was probably unlikely that it would work. And anyway, she would have to get access to the jewelry somehow and that meant asking Quinn. It seemed impossible.

She was walking along Newbury Street when she saw, high up in the window of a second-story gallery, a line of painted words reading JACK PUTNAM. WORKS IN WOOD AND METAL AT THE DAVIS GALLERY. She could see people milling around up in the window. It was only nine and there was something about the warming air that made Sweeney not want to go home. So she climbed the stairs to the second floor and found herself in an airy gallery filled with graceful sculptures made of pale wood, the components bracketed together in gracefully human forms calling up people dancing and embracing.

Sweeney wandered around, putting off the gallery worker's question about whether she needed help with a friendly, "Just looking, thanks."

She was standing in front of a disturbing sculpture of a vaguely human form curled into a fetal ball when she felt someone come up behind her. "Very strange, isn't it? Kind of makes you wonder about the artist."

Sweeney turned around and grinned. "Absolutely. I'm ready to call the crazy artist police and order a psychological examination."

Jack's hair was wet from the shower and he was wearing a black leather jacket. He had a pale blue sweater tied around his neck like a scarf and it made his eyes look a lighter shade of blue.

"Are you checking up on the work?" Sweeney asked him. She wasn't sure why, but she was embarrassed that he had found her here, embarrassed that he knew she had gone to the trouble of finding out more about him, and embarrassed by how attracted to him she was. "Making sure it's selling?"

"I wish. Actually the gallery called because someone stuck a piece of gum on one of my pieces."

"No!"

"Yes. I had to scrape it off. They were afraid to touch it."

"That's horrible." Sweeney was secretly sort of delighted with the idea of someone sticking a piece of gum on a sculpture in a high-end gallery. Had they been registering protest or merely caught without a tissue?

"I know." He looked around and then down at her. He was pale, and thinner than the last time she'd seen him, she noticed, as though he'd been sick. They stood for a moment staring at the piece and Sweeney had the sense that he was reliving emotions he had felt while making it. It was a powerful work, and it made Sweeney monumentally sad. She had an image of herself lying on a bed in the days after Colm's death, wrapped into a ball, trying to get beyond all feeling, trying to return to a state beyond all sense.

"I hadn't seen your work before," Sweeney said. "I really like it. They remind me of those little wooden sculptor's models that you can move into different positions. But that sounds terrible . . . I didn't mean . . . I love them."

"No. No. That's where they came from. I was taking a figurative sculpture class in grad school and I was working with one of those little guys—I named him Pablo. And I kind of got more interested in Pablo than in the piece I was working on. I'd always been into woodworking and I decided to make my own model, but I couldn't figure out the scale and I made a huge one. There was something about it that I really liked and I got some more wood and I just kept at them."

Sweeney wandered over toward a tall male figure standing and looking up at the sky, his hands behind his back.

"That one reminds me of a Giacometti," she said. There was something about the way the long-legged figure stood at attention that called up the sculptor's loping, melancholic subjects.

He looked pleased. "You've made me blush. Giacometti is one of my heroes."

"How do you make them?"

"I buy blocks of wood and then cut them with a bunch of different table saws I have. Then I'll carve the different components to get the finer details, sand them down and stain and varnish them. Then I put them together. Hey, you know what? Why don't I show you my studio. You can see for yourself, and I can probably even rustle up a drink. I'm literally around the corner."

"Well . . ."

"Come on, I'm a bit depressed after the gum incident."

Sweeney laughed. "I guess I can't just leave you in a state of gum-induced depression. All right."

"Great." He grinned and they waved good-bye to the gallery workers and then walked along Newbury Street and down Fairfield to Commonwealth Avenue.

They crossed, walked along the mall, and stopped in front of a large brick Beaux Arts mansion. "It looks pretty nondescript on the outside, I know," he said. "I wanted to put in a wall of glass on the side and paint it blue, but they're pretty strict about historic preservation. Wait until you see the inside, though."

They entered through a street-level door painted red. "The house has been in the family for years and my dad gave it to me a couple of years ago," Jack said. "I've been working away on it. The second and third floors are where I live and I gutted the first floor and turned it into the studio. I have a lot of really heavy equipment, saws and sanders and stuff, so I had to keep it all as close to the foundation as possible."

He opened the front door and stepped aside to let her in. They were standing in a cavernous room, with a stainless steel circular stairway at one side climbing up past the second and third floors to a giant skylight. She stood underneath it and looked up at the night.

The walls of the studio were painted bloodred and there were a few huge canvases, white fields scrawled with lines of dark red paint. One whole side of the studio was taken up with huge pieces of machinery, circular saws and other tools that she didn't know the names of.

But all around the rest of the studio, as though it were a park full of moving, walking people, were his strange wood and metal figures, their limbs at so many different angles that they really did seem to be moving. Though they were made of many kinds of wood and held together with varied mechanisms—bolts, screws, lengths of string—the pieces all looked vaguely related. It was clear they were made by the same artist. But they represented many different emotions. A running figure, his long, Giacometti-like legs caught in mid-stride, his arms pumping at his side, was pure joy. Another man stood tall and upright, his arms gesturing as though he were giving a speech.

"What was this?" she asked, pointing to a pile of heaped debris. She could spot a limb here or there, the edges of the cut wood raw and splintery.

"Oh . . . that was a . . . a mistake." He led her over to a tall figure, obviously feminine, that stood shyly, her limbs in an attitude of demure flirtation.

"I've started doing women," he said. "When my last girl-friend was breaking up with me, she threw in my face the fact that I've never done women. She said it was because I had a total lack of understanding of them. What do you think of this one?"

Sweeney studied it for a few moments. "It's pretty, but . . . I don't know."

"It's limited?"

She looked up at him in surprise. It had been exactly what she was thinking.

"Not in a bad way. In kind of an innocent way actually. Kind of . . . I don't know . . . boyish."

"Great." He put a playful arm around her shoulders and she felt competing urges to lean into him and to stiffen against his arm. "Want a drink? I'll show you the rest of the place."

She hesitated, then said, "Okay."

"You don't have to look so afraid. I'm not going to bite you." He laughed.

Sweeney tried to laugh too. "I'm not afraid. It's just . . ."

"What?"

"Nothing. Let's have that drink."

They climbed the circular staircase and were suddenly in an open-plan living space, with a brand-new restaurant-quality kitchen separated from a large living room and dining room by a maple and marble island.

Jack went into the kitchen and poured two glasses of scotch. He handed one to Sweeney and pointed to the couch in the living room. It was old, with art deco wooden detailing, and upholstered in pale blue silk, but somehow it fit perfectly in the otherwise modern room. Sweeney walked around looking at a series of canvases featuring blue fields of various shades and sizes. On one wall, he had hung a long black bully whip. The dark leather made a snaking shadow on the pale wall.

"I like your house," Sweeney said, sipping the scotch and then setting it down on a coaster that appeared to be a butterfly caught in epoxy. "But what about that?" She pointed to the whip. "Isn't it a little kinky for home decor."

"I don't know," he said. "Kinky can be good." He winked at her and sat down next to her on the couch, kicking off his shoes and turning to face her.

"How are your parents doing?" Sweeney asked, flushing from his comment.

"All right. Getting through the memorial service was important," he said. "I think that doing it on their own is hard, though. I even wondered if . . . Anyway, I think they're getting through it."

"How old were you when they split up?" She knew the answer, but she wanted to see how he'd describe it.

"Oh. It was just a few years ago. After Petey died. It happens, you know. When a child dies. To almost everybody. I was seeing a headshrinker around that time and he told me the statistics. They're pretty staggering. The strange thing to me was that Petey's death was the thing that finally did it. They'd almost broken up so many times before. You heard the stories. Our house was . . . I mean, you can imagine. He was not the nice guy he is now." He paused. "What about you? Are your parents still together?"

Sweeney took a deep breath. "My father committed suicide when I was thirteen and my mother is something of a drunk herself. I don't even talk to her anymore. They never got married, but they lived together until I was five. Then my mother caught him screwing around and he moved out. She was an actress and we moved around, all over the place, but when things were really bad, she'd send me back to Boston to live with him."

His eyes were wide. "Was your father Paul St. George? I didn't put it together before."

"Yeah. That was him." She looked away from his intense gaze.

"He was another one of my heroes. Seriously. I love his work. I always said that I'd buy one if it came on the market. Wow. I can't believe you're . . . Wow!"

She focused on a metal and leather mask that was hanging on the opposite wall.

"How do you think it's affected you? Growing up like that?"

"I don't know," Sweeney said. "I suppose a shrink would say that I have a hard time trusting, all that. I don't put a lot of stock in shrinks. What about you?" She put on a German accent. "How has your childhood affected the vay *you* deal with things?"

He laughed. "Well, I told you about my relationship history." He grimaced. "No, no. I've dated some really great woman. I guess that ultimately I just wasn't ready to take it to the next level or whatever. I think in some ways seeing Drew and Melissa's marriage was what did it for me."

"What do you mean?"

"Don't get me wrong. I think they actually really love each other. But it hasn't been easy. They were always kind of volatile, even before they got married. Breaking up and getting back together. And then they've been trying to get pregnant for years. Melissa keeps having miscarriages. There was even one baby that made it to six months and then she lost it. It was awful. They buried it and everything. We all went to the service." Sweeney thought of the little marble angel she'd seen at Mount Auburn. "Anyway, I guess I shouldn't judge, but it always seemed like life would be a lot easier if they hadn't gotten married."

"It's a platitude, but I think the thing about being married, or loving someone or whatever, is that it isn't easy."

"Yeah, and lately I've been feeling like I understand that. I can see having kids someday, more so than I ever could before. Maybe it's turning thirty." He grinned. "Who knows?"

He was getting drunk. Sweeney could see the signs, his bright eyes, the deliberately unslurred speech. It struck her that he must have had a couple of drinks before he came to the gallery. But he was someone who knew how to drink. She watched him carefully modulate his words, determined to appear alert and together.

"Do you think you were helped by seeing a shrink?" she asked him.

"Do I think I was helped? I think I came to know myself better. But whether I have the wherewithal to do anything about it is another question."

She gulped her scotch and realized that just to keep up with him, she was drinking faster than she usually did. It was like that thing she'd heard about where people who were effective conversationalists learned to match their tone of voice and way of speaking to the person they were talking to. It made them feel good and it made them feel like you were like them.

Uncomfortable under his gaze, she looked around the room. "So how long has this building been in your family?"

"I think my great-great-great-grandfather bought up the land in the 1850s, before the Back Bay existed at all. They put up a bunch of buildings and we've held on to them. Now Drew has some scheme to turn them into luxury apartments or something."

He leaned toward her and dropped his arm along the back of the sofa. "I hope you don't think I'm being too forward," he said. "But I just have this kind of feeling about you. I want you to be in my life."

Sweeney looked away. She felt somehow pleased, but she wasn't sure what to do.

"I'm sorry. It's kind of crazy."

"Do you think it has to do with Brad's death?"

"Maybe. I don't know. I'm sorry. I'll stop making you uncomfortable."

He drained his scotch and got up to pour himself another one.

"It's different than it was with Petey, you know. There's a sense that we haven't put him to rest yet, that there's all this unfinished business, if you know what I mean. I think that we're so used to death just being the end of something and this feels open, raw. And all the media interest and everything just keeps on reopening the wound. Somehow I feel ill-prepared to deal with it, if you know what I mean. My last girlfriend was Jewish and when her father died I remember sitting shivah with the family and thinking that it made sense. There was something they were *supposed* to be doing. It was all scripted for them and it was kind of a relief."

"I know what you mean," Sweeney said. "I think that by giving up some of the ritual surrounding death, we've given up some of the most important effects of that ritual. That's what ritual does—it kind of puts an end to suffering. It allows you to go on."

He was staring at her and his hand had crept from the back of the couch to her shoulder, where it was playing with her hair. She was tempted to lean back so his hand was on her neck. Instead she sat up. "I should get home, I guess."

"Yeah. I bet you have to be up early and all that. But you haven't seen my roof deck. You have to see the roof deck! Come on!" He jumped up and pulled her up too, then ran up the circular staircase. Sweeney laughed, though she was still uncomfortable, and followed him. The stairs led past a hallway with four doors leading off and up to a little landing with a storage area and wide French doors. Jack opened them and they stepped out onto a large wooden deck surrounded by a low railing. There were five chaise longues and a bunch of chairs around the deck and, over in one corner, a hot tub. Sweeney stood against the railing and looked up into the night. A few billowy clouds floated by and from somewhere off in the distance she heard music—Miles Davis, she thought. Before she could be sure, he was standing directly behind her. He put his hands on her shoulders and he turned her around to face him.

Their faces were very close and at the same moment, they leaned in, knocking noses, then finding each other's lips. There wasn't anything tentative about the kiss. Jack kissed her hungrily, his hand at the back of her head, pressing her into him and she could taste the alcohol on his breath, smell the tobacco, feel his unshaven face pricking her cheek.

She was breathing hard and he smiled at her before he leaned in, pressing her hard into the railing, his knee between her legs, his lips all over her neck, biting her, not quite hard enough to hurt. She was turned on and she pushed back, arching her neck to give him access to her throat. He bit and licked her skin and she felt his hot breath against her skin.

"Jack," she whispered, but he didn't answer. He kept biting her skin and Sweeney felt little pinpricks of sensation, not quite pain, but something like it. His breath in her ear was harsh and ragged.

She turned quickly out of his grasp so that they had switched positions and he was pressed against the railing. He smiled again, then roughly caught her hands behind her back and held them there. His grasp almost hurt, but she let him kiss her again, her body useless against his strength.

Breathless, she stepped back and looked at him. He was grinning and he was about to reach for her again when she wrenched her hands away, moved out of his grasp, and sat down on one of the patio chairs.

"What's wrong?" He was breathing hard.

"Nothing. I just . . . things are moving a little fast."

"I'm sorry. I thought you wanted to."

"I . . . I do. I just, let's sit down and talk."

"Okay. That's fine. Let's talk." He sat down across from her and grinned, then reached forward to touch her knee. "What do you want to talk about?"

"I don't know. Let's talk about Brad."

"What about Brad?"

"Who do you think killed Brad?" It was cruel, but she wanted to say the one thing that would slow down whatever was happening between them. She watched his face crumple with anger, then recompose itself.

"How should I know? I'm not a detective."

"But you were there. You must have some idea about it. You saw the room."

"Yeah, but it just looked . . . I don't know. It just looked the way it always did. There wasn't anything strange about it at all." Not looking at her, he ran a hand through his hair nervously. She could still hear Miles Davis, climbing in the air, bouncing off buildings, and sailing off toward the water.

"What about when you left the apartment? How did he look when you left him?"

"He was on the bed, passed out, with the ropes around his hands or whatever and he . . ."

She interrupted him, staring. "But it wasn't ropes, he was tied up with neckties. The police . . ." The realization hit her as she watched his face. "It wasn't you, was it? It wasn't you who tied him up that night." She stood up, her heart beating, her eyes searching for the stairs.

"Sweeney . . ."

"Why did you lie about it?" She was whispering and when he stood up, his hands out, reaching for her hands, she turned away from him and started down the stairs. She was afraid now and she heard him behind her.

"Sweeney, wait . . ."

She didn't say anything as she ran down the two flights of stairs, grabbed her coat from the banister, and kept going out the door.

"Jesus Christ! Hang on." She heard him calling again, but

she pushed the door closed and ran across the street to the Comm. Ave. mall.

The mall was almost empty and she stood for a moment, confused and dizzy. It was late. What if she couldn't get a cab? But when she reached Newbury Street, she saw one heading toward her. She put a hand up and miraculously it stopped for her.

"Can you take me to Somerville?" she asked the man behind the wheel.

He studied her for a moment and then he said, "Of course I can. I'm a cabdriver, aren't I?" She smiled and got in.

As he pulled away from the curb, he watched her for a moment in the rearview mirror. "You look as though you'd seen a ghost," he said, and she glanced up at her reflection in the mirror.

"No," she said, "Not a ghost."

TWENTY-EIGHT

Sweeney found Quinn's address in the phone book once she got home. His little double-decker, in a section of Somerville that was only starting to be gentrified, was well kept, with rows of tulips and daffodils blooming all along a stone path, and a new doormat printed with "Welcome." The other houses on the quiet street were all tidy too, and there was a kind of Old World feel to the neighborhood—tiny front gardens, vinyl siding, a few with flamingoes or garden gnomes keeping watch.

Sweeney looked at her watch. It was eleven. She had no right to be bothering him at home, but she felt like she had to tell him what she had found out in person. Hell, he was a cop. He was probably used to getting interrupted at ungodly hours.

And besides, it appeared that he was still up. Lights burned in the house and she could hear a TV blaring from somewhere inside.

She knocked on the door and listened to footsteps come closer and closer. The inner, wooden door opened and a woman stood behind the glass, staring out at Sweeney. She had short blond hair that looked as though it had been dried in a hurricane, and a face that was distinctive for its high cheekbones and perfect skin. She was petite—no more than five foot one or so, but she seemed somehow swollen, as though she had suddenly put on a lot of weight. She was dressed in sweatpants and a man's flannel shirt and she had been crying. As soon as the door opened, Sweeney had a sense of crisis, the feeling that something disastrous had happened in this house. The woman stared at her.

"Is Detective Quinn here?" Sweeney asked.

"Who are you?"

"Can you tell him that Sweeney St. George is here to see him? It's kind of an emergency."

"What do you want?" The woman stared at her in silence for a couple of minutes and then said, "Who are you? Are you having an affair with him?" But she didn't seem to be angry, rather she stared at Sweeney dreamily. "Do you love him?"

"I . . . No . . . I . . ." She was starting to be consumed by panic when she heard Quinn's voice from inside the house.

"Maura, who is it?" he called out. "What's going on?"

The woman stared at Sweeney for another moment and then she just turned away, as though she had answered the door to find that there was no one there.

"Maura, hold on, I . . ." Quinn's voice came from a room somewhere inside the house and Sweeney just stood there in the doorway, unable to move.

"Who is it?" he called out in a panicky voice.

Through the open door, Sweeney saw him come into the room. He looked terrified, as though he didn't know what he was going to find out there.

She stared.

Quinn was holding a very new baby. And as he stood there, staring back at her, as though she were the absolute last person he had expected to see on his doorstep, the baby began to whimper, and then to cry, horrible, despairing cries that seemed as though they could never be soothed.

"My wife . . . she's . . . she's had a hard time since Megan was born," Quinn said finally.

After she had explained why she was there, Sweeney had sat down on the couch and held the baby while Quinn took his wife upstairs. She was still new-baby light and she stopped crying after a few moments and let Sweeney hold her in the crook of her arm and stroke her tiny hands.

"It was a difficult birth and she's been kind of depressed," he said, putting the baby into a little carrying cradle and setting it on the floor next to him. The room was overly warm, with floral wallpaper that was too busy for Sweeney's taste and slipcovered furniture. On the wall over the couch was a shamrock encrusted plaque with the words "May the road rise to meet you. May the wind be always at your back. May the sun shine warm upon your face. May the rains fall softly upon your fields until we meet again. May God hold you in the hollow of his hand."

"That's really normal, you know. The hormones and all." The baby was making tiny kitten sounds, and Sweeney leaned forward to smile at her.

"Yeah, well, this is . . . something more serious. I don't know."

"Has she seen a doctor? Sometimes medication can help."

"Yeah, yeah. I made sure she was seeing a doctor. She's taking the antidepressants and all. It didn't seem like it tonight, but I think she's actually getting better. We were hoping that . . . Anyway, I'm sorry about . . . that."

Sweeney wanted to say something that would make him feel not so ashamed and so she said, "I've got lots of depression in my family. Nothing shocks me."

He smiled. "Good. So how did you figure out he was lying?"

"He mentioned something about finding Brad tied up with ropes." She watched his face. "Not neckties."

Quinn didn't say anything.

"I know I probably wasn't supposed to know about that, but Becca Dearborne called a few friends before you got to the apartment. I heard from a friend of mine that he was tied up with neckties."

He stood up and went over to the window. "Shit. We were holding that information back. Half the kids in Boston probably know by now." The baby started to cry and Quinn picked her up, hoisting her so she could peer over his shoulder and pacing around the living room as he talked. "I'll have to talk to them again tomorrow. And don't even ask if you can be there."

"Don't worry. I don't think I want to be there when you lay into them."

He grinned. "You're telling me."

"I figure it has to be Camille," Sweeney said. "I mean, she's the one with the most to lose from being involved in this. It could be Drew, but somehow . . . I don't know. I just don't buy it."

"You may be right. We'll see," Quinn said quietly. "I really appreciate your telling me all this."

They were silent for a little while, watching the baby.

Finally Sweeney said, "There's an idea I have and it's going to sound kind of crazy to you, but I'll throw it out there anyway. You remember the mourning brooch that said 'Beloved Son, Edmund'?"

He nodded.

"Well, as you know I had been kind of interested in it and when we found out that the jewelry came from the Putnam family, I tried to figure out who the brooch had belonged to. It turns out that it belonged to Belinda Putnam, whose son Edmund died in 1888.

"Remember, the brooch had the dates of his birth and death on the back? March 4, 1864, to June 23, 1888. Well, I got interested in Belinda Putnam so I went to Mount Auburn Cemetery, where the family has a plot, and I found Edmund's stone."

"Okay?" Quinn said, looking impatient. "And?"

"And the date of birth on his stone is different from the one on the brooch. The stone says he was born on December 4 and the brooch says March 4, three months later."

"It must have been some sort of mistake," Quinn said. "I'm sure people got things wrong on gravestones all the time."

"But remember the mourning necklace," Sweeney said. "Belinda Putnam made it or had it made after her husband Charles died—in April 1863." The implications dawned on him as Sweeney said, "I don't think it's humanly possible for a woman to be pregnant for twelve months."

"So if the date on the brooch is right, it means that Edmund Putnam wasn't his kid."

"Yeah."

"So you think Brad figured this out?"

"I don't know. He may have been about to figure it out. I've looked at some of his notes for my class and I think he was looking into it. What if he had suspicions and expressed them to his family? What if someone in the family became concerned that he was going to reveal that their ancestor was illegitimate?"

"But what would it all mean? This was a hundred years ago. It's not like they'd take back all the Putnams' money, is it?"

"I don't know. It would depend on what his will said. Charles Putnam had a brother and his descendants might have a case to make that some of the Putnam fortune should go to them."

"Can you get hold of wills that old?"

"Well, I've done a bit of genealogical research and I know you can get copies of probate documents from the Massachusetts Archives. I suppose the birth records for Edmund Putnam might help too, though I imagine that if there was any kind of subterfuge, they would have filed a birth certificate with the earlier date." She paused. "There may be another way, though."

Quinn was rubbing the baby's back and he looked up at her. "Yeah?"

"What if we could establish paternity by doing a DNA test?"

"But how could we possibly get samples from people who have been dead for a hundred and fifty years?"

"There's the jewelry," Sweeney said. "The necklace and the locket both have samples of Charles Putnam's hair. All you'd have to do is take a small piece. It's iffy—apparently you have to have a piece of the root, so if the hair was cut it won't work. But if it was pulled out, there may be enough genetic material to do a test. There's a chance anyway. You have access to a forensics lab, right? Apparently a small sample of hair is enough to tell us whether the two people are related. If they're not, then we know that Edmund Putnam wasn't the son of Charles Putnam. And if that's true, and if Brad figured it out when he was studying the jewelry, it gives us a motive for his murder."

"Okay, but even if I could do this, which I don't think . . . But even if I could, where are you going to get a sample to compare it with?" he asked. "The Putnams are acting pretty suspicious, but I don't think I've got grounds to request DNA samples."

Sweeney waited a second. "Well, that's what I was thinking. I'm sure that the lab has examples of Brad's DNA, to compare later in case something turns up."

Quinn raised his eyebrows and nodded, warming to the idea. "I don't know. I have a friend down at the lab. Let me see what he says. But I'm not promising anything."

"I know, I know." She yawned. The clock over the television said 2 A.M. "In the meantime, I'll look into the probate and birth records, see if I can find anything."

"I'll let you know what my friend says." The baby started fussing and he lifted her up in the air, holding her over his head and smiling at her. Her tiny, wizened face broke into something like a smile.

"It was nice to meet you, Megan," Sweeney said, smiling at her too, then turning to Quinn. "She's really beautiful."

"Thanks." He grinned, for a moment anyway, then got up and walked her to the door. "If you learn anything else, let me know."

TWENTY-NINE

❦

The teakettle whistled.

Andrew Putnam sat up. He had dozed off for a moment, sitting at the kitchen table and reading the paper, and now he went to the stove and turned off the gas, then searched through four cabinets before he found the box of Earl Grey tea bags.

Normally, Greta was there to do it for him. But since Brad's death, he'd been unable to stand having her in the house and he'd given her a month off to visit her mother in Munich. The kids had worried about him being alone, picturing him falling off the wagon no doubt. Cammie had even offered to move in for a while, but he had convinced her that he'd be okay.

He poured the hot water over the tea bag in a mug and let it sit for a few minutes before taking the bag out and adding milk. The warm mug felt good in his hand. It was one of the first things he'd noticed at AA meetings, the steaming cups of coffee or tea, the compulsive little knots of people smoking outside before the meetings started. Alcoholics replaced one ritual with another, one addiction with a less harmful one. But the gurgle of hot water into a mug was a poor substitute for the sharp rattle of ice in a cocktail shaker.

He took his tea into the study and sat down at his desk.

And then, for what must have been the fortieth time that day, he reached for the phone to call Kitty.

Kitty. He had seen her more in the last two weeks than he had in the last two years and he felt almost guilty when he realized how welcome it had been. When he had gone down to

Newport right after he had heard about Brad, he had almost wondered if she felt the way he did, but she was able to shut him out so quickly. It was like getting a glimpse of a distant vista through a window and then having the curtain drawn before you could really see it. Kitty. She had let him hold her for a second and he had felt that old pull, the base urge that had never really waned, even when everything else had been shit. He knew that she had been thinking about it too in the moment before she pulled away, the night Petey had died.

In spite of himself, he found that he was aroused, and he picked up the hot mug of tea for something to do. But it was much too weak and he put it down again, the pale taste lingering on his tongue. He didn't know what to do with himself, so he took out Drew's plans for the Back Bay town house development.

Andrew had always liked looking at architectural plans. There was something so promising about a project when it existed only as a series of small lines on paper. Drew had been talking for a while about renovating the unoccupied Back Bay residences and he'd finally asked the architects to go ahead and come up with some design ideas. The town houses would be designed for young single professionals, with large master bedrooms and offices, plus space for entertaining. Drew wanted to call it Commonwealth Place and incorporate a courtyard with a pool, exercise room, and outdoor barbecue area into the design. Andrew had an image of a bunch of well-dressed young Bostonians milling around on a roof.

It looked fine and Drew said it was the best use for the property. In truth Andrew didn't care much about the development side of things. He didn't care much about any of the things people said he was supposed to care about. When he was twenty-three, his father had taken him out to lunch. "Andrew, what do you love to do?" he'd asked. "Now that you have your law degree, you have a great many options in terms of what you will spend your time doing within the firm."

When Andrew hadn't been able to come up with anything, his father had seemed furious. Finally, just for something to say, he had blurted out, "I always liked the idea of buying and selling houses."

It had been something of a dream for him, to buy a house and work on it, sand the floors and paint the walls cool, soothing colors, replace the heavy, old Victorian fixtures with clean, modern ones, then sell it to someone else and perhaps buy another one. He had always liked woodworking and thought he could do some of the work himself. He had built Kitty a chest for Christmas and had been pleased with how it had come out.

But his father had misunderstood.

"Excellent. Real estate law," he had said. "I've been thinking that we ought to develop our real estate holdings. If you can become expert in the areas of the law that apply to our work, we could have quite a nice little thing going here."

Andrew had put a good face on it, but he wasn't much good at the business and everybody knew it. Gradually, they had hired lawyers younger than him to do the work and he had found that he could go home by two or three every day.

But he hadn't been bored. He had loved being there when the kids got home from school and he had enjoyed just being in the house with Kitty. It hadn't been good for his drinking, of course, the empty afternoons. It had taken five years of psychoanalysis for him to figure that part of it out. He had gotten into the habit of having a drink or two when he came home and then more throughout the afternoon as the hours stretched on.

Again, he reached for the phone, and this time he allowed himself to pick it up, dial the familiar number.

It took her eight rings to answer. They had often fought about her unwillingness to install additional phone extensions in the Newport house. It was ridiculous! The house was huge. If you were on the second floor and the phone rang downstairs, it was almost impossible to reach it in time.

But it was one of the things about Kitty that he'd never been able to change. She'd grown up in a modest suburban house in Brookline, where she and her five brothers played rough and tumble games and their Irish setters wrecked the furniture, and she'd never much liked the business of houses, the redecorating and improving and changing that had been so important to his mother.

When they'd first started going to Newport as a young married couple, she had been stiff and uncomfortable in his parents' house, retreating outside for swims or walks along the Cliff Walk whenever she could. But after his parents were gone, and the house was theirs, he'd noticed that she'd gradually settled into it, making it hers. His parents' things had slowly disappeared, vases and figurines and silk pillows put away up in the attic, replaced by her birding books and bags of potting soil. She'd had beige canvas slipcovers made for the furniture, and the dogs left mats of golden hair on them. When they'd split up, she'd said she wanted to stay there and it had been fine with him. He hadn't been able to stand being in Newport anymore. Too many memories of Petey, too many memories period.

"Hello," she finally said into the phone.

"Hi."

"Andrew." She said it quietly, a warning to herself about what was coming.

"How are you?"

"All right. I guess. Considering." He couldn't tell if it was annoyance or exhaustion, but her voice sounded flat.

"I'm sorry to call . . . I just wanted to hear your voice."

"No, that's okay. I was just outside with the dogs. I'm not sure what to do with myself."

"I know. I'm sitting here looking at Drew's architectural plans. Wouldn't he be happy if he knew?"

She laughed. A short, bitter laugh. "So, how are *you* doing?" They both knew what she meant.

"Okay. I've got a wicked tea habit going, though. Greta bought something like a case of it before she left. Even so, I think I'll have to restock."

"Have you heard anything from the police?"

"No, except I wish they'd lay off poor Jack."

"I know. Well, I'm going to go." She sounded suddenly as though she were going to cry. "I haven't been sleeping."

"Kitty, can I . . . can I come down?"

"No. No, that's not going to help anything."

"Of course it isn't, but if I could just . . . Please. I don't want to be alone."

She hesitated, but finally said, "No, I'm tired. I'm sorry." He heard a last sound, the start of a sob, before she hung up the phone.

He listened to the dial tone for a few moments, then looked up at the clock. It was almost nine, too early to go to bed. The old sense of restlessness had taken over. He wanted a drink. It wasn't the kind of urgent want he'd known when he first quit. Then, the wanting had been a kind of question. He had never known the answer until he'd made it through the evening or the afternoon. Now he knew its shape, its arc. He knew where it began and ended. He knew from experience that he could handle the craving. He knew what he had to do.

His head buzzing with the start of a headache, he got up, took his keys from the key rack in the hall, and went out into the night.

THIRTY

Sweeney was coming out of the shower the next morning when she heard about the accident. She liked to listen to the morning news while she was getting ready and she had left the overperky TV host talking about Mother's Day crafts projects.

But as she toweled her hair, she heard the cheery voice coming through from the living room. "University officials and students are this morning mourning the death of student Alison Cope, a junior who was killed in a hit-and-run accident last night near her Cambridge apartment. There were no witnesses to the accident, which occurred sometime between one and two A.M. this morning. Cope's body was spotted by a passing cabdriver who tried to resuscitate her at the scene. Cambridge police are asking anyone who may have been near the scene of the accident to call the CPD hotline. Cope, twenty, was from Minneapolis and was majoring in Biology. University officials expressed sympathy for Cope's family and said that the university community, already in mourning after the recent and still unsolved murder of student Brad Putnam, would be greatly affected by this second death."

Sweeney toweled her hair and watched the footage of the accident scene. Alison Cope. The name didn't ring a bell. Sweeney didn't think she'd ever met her. But it was strange, a second death—a homicide, really, though it was likely an unintentional one—in three weeks.

"Cope's family has flown in from Minneapolis," the anchor was continuing, as a picture of a blond girl in a high school graduation cap and gown flashed on the screen. Sweeney stared. She had met Alison Cope after all. Her good memory had it immediately.

Alison Cope was the girl who had been at the Putnams' house after Brad's memorial service. Alison Cope was the girl who had angered Jaybee by coming to the Putnams' house and pretending that she had been friends with Brad.

As she walked through the yard to her office, Sweeney was aware of an oppressive sort of nervous tension. Students stood around talking in small groups. As she unloaded her bag onto her desk, she looked out the window and saw two girls crying and hugging each other on Quincy Street. She wasn't teaching today, but she had a pile of papers to grade and she'd been planning on cleaning off her desk when the phone rang.

It was Quinn.

"I heard about the accident," she said, once he had identified himself. "Do you know what happened?"

"Not yet," he said. "I was calling because—"

But Sweeney cut him off. "Wait, you may know this, but she was at Brad's memorial service. I don't think they knew each other very well, but she was there, which means they knew each other a little."

"We'll look into that, of course." He sounded distant, distracted. In the background, Sweeney heard someone laughing.

"But she was there . . . Don't you think that it's strange that she was connected with him at all?"

"Right now, it looks like it was a straightforward hit-and-run. There's no reason to believe it was anything like that. But we'll look into it."

"But—"

"I said we'll look into it," he said, closing off the line of conversation. "Look, you were right about Jack Putnam not being the one who tied Brad up. It was Camille. They made up the story about Jack doing it because they realized what the press could do to her campaign. They seemed kind of relieved to get the truth out actually."

"So what about that phone call to Jack?"

Quinn hesitated. "He claims that it went straight into his

voice mail and he got the message later that night. It was Brad, obviously drunk, and he was going on about how Jack was a great brother and he really loved him.

"And Drew didn't come out with any revelations?"

"No. Hold on."

She heard him talking to someone for a few seconds.

"Sorry," he said, when he was back on the phone. "Anyway, the main reason I called is that I took the jewelry down to the forensics lab this morning and talked to my friend. It turns out that the necklace isn't going to yield anything. The hair was trimmed and had been treated and there weren't any intact roots. But the locket is actually pretty promising, my friend thinks. The sample had been pulled rather than cut, which is kind of odd, but anyway, he said that it had been extremely well preserved in the locket all these years and that he found a couple of intact roots for testing. So he thinks he might be able to do something with it, but before I tell him to go ahead, I think I'd like to see the gravestone. I'm certainly not doubting you on the dates, but I'm kind of calling in a favor here and I'd like to see it for myself."

"Absolutely," Sweeney said. "I'd be glad to show it to you."

They agreed to meet at the main gates of the cemetery later that afternoon.

THIRTY-ONE

Quinn was getting a cup of coffee out of the machine when Marino came out into the hallway. "Jesus, Quinny! Every time I try to find you you're getting a cup of coffee. Have you ever thought you might need to cut down on your caffeine habit?"

Quinn waited for the machine to stop spraying the awful stuff into his little Styrofoam cup. "What's going on?"

"I want to get down there and interview anyone who lives in that neighborhood. Anyone who may have been up last night, convenience store clerks, bartenders, anybody like that. Get the names of any cabdrivers who got called out in that area. You ready to go?" He was drinking a Coke and in between orders, he paused to take swigs from the can.

Quinn took a deep breath. "But what about the Putnam thing? I was thinking we could interview the family again and there are a couple of leads I want to follow up on related to the jewelry."

"We've gotta focus on this," Marino said. "The lieutenant said he's got Yolen and Anderson on the Putnam thing." He looked away. Yolen and Anderson were senior homicide detectives and Quinn knew that it wasn't the first time Marino had been pushed out to give them a chance on a case.

"Besides I don't think there's anything more we can get from the family," he went on. "We're running the details through the database again. See if we get any matches."

"Is he taking us off Putnam?"

"I don't know. He was saying just for today." Marino looked embarrassed.

"Marino, I'm telling you. This doesn't feel like a ritual killer thing. I think Brad Putnam's killer knew him, I think . . ."

"Yeah well, it doesn't matter what you think. It matters what you know. And the lieutenant wants us on this hit-and-run."

"But—"

"Be ready in five, Quinny," Marino said before he left the room. "We'll take two cars 'cause I got some stops to make later."

They spent the morning stopping at every house or apartment that looked out on the accident scene. There were mostly students or senior citizens in the neighborhood and so they found that most of the residents had been either not home yet or long asleep when the accident had happened.

They stopped in at the couple of twenty-four-hour stores and Laundromats in the vicinity, but the first anyone had heard of the accident was the ambulance and police sirens responding to the scene.

It seemed that Alison Cope's death had been witnessed by no one.

Except for the person who had killed her, Quinn reminded himself.

Marino had headed back to the station, and Quinn was on his way to Mount Auburn Cemetery when he passed the apartment building where Brad Putnam had lived. They had already interviewed the residents, but one guy hadn't answered his door and Quinn thought he could try him again. Marino hadn't told him to do it, of course, but it was really just a question of tying up loose ends.

He parked in front of the building and checked his notebook. The apartment he'd struck out at was at the back of the building. He went around and knocked on the door. No answer. He knocked again. Still nothing.

So he went up and knocked on the door next to Brad's and Jaybee's apartment. He had already interviewed the guy who lived there. He was a musician, Quinn remembered, and he hadn't heard or seen anything the night Brad Putnam was murdered. He'd been practicing for some kind of concert and he'd gone to bed early and slept through the night.

He seemed to do a lot of practicing. From behind the door Quinn heard the strains of some kind of classical music. Nothing very well organized, more like someone practicing scales. Quinn knocked.

The music stopped. "Yeah?" a male voice asked.

"Cambridge police," Quinn said. "Can I come in and ask you some questions?"

The door opened and a guy in a blue bathrobe stood there, holding a mug of what smelled like coffee.

"Hi, I'm Detective Tim Quinn. Cambridge police. I think I already interviewed you about the night of Brad Putnam's death."

"Yeah, I remember you. Come on in." The guy had the kind of accent that made Quinn hyper aware of his own, Boston, but not the part of Boston Quinn had been raised in. This guy sounded like a Kennedy.

Quinn nodded and stepped into the messy apartment. A couple of music stands were arranged in a half circle, and a cello was lying on its side on the floor. A bow was resting on the music stand.

"Do you know who lives downstairs around back?"

"Oh. Yeah. Lorcan. He's Irish."

"Does he work a lot or what? I've tried a couple of times and haven't been able to talk to him."

"He's away. Florida."

Quinn wrote that down. "Know when he's back?"

"I think he said he was going for three weeks. He just finished up a big paper or something. Maybe his thesis."

"Yeah? What'd you say his name was?"

"Lorcan something. You know how it is when you live next door to someone. You never really get their last name. Oh. No, I do know what it is. Lyons. I had to sign for a package for him once."

Quinn wrote that down. "Okay. Guess I'll have to try him again. Thanks for your help."

It was only three-thirty. He was meeting Sweeney at four, but he figured he'd head up to the cemetery and look around before she got there. He drove through the imposing archway, which looked a little like the entrance to a prison, and parked along one of the side roads, as the signs told him to do. Then he got out and walked back toward the main gate, stopping to read some of the stones along the way. He had never thought that much about gravestones. During his childhood, they seemed to kind of always be there, in the neighborhood, when he was forced to go to the funeral masses and burials of relatives or neighbors. His father's stone was just a big block of— what kind of stone was it? Granite, marble? He realized he didn't know. It was gray, with black flecks, so that was probably granite, he decided. Quinn and his mother had ordered just his name and dates and a cross. It had been years since he'd gone to see it. When his mother had died, she'd told him she didn't even want a stone, so he'd had her cremated and he and Maura had sprinkled the ashes in the ocean off Cape Cod. Back to Ireland, she'd told him one of those last days in a painkiller-induced haze. I want to drift across the ocean back to Ireland.

But these stones were different from his father's. They were in the shapes of things, coffins or pyramids or angels, and they had beautiful flowers carved on them. As he wandered along the rows, reading the names on the stones, he recognized some of them from buildings he'd see around town, street names.

He stopped in front of a small statue of an angel, inscribed with the words, "My Wife and Child." That was it, no names, no dates. He stood for a moment, reading the words, conscious that his eyes were filling up, and embarrassed, he wiped them away.

"Hi, sorry I'm late."

Sweeney St. George's voice broke the still air and he turned to find her standing behind him, wearing a bright yellow raincoat and carrying a brown paper shopping bag. Between the raincoat and her hair, she was the only bright thing in the sea of gray and white.

"That's fine. I was just . . . looking around." He turned away from her so she wouldn't see his eyes. "Why don't you show me where it is?"

She led the way down one of the side streets and on to a dead end walking path with four family plots. "Here," she said, gesturing to a small square of gravestones with a little fence around it. In the middle of all the other stones was a tall one, shaped almost like a church steeple. It had to belong to someone important, he decided, someone rich.

"Whose was that?" he asked. He was standing outside the little fence, but Sweeney walked right in, going over to the stone and gesturing him over to look at it. "Is it okay?" he asked nervously.

"Yeah, this is what gravestones are for," she said. "You're supposed to look at them, touch them. Think about people you know who have died. Would they want you to be afraid?"

"No, I guess not." He joined her next to the stone, conscious the whole time of what he was probably standing on.

"This is Charles Putnam's stone," she said.

"Edmund's father?"

"Yeah. It's a little ostentatious, don't you think?"

"Just a bit." He grinned, looking up at the high tower.

"I think it's safe to say that Charles Putnam saw himself as the patriarch of the family. I suppose, though, that he was right. He has a lot of descendants. Now here's Edmund's stone."

It was large too, made of white stone that had been dirtied with age. It was a masculine stone, he decided. The squared-off top had been carved so that it looked as though pieces of cloth were draped over it. It was so perfectly done, you could almost imagine the way the cloth would feel, soft and rich, like velvet, and there were little tassels at the corners that seemed to move in the slight breeze. The words, carved in plain, straightforward letters, read "Edmund Danforth Putnam. December 4, 1863–June 23, 1888. All Is Bright."

"What's the cloth for?" He tentatively put a hand out to touch it. The stone was cold and rough.

"It's supposed to be a funeral shroud. But see what I mean about the dates? It's December here, not March."

He leaned down and looked carefully at the letters, trying to determine if it had been tampered with. But the date of Edmund Putnam's birth was in the same plain type as his name and the date of his death. All of the carving had worn away at about the same rate, he decided. It was becoming harder to read and he wondered suddenly if there were ever stones that were so worn away you couldn't read them at all.

"It is strange," Quinn said. He didn't want to let Sweeney know how excited he was. He got the same feeling he got when he got a new lead in a case, a sense that someone had opened a door for him. But he wanted to think about it for a minute.

"It's different, this cemetery," he said. "I mean, it doesn't seem like other ones I've been to."

"Well, Mount Auburn came out of a change in the way Americans saw death and by extension, burial and mourning," Sweeney said. "As America moved away from the skull and crossbones sense of death of the Puritans, it began—especially in Boston, which was kind of ahead of its time—to see death as a more natural process, something not to be feared but accepted. And it began to think of burial grounds as natural places for spiritual refreshment and melancholy contemplation, rather than festering yards of corpses buried four or five deep because of space constraints. Before Mount Auburn, everyone who died in Boston was interred in one of a few church cemeteries in the city. The churchyards had become completely overcrowded as the city's population grew in the early 1800s and by the 1820s, the city was embroiled in controversy over the sanitary implications of continuing to bury bodies in the city."

She remembered reading an account of the controversy in a history of the cemetery. On the one side were the religious leaders who felt it was imperative for their parishioners to find their final resting place next to the church. On the other side had been city leaders who saw continued city burial as a public health disaster in the making.

Inspired by the growing Unitarian and Universalist movements, a group of prominent Bostonians allied with the Boston Horticultural Society had banded together to create Mount Auburn, a green oasis of trees and flowers, shaded groves, and pastoral ponds.

"It does feel peaceful," he said. "I see what you mean."

He wandered back over to Charles Putnam's stone and read the epitaph again.

" 'Amid the mansions of the dead.' What does that mean?"

"Oh, most people know the line from a poem by Robert Blair," she said. "In fact, there are references to the 'mansions of the dead' as far back as Sophocles. But it became kind of a popular way to describe cemeteries. There are a couple of Protestant hymns that use the term. It's in Mark Twain even. I think he uses it describing Père Lachaise in Paris." Quinn had no idea what she was talking about. "Blair made it well-known though."

When she spoke again it was in a strangely formal voice, deeper than her own. "See yonder hallow'd fane, the pious work/Of names once fam'd, now dubious or forgot,/'And buried 'midst the wreck of things which were;/There lie interr'd the more illustrious dead./The wind is up—hark! how it howls!—Methinks/'Till now, I never heard a sound so deary:/Doors creak, and windows clap, and night's foul bird,/Rook'd in the spire, screams loud; the gloomy aisles/Black plaster'd, and hung round with shreds of 'scutcheons,/And tatter'd coats of arms, send back the sound,/Laden with heavier airs. . . ." She paused, then said dramatically, " 'From the low vaults,/The mansions of the dead.' "

"Wow." He felt a little chill go up his spine, and looked around at the gravestones, spotting the spire of some kind of church up above them on the hill. The words acted on him like a drug, chilling his blood. " 'From the low vaults, the mansions of the dead,' " he repeated, in his own mind hearing the dark rhythms of the verse.

He was disappointed when she said, "It's all so melodramatic. But Blair and all the Graveyard Poets were in the business of scaring people. These were pretty much evangelical poems. They were trying to tell people how awful the grave was so that they could . . ." She stopped talking and a look of confusion came over her face. "It's funny actually."

"What?"

"Nothing, just that Brad and I were talking about Robert Blair. Almost two months before he died." She was silent for a moment. "Anyway, places like Mount Auburn were built because people were tired of that scary, Puritan view of death as something horrible and macabre. The idea was to create a peaceful place where mourners could appreciate nature and feel sort of melancholy and think about the person who had died. As you can see, death was thought of as kind of a pastoral, natural experience; you would hear the birds singing, smell the flowers. In creating the landscape here, they were recreating the idealized notion of death."

Quinn took a deep breath. He felt a kind of understanding of what she was saying hit him as though he'd been punched. He couldn't think how to articulate it, though, so he quoted from the poem he'd read so many times, surprising himself with his perfect memory of it.

" 'Darkling I listen; and, for many a time:/I have been half in love with easeful Death,/Call'd him soft names in many a mused rhyme,/To take into the air my quiet breath;/Now more than ever seems it rich to die,/To cease upon the midnight with no pain,/While thou art pouring forth thy soul abroad/In such an ecstasy!/Still wouldst thou sing, and I have ears in vain—/To thy high requiem become a sod.' "

" 'Ode to a Nightingale?' " To her credit, she didn't look at all surprised. Quinn decided that she must be used to people who randomly quoted poetry as they stood in cemeteries.

"Yeah."

"I always wondered what a darkling is. Who is it who writes about the darkling thrush, Hardy, right?"

"I think it just means that he's listening to the nightingale's song in the dark." He wasn't sure, but it was what he'd always thought.

Sweeney looked off into the distance. "Yeah, I think you're

right. I never liked 'Ode to a Nightingale.' I find the idea of easeful death disturbing. It shouldn't be easy. It should be a fight, you should go out kicking and screaming. 'Do not go gentle into that good night' and all that."

"I think you can only think that if life is something good to you. There are people who have such a tough time, who are in so much pain or whatever, that death can only be a relief."

"Well, that's how old Keats felt," Sweeney said. "Wasn't his brother dying of consumption or something when he wrote it?"

"I don't know," Quinn said honestly. "I don't know a lot about it. I just know I like it."

Sweeney studied him for a moment and he found that her strange green eyes were more gray in the spring light.

"Were you an English major in college?"

"Nah," he said. "Criminal justice. I should have done English. Always liked poetry and stuff. I was thinking I might take a class sometime. Night school."

"You should. They have continuing ed. at the university."

A breeze came up and he was cold all of a sudden. "Yeah, I don't know. Might be hard with the baby and all that."

Sweeney didn't say anything. She just watched him with those strange green eyes.

"Well, I'm going to go ahead and tell my friend to do the test," he said, to break the silence, and they began walking back toward their cars. "Now he just has to find out if it's been too long. But he should let us know in a few days, a week at the most."

"Okay," she said. "Thanks."

"You can wait until then, right? You're not going to go off and do anything crazy."

"What do you mean? What would I do?"

Quinn laughed. "I shudder to think."

She hesitated a moment and then said, "Well, I might do some looking into the will and the birth records. Is that okay?"

"Yeah. Just let me know what you find."

"Okay." She looked up at him and said, "Can I ask you something?"

"Sure."

"What do you think happened to Brad?"

"If I knew that," he said, smiling, "I wouldn't be standing here quoting poetry to you."

THIRTY-TWO

Sweeney was uncertain about what to do next.

Quinn had told her not to go off and do any hunting around until he got back to her about the jewelry. But he had said she could look into the will and, by extension, she figured it was okay to keep looking into the jewelry. Because it wasn't just about Brad, was it? If Edmund Putnam had been illegitimate and the date on the gravestone had been changed while the mourning brooch had the right one, well, that was significant, not just for history and for the Putnam family, but for Sweeney's own work on mourning jewelry.

Either way, it made sense for her to keep looking into it. She wouldn't know about the DNA until Quinn called, but she could go ahead with trying to find out how the subterfuge might have been accomplished. She tried to put herself back into the mind-set of the 1860s, to imagine what Belinda might have done.

This early Mrs. Putnam had found herself a young widow, and sometime in those few months after her husband's death, she had met someone else. Sweeney took out the postcard of Belinda's portrait that she'd purchased in the museum gift shop. Belinda stared out coolly, her eyes serious and her pretty face set in a determined expression.

She tried to put herself in Belinda's shoes. What would she do if she found herself with a husband in the ground three months and a baby on the way?

Sweeney remembered reading that, in colonial times, some huge percentage of babies were born less than nine months after their parents were married. She even remembered that there was implicit approval of a young couple sleeping together before they were married and waiting to see if the woman got pregnant in order to make sure she was fertile. People referred to the babies as premature and let the neighbors talk.

But this was the other way around. You couldn't pretend that a baby had gestated for eleven or twelve months. So what would you do?

The only option would be to say that the baby had been born earlier than it had. But you couldn't do that, could you? People would see that you were still pregnant and they would wonder where the baby was.

Unless . . . unless you went away somewhere and sent a letter home saying that the baby had been born. You would have to hope that the baby was big for its age and that when you eventually returned home, no one would question your story.

She found a few references to Belinda's life in Henrietta's book and a couple of other histories of the family, but they were all in relation to her charitable activities and were from a much later period of her life.

"Belinda Putnam, the widow of one of Boston's most prominent businessmen Charles D. Putnam, established a charitable home for unwed mothers called the Hatty Hope Home, which caused great consternation among the city's ruling elite," Henrietta's account went. "But Belinda Putnam was a determined woman who felt strongly about her causes and wanted to make sure that unfortunate girls who had been cast out from their families had a place they could go. She taught them various arts and crafts and when their babies were born she arranged for their adoption among the wealthy classes of the city."

Sweeney read the passage over again. It seemed to support her theory about Belinda Putnam. If she had had her own experience of being an unwed mother, however well it had turned out for her, perhaps that's what had given her the feeling for the poor young girls in such dire straits.

In the second book, there was a reference to the fact that Charles Putnam had been on the board of directors of Mount Auburn Cemetery. That was interesting. Sweeney hadn't known that the Putnams had had a formal connection with Mount Auburn. But of course, most of the city's prominent families had been associated with it in some way or another.

Charles Putnam had written a letter in 1863, a few months before his death, expressing concern about the rapid expansion of the cemetery. The book told her that the cemetery was full of laborers that year, many of them recently arrived from Ireland or other countries and that those who were not off fighting the war were put to work building new roads and improving the cemetery grounds. Putnam's letter was reprinted: "Sirs. I cannot see the benefit to any of us in frenetic expansion. Soon the cemetery will become a tourist attraction and will be full of people looking upon the graves as curiosities. There will be no rest for the poor dead entombed within the gates, no rest for the poor bereaved visiting those graves."

Charles Putnam had lost his fight. The cemetery had gone on to expand greatly in the years after his death.

Sweeney sat back in her chair, her eyes tired from reading. She hadn't learned much. So what if Belinda Putnam had had an affair after her husband's death? Who was she to go revealing it to the world? She was kidding herself that she was interested in the jewelry. When it came right down to it, it was the connection to Brad's death that really intrigued her. But why would someone kill Brad to prevent news of the illegitimate birth getting out? It had to be that there was some kind of incentive to do so. It had to be that if Edmund was illegitimate, then his inheritance had been gotten by fraudulent means.

It depended on the will, she realized. If Charles Putnam had left his property to Belinda, assuming that he didn't have an heir, then it didn't matter who Edmund Putnam's father was because Belinda had acquired the fortune honestly and had passed it down to her son honestly. But if the will was in favor of someone else, and had been voided because Charles Putnam ended up having a legitimate heir, then the legitimacy was the most important point.

What would Belinda have done? She would have had to go
to the lawyer and claim that she didn't realize she was pregnant when her husband made his will.

There was only one thing to do. She had to see the will.

Sweeney had always loved the Massachusetts Archives. The
repository of public records was located on the UMass Boston
campus on Columbia Point, and as she got out of her car, she
caught a whiff of the thick, salty air rolling in off Dorchester
Bay. A jet flew low, heading for Logan.

The next Monday morning, she signed in at the front desk
and then went through to the big library room where the microfilm records were kept. The probate documents were indexed
in black leather books, stamped with gold letters reading "Index to Probate Records," and Sweeney found the Suffok
County records, flipping through the stiff pages laced with
black print until she found the entry for Charles D. Putnam.

She had done probate record research before and she remembered that you had to get a reference number and then
check the microfilm indexes to find out where the will in question was. She fitted the roll of film into one of the clunky old
manual viewers, found Charles Putnam, and copied down the
volume and page numbers for his will. There were a number
of other probate documents indexed too and she wrote down
those numbers in case she needed them later.

The will, once she'd found it toward the middle of another
roll of microfilm, had been copied over by some anonymous
clerk in a restrainedly embellished hand.

Sweeney got out a notebook and the pencil they'd given
her at the front desk, excited about reading Charles Putnam's
words for herself.

"In the name of God Amen, I Charles D. Putnam of the
City of Boston, being in good bodily health and of sound and
disposing mind and memory, but calling to mind the uncer-
tainty of human life and being desirous of settling my worldly
affairs while I have the strength and capacity to do so, make
and publish this my last will and testament."

Winding the film back to the first page of his entry, she

checked to see when he had written it: 1861. Two years before his death.

"I commend my mortal being to Him who gave it," the will continued. "And my body to the earth and as to the property, real, personal and mixed, I devise, bequeath, and dispose thereof. To my beloved wife Belinda, I give and bequeath all my household furniture, and all provisions I may have at the time of my decease for her use during her natural life. I further give and devise to my said wife for during her natural life, tenancy of the lot of land and buildings on Beacon Hill in the City of Boston, and after her decease, to be distributed to my brother, James F. Putnam."

She read on and found what she was looking for. "Should a natural male heir be born to my wife and myself, said property, along with all my other worldly goods, will be distributed to said male heir upon my death."

It was pretty straightforward. Charles Putnam had made the will not knowing he would ever have a child, but allowing that if he did produce a male heir, the money and real estate would go to the child rather than to his brother. To the child, not Belinda.

It was a bit mean to his wife, slightly unusual, but not out of the realm of possibility. People back then had strange ideas about women and Charles Putnam must have believed his wife incapable of managing her own money.

But the child had changed everything. The child had virtually secured the family fortune for Belinda Putnam. A young woman still when she'd had her son, Belinda Putnam had gone on to live for a number of years—and do a lot of good with the money her husband had left behind.

It had been a gamble. If the child had been a girl, the subterfuge would all have been for nothing. But necessary just the same, Sweeney reminded herself, if Belinda Putnam was trying to avoid a Scarlet Letter scenario.

She took some notes on the will, rewound the microfilm, and then thought of something. How had Belinda falsified the birth record for her son? She would have had to file a birth record. Had she filed a false one?

The answer was easy to find in the green cloth-covered indexes of birth records. Belinda hadn't falsified the record. There wasn't any record of Edmund Putnam having been born in Boston, in 1863 or anytime else.

Bill Landseer had been Sweeney's father's lawyer and, after his death, the executor of his estate. He had been something of a bohemian in his twenties and he and Sweeney's father had shared an apartment—and a girlfriend, Bill always said—for three crazy years when Paul St. George was establishing himself as an artist and Bill was fending off his family's suggestions that he become a lawyer.

Sweeney's father had found eventual success and Bill had eventually given in. But he had liked to remind himself of his misspent youth by staying in touch with Sweeney's family. After Sweeney's father's suicide, Bill had been the one who had made sure there was money for Sweeney to go to college, who had made sure that some of the paintings went to places that Paul would have approved of.

Since he'd been wanting to talk to her anyway, she was hoping he could tell her something about Charles Putnam's will in return.

After hugging Bill and catching him up on her job, Sweeney sat down in the comfortable leather chair opposite his desk, feeling the sense of calm and security that all of his clients felt when they sat there in that chair. He looked the way he always looked, an aging hippie dressed up for lawyering, his gray hair in a little ponytail, an exuberantly patterned yellow tie under the conservative blue blazer.

"I have a hypothetical question to ask you. Say that there was a family that had, over the years, through inheritance, acquired a lot of very valuable real estate, lots of other assets too."

"Yes?"

"And say that a member of that family found out that one of the antecedents was illegitimate. In other words, all of the inheritances from that point on were based on a falsehood. What would happen, legally, in a case like that?"

"How long ago would the illegitimate heir have been born?"

"The 1860s."

"God, that's . . . Well, the inheritance itself would likely be deemed void by a court, but it would depend on who's bringing the case. Would it be alternate heirs, the father's legitimate children?"

"No, it's kind of complicated. From what I can tell, this heir is the only child."

"So what leads you to think he's illegitimate?"

"It's a Scarlet Letter kind of thing. I've found evidence that the son was born more than nine months after the death of the father. But I think it was, you know, hushed up or whatever was done in those days. She must have gone away to give birth and then said that the baby had been born earlier than it had. I think it was a matter of a few months, so it wouldn't have been too hard."

"Can I ask . . . ? This isn't your family you're talking about, is it?"

"No, no. I don't know if I should say."

"Okay, well. This would all depend upon a lot of things. If the father never knew that his son was illegitimate, never knew in fact that he was going to have a son, then it would have been typical in those days for him to leave his wife something to live on and to leave the rest of his estate to the closest living male relative. So let's assume that that was the case. Presumably, then, when the wife discovered she was pregnant, she would have said she was farther along than she really was. When a son was born, the will would have been voided and the son would have inherited everything. Have you seen the will?"

"Yeah. That's pretty much what it says. What would happen if someone found out about this now? Could everything be taken away from this family?"

"I highly doubt it. For one thing, there's no way to prove that the son was illegitimate. There wasn't DNA testing back then. Unless there was some kind of document that existed that proved absolutely that the son was illegitimate, say a letter from another man acknowledging that he was the father or a signed testimony from the mother."

Or a piece of mourning jewelry, Sweeney thought.

"But this is all so long ago now that I have trouble believing any court would go back and try to change it. There would have to be another family member bringing the case, a descendant of the person who would have inherited instead of this person. I assume that's not the case?"

"Not that I know of. Although there must be cousins, I suppose."

"And there's the question of what the remedy would be. I mean, do you go back and give the inheritance to the rightful heir in real dollars, or do you account for what's been done with the inheritance over the years? It would be such a mess that I have trouble thinking anyone would even touch it. But you never know. It's an interesting case. Can't you tell me any more about it? How did you get involved anyway?"

"Oh, it's a cemetery thing. I found a discrepancy on a gravestone and I'm trying to figure out whether I should say something to the family about it. I'm just wondering if it would even change anything."

"If I were you, I'd leave it alone," Bill said. "It was so long ago. It doesn't seem like there's much good in bringing something like that out. Now, if my client was a descendant of the wronged family member, I might feel differently. In that case, I would go back and start looking into the family, see if there were any documents that proved the child had been illegitimate. But I don't think I'd start spending the inheritance."

"Okay," she said. "Thanks."

"Now my turn: I've been wanting to talk to you. Have you thought anymore about what you're going to do about your father's work?"

Sweeney looked up at the brown and orange desertscape that her father had given Bill. It was a horizontal oil, the brown desert sweeping out toward a little gas station, the red, white, and blue Texaco station.

"There are something like a hundred paintings in storage,

Sweeney. With the way the market's going right now, we could get a fortune for them. . . ."

"I'm not ready to sell them, Bill."

"Then put them on your wall. Loan them to a museum. You're an art historian, for God's sake. Don't you see that it isn't fair to keep them locked up?"

"I know, I know. I just . . . There's too much going on right now for me to think about it. I have to do it properly."

"How are you doing for money? Have they given you anything more secure at the university?"

"No," Sweeney said grumpily. "They only gave me two classes for the fall semester. There's a tenure track job open, but I don't think I'm even in the running."

"You working on a new book?"

"Yeah. I think I've got the premise. I'm going back to colonial stones, looking at the early history of the country and a couple of very important carvers."

"Wouldn't you like to be able to work on it and not have to worry about money?" When she didn't say anything, he raised his eyebrows at her. "Sweeney . . . ?"

"I'll start thinking about what I want to do and I'll call you. Okay?"

He hugged her. "Okay. Stay in touch."

THIRTY-THREE

By the time Sweeney got to the Memorial Hall theater that
night, it was about three-quarters full. The stage was decorated with bouquets of red carnations, and a huge red, white,
and blue banner swagged across the front of the stage, read
YOUNG DEMOCRATS AND YOUNG REPUBLICANS WELCOME
STATE SENATOR CAMILLE PUTNAM AND CONGRESSMAN GERRY
DIFLORIA. Since it was the first time the two candidates had
debated, television cameras were everywhere.

Sweeney had arrived late on purpose, hoping to slip into a
seat in the back and therefore avoid Jack Putnam. He had
called her a couple of times since the night she'd been at his
house, never referring to Quinn or to the lie, but saying that he
wanted to talk to her. She hadn't called him back.

But as she scanned the crowd, she realized she needn't
have worried. Jack wasn't there. She spotted Drew standing
up near the stage talking to a group of people and Andrew and
Kitty Putnam sitting in the front row. A young guy in a tweed
jacket came up and said something to Drew, motioning for
him to step off to the side. They talked privately for a few
minutes, the guy writing down whatever Drew said in a notebook. Sweeney watched them. There was something familiar
about the guy, but she couldn't figure out where she knew him
from. Finally, Drew shook his hand and took a seat.

As it got closer to seven, the activity in the hall increased
until finally, a young woman wearing a bright red miniskirt
and blazer stepped up to the podium and adjusted the microphone. The room quieted as the student began to speak.

"Hi, everyone. It's great to see such a big crowd here tonight. We feel very lucky to have State Senator Camille Putnam and Congressman Gerry DiFloria with us here tonight. We want to extend our deepest sympathies to Senator Putnam and her family at this very difficult time.

"Now, let me introduce the candidates. Camille Putnam is a state senator from Charlestown. She attended Choate Rosemary Hall and got her bachelor's and law degrees from our own university. She was elected to the Massachusetts assembly at twenty-five. After two terms, she was elected to the state Senate, where her legislative work has focused on the rights of women and children and health care issues. She is now a Democratic candidate for Congress from the Eighth Congressional District. I present Senator Camille Putnam." There was a round of applause as Camille came out. In a blue power suit that was a bit too big for her, she looked more petite than Sweeney remembered. But she was smiling broadly and had put on lipstick for the occasion. She waved to the crowd and took her place behind one of the podiums on the stage.

"And now I'll introduce Congressman Gerry DiFloria, a Republican from Somerville. Congressman DiFloria attended St. John's University. He attended law school here at the university and served as chief of staff to former Senator Chris Bartholomew for twenty years. He started his own law firm before running for Congress two years ago. Let's welcome Congressman Gerry DiFloria." There was another round of applause and a good-looking man of sixty-five or so came out onto the stage. He wasn't that tall—five-nine or so—but he carried himself like a tall man and his suit made the most of his height. He smiled and waved at the crowd, then stood next to Camille at the second podium, resting his hands casually in front of him. Camille was nervously picking at her skirt.

The young woman waited until the applause subsided. "We're going to use a fairly straightforward format here. I'm going to give each candidate three minutes to introduce himself or herself. Then I will ask five questions and give each candidate five minutes to answer. We'll finish up by giving each candidate three minutes to wrap up. Then we'll take some questions from the audience. By coin toss before the debate, it was determined that Senator Putnam will go first. Senator Putnam?"

Camille leaned toward the microphone. "Hello. First of all I want to thank all of you for coming out tonight and getting involved. I wasn't much older than many of you here when I first ran for the state assembly. People said I was too young, that I hadn't had enough real life experience. But I knew that I cared about where our state and our country were going and I knew that I had something to contribute. You know, people said that my generation didn't care about politics, that we were only interested in watching TV and playing video games. They say the same thing about your generation. But I got involved because I didn't like being told that my generation wasn't interested. *I* was interested. I cared about having an economy that would pay a decent wage to hardworking people, about having a health care system that would take care of the most vulnerable members of our society. I cared about having a clean environment, I cared about having the right to make my own reproductive choices, I cared about giving people a reason to believe in government again."

She got an enthusiastic round of applause and went on.

"I hired some other young people to run my first campaign for the state assembly and we set out to do things differently. I wanted to run on a platform made up of the things I cared about. And you know what, there were people out there who didn't agree with me on a lot of the issues, but they respected that I spoke my mind.

"Politics isn't some obscure thing that happens in Washington. It's what affects your everyday life. It's whether your school has enough money for books and paper, it's whether families with two working parents can find quality child care. Politics is what keeps the environment clean and the world safe from war and social injustice. I jumped into this race because I feel that the people of Massachusetts need an energetic voice in Washington. A voice that isn't afraid to stand up for what's right, that isn't beholden to special interests. A voice that respects you and your problems and concerns, not just those who have enough money to give to your campaign. Thank you!" There was wild applause and Sweeney found herself clapping right along.

Gerry DiFloria waited for the applause to stop and then leaned forward, gripping the podium. "First of all, I would like to start out by offering my deepest sympathies to Senator Putnam on the untimely death of her beloved brother. My wife Cheryl and I are thinking about the Putnam family at this sad time. I don't know if Senator Putnam knows this, but I knew her grandfather—well, I knew both of her grandfathers, but I worked with Senator John Putnam—when I was a Senate staffer. He was a good man." It had been a pretty sly thing to slip in there, Sweeney decided. The comment reminded the audience both that DiFloria had been helping to make laws when Camille Putnam was in diapers, and that Camille Putnam's grandfather had been a Republican and a friend of Gerry DiFloria's.

"I believe in your generation too. I believe that your generation wants opportunity and freedom. I believe you want a chance to work hard and make something of yourself, a chance to see your dreams and hopes become a reality. And I believe that I have a proven record of helping the people of Massachusetts to realize their hopes and dreams. Whether it's my small businessperson's grants bill or my support for the 'Get America Started' tax cut, I have fought for you and your family and I will continue to fight for you and your family. Thank you."

The first question was about tax policy and Sweeney, not knowing anything about the subject, tuned out and looked around her at the crowd. There were a fair number of students, but a good percentage of older people as well. A group of young women sitting on one side of the theater were wearing T-shirts that said, "A Woman's Place Is in the House."

The candidates answered four more questions and then finished up. In her closing statement, Camille Putnam said, "I appreciated Congressman DiFloria's acknowledgment of what a hard time this is for our family. As many of you know, my younger brother, who was one of your classmates, passed away recently. I think about him all the time as I'm out there talking to people his age, talking to them about their hopes and dreams and about the world they hope to inherit. So, what I want to say to you is get out there! I don't care if you vote for me or my opponent, I just hope that you'll find some issues that you care about and you'll get out there and change the world. Thank you."

The audience, and Sweeney too, rose to its feet, clapping and cheering. Camille waved and acknowledged the applause, then came down off the stage, running a hand through her hair as though it had driven her crazy to have it hairsprayed into place for an hour and a half.

Sweeney stood at the back of the hall and watched Drew come forward to hug Camille as a group of students crowded around her. The guy in the tweed jacket who had been talking to Drew earlier was interviewing a couple of young women who were waiting in line to talk to Camille, and as she watched him nodding earnestly and writing on his notepad, Sweeney was again struck that she knew him from somewhere.

She watched as he shook hands with the women and then started up the aisle, flipping back and forth in his notebook. Who was he? It was bothering her.

Out in the hallway, he paused for a moment as though he were trying to decide what to do. Sweeney stopped a couple of yards from him and stood against one wall, out of the way of the groups of people milling around in the lobby, trying to watch him without bringing attention to herself. He was about her height, with graying dirty blond hair, a close-cropped beard, and friendly brown eyes behind John Lennon glasses. He looked like a stereotypical English professor. He even had the dark circles under his eyes.

It was when he looked up to check the clock on the wall that Sweeney realized where she knew him from. He had been in Brad's apartment the day she and Toby had hidden in the closet.

Right then he looked up at her and flashed her a smile. "Hi, can I talk to you for a minute? My name's Bill McCann. I'm a reporter for the *Globe* and I'm covering the campaign here. Can I ask you what you thought of Ms. Putnam's speech here tonight?" He raised his eyebrows speculatively, his pen poised over his little reporter's notebook.

"Oh," Sweeney said. "I'm not . . . I mean, I'd really rather not."

"Just tell me, do you think you're likely to vote for her? Based on what you heard here tonight?"

"I really would rather not comment." She zipped up her jacket and found her car keys. "Sorry."

"That's all right," he said. "Have a good night." He smiled and turned away, looking for another likely source.

Sweeney walked out into the evening, her heart thudding in her chest. One thing made sense to her all of a sudden. Quinn had said that the notebook they found in the apartment was a reporter's notebook. And Bill McCann had been looking for something the day she and Toby had been there. The notebook that Quinn said had been found under Brad's bed must have belonged to McCann.

She remembered the conversation with Quinn. The notebook had only had a few words in it, something about the Putnam family's real estate holdings in the Back Bay. Had McCann been looking into a story on the Putnam family and gone to interview Brad? That would make sense. So maybe he had somehow left the notebook behind. Then Brad had died, and he had feared that someone would find it, so at the first chance he had gone back to get it.

It was after ten by the time she got home. She did a quick check of her mail and pressed the play button on her answering machine.

"Hi, Sweeney," came an unfamiliar voice, hesitant and soft. "This is Melissa Putnam. I just wanted to ask you something. No big deal. Don't even worry about calling back. I'll try you tomorrow."

Sweeney looked up at the clock. It was probably too late to call, and besides, Melissa had said that she'd call tomorrow.

But it wasn't too late to call Paul Blum. She dialed his extension and he picked up on the first ring. "It's Sweeney. Are you on deadline?" she asked him.

"Nope. Just filed. I have a few minutes before anyone gets back to me."

"Listen, Paul, do you know a guy named Bill McCann?"

"Yeah, he sits a couple of desks away from me. Nice guy. Why?"

"What can you tell me about him? I met him tonight and I was just wondering . . . well, if he's single." It was the best excuse she could come up with and she knew it was one that Paul, an inveterate matchmaker, would jump on.

"Oh," Paul said, sounding suddenly interested. "Yeah, I think so. I've never heard about him dating anyone. He's a good guy. One of the stars around here."

"What does he write about?"

"Well, he was on the statehouse beat, but they just switched him over to covering the Putnam-DiFloria congressional race. He's written some great stories."

"Did he cover the Putnam family before he started the congressional beat?"

"Funny you should ask. He'd done this big Sunday feature a couple of months ago. The story didn't reach any conclusions, if I remember, it was looking into the family's real estate holdings and whether they'd benefited from the Back Bay Tunnel project. Anyway, when Brad Putnam died and I was writing those stories about the family's long string of misfortunes, Bill helped me out with a lot of the history."

"Thanks. Hey, could you e-mail me that story? I'd go into the archives, but it costs money."

"Cheapskate. Hang on." She could hear him tapping away at his computer keys. "Okay, you should have it."

"Thanks."

"So do you want me to give him your phone number or something?"

"No, that's all right. I have his and I'll figure out a way to meet him that won't seem obvious. Don't say anything, okay?"

"Okay. But I get to give the speech at your wedding."

Sweeney checked her e-mail and opened the message from Paul. As far as she could figure it out after three readings, McCann's concerns centered around the Putnam family's ownership of much of the land that the Back Bay Tunnel was being built on. In the late seventies, when the project was being proposed, Senator John Putnam had been the chair of the senate. There had been some question about whether it was ethical for Putnam to vote on the project since his family owned some of the land the new road would go on. But he had quelled the concerns by effectively giving the federal government the parcels that were needed. McCann's article centered on whether the Putnams had benefited from their ownership of the land around the parcels. The family still owned ten residential properties in the Back Bay: Jack's building on Comm. Ave., and nine other nearby buildings.

McCann had found the tax records and listed the real estate values for the buildings—3 million for Jack's building and amounts between 2.5 million and 7.2 million for the other buildings. Sweeney did the math. They were sitting on a small fortune in real estate. And they owed it all to Charles Putnam, who had had the good foresight to buy the land in the first place.

McCann quoted a couple of real estate agents, half of whom said that the buildings would increase in value because of the Back Bay Tunnel project; the other half said that the project might actually deflate the value of the buildings because of the long construction coinciding with the spike in the market. There weren't any conclusions and what Sweeney took away from it was that the family hadn't either benefited or lost out from the tunnel project.

But again, she was struck by what a wise investment Charles Putnam had made all those years ago. So how did it all fit together? If Brad had realized—because of his research into the jewelry—that his family was not the rightful owner of the Back Bay property from which it had made a fortune, he was a danger if he was talking to a reporter like McCann. Had someone killed him to stop him from telling what he knew?

But what did he know? Until she knew if her suspicions about the jewelry—and what it signified—were correct, she had nothing to go on.

Or not nothing, she realized, because she had McCann. McCann coming back to Brad's apartment to look for the notebook. She didn't understand why he hadn't told the police about being there. Presumably he had gone to Brad's to interview him at some point over the past few months. Why wouldn't he just have come forward? It didn't make a lot of sense, but she had the feeling that the reporter might be able to lead the way.

THIRTY-FOUR

Sweeney was working in her office when she heard the motorized hum of Fiona Mathewson's wheelchair and looked up to find her colleague smiling at her from the doorway.

"Hi, Sweeney. What are you up to?"

"Getting ready for seminar." Sweeney was hurriedly trying to organize her slides.

"Which one?"

"Mourning Objects."

"Oh, that's the one that Brad was in, right?"

"Yeah."

"They're a pretty tight group, huh? Had you had them before?"

"Yeah. Then they all took the seminar together." Sweeney looked up. "Wait, Fiona. Why do you say that?"

"I don't know. I guess I've just seen them around together a lot. They seem pretty tight. Seem to have a good time together."

"Yeah. I think they are. See you later, Fiona." Fiona was gone when Sweeney looked up again. They *were* pretty tight. And they spent a lot of time together. Why not the Saturday night that Brad had been killed? She remembered Raj's face when she'd asked him about it that day in his apartment. She wasn't entirely convinced he hadn't been lying to her. She'd just have to ask again.

When Sweeney came into the seminar room a few minutes later, the first thing she said was, "Where are Becca and Jaybee?"

Nobody said anything. "Well, we'll just have to go on

without them." She stood up at the podium, but didn't take out her notes or set up the slide projector. They all looked around at one another, nervous now.

"I want to know something. Were you guys all together the night that Brad died?"

There was a long silence.

"It's going to come out somehow," Sweeney said. "And it would look a lot better to everyone if you were the ones to come out with it."

"Okay, okay," Jennifer finally said. "We were."

It was beginning to make sense to Sweeney. "Had you been out in a cemetery that night?"

Ashley started to say something, then stopped, and finally Raj broke in. "I'll . . . I should have told you when we talked before. I'm sorry I lied. I knew that we'd all be suspected if you knew. We didn't have anything to do with it. It was just . . ."

"Why didn't you tell the police? There's nothing illegal about . . ." She looked around at them. "But there was something illegal about it. What were you doing?" Raj hesitated for a few moments before she went on. "Look, I'm only twenty-eight. It was pretty much last week that I was doing whatever it is you're afraid to tell me about."

"That's what I told them," Raj said. "I said we should invite you to come too."

"Thanks. So what happened?"

He glanced at the others. "All right. As I told you, we'd been going to cemeteries and just kind of hanging out. We'd gotten drunk a few times and it was kind of cool, running around in the cemetery, kind of spooky. But Ashley said that we should eat mushrooms and go there. She said it would be amazing, that we might see ghosts and it would be like breaking down the walls between the living and the dead."

"It was like that," Ashley said. "Even if you want to deny the experience."

Raj rolled his eyes. "I wasn't going to do it with them. It sounded like kind of a bad idea to me, but then . . ." He stopped. "Anyway. We decided to spend the whole day—that day—in the cemetery."

"Which one?"

"Oh, Mount Auburn. We didn't want to have to drive. So Ashley got the mushrooms and I gave some to everyone beforehand, because they take a while to kick in. And we went out to the cemetery and for a while it was really cool. We just walked around looking at all the stones, and I felt just really happy, you know. I remember that everything looked sunnier and brighter and I had this feeling that all the dead people in the cemetery loved me, that they were all kind of embracing me. It sounds stupid to say it, but . . . there you go. That's how it was. We had brought lunch—Brie and grapes and chicken and all this good stuff, and I remember that I didn't think I'd ever tasted anything that good. Even Brad, who always seemed kind of depressed, seemed kind of happy that day." He stopped and his face appeared to cloud over.

"But . . ." Sweeney prompted him. Jennifer and Ashley were staring down at the table.

Raj grinned at her wryly. "But. But then there were all these other people in the cemetery. Tourists or something, and it started to get cold, and it was late afternoon and it was getting dark, or seemed like it was. It seems now like it must have happened slowly, but I think it was pretty fast actually. The whole mood changed, and all of a sudden I felt so sad. Just . . . monumentally sad." As he described it to her, Sweeney almost sensed that he had enjoyed feeling that way, and she knew that someday she would pick up a book by Rajiv Patel and she would find a passage that described that feeling of monumental sadness.

"It was awful," he said. "We all started getting really freaked out. Ashley was convinced that all these people in the cemetery, all the tourists, were actually dead people, and they were coming after her. She was screaming and I have to say—obviously I was kind of suggestible, because I was so freaked out—I started believing her. I didn't know what to do. Anyway, I decided to take her home. We were getting worried that someone might call the police. I don't know. We just got really paranoid."

"So you left?" Sweeney asked him.

He nodded. "I took Ashley home, then I went home and went to sleep."

"I went right to sleep when I got home," Ashley said. "I swear."

Sweeney turned to Jennifer. "What did the rest of you guys do?"

"We took Brad back to the apartment," Jennifer said. "He had gotten really angry and he was acting weird and started drinking tequila. We were trying to get him to stop, but he just kept getting more and more angry and finally we just left and I went home and Jaybee and Becca went to Becca's."

"You left him alone?"

"Well, it didn't seem like the mushrooms or being drunk were going to hurt him. You just have to sleep it off. And Brad wasn't a big drinker. We figured he'd just pass out and be fine in the morning."

"What was he so angry about?" Sweeney watched their faces.

"I think he was kind of freaked out from the mushrooms," Raj said finally. "He was really out of it. The whole night. He kept disappearing and he wasn't himself at all."

"What about when you got back to his house?" Sweeney asked Jennifer. "Could you tell what it was about?"

Jennifer thought for a moment. "I don't think he was mad exactly. Not at anyone. It was more like he was mad at himself. He just kept saying he was a coward and that he didn't have any balls. Stuff like that. That he was so afraid of everyone, afraid to do anything, afraid to say anything."

"Afraid of who?"

"He didn't say, but for some reason I had the idea it was someone in his family. He said something about how no one he knew talked about anything, how they were all so silent about the things that mattered. But I guess that could be anyone."

Sweeney studied them. "Okay," she said. "I may need to tell some of this to the police. But you won't get into trouble for any of it, so don't worry about that. Now, let's have class."

THIRTY-FIVE

❧

"Did Alison have any enemies that you know of?" Quinn was asking. "Anyone who had been bothering her lately, who might have been mad at her?"

"I don't think so," said the girl named Emma. "I mean, she and her stepmother didn't really get along. But her family lives in L.A."

He and Marino were interviewing Alison Cope's roommates, a pair of skinny blond girls who seemed to have come to resemble each other in the time they'd been living together. Emma and Angela had almost identical straight blond hair falling below their shoulder blades, and their arms—on full display in the tank tops they wore—were stick-thin, making them look emaciated to Quinn. He found himself bothered and oddly disturbed by the extremely low riding jeans they were both wearing—he could see the elastic bands of their underwear peeking out at their hips, underwear decorated with childish floral patterns.

They hadn't called ahead to tell Emma and Angela they were coming, and the girls hadn't wanted to let them in until they'd confirmed their identities with the officer on duty down at the station. Once they'd gotten a satisfactory answer, though, they'd been remarkably friendly, and Marino had taken them up on their offer of a glass of Diet Coke.

Quinn took a quick look at the bookshelf. Kant. Nietzsche. Kierkegaard. Schopenhauer. And on the next shelf, Jane Austen, Charlotte Brontë, and Emily Brontë. He didn't need those books to know they were smart girls. They'd figured out right away that Quinn and Marino were exploring the possibility that Alison's death hadn't been an accident. "You think someone killed her on purpose?" Emma had asked, and he had said that they weren't sure but that they had to look into all the possibilities.

He looked around at the walls. One end of the living room was decorated with a large flowery poster. "Monet at the Metropolitan Museum of Art" it read. The other wall was covered with band posters, Bruce Springsteen, Crosby, Stills, and Nash, the Grateful Dead. Quinn and Maura had the Dead poster at home in their basement.

"Did she have a boyfriend?" he asked Emma once Marino was settled on the couch with his Coke.

"No. She'd been dating this guy in the fall, but they broke up at Christmastime." Quinn nodded. They'd already looked into him.

"No one else? Even something casual?"

"Well . . ." Emma hesitated. "I don't know. I mean, she didn't say anything. But there were a couple of nights where she didn't come home and when we kidded her about it, she didn't seem to want to say where she'd been. The last time she got kind of mad at me."

She raised her eyebrows, smiled, and gave a little what-are-ya-gonna-do shrug.

"She didn't say anything to you either?" Marino asked Angela. Quinn could just about hear the sound of a good lead going nowhere. Whoosh.

"Un—unh." She shook her head. "I was up early writing a paper and she came in at seven-thirty or something and I asked where she'd been. She kind of smiled but then she just said that she'd stayed at Genevieve's place."

"Genevieve?"

"Oh, a friend of hers."

"Do you remember when this was?"

"Yeah. It was the night that Brad Putnam died. I remember because we all went to lunch and we were giving her a hard time about where she'd been and then someone told us."

"What's Genevieve's last name?" Quinn asked. He'd have to check with her, but he was already pretty sure that Alison had been lying. "Alison was friends with Brad Putnam, right?"

They looked at each other and Emma shook her head. "I don't think so. She may have met him at a party or something, but they definitely weren't friends."

"Are you sure? I've heard that she was at his memorial service. Why would she have gone if they weren't friends?"

"I don't know, but I remember talking to her about him once and asking if she knew him. She didn't."

"What about casually? Hanging out at parties, that kind of thing? I mean, you guys weren't with her every single second, were you?" Marino drained his glass and put it down on the coffee table.

"Maybe," Angela said doubtfully.

Quinn walked over to the bookcase. "Who are all these guys then? You studying German?"

Emma and Angela exchanged a quick look.

"They're philosophers," Emma said, smiling up at him. "They philosophize."

"Oh yeah? What's their philosophy then?"

"Depends on who you mean." Emma got up and joined him at the bookcase. She took the Kant down from the shelf and handed it to him. "Immanuel Kant. Kant believed that man wants to answer three questions for himself. What can I know? What may I hope? How should I live?"

Quinn look at the book, turning it over in his hands. He'd thought it was "Can't" but she pronounced it "Cahnt." "Oh yeah? And what's the answer? How *should* I live?"

Marino laughed.

"Morally," Emma said, looking up at him again. "Kant believed that it is always better to do what is moral than to do what makes you happy, or makes other people happy."

Embarrassed, he put the book back on the shelf. "And you're sure you don't have any idea about who the guy was? The guy she was dating?"

The girls looked at each other. "I always thought it was an older guy," Emma said finally.

"Why's that?"

"Because we were having this conversation about guys and she said something about it."

"She just came out and said that? Why would she say that?" Marino asked her.

Emma looked up at them. "Well, I'd been saying that I thought older guys were really sexy or something. And she started to say something . . . You know how people start to tell you something and you can almost see where they're going with it?" Quinn nodded. "Well, she had this look on her face, kind of a triumphant look, like she wanted to tell me that she knew that older guys were sexy or something, because she had one."

Emma blushed. "I don't know, it was kind of a feeling I got. But I don't know for sure."

"You believe all that stuff about doing the moral thing all the time, Quinny?" Marino was driving and turned to look at Quinn. "What do you think she was getting at with all that?"

"I think just what she said. You should do what's right, rather than what makes you happy. So you shouldn't have an affair or go out gambling just because you like sex or cards."

"Yeah, yeah. I see what you mean."

Marino was silent for a few minutes as he waited to turn on to Mass. Ave. "Old Leary didn't agree with that kind of thing. He was a guy who liked to make himself happy. Other people too. He was a good time, Leary."

Not for his wife, Quinn wanted to say, but didn't.

Leary had been Marino's partner for eighteen years before he'd been killed by his five foot two wife with a butcher knife, in self-defense after years of beatings, everyone said. Marino hardly ever talked about him, except to say things like "When me and Leary were working together, we would have picked up on that guy's lie the first day of the investigation" or "Leary would have liked that sandwich. He'd go miles for a good roast beef."

But now he glanced over at Quinn and said, "But he wasn't such an upstanding guy really, when it came right down to it. He wouldn't have liked what that German guy had to say. Wouldn't have liked him at all."

Quinn tried not to smile.

THIRTY-SIX

Camille Putnam was attending a fund-raiser at the home of Londa and Barry MacAdam in Cambridge that night. Sweeney had found this out by calling the "Putnam for Congress" office downtown and telling them she was a reporter for the *Hartford Courant*.

"My editor asked me to cover the thing tonight, but he didn't have any details."

"The fund-raiser? Hold on. I can get you the address." The woman put the phone down for a moment and Sweeney could hear phones ringing and people talking in the background. "Okay, I got it," she said, once she was back on the line, giving Sweeney an address off Fresh Pond Parkway.

"Great, thanks," Sweeney said, writing the address down. "Hey, by the way, do you know if the *Globe* is sending anyone?"

"Yeah, Bill McCann is covering it," the woman said. "He called to get directions too."

"Great." Sweeney tried to imagine how a cynical reporter type would sound. "Thanks a lot."

The MacAdams' house was a rambling Victorian on one of the side streets off Fresh Pond Parkway. It was painted a vibrant blue and had a porch swing and lots of potted plants. Through the big bay windows, she could see people moving across the windows, the whole house filled with warm light.

Parked across the street so she could keep an eye on the door, she looked up from her book every few seconds for Bill McCann.

Around nine-fifteen, he came out of the house and got into a little red Toyota pickup. Sweeney started the Rabbit and waited until he had turned off the MacAdams' street before speeding up and catching him at the intersection with Fresh Pond Parkway. They turned left, toward Mount Auburn Cemetery and Sweeney thought that was where they were headed until he turned left on Mount Auburn Street and headed down Mass. Ave. toward Central Square and over the bridge.

They were heading into the Back Bay.

He drove along at a good clip, and she had to focus all of her attention on the road so that she didn't lose him. The traffic was snarled because of a broken-down car and Sweeney almost lost McCann's pickup when he quickly changed lanes and then pulled in front of a delivery van and made a quick left onto Marlborough Street. It took her a few minutes to get over and by the time she was able to turn, she'd lost him.

She cursed loudly and slammed her fist on the steering wheel, but miraculously, when she reached the intersection of Marlborough and Dartmouth, the red pickup was disappearing down toward Comm. Ave.

She turned left and watch the pickup's brake lights come on, slowing so he wouldn't see her behind him. Then he turned onto Gloucester and quickly made a right into a public alley.

She drove past the entrance and found parking a little farther down Gloucester. It was Back Bay resident parking only, but she decided to risk it. She got out of the car and stood at the entrance to the alley, peeking around the brick corner of a building. McCann had parked in one of the parking spaces behind a tall residential building and he got out of the truck.

Like most of the public alleys behind Comm. Ave., this one had been fixed up to suit the upscale residences it backed. Most of the buildings had newly paved parking areas behind them and a few had tiny back gardens, surrounded by high fences. There were cars parked behind almost all of the buildings, but the one that McCann had parked behind—as well as the two other huge buildings next to it—didn't have any cars at all. Sweeney wasn't sure why, but the buildings seemed uninhabited to her. It was the windows, she realized, looking up at the rows of dark rectangles. There were lights on in the windows of the other buildings. They were a couple of houses down from Jack's building, and as she started counting, she realized that these were the buildings owned by the Putnams that McCann had mentioned in his story.

Sweeney watched him go to the back door of one of the buildings, get his wallet from his pocket, take a credit card out, and then fiddle with the lock. After about thirty seconds he opened the door and disappeared inside.

She approached the door and found that he had propped it open with a brick. Because of the light coming into the building from the street, and the almost-full moon, she could see pretty well and, her heart pounding, her mouth suddenly dry, she entered the building.

She was in a first-floor apartment, and she looked around at the empty living room and almost whistled. At one time, these had been pretty fancy pads. The ceilings soared high above her and the crown molding, hardwood floors, and stained glass windows were the original stuff.

She stood still and listened, not hearing any sign of movement in the building. Very quietly, she looked around the empty apartment and then found the door open to a hallway flanked by two staircases.

The hallway was typical upscale apartment house fare—a row of mailboxes and a little desk on one side, a stripey, formal-looking wallpaper on the walls. But everything looked worn and damaged, as though the place had been vandalized. Paper hung off the walls in strips and there were holes in the ceiling. Sweeney stood in the hallway for a minute. Where had McCann gone? She couldn't hear his footsteps upstairs.

She was about to climb the stairs when she felt a quick premonition of danger and then someone's arm around her chest.

She tried to scream, but there was a hand over mouth and all she could do was bite the soft flesh. She heard a man's voice swear and then she was able to get some leverage. Her assailant wasn't as tall as she was and she bucked sharply, loosening his hold on her, then turned and kicked, aiming for the groin area. He cursed again and she was able to twist around and get a look at Bill McCann, sweating and looking as surprised as she was to find himself engaged in a wrestling match on the floor of an abandoned building.

"Shit!" He was clutching at his groin and breathing hard. "Why were you following me?" he groaned. "Why the hell were you following me?" He opened his eyes and squinted up at her. His glasses had fallen off and she picked them up and handed them to him. It took him a moment to clean them off and put them on again. "I know you," he said when he'd gotten his breath. "I tried to interview you the other night at the debate."

She didn't say anything.

"What are you doing here?"

"I know that you were in Brad's apartment and that you'd left your notebook there." It was all she could think of to say. "If you don't tell me why you were in Brad's apartment and what you were doing, I'm going to tell the police. I don't know what's going on, but . . ."

"Just hold your horses," McCann said, surprised. "I have to make a phone call." With effort, he got to his feet and led the way out to the alley, taking a cell phone out of his jacket pocket, scrolling down through a list of programmed numbers.

"Hey, it's me," he said quietly into the phone. "I know, I know, I'm sorry. But listen, there's a woman here who says she saw me in Brad's apartment. No, I'm in the Back Bay. Comm. Ave. and Gloucester. The public alley behind the houses. She knows about the notebook and she's asking . . . Yeah. I know. No, I think we should just . . . Okay. Drive carefully." He hung up the phone and put it back in his pocket.

"All will be explained," he said to Sweeney. "Jesus, you got me good. I think you kicked my balls up into my lungs." He took a deep breath, then laughed out loud. "What the hell were you thinking, following me like that? I knew you were there from the moment I got into the truck. Jesus!" He sat back down on the ground and took a few more deep breaths before he began to look more relaxed.

They lapsed into uncomfortable silence again and Sweeney

was beginning to be afraid, when a black Jeep Cherokee drove up and parked behind McCann's Toyota.

The door opened and Camille Putnam got out.

"You're right, I was there the night that Brad died," McCann said from the backseat of Camille's Jeep. "But it's not what you think. Do you want to, Cammie, or should I?"

"You," she said. Sweeney turned in her seat to listen to his story.

"I covered the statehouse until recently," he said. "It was a good beat, where they put the up-and-comers and I was pretty happy there. I'd interviewed Cammie a few times and she'd given me some good background on a few stories. And then when she got really involved with women's issues, she went on this junket to Zimbabwe."

Camille turned around and grinned at him. "It wasn't a junket!"

"Yeah, yeah. Whatever. A fact-finding mission. Anyway, my editor thought it would be a good story. I went too, and well, one thing led to another." He smiled. "It wasn't too bad once we got back. I wrote the story and then I dodged writing other stories about Cammie. We kept our relationship mostly secret. She decided to run for Congress, which meant she would eventually be off my beat, but then they offered me the campaign. Covering a campaign is how you prove yourself in the big time. I was going to turn it down . . ."

"But I wouldn't let him," Camille finished. "It's what he's been working for his entire career. I said that we could stop seeing each other during the campaign and then when it was all over we could see where we were."

"I didn't like it," Bill said. "But it seemed like a solution. And we were good. From the moment the campaign started, we didn't see each other at all, or not that way. It was sort of okay at first because we were seeing each other every day, and we were talking on the phone. But then it just became kind of painful, to see her and not be able to . . ." He reached forward and rubbed Camille's arm.

"But we sort of felt that if we could make it until November everything would be all right," Camille said. "Or at least I felt that way. But then on the . . . on the night that Brad died, I got home early from a fund-raiser and it was the first time in months that I was home, alone, with no staff making me practice speeches, no cocktail parties or fund-raisers to go to. And I . . . I called him."

"I think I said something like, let me just come over and we'll talk about the campaign," Bill said, and laughed. "When she said she wanted to get together, I can't describe it, I felt as though all was right with the world, I was happier than I'd been in months, and I realized that I had to do something about our situation. I suddenly realized that I didn't care much about my career, or about what people thought, or anything. I decided I was going to quit and ask Cammie to marry me.

"So we met at this diner and I was just starting to explain all of this to her—God, it seems so long ago, doesn't it?—and then her cell phone rang. Do you want to . . . ?"

Camille took over. "It was Brad. He was drunk. I had never thought of him as a drinker. But he was going on and on about Petey and the spirits. I don't know what he was talking about, something about how I was the only woman who cared about him and he knew I would come. And that I was a good woman, not cold like her. I had no idea what he was talking about, or who, but I was concerned because he was just so drunk, and sounded so *desperate*. So I asked Bill to come with me. It was stupid, I know, anyone could have seen us, but we'd been, well, talking about the future and it seemed like we were going to be together and I just felt like . . . like anything was possible." She took a deep breath. "So we went to Brad's apartment."

"Did he let you in?"

"No, he was passed out on the floor of the living room. But we'd all had to feed those damn fish when he was away and I knew that there was a key they kept outside, by the door. Anyway, he was in bad shape. He had thrown up and I cleaned him off. Bill helped me drag him into the bedroom and take his clothes off and I . . . well, you know this part of it. I put him on his stomach and tied his arms to the bed so he wouldn't choke." She started crying. "I should have stayed."

"It's my fault," Bill said. "She would have stayed if I hadn't been there. She was worried about me being involved."

"So you dropped the notebook when you were helping to get Brad into bed?" Sweeney asked.

"I must have. But I didn't realize it until the next day and by then I'd heard the news about Brad. There was no way I could get it back then. So I waited and went back a week or so later. I thought there was a chance that they hadn't found it, but as soon as I looked around I realized it was gone. How did you know about that anyway?"

"Oh, I happened to be outside and I saw you go in," Sweeney lied.

"You don't know how scared I was when that cop called," Camille said. "I thought he'd figured it out. When I realized he'd just figured out the part about it being me and not Jack who had tied Brad up, I was so relieved I couldn't believe it."

Sweeney thought for a moment. "You've got to tell the police. They know about the notebook and they're going to find you. The fact that you didn't tell them is going to be a problem."

"If this comes out, it could end Bill's career, it could affect the campaign. I'd be letting so many people down. I mean, we've been good, but it just looks terrible." Now Camille sounded very young.

"It would look a lot better if you called them and told them."

She almost asked Camille about the mourning jewelry, about whether Brad had said anything to her about discovering something odd about their family, but she realized that she had ceased to trust that anyone in the Putnam family was telling her the truth.

She thought for a moment. Something still wasn't computing. "But I don't understand," she said finally. "I read some of your old stories about the Back Bay properties. You were interested in whether Camille's grandfather had benefited from the tunnel project. Why did you come here?"

Camille looked up at him questioningly. "I didn't get a chance to ask you that," she said. "Why are you here tonight?"

Bill looked uncomfortable.

"Did you find out something new about the Back Bay Tunnel project?" Sweeney asked.

That was it. He looked up quickly, then over at Camille.

"Billy?" she said nervously. "What's going on?"

"I did find out something, Cam. It's . . . not good about your family. It could affect things. I was hoping you wouldn't have to know."

"Whatever it is, I want to know."

"But . . ."

"I don't care about Sweeney. She's already shown we can trust her. Come on. I'd rather know as soon as possible."

McCann hesitated. "All right. Here's what happened. A couple of months ago, I was working on a story about the campaign." He turned to Sweeney. "We hadn't seen each other in a while at that point and I was feeling optimistic about things, like we'd be able to get through it. Anyway, I was thinking about doing sort of a color piece on Cammie's grandfathers and how she was following in their footsteps and I was going over some old pieces about the negotiations over the Back Bay Tunnel project. There was a mention of how initially there had been some suspicion of Senator Putnam's motives because of his real estate holdings in the area, but he was able to allay them by giving the land that they wanted for the tunnel to the federal government. It was fairly worthless anyway, a swampy little strip that wasn't fit for building on. The Puntnams' really valuable holdings were on Comm. Ave.— right here—and it was hard to argue that ten years of drilling and noise were going to make those properties worth anything at all.

"Anyway, I got interested in what had happened to that land. Had it become worthless? Had Putnam committed basically a totally selfless act in allowing the government to build on it? Or had he actually made a profit? I interviewed some real estate agents. There wasn't any clear answer.

"But then I came down here and discovered that about half of the houses had been vacant for almost ten years. I started getting interested in why that was and discovered that during the initial drilling for the tunnel project a couple of years ago, the depths had been misfigured and the buildings were permanently damaged during the drilling. It was too close to the surface and it permanently wrecked the foundations. They were condemned."

"Yeah," Camille said. "And Drew has this plan to fix them up and connect them and make them into apartments for yuppies or something."

"But I don't understand," Sweeney said. "If anything, that would suggest that John Putnam—or his family—was hurt by the tunnel project."

"Except there was some kind of insurance policy on the houses," Camille said. "I got some in my trust. We all did."

"Yeah, so I found out about the insurance settlement and started wondering. The insurance company's trying to get it back from the government, but that could drag on for years and in the meantime, the family did very well. I started looking into it and I started wondering if the drilling mistake wasn't a mistake."

"But John Putnam couldn't have organized . . ."

"He wouldn't have had to organize anything. He was the chair of the transportation committee. He saw the engineering plans and he'd studied up on this stuff. He would have realized that it was too close to the surface, especially in the Back Bay, which was basically swamp anyway, and that it would do damage to the buildings."

"So he let the plans go forward to get the insurance money?" Camille was looking dismayed.

"I don't know. I stopped looking into it."

"Why didn't you write the story, Bill? We agreed when we started this thing that you weren't going to pull any punches. It would have been a two-week story, three weeks tops. I could have very convincingly said that I was like ten years old when this was all going on."

"I just . . . I don't know. It wouldn't be good for the campaign. You know that. And what does it really matter? Who cares about all this old stuff anyway?" He reached forward and rubbed her shoulder.

Suddenly, Sweeney thought of Brad's face as he'd sat on

the floor of her office and asked whether he should reveal something he'd learned, something that could hurt someone. And then, the night he'd died, he'd been berating himself for not having enough courage. Courage for what?

"Did Brad know about this?" she asked McCann.

"Brad? I don't think so. I mean, how could he?"

"I don't know. He was very interested in his great-great-great-grandparents, who bought the Back Bay land. Maybe he looked into it further."

"Brad wasn't interested in stuff like this," Camille said. "He liked gravestones and old books and paintings."

"Still," McCann said. "You never know."

THIRTY-SEVEN

Quinn and Marino were having their lunch at the Starbucks across from the station when Sweeney called Quinn's cell phone.

"What do you want?" he asked, trying to sound busy.

"I understand why you didn't tell me," she said. "But I found out about it from his friends so now we can talk about it. I hadn't thought about this before, but what if it was about the drugs?"

"What?" Quinn looked over at Marino, who was reading *The Man from Comanche Falls*. On the cover, a blond, buxom cowgirl was being ravished over the back of a horse. "What are you talking about?"

He sensed her exasperation over the phone. "You know, the drugs he'd taken that night. No, that's stupid. It's not like there's a rip-roaring psychedelic mushroom trade at the university. It's not the kind of drug that drug dealers kill people over is it? I mean it's the kind of thing that philosophy Ph.D.s do on the weekend, mushrooms."

"I don't know what you're talking about." Marino looked up, curious now about who he was talking to.

Sweeney said, "Brad ate psychedelic mushrooms the night he died. Didn't you know?"

"Are you sure about that?" he asked after a moment.

"Not completely, but my students told me that they'd all been doing them. I just assumed that Brad . . ."

"No." He said it as though he was trying to convince himself. "They would have tested for it. College student? They have to do a special psilocybin test, but I'm sure they did it."

"Well, maybe all his friends ate them, but he didn't. But if he didn't, why was he so out of control? The way his friends were describing his behavior, it was like he was completely tripped out. If it wasn't the drugs, then what was it?"

"I don't know." Marino was looking up from his book now and was listening to Quinn's side of the conversation. "Listen, let me look into it. Thanks for calling." He disconnected before she could ask him if she could help.

"What was that all about?" Marino asked.

Quinn looked around the café, just to make sure there wasn't anybody they knew. "What if I told you that the Putnam kid was taking magic mushrooms the night he died?"

"I'd say it didn't show up at the lab. And they would have tested for psilocybin. They always do with something like this."

"Well, maybe they missed it. Or maybe he didn't take them that night, but he took them some other night. Besides, if all the kids he was with that night were taking them, maybe that's what the murder was about. What do you think?"

Marino put the book facedown on the table. "I think that's not a bad idea. Maybe we should look into it a little."

"Okay," Quinn said. "Why don't you say good-bye to . . ." He picked up Marino's paperback and read the back cover. "Savannah West. And we'll hit the trail."

They started with Jack Putnam.

"I'd say he'd be the most likely to know about his brother's drug habits," Marino said as they drove into the Back Bay. "He's the closest in age, an artist and whatnot. If he doesn't know anything, maybe the other brother. I'm reluctant to get into it with the sister. We say the word drugs and she's going to have her people down on us like nobody's business."

"The lab said they did test for psilocybin. Negative. So whatever he might have been doing, he wasn't doing it that night."

Quinn turned onto Comm. Ave. and parked a couple houses down from Jack Putnam's in front of a fire hydrant.

As he got out of the car, Marino said, "I called the university police again. They weren't aware of any kind of psilocybin ring or anything, though they said it's fairly common around campus. Every couple of months they'll get a kid who's had a bad mushroom trip coming into the health center. But they didn't seem overly concerned."

They knocked on the street level front door, and when there was no answer, Quinn pressed the buzzer. Still no answer.

"Not here," Marino said. "We can call and make an appointment to see him, but I want to ask someone in the family about this before they get warned. You know what I mean? See what happens when we say, 'Did your brother take drugs, Mr. Putnam?'"

"Yeah, maybe we should head out to Weston. It's what—?" Quinn checked his watch. "Four. They might be home. Worth a shot."

With rush hour traffic out of the city, it took them nearly an hour to get out to Weston.

"Pretty nice out here, huh?" Marino was looking out the window as they passed a couple of construction sites, the big new houses sprouting up where the old ones had been.

"Yeah. Think of it. I'd kill for one of those houses, and they're knocking 'em down to put up something even bigger and better."

They turned into the Putnams' long driveway and as they approached the big house, Marino gave a low whistle.

"Yeah, I know," Quinn said, getting out of his car. In the dusky light, the house was dark and lonely-looking. They walked up to the front door and rang the bell, but were met with the same silence they'd been met with at Jack Putnam's.

"What's the deal? They all go away somewhere?" Marino went and looked in the window next to the front door, but it was obscured by a lace curtain.

"I don't know. I guess we'll have to try again."

They were driving back down the long driveway when a

teenage girl pushing a baby carriage came out of some hedges along the driveway, causing Quinn to slow down and wait for her to cross the road. She seemed to be heading for another one of the large, new houses.

He rolled down the window and called out, "Hey, do you know where the Putnams are? We're trying to get in touch with them."

She turned around and he saw that she was older than she'd appeared from behind. Her pretty, fair face, framed with stringy blond hair, was afraid.

"We're police," he said, to try to allay her fears, but she only looked more nervous than before and leaned forward to take a chubby newborn out of the stroller, cuddling it to her as though she thought she had to protect it from them.

"I don't know," she said finally in lightly accented but otherwise perfect English. Swedish, Quinn thought, that or German. "They might have gone down to Newport. His brother died and they've been gone a lot. You probably read about it in the newspaper."

"That's kind of what we're here about. You know them very well?"

"Not really. I work for the Sorensens." She pointed to the big house behind her. "They just moved in and Mrs. Sorensen had the baby right when they got here, so they don't really know any of the neighbors."

"Do you live with them?"

"Ya," she said. "I'm the au pair."

"Oh. So you don't have any idea where the Putnams are?"

"No. Maybe he's working. He works a lot of nights."

"Nights? Isn't he a lawyer?"

"I don't know. I guess so. But he goes out at night a lot. I always assumed it was work."

"What do you mean?" Quinn watched her eyes flick past him to Marino, who was leaning across so he could hear what she had to say.

"He goes out at night. Late."

"What do you mean when you say late?" The girl had Marino's attention now.

"Uh . . . You know, ten, eleven. Sometimes later. The only reason I know is that we're up so much these days, with the baby. I always assumed it was work. But . . . I hope I haven't gotten him in trouble."

"Not at all. Thanks a lot." Quinn gave Marino a look. "He does this every night?"

"No, not every night."

"What would you say, four out of five nights?"

She thought for a minute as the baby grabbed at her blond hair. Expertly, she loosened the baby's grip and replaced the hair with a finger. "Maybe three out of five."

"What about the weekends?"

"Yeah, sometimes the weekends too."

"How about last Saturday or the Saturday before that?"

"I think so. I'm not positive, though. The days all seem to kind of run together now, you know. With the baby. Mr. and Mrs. Sorensen have to be at work early so I get up with him in the night. But I think I do remember seeing him the last couple Saturdays." She looked worried again. "Maybe I shouldn't have . . . I don't want you to think I was spying on him or anything. It's just that the nursery looks out on their driveway and when I'm trying to get the baby to sleep, I like to walk around the room with him. He likes looking out the window. I don't know if he can see anything, but it kind of seems like it."

"No," Quinn said, trying to look reassuring. "You've done the right thing."

"We shoulda talked to her before," Marino said once Quinn had rolled the window up.

"Yeah," Quinn said. "I think we talked to the parents, but we didn't think about the nanny. So what do we do now?"

"I don't know. We can call them, figure out where they are, but it gives them a chance to come up with a story. Like I said, I just want to see his face when we ask him."

'Yeah." Quinn was thinking about it when a set of headlights turned onto the driveway. A black SUV slowed and Drew Putnam's face appeared as the tinted window came down.

"Can I . . . ? Oh, hi, Detective Quinn."

"Hi, Mr. Putnam. Sorry about this, but we just wanted to talk to you and your wife for a second. Could we come in? It won't take long."

Drew Putnam turned to look at his wife, who was sitting next to him, and in the instant before he turned back and said, "Yes, of course. We're happy to help you any way we can," Quinn saw raw fear pass across Melissa Putnam's face as she glanced at her husband.

Quinn pulled up next to the SUV and raised his eyebrows at Marino, who grinned.

"Lucky break," Marino said, getting out of the car.

"We had to take Melissa's car to the shop," Drew said apologetically as they all walked toward the front door. "I hope you weren't waiting long.

"No, no. We just got here."

Drew let them in and as he flicked on the lights in the hallway, Quinn was shocked to see that the entryway and the rooms beyond it were completely emptied out, that the walls had been stripped of all their wallpaper, leaving behind desolate-looking expanses of gray.

"We completely forgot that we'd arranged to have all the rooms done," Melissa said when she saw the look on his face. "It was awful. They just showed up and there wasn't anything we could do."

She led the way into the kitchen and told Quinn and Marino to sit on stools pulled up to a marble island in the middle of the room. She didn't offer them anything to drink. It struck Quinn that she had been sick. Her blue eyes seemed sunk deep into their sockets and her lips were so pale they almost disappeared against her skin. As they sat, she took a lipstick out of the leather purse she'd carried in from the car and, leaning close to the refrigerator to see her reflection in the stainless steel surface, she rolled the pinkish color onto her lips.

"We're just trying to get everything pinned down about where everyone was the night of Brad's death," Quinn said. "Now, you say you arrived home and went straight to bed."

"Yes," Melissa said. She did look better with the lipstick. Drew didn't say anything.

"And, Mr. Putnam, you went out again. What time was that?" Marino said it so nonchalantly that Quinn almost thought he was going to walk into it. But when he looked up, Drew's face was red.

"What do you mean?"

"One of your neighbors saw you leaving around eleven on the Saturday night that Brad died. You didn't tell us this before. Where did you go?"

"Out for a drive. I couldn't sleep and I was gone for about ten minutes." Nobody said anything. "Surely you can't blame me for forgetting about it."

"Where did you go?" Marino was angry now. Quinn could see the signs, his eyes narrow, the cauliflower ear reddened.

"I drove around the neighborhood."

Quinn turned to Melissa. "And you said that you took a sleeping pill when you got home and went straight to bed?"

"I took a sleeping pill, yes."

"So you wouldn't have known what time he came home?"

"He said he came home ten minutes later."

"But you wouldn't really know, would you? Because you'd taken a sleeping pill?"

She looked startled, but didn't answer him.

"Can I ask why you take sleeping pills?"

"That's kind of a personal question, isn't it?" Drew sneered.

"Well, it doesn't seem like there's a lot of sleeping going on in your house."

"No, no. It's okay." Melissa looked up at him. "I've had seven miscarriages in the last four years. The doctors say there isn't anything wrong, but . . . I have trouble sleeping."

It was more information than she'd needed to give and Quinn wasn't sure if she'd told him because she really wanted him to understand or if she was just trying to shock him.

"So you took a pill that night. Was it before or after your husband came back from his drive?"

She looked almost triumphant. "Before. But as I was going off, I heard him come in. Sleeping pills don't knock you out immediately, you know. It's not like it is in the movies."

"But there's no reason he couldn't have gone out again, after you were asleep?"

Drew stood up and went to Quinn with his arms outstretched. For a moment, Quinn thought he was going to embrace him. "But I didn't, I'm telling you that I didn't." He turned away and put his head in his hands. "Why won't you believe me?"

"Okay, okay," Marino said. "As far as you know, Mr. Putnam, did Brad take drugs?"

"What?"

"Did Brad take drugs?"

"I don't know. If he did, he never told me about it. He was in college, for God's sake. He wouldn't be the first college kid to try drugs."

"Yeah," Marino said. "But unlike most college kids, he got murdered. And we're just trying to find out by who."

They were almost back to the station when Quinn's phone rang. The display listed his home number and he answered it, feeling his stomach seize up.

"Tim, it's Debbie. I'm sorry to bother you at work, but Maura was acting really weird this morning and I just went up to change Megan and when I came down again she was gone." Debbie was breathless, and Quinn could tell she'd been crying.

"What do you mean?"

"I mean she's gone. I don't know where she is. I took Megan outside and looked around a little, but now she's gone down for the night."

"All right, all right. I'm coming home. Just stay with Megan and I'll be right there."

"Everything okay?" Marino asked.

Quinn glanced over at him. "Can you drop me at home. I'll take the T back for my car later."

"Sure."

It was six-thirty now and the traffic was light on Mass. Ave.

Marino left him and Quinn stood for a moment looking up at his house. Everything looked all right from the outside, just the way he'd left it that morning. The grass needed to be cut, and there was a bag of trash on the porch that he'd forgotten to take out that morning, but otherwise everything looked fine.

"Debbie," he called out as he came in the door.

She appeared at the top of the stairs, a finger to her lips.

"Shhh. Megan's gone down."

"Is she back?"

She shook her head.

He rushed out into the street and took in the darkening, empty sidewalks, the houses illuminated by the bluish light of televisions. She couldn't have gone too far without the car, he told himself. He started down one side of the street, calling out, "Maura? Honey?" and looking into driveways and side yards as he went. He was almost halfway down the street when Mrs. Maiorelli, a grandmotherly type who had brought them veal Parmesan when they first moved in, came hesitantly out of her front door and said, "Are you looking for your wife?"

"Yes. Is she . . . ?"

Mrs. Maiorelli pointed toward her backyard. Behind her, he could see her television going, could smell fried onions wafting out into the spring air. "She's back there. I tried to talk to her and she didn't want to. So I just let her sit."

"Thanks, Mrs. Maiorelli. Can I . . ." He pointed to her side gate.

"Yes, yes. Go around."

Quinn had never been in the Maiorellis' backyard and he was amazed at what a beautiful little oasis they had made of the eighth of an acre they had behind their house. There were flower beds all around the edges of the lawn and at the back they had constructed a little raised area, faced with a rock garden. At the top was a dwarf cherry tree shading another little garden and under the tree was the statue of an angel and a little bench. Maura was sitting on the bench, looking desolate and in the low light from the fixture perched on the back of the house, he could see the tears streaming down her face.

As he walked across the lawn to his wife, Quinn remembered the first time he had seen her. He had been home from college and had gone to a party with some high school friends. Late in the night, he had gone out into the backyard to get some fresh air and he had seen a young girl sitting on a chair at the edge of the yard, looking forlornly out into the dark. He had been attracted to her because of that, he knew now. He had sought her out that night, and all the other nights he had held her when she was depressed, because he had liked the idea of someone who felt things that deeply.

"Maura," he said quietly. "I was worried about you."

"Yeah," she said, looking up at him and, miraculously, smiling. "I'm sorry. I just . . . I wanted to come and sit with the angel." She pointed to the little statue.

He didn't know what to say to that so he just sat down next to her on the bench and took her hand. She let him hold it and just as he was about to suggest that they go back to the house, she turned her face to him and he saw her there, saw the old Maura in her eyes.

"I feel better," she said, smiling again. "I woke up this morning and I felt new, like I could handle things."

"Yeah?" He tried to keep the joy out of his voice. The doctor had said he needed not to let her see how much he wanted her to get better.

"It's so strange," she said. "It was like I'd given something up. I think I'm going to be okay."

He looked up and saw Mrs. Maiorelli in a back window of the house, watching them. The angel statue glowed white in the dusky night.

"I'm so glad." He turned to her to hug her, stroking her hair, and he realized that he too was crying.

THIRTY-EIGHT

꧂

Sweeney spent the next day working at home, trying to catch up on grading and on her own work. She got through the first draft of an article on a 1690 stone in a Connecticut cemetery that she'd been working on for a while and by nine, she was exhausted and dazed. She put on her leather jacket against the chilled air and walked over to Easter 1916, hoping there was a traditional music session on. As she walked in, she knew she'd gotten the right night; the steady thump of the bodhran and the high reedy chirping of the flutes came out to greet her as she entered, the music chasing the chill in the air.

While Easter 1916 was one of her favorite hangouts, it had been a long time since she'd come to a session. Consciously or unconsciously, she'd steered clear of the sessions, and now she had a sudden memory of Colm, hunched over in the corner of an Oxford pub, playing his flute while the lovely music rose up around him. He had always played with his eyes closed, his fingers and lips translating the music, his ears taking cues from his fellow players, his eyes not coming into it at all. She had sometimes felt threatened when he was playing. He seemed to go off somewhere else, somewhere she couldn't reach him. Wanting to be a part of things, she'd even tried to pick up the bodhran, but she wasn't any good.

He had known all the best places to go, in Oxford, and in London too, and it was something they had loved to do together. The couple of times she'd gone to Ireland with Colm, they'd found sessions in his local pubs, and she had come to

love the camaraderie, the way old and new players just wandered in and joined the playing.

The bar was busy and she ordered herself a Guinness and
then slipped into the crowded back room where the music was
just starting up. A fiddle player, a flutist, and an accordion
player had already started and the bodhran player was listening, trying to find his rhythm before jumping in. Sweeney
found a seat and set her Guinness down on the table, listening
to the tune, trying to tease it out of the lines followed by the
different instruments.

*Dee Da Da Da, Dee Da Da Da Deedle Dee Dee Da Da, Dee
Dee Dee*. What was it? She sipped her Guinness, smiling at an
older couple sitting at the next table. The old woman's foot
was tapping away on the table leg. Her husband was holding
her hand on top of the table, tapping a finger against her own.
Sweeney watched them for a moment. They seemed full of
joy, as though there was nothing they would rather be doing at
this moment than listening to this music.

Everyone clapped when the players wrapped it up and they
moved on to another tune. This one she knew. It was a jig,
"The Lark on the Strand," a tumbling collection of notes,
gathering on themselves, doubling back and moving the tune
forward. *Na Na Na, Na Na Na, Na Na Na Nah. Na Na Na, Na
Na Na, Na Na Na Nah*.

She closed her eyes and lost herself in the sounds of the
flute, reaching and arching, the notes high and flinty. The fid-
dler was very good, and a bodhran player kept time while the
accordion player jumped in, the whiny, whimsical notes rising
and climbing.

The music put her into kind of a trance and she found that
her mind cleared suddenly. Colm had always said that when
he was having trouble with his thesis, he found that going out
to a session helped to get his thoughts in order. She understood what he meant now. There was something about the
background of the seemingly disordered but quite logical
notes that allowed her to reach for the facts and tidbits of information that were bothering her.

Brad had been worried about something before he died,

perhaps the jewelry, perhaps the Back Bay houses, perhaps something else. That much she knew. And the night of his death, according to Jennifer, he had been angry at someone, or no, scared of someone. Someone he was close to, by the sound of it. Okay, so she had that. Then what had happened? Well, then Brad had been killed. Someone had put a bag over his head and then put the jewelry on him. That was the important thing. There was something about that fact that seemed at the very heart of all this, but she wasn't sure what it was.

If Brad had figured out that the jewelry was evidence of Belinda's subterfuge, he might have told someone that he was going to reveal it. And he may have been scared of that person whoever he or she was. That tied in with what Jennifer had said, didn't it? Brad had been going on and on about how he didn't have any balls, and how his family never talked about anything. What if he'd been about to talk?

But she'd run up against this before, hadn't she? If that was what had happened, then why would the killer leave the jewelry there, on his body, pointing police in the right direction?

The tune ended with a flourish and she opened her eyes and clapped with the rest of the audience. As the musicians smiled and accepted the applause, she looked up to see a man holding a drink and looking around for a seat. It took her a few moments to recognize him.

It was Quinn.

He was wearing jeans and a windbreaker and it was a few moments more before he saw her. When he did, she saw something on his face that she couldn't quite identify. He looked down at the ground. He seemed guilty, she thought. That was it. Once he'd seen her, there wasn't anything he could do but come over and sit down in the seat next to her.

"Hi," he said. "I'm surprised to see you here."

"Yeah, well, I was craving a session. What about you? Are you a regular?" The new song had started and was getting louder, musicians joining in.

"Yeah, well, it's not so far from the house. Maura and the baby were both sleeping and this Brad Putnam thing was really on my mind, so I thought I'd get out and grab some music." He looked guilty again and Sweeney realized that he'd been afraid she'd disapprove of him coming out by himself. "My father was a bodhran player. I have good associations."

Sweeney smiled. "I was engaged to an Irishman. When I used to live in England. He was a flute player. He'd always bring me out to sessions."

"Really?" He seemed surprised. "They're good tonight." Sweeney nodded and they lapsed into silence, listening to the music. At one point, Sweeney looked over and saw that Quinn was sitting with eyes closed, a foot tapping out the music's rhythm on the floor.

The musicians had just finished one long piece and the observers were applauding when Quinn's cell phone rang. He reached for it and stood up, answering it as he left the back room. Sweeney watched him duck into a little alcove outside the door. He talked for only a few minutes before he came back to get his coat.

"Good to see you," he said, slipping out through the crowds of people.

"Wait . . ." But he didn't wait and Sweeney followed him out onto the sidewalk. "Is everything okay?" she called out.

"I have to go," he said. "There's been another hit-and-run."

Sweeney felt herself go cold. "Who was it?" A couple came out of the bar, laughing and stumbling, and she stepped out of the way to let them pass.

Quinn hesitated for a few moments before walking back to her. "Melissa Putnam," he said. "Down in Newport."

THIRTY-NINE

It was after one A.M. now and Sweeney drove a little too fast down Mass. Ave., back toward the university, and Becca Dearborne's dorm. Quinn had allowed her to drive him home and she had told him about Melissa Putnam's message.

"What did she say?" he'd asked once they were in the Rabbit.

"Just that she wanted to talk to me and that she'd call back. She didn't leave a number or I would have gotten back to her. What happened?"

"Apparently, she couldn't sleep and told her husband she was going for a walk around nine-thirty. Then an hour or so later, someone was coming home early from the bars in town and their headlights caught her lying by the side of the road. She hadn't been hit very hard—it was probably an accident—but she'd hit her head on the pavement and that accounted for her being unconscious. They think she'll be okay though."

"God, could it have anything to do with Brad?"

"That's what I'd like to know," Quinn said. "I asked if I could go down, but they said no. I guess it's being handled by the Newport police for now. We'll have to see what happens. It may be that it was just somebody driving drunk and they didn't see her."

"But you have to admit that it's pretty strange that she called me. I've only met her once or twice. I guess she knew I was looking into the jewelry . . ."

Quinn looked at her quickly. "You think maybe she was calling you about the jewelry?"

"I don't know."

"My friend said he should know in a day or two. I don't know how this all works, but I think it took longer because he's doing it on his own time. I'll call you as soon as I know."

"Call me on the cell. I might be in Newport this weekend, visiting my aunt."

"In Newport?" He raised his eyebrows.

"Yeah, well. I was planning on going down there to see her."

"I don't know if I believe that." He laughed. "But do me a favor and don't get into trouble."

Sweeney had pulled up in front of the house, but Quinn didn't undo his seat belt. He sat there for a few moments, thinking.

"It's strange that it's another hit-and-run, isn't it?" Sweeney asked him. "Have you found out who might have hit the other girl? Alison Cope?"

"We're following up on some leads. Nothing so far. According to her roommates, she knew Brad Putnam only by sight, so there's no connection there, but we'll have to see if we can establish one between her and Melissa Putnam." He sounded very tired.

"What do you think happened?" she asked him. "What did you think when you found him?"

"What do you mean?"

"I mean when you first arrived at the apartment. What struck you about the room? Was there anything strange?" She wasn't sure what she was asking him.

"I don't know," he said slowly. "It struck me as being a very disorganized murder."

"Disorganized?"

"I mean, it was messy. I had the feeling that someone had been looking for something. Things were pulled out, drawers you know. And there were books and things on the ground. But there wasn't anything missing and we decided eventually that there must have been a struggle, or that perhaps he was killed by someone in a rage and they kind of lost it."

There was something hesitant about the way he said it.

'What?" Sweeney asked.

"Nothing, it's just that it didn't seem like the person was in a rage. Not to me. It was like when you're looking for something, you know? And you really want to find it and you just kind of turn everything upside down, planning to put it back later. I don't know. That's crazy."

"No, it's not. But what could the murderer have been looking for?" Suddenly, she thought about the files she'd taken from Brad's apartment, sitting at home on her desk. But she couldn't tell Quinn about that. There were laws about breaking and entering, even if she'd used the key.

"I don't know." He looked awfully troubled.

"Remember to call me," she said. "And I'll ask around, see if I can find out anything else from the kids in my class."

He looked as though he were about to say something else, then thought better of it.

"What?"

"Nothing. Thanks for the ride," he said. "And remember what I said about staying out of trouble. I'll call you when I hear about the jewelry."

Now she clutched her class roster listing Becca's dorm address. She knocked on the wooden door.

Jaybee came to the door first, wearing only boxers and looking surprised to see Sweeney.

"I need to talk to you," Sweeney told him. "To you and Becca. Melissa Putnam was hit by a car tonight. Hit-and-run."

Jaybee's eyes widened. He didn't say anything, but he held the door for her, then shut and locked it behind her and turned on a couple of table lamps in the little living room/kitchen area. Without a word, he disappeared into the bedroom, not bothering to close the door.

"Bec," she heard him whisper. "Bec, you have to get up."

They came out a few minutes later, Becca in flannel pajamas and Jaybee wearing jeans and a T-shirt. "What happened?" Becca asked. "Is she dead?"

"No, but they don't know how seriously she was hurt." Without being asked, Sweeney sat down on a low futon in the little living room. Jaybee and Becca sat down across from her, on the floor. "Listen, I have to ask you guys something. Raj and Jennifer and Ashley told me about the mushrooms and the cemetery, the night Brad died. Was he taking mushrooms too?"

"No," Jaybee said. "The rest of us were. But Brad chickened out at the last minute."

"Why?"

"It was because of his sister. He was all nervous about getting caught and wrecking her campaign. At the last minute, he didn't take them. I was the only one he told, though. Everyone else thought he was tripping out too."

"So why was he so angry? Jennifer said he was really upset."

Becca looked at Jaybee.

"Becca," Sweeney said. "I think someone tried to kill Melissa Putnam tonight."

"It's okay," Jaybee said. "Tell her."

Becca sat up, holding her knees to her chest and rocked back and forth a few times, as though giving herself strength. "It was me and Jaybee. He had just found out about me and Jaybee." Tears came to her eyes. "We were in the cemetery and Jaybee and I went off and we didn't think anyone could see us and we were kissing. And then we turned around and Brad was there." Her voice was very low, almost a whisper.

"He was furious," Jaybee said. "It had been going on for a couple of weeks and we wanted to tell him, but I knew he wasn't going to like it. He'd been in love with Becca since he was like ten, and he used to talk to me about it all the time, about how he knew that they were going to be together someday and how she was the only one who understood him. When I realized that I . . . well, that I wanted to be with her, I didn't know what to do. I couldn't tell him, but then we got together and it just seemed easier and easier to pretend. He thought I was seeing someone because I would spend nights at Becca's, and it totally sucked, lying to him. I hated it, every time I did it. But I didn't want him to know."

"But then he saw you?"

"Yeah, he saw us kissing and we . . . it was like we knew he was there and we turned around and to tell you the truth, it scared the shit out of me," Jaybee said. "He was just staring at us and then he said something about how he should have known and how it was probably his fault and he didn't deserve Becca. It was awful."

"And he was really angry?" Sweeney asked Jaybee.

"Yeah. At first anyway. He was going on and on about what a coward he was. What a wimp and how afraid of everyone he was. But then, once we got him home, he wasn't so angry anymore. It was more . . . I can't describe it, like he had, like he had decided something. Like he had made some kind of decision."

Becca said, "I think maybe it sent him over the edge, finding out about me and Jaybee. Brad had always had this weird thing about me, because of Petey's death, because I was there. He couldn't let go of it."

Sweeney stared at the poster on the opposite wall. It was a Rothko, one of the black and burgundy ones. It wasn't a painting she would have expected Becca to like. "Wait a second. What do you mean? You were there the night Petey died?"

They exchanged a quick glance and Jaybee said, "Becca was at the bar. Nobody was ever supposed to know that she was there. Her parents got a lawyer."

"Do you know which one of them was driving?"

"I swear I don't," she said. "We were all hanging out at the Full Fathom Five and we were all drunk. Brad and Petey and I were excited because they didn't ask for ID and Drew and everybody were buying us drinks. It was really fun, but then their dad came in."

"Andrew Putnam was there that night too?"

"Yeah, he came in and he was completely toasted. I mean, just wasted. And he was being really embarrassing, pretending he was our age or something, and flirting with Melissa. It pissed Drew off. That's why he wanted to go home. Because his father was there. But no one else wanted to go. This friend of mine from boarding school was there and she said she'd give me a ride home, so I stayed. But Drew wanted everyone to go home and he was getting kind of, I don't know, just really angry. And Melissa got really mad, I guess at the way he was talking to her, and so she took off and took their car home, 'cause we'd all come in separate cars. That really pissed Drew off, so he said it was time to go and they all took off and that was it."

"Do you think Drew was driving?" Sweeney almost whispered.

"I told you I don't know. They never told us. I asked Brad once but he said he'd promised not to tell."

"Promised who?"

"I don't know. I told you I don't know." She seemed on the verge of tears and Sweeney let her turn to Jaybee and bury her head in his chest. "This is really important you guys. Do you think that Brad was killed because he was going to say who was driving that night?"

"No! What are you . . . ?" Jaybee looked horrified. "It's his family."

"Someone was driving that night. Brad knew who it was." Sweeney felt her stomach sink as she said the words. There was truth to them.

"No," Becca said. "It's impossible."

They sat in silence for a few moments, listening to a ticking clock on the wall.

Sweeney waited a few more minutes. "Becca, why didn't you say anything about the night Brad died?"

In the strange, low light from the desk lamp on a side table, Becca suddenly looked very young. She was crying and she wiped her eyes across her sleeve, like a little girl.

"Because I was guilty. Can't you see? It was my fault. If I had just loved him, none of this would have happened."

"But that's not how it works. That's not how love works." Sweeney watched Jaybee try to comfort her, pain shadowing his own face. "That's not how anything works."

FORTY

The air grew saltier as Sweeney drove south toward Newport.

So exhausted that she knew she wouldn't be able to sleep, she had gone home, packed a bag, and set off. Now the tangy air seeped through her thin sweater, so that she grew more awake as she drove.

She listened to the wind whistling in her open windows. It didn't take her long to reach Newport on the empty roads, and she turned onto Bellevue, then left onto Narragansett. In darkness, the big houses and dark drives seemed mysterious and sinister. She turned into Anna's driveway—she realized that she now thought of it as Anna's house, whereas the last time she'd thought of it as her grandparents'—and got her bag out of the backseat.

The ocean roared as she walked along the dark path to the front door and pressed the doorbell. When no one came, she pressed it again.

"Hang on, hang on," came Anna's voice. Through the glass panels next to the door, Sweeney saw her rush down the stairs in her bathrobe, looking sleepy and afraid.

"Hi," Sweeney said, when she'd opened the door. "I was thinking maybe I could stay here for a few days."

When Anna saw who it was, she smiled. "You were born in the middle of the night, you know," she said. "I should have known you were establishing a pattern."

"Melissa Putnam was in a hit-and-run accident tonight," Sweeney said. "It looks like she's going to be okay, though."

Anna had made tea and they were sitting on the back patio, a couple of candle torches lighting the pitch black night. It was three in the morning, but miraculously, Sweeney found she wasn't tired anymore.

"Where did it happen?" Anna asked. In the man's bathrobe she looked small and sleepy, her gray hair sticking up and her blue eyes fogged with sleep.

"Up on Ocean Drive. Apparently she must have gone for a walk and someone came along and didn't see her in the dark. At least that's what the police are saying. I'm wondering if someone didn't come along and hit her on purpose."

Anna raised her eyebrows. "It sounds like you've gotten involved."

"Yeah. You don't know the half of it."

The eyebrows went up again. "Does your involvement have anything to do with Jack Putnam?"

Sweeney felt herself flush. "Why would you say that?"

"Because he's your type. And because you just blushed as red as your hair."

"How do you know what my type is?"

"I've known you since the day your parents brought you home from the hospital. I know you better than you think I do. And I met Colm, remember?"

She had forgotten. Anna had been in London for a friend's daughter's wedding and had come up to Oxford for the day. They had gone out to lunch and Colm had told Anna about his thesis on Yeats's role in the Easter Uprising. Sweeney choked up for a second and took a quick gulp of her tea to help it pass.

"I don't know. Jack's interesting. Talented. Good-looking. But this whole thing has gotten so complicated. I don't think there's even a possibility of it anymore."

Anna studied her for a moment, as though she were determining whether Sweeney was strong enough for her question. "Has there been anyone else? Since Colm, I mean?"

Sweeney leaned back in her chair and looked out over the flower beds that edged the backyard, strange in the twirling light from the torch candles. There were late-blooming tulips and the greenery of the daylilies that would bloom later in the summer. The peonies—always Sweeney's favorite for their fleeting audaciousness and singular scent—were just starting. She could see the tight round buds that would give way to the prettily ragged petals of pale pink. "There was a man I met over Christmas. I went up to Vermont with Toby." Sweeney told her about Toby's family, about the murders. "His name is Ian and he lives in London. I thought that . . . I don't know. There was something there and it could have gone on, but when it came right down to going to London to see him, I couldn't do it. I told him I'd come visit in the spring."

"It's spring now," Anna said quietly.

"So he tells me." She took another long sip and looked up at Anna. "How could I?" she asked. "It doesn't seem possible."

"You do," Anna said. "You just do."

"What about you? Has there been anyone since Julian?" Sweeney tried to put a little bit of challenge in her gaze. Anna liked asking people personal questions but she didn't like answering them.

But she surprised Sweeney by grinning. "There was a man a couple of years ago. I was doing this studio residency thing and he was too. Gordon. He was from San Francisco."

"So what happened?"

"We stayed in touch for a while. I even went out there for a weekend." Sweeney had a vision of her aunt on an airplane, smiling secretly in the air over California. "But we were two old people, set in our ways. Neither of us wanted to move. We reached something of an impasse. I feel sometimes as though I have too many things to do, too many things to finish. How I will finish them all, I don't know. I spent so many years making Julian's art possible and now I just want to paint and never stop."

Sweeney thought, That's what would happen with Ian. She had a vision of herself in an airport after a weekend visit, walking alone down an empty hallway.

"So tell me about the English guy. What does he do?"

"He's an art and antiques dealer. He's divorced, has a daughter. That part of it scares the bejeezuz out of me. He's . . . I don't know. He makes me nervous. I can't figure out if that's a good thing or a bad thing. I feel sort of universally unsettled around him."

"You don't think that's because of what happened when you were up there in Vermont?"

"Maybe. That's the thing. We . . . whatever there was of 'we' is so tainted by what happened that I don't know how we would begin again. But now the same thing may be true of Jack Putnam."

"Yeah, but it can happen the other way too. I remember when Peter Putnam died, everyone always said that it had brought Melissa and Drew together, strengthened their relationship. They'd always been kind of unsure, I think, but Petey's death kind of brought them together, made them put aside whatever it was that was the problem with their relationship."

"You were here when Peter Putnam died, weren't you?"

Anna looked up at the ceiling as though she were thinking. "Oh yes, of course. It wasn't that long ago. Everyone in town felt so bad for them. We had all known Petey and the other kids of course. He was a good kid. Mischievous. Very much the youngest child."

"Who did everyone think had been driving?"

"Well, the family really circled the wagons. The police tried everything but those kids stuck to their story. You had to give them credit. And frankly, I think everyone around here felt that whoever had been driving had already been punished. There wasn't any point. But the police had had some episodes with the Putnams before, felt the weight of their influence so to speak. They weren't going to let it go. They kept bringing them down to the station to question them, kept getting stymied by all the high-priced lawyers, and ultimately they didn't find out anything. Those kids, it was amazing, it was as though they'd been lying all their lives. They just kind of outlasted them. Of course if it had been anyone else, they probably would have been brought in for not cooperating with the investigation or something, but because it was the Putnams, they finally had to let it go. People in town put a lot of pressure on them too."

"Was there ever any sense that it was more likely to be one

of them? I mean, who did everyone think was being shielded?"

"Well, I always thought that it would be Drew if it was any-body. I guess because he had the most to lose. But of course now that Camille's running for Congress, she's got a lot to lose herself. Something like this, well, it would always hang over you, wouldn't it?"

"But she didn't know that she would be running back then, did she?"

"Oh, I think Camille Putnam always knew she was going to run for Congress."

"What about Jack?" Sweeney felt the beginnings of a blush when she said it.

"I felt as though Jack Putnam would have just come out and said it if it had been him. There's something kind of wild about him. But then again, he's a Putnam. And his parents might have put their foot down and said that they weren't go-ing to tell, under any circumstances. I used to teach Jack painting in the summers, you know. He was really good, even then."

Sweeney had forgotten about Anna's summer art camp. Sweeney had even participated one summer. She wondered if she'd known Jack then, but of course he was a couple of years older.

"I can't believe nobody ever said anything. I mean some-one must have been in the bar that night who saw who was driving."

"The police tried."

Sweeney thought for a moment. "There was something about him . . . about Brad . . . that reminded me of . . . It's hard to explain. He was so alive and so dead at the same time. So joyful and so depressed, all in one. You just wanted to save him."

"He reminded you of your father," Anna said quietly. She looked at Sweeney and smiled.

Sweeney looked away.

"There's something I always wanted to say to you, Sweeney." Anna was looking off in the direction of the water.

"The way Ivy always talked about Paul, and the way Paul always talked about Ivy, well, it was—"

"They hated each other," Sweeney cut in.

"Yeah, after they split up, they really did," Anna said, smiling regretfully. "But before that, when they met, when they had you. It was magic. It was magic being in the same room with them. They . . . actually, hold on a second. I was going through some old letters the other day and I found something. I was going to send it to you."

She was gone for a few minutes and when she came back, she handed Sweeney a letter. "Your father wrote it to me when Julian and I were in London. It was just after he'd met your mother. Read it."

Sweeney recognized her father's sprawling, untidy handwriting, the frequent cross-outs and ink blots where he'd left pen to paper a little too long. As on her own letters from him, this one had little drawings in the margins, animals and people dancing and strange little ornaments.

"Anna dear sister," it read. "Isn't it lovely out today? Well, I suppose it may not be lovely in London, but here in New York, where I am for the weekend (and perhaps longer—read on!), it is glorious and sunny and the birds are singing. Pat and Delia took me to see a show last night, a horrid little modern play about a couple who are in jail together for some crime we never learn about and spend all three acts fighting and needling each other. Quite bad, but the woman playing the wife was terrifically good. Ivy Williston-Mount, her name is. Veddy English, veddy posh, but with a veddy naughty mouth, gorgeous red hair, and perfect little legs. Her family owns some huge estate in Somerset or something, called Summerlands. But she, it seems, is quite the prodigal daughter. Ran away from home for the the-ah-tah when she was sixteen. Completely estranged from Mummy and Daddy. Don't you just love it? I was smitten immediately and as it turned out, Pat knew her from somewhere and she came out with us afterward. We met her in her dressing room and everything and when we came in, she was taking off her makeup and Pat introduced me and she turned around and said, "Ah yes, the rising young artist," in this withering sort of way.

"We caroused and caroused all night and then she spent the night, or rather day, and I'm in love, love, love!!!!! Anna dear, you will meet her soon enough, but until then, just imagine a small, slim, deliciously lovely gal with nice tits, perfect legs, and long straight red hair. She has flashing green eyes, and a huge brain, and she's so wickedly funny you can't imagine.

"So love to you and Juli. Hope all's well. Paul."

Sweeney put the letter down on the patio table. "He was having a manic episode," she said. "You can tell from the letter."

Down on the rocks the waves lapped tentatively, their hushed, watery tread a far away song.

"Sweeney, you big dope." Anna looked at her with sad eyes. "He was in love."

FORTY-ONE

❧

After the late night, Sweeney slept in until nearly nine. On her way to the bathroom across the hall, she saw Anna working in her studio and poked her head through the half open door.

"I'm a lazy niece."

"No, we were up late. You must have needed the sleep." Anna dabbed at a white dress on the canvas propped up on her easel.

"Snow White and Rose Red?" Sweeney asked, looking over her shoulder at the blond girl in a long white dress and her sister, a brunette, in a scarlet one.

"Yeah." Anna looked up, blinking as though she'd been in a trance. "There's coffee and toast in the kitchen."

"Thanks. I'm going to take a quick shower and then go down to the historical society. I'll see you tonight?"

"Sure. You won't mind if I don't make dinner, will you? I'm hoping to get this finished and I think I'll probably be at it most of the night."

"Course not. I'll find something in town."

Sweeney found Anna's copy of the *Newport Daily News* out in the newspaper box and read the update on Melissa Putnam's accident while she had her coffee.

"The investigation into a hit-and-run accident last night on Ocean Drive continues today as Newport residents express their gratitude that accident victim Melissa Putnam wasn't killed when she was struck while walking along Ocean Drive near her husband's family's Bellevue Avenue home.

"Putnam, thirty-four, had gone for a short walk, when she

was struck down sometime after nine P.M. Around ten P.M. Providence resident Michael Mabee, twenty-one, was returning to a friend's home on Harrison Avenue when he found Mrs. Putnam unconscious by the side of the road. He called 911 from his cell phone, and the victim was taken to Newport Hospital with facial lacerations and head injuries. She is in stable condition this morning at the hospital. Police will be questioning her today, according to a source."

Sweeney tried to picture Ocean Drive at night. There wasn't much of a shoulder and hardly any light; it would be very dangerous to walk there without a reflective vest or a flashlight. Sweeney had been to the Putnams' house. There was plenty of lawn to walk around on. So what had Melissa been doing up on Ocean Drive after nine?

She showered as best she could with Anna's spartan shower supplies, which consisted of an old bottle of Pert shampoo and a tiny bar of Ivory soap, and put on a red-polka-dotted sundress she'd found at a thrift shop, a white cardigan, and sandals, and walked down Bellevue Avenue toward the old part of town.

It was a brilliantly sunny day, the kind of early spring morning when the sunny side of the street is warm and the shade side is chilly. Sweeney was glad to be outside, and the sun and Anna's strong coffee gave the day a sense of promise and good fortune. She sensed that the answer to this mystery lay somewhere in Newport, somewhere in the winter of 1863. And she was going to figure out where.

The Newport Historical Society was located on Touro Street, just off Bellevue Avenue in the old part of town. It was fairly shabby inside, with a few offices for historical society employees and a small collection of paintings depicting various important Newport residents. But it wasn't really a place for the public to visit, and Sweeney was struck by how the functional interior contrasted with the historical society's public persona—the grand houses on Bellevue Avenue, owned by the historical society, and even the patrician exterior of the building.

She introduced herself to the harried-looking woman behind the desk and asked if there was anyone who specialized in the history of Newport in the 1860s. "I was wondering if you had any information on a woman named Belinda Putnam—Belinda Cogswell, her maiden name was—having been in Newport in the winter of 1863. I don't know where or what it would be, maybe a reference in a letter or something. She wasn't from here, but I think that her family may have started spending summers in Newport starting in the 1850s or so. I'm looking for any evidence that she came down here in the off-season.

"Oh, that's George you want," the woman said. "Hold on." She disappeared for a moment and came back with a middle-aged man dressed in bermuda shorts and a "Newport Mansions" T-shirt. He looked up shyly as Sweeney explained what she wanted.

"It's interesting, you know," the man said. "How Newport developed as a summer destination. We had our heyday in the 1750s, before the British occupation during the Revolutionary War. We fell on hard times after the war, of course, but it was as a summer destination that we had our second heyday. It had always been the custom for wealthy Southern plantation owners to bring their families up in the summer months. The air was considered healthier and they were familiar with the area because they had been up for the slave markets. But Easterners didn't come until the mid-1800s. Our first tourist hotel was built in the 1820s and then more went up in the 1840s. That was when Newport became a destination for Boston intellectuals."

"That's when I imagine Belinda Cogswell's family started coming," Sweeney said.

"Well, let's see. I have an index of some of the material we have here, but I don't know that we'll come up with any thing." He went to a brand-new Macintosh on the desk and started typing.

"Well, we've got a lot of references to the Putnams, of course. Let's see, B. . . . B. Belinda. There's one reference but it doesn't look promising. It just says gift to Newport Ladies' Society. 1880. That's much later than you're looking for, isn't it?"

"Yeah. What was the gift?"

"A set of framed sketches. By the donor, it says. But there's . note that says the Ladies' Society gave them back to the amily in the 1950s when they lost their meetinghouse."

"Hmmm. What about under Belinda Cogswell?" Sweeney .sked.

"Cogswell, Cogswell. I've got Nathaniel Cogswell, but no 3elinda."

"That's okay. It's kind of a long shot anyway. Is there any hance that there's material that isn't cataloged?"

"Well . . . I suppose if there was a reference to her that vasn't indexed, maybe because her name wasn't used, or vasn't correct. I don't know." He took a stack of books down rom a shelf. "You can look through these if you want. I'm orry we can't be more helpful."

"No, no. I think you might be on to something." Of course. he wouldn't have used her name, would she, if she were hid- ng out, waiting to deliver her baby? "Is there a place I could pread out a bit?"

"Sure." Carrying the books for her, he showed her into an mpty office and pulled the desk chair out for her. "Take your ime, and let me know if there's anything else you need."

"Thanks." He shut the door behind him and Sweeney took uick stock of the books he'd given her. There were a couple of eneral histories of Newport, published by academic presses, nd then one trade history with a picture of the Viking Hotel on he front cover, *Newport: America's Summer Holiday*.

The histories proved useless, but she was more hopeful bout the summer vacation spot book.

Sweeney started searching the index for anything vaguely elated to the Putnams. When she struck out there, she earched the chapter titles, and chose a few that looked prom- sing that focused on the building of the big tourist hotels rom the 1840s on.

But there wasn't anything on the off-season, and Sweeney lidn't find any references to a woman, pregnant or otherwise, vho came to Newport in the winter of 1863.

She looked through the last of the books and, striking out

again, leaned back in her chair and looked around the little o
fice. The walls were covered with posters advertising the Nev
port mansions, Rosecliff and Marble House and The Breaker
and The Elms. The room had mostly been cleared out but the
were a few books and papers lying around. As she looked
them, Sweeney decided that the former inhabitant of the offi
must have been interested in the history of African-America
in Newport. Sweeney had always been interested in this aspe
of Newport's history too. She knew that the town had had a su
stantial population of African-Americans before the Civil W
and then more had moved to the town to work in the burgeonir
tourist trade. There had been black hotels and boardinghous
and many black institutions had sprung up in town, beauty pa
lors and restaurants and banks.

It gave her an idea.

"Can I ask you something?" George was working in his o
fice again and he looked up when she poked her head in.
didn't find anything at the fancy places, but I'm wonderir
about the less fancy places. There must have been boardin
houses for the people who worked at the big hotels. Plac
that were more out of the way. Do you have any informatic
about those?"

George grinned. "I've always found that part of Newport
history interesting. Unfortunately, most of what we've got c
the workers' residences is either self-published or in man
script form." He winked. "The tourists aren't interested
glossy coffee table books unless they have pictures of t
Vanderbilts' living room. But I'll get you what we've got c
the boardinghouses."

He reached up and took a selection of thin books and pan
phlets down from his bookshelf and handed them to Sweene
"Have fun."

She skimmed three or four of the books in the pile, readi
about the cramped and drafty budget hotels and apartme
buildings where the people who served the summer residen
of Newport lived, before she came to a small book unimag
natively titled *An Interesting Life: Recollections of
Boardinghouse Owner*. The text was a transcription of an or

history recorded in the 1920s, and had been self-published a few years before as part of a series on African-American life in Newport. The boardinghouse owner, one Harold J. Johnson, had a bland and unappealing storytelling style, and it was a tough slog through the accounts of "interesting" guests (none of whom seemed the least bit interesting to Sweeney) who had stayed at the boardinghouse over the years.

She was about to put it back when she came upon a chapter titled "A Mysterious Visitor" and was finally rewarded with what she had been looking for all along. "In December 1863," Harold J. Johnson recounted, "we had a curious event at the boardinghouse that I have never forgotten. I had just gone to bed when I heard knocking at the door and a young woman, who appeared to be with child, though not heavily so, appeared on my doorstep and asked if she could have a room.

"I looked at her and asked if she was in the right place and she said, 'Sir, I assume you are referring to the color of my skin. I can only tell you that this is the only place I feel I can come. I will ask you not to make much of it.'

"Well, we had never had a white woman stay before and I was concerned about how she would find our little boardinghouse. But she seemed quite comfortable and she settled in, telling me she wanted to stay for about three months. On the third day, she took me aside and asked me if I could do her a great favor. If anyone came looking for her, she said, would it be possible for me to pretend that she was not here. She did not think this would happen, she said, because it was unlikely that it should be guessed that this is where she was staying.

"It never came to pass that I had to tell my lie, for which I was exceedingly grateful. She lived with us unmolested for the three months, as she grew heavier and heavier with child.

"In all this time, she never told us what she was fleeing. Every once in a while, she would post a letter—to London, I saw when she asked me to post them for her once—but she seemed not to have any contact with anyone, other than the letters."

"Finally, in the third month of her stay, one of the chambermaids heard her moaning in her room and went in to see what was the matter. She found her in the throes of childbirth and asked if she could send for a doctor. But the lady said that she did not want a doctor. I sent my wife, who had some experience with childbirth, and my wife helped the lady to deliver a healthy baby, a boy. She stayed with us for two weeks more, hardly ever venturing out of the boardinghouse, and we all became quite attached to the little boy, who she called Eddie.

"I will not ever forget this strange episode in the history of Johnson's boardinghouse. I never asked the lady her name, but the day she left, I told her that I wanted to remember her and her little son and I will never forget what she told me.

" 'You can call me Hatty Hope,' she said. And that is how I have always thought of her."

Sweeney sat back in the chair, her heart thudding, her stomach suddenly queasy. It was what she'd been hoping she would find—proof that Belinda Putnam had come down to Newport in the winter of 1863 and carried out exactly the kind of subterfuge that Sweeney had pictured.

Those letters to London suggested something like what Sweeney had suspected all along. She must have told her family that she was going to London for her confinement, but instead had gone down to Newport, a place she knew well. She had posted letters to someone she knew in London, who in turn posted them back to her family in Boston, and no one was the wiser.

She must have written a letter in December, announcing the birth of the child. How had she done so without knowing what sex the child would be? Had she taken her chances and assumed it would be a boy? There were old wives' tales about these kinds of things. How the pregnant woman was carrying, how hungry she was. It had been an audacious act. But of course the alternative was much worse and people had done far crazier things out of desperation, Sweeney thought.

And if anybody secretly thought that the baby looked younger than he should when she returned home, people would have been willing to let it go and believe her story.

Still shaking, she replaced the books on the shelf and

brought the stack of books that George had given her back out into the main office.

He was bent over a file cabinet, flipping through index cards and when Sweeney said, "Thanks so much for these," he stood up too quickly and knocked his head on the top file cabinet drawer, which was pulled out. The file cards he'd left sitting on top of it fluttered to the ground.

"Ow!"

"I'm sorry," she said. "I didn't mean to startle you."

"No, no. Oh, you can just put them on that desk. Did you find anything?"

"Not really," Sweeney said, feeling guilty. "There's some interesting stuff there, but not exactly what I was looking for."

"Well," he said, still rubbing his head. "I took the liberty of going through our cemetery records. We got a grant a few years ago to catalog everyone buried in cemeteries within Newport city limits. It's not computerized yet, but we've got a nice card index, and I found an entry for Belinda Cogswell Putnam. 1840–1925. That's her, right?"

"Yes, it has to be. Thank you so much!" Sweeney could hardly believe her luck. He handed the card over and she copied down the name of the cemetery, the Island Cemetery, one she knew well, and copied out the little grid that someone had photocopied onto the card, as well as the little star indicating where the stone was located. "You can't imagine how helpful this is. I was planning on walking around every cemetery between here and Boston and just looking for it."

"No problem," he said. "That's Putnam as in Putnam, right?" Sweeney nodded. "I just heard about the hit-and-run. That poor family. As if they hadn't been through enough, huh?"

"Yeah. Well, thanks for this. I'm going to walk up there right now and see if I can find it."

He blinked at her. The bump on his forehead was starting to show. "Feel free to come back and visit," he said shyly. "Anytime."

She hadn't been up to the Island Cemetery—the biggest on the island and where most of the residents of Newport would find their final resting place—in years, and she was surprised at how surrounded it was now by the residential neighborhoods. The cemetery was virtually packed in by the small houses that seemed a world away from the ones on the other side of town. It had been a good twenty-minute walk and by the time she arrived, Sweeney was damp with perspiration. She sat on the bench just inside the gates and looked out across the city of stone.

The cemetery was well-cared for, with rose gardens and perennial beds near the entrance gates and well-trimmed grass around the stones. There were a lot of modern stones as well as older ones, many with wilted bouquets left at their bases.

She consulted the little grid and counted out the stones as she walked down the right row. It was a white marble headstone, somewhat stained with age but still gleaming brightly in the afternoon light, a slim rectangle with a simple garland of roses along the top. The inscription read simply, "Belinda Cogswell Putnam. 1840–1925." It did not say anywhere that she had been the wife of Charles Putnam or the mother of Edmund Putnam and for some reason Sweeney felt that that was exactly the point of this simple, lovely stone.

Below her name and the dates of her life, the epitaph read only "To help one's fellow man is truly divine."

With this simple stone, Belinda Putnam had exiled herself in death, away from her family, away from family privilege, away from the benefits of her family name. Sweeney tried to imagine. If Edmund had been illegitimate, perhaps she had felt guilty, unworthy of being buried next to her husband. But wouldn't she have asked that her son be buried near to her? It didn't really make sense. Sweeney made some sketches of the stone and stared at it awhile longer before heading back toward town.

She was almost back to Anna's when her cell phone buzzed in the pocket of her dress.

"Hello?"

"Sweeney? Tim Quinn." Static crackled his voice.

"Hi. Has something happened?"

"No, no. I just got the results back from the DNA tests. I wanted to let you know."

"Oh, that's okay. Were you able to prove—?"

But he cut her off, his voice businesslike and short. "Actually, I think you're going to be disappointed. We tested the hair in the locket and Charles Putnam *is* related to Brad Putnam. I think there must have been some mistake about the date on the brooch."

"But . . ." She hadn't realized until now just how much she was counting on proof of her suspicions. "Are they sure? There must be some kind of mistake."

"Yes, they're sure." She heard voices in the background.

"But I found this book, at the historical society. I think that Belinda must have come down here in the winter of 1863 and she must have—"

"I'm sorry, I have to go." He sounded annoyed.

"But it doesn't make sense!"

"I'm sorry. I know you were counting on this. But I have to go."

"Wait, I wanted to tell you that I talked to some of my students and they said that Brad didn't take any drugs the night he died. I just wanted to let you know."

"Yes, thanks. We're looking at something else now. And I really do have to go. Good-bye." The phone went dead.

Dumbfounded, she put it away. But she had proof! She knew that Belinda had been in Newport and she knew that she had stayed until March. There was no other explanation for it. How could Brad share DNA with Charles Putnam if Edmund Putnam wasn't Charles's son? It didn't make any sense.

The only way it made sense was that she had been wrong about everything, that the murder had nothing to do with the Putnam family, that it had in fact been an anonymous person who had come into Brad's apartment and found him tied up and killed him. That must have been what Quinn meant when he said that he was looking at something new.

She let it settle in. She had been wrong. She had made a big deal out of something that had nothing to do with Brad's murder. She had wasted Quinn's time and perhaps hurt the investigation.

Disheartened, she walked back along Thames Street, wandering in and out of bookshops and the posh little boutiques that supplied well-heeled summer residents with beachwear and beach reading. Attempting to console herself, she stopped for an egg salad sandwich at a little deli by the water, and read the *Globe* while she ate.

She had just stood up to go and was putting her things back in her bag when someone touched her arm and said, "I thought that was you. You're distinctive, even from a distance."

The blue eyes were like granite under the shade of the deli's awning. She hadn't seen Jack Putnam or talked to him since the night at his apartment.

"What are you doing down here?" he asked when she didn't say anything. He put a hand up to his forehead to shield his eyes from the low afternoon sun. In a pair of old Hawaiian print swim trunks and a faded blue T-shirt, he looked younger than she'd ever seen him, though he still seemed pale under his tan, and his eyes were still tired.

"Visiting Anna. What about you?"

"We all came down to be with Drew. You heard about Melissa?"

"Yeah. I'm so sorry," Sweeney said. "I was thinking about all of you. How is she?"

"It looks like she's going to be okay. She doesn't look great, and she doesn't remember anything, but she was pretty lucky."

There was an awkward silence and finally Sweeney said, "Well, I guess I should be getting home."

"Okay, well. Good to see you." His hand rested on her arm for a moment and she felt her heart speed up.

She'd turned away and had walked a block down Thames Street when he came running up behind her, saying, "Just . . . Sweeney, just hold on a second," taking her hand and pulling her into one of the little side alleys that led down to the waterfront. "I've been wanting to talk about what happened that night I ran into you at the gallery. I called a few times and I should have tried again, but I was afraid you'd hang up on me."

"I'm sorry I told the police."

"No, it's my fault. I shouldn't have put you in that position. And I shouldn't have lied. It just seemed like it would make things so much easier for Cammie."

Sweeney nodded. They were standing very close together and he was still holding her hand.

"Look," he said, "why don't you come over for dinner tonight?"

"I don't know . . ."

"Please," he said. "I've been secretly hoping that I'd run into you. I wanted to explain about everything. I feel like you've seen the absolute worst of me. Hardly a way to start off a relationship."

They were standing against a brick wall and she put a hand back to steady herself, feeling the roughness. "Is that what this is?"

"It's a possible relationship, don't you think?"

"Jack, I . . ." She had been about to tell him that they couldn't know what it was until things were more normal, until all of the immediate aftermath of Brad's death had passed, but as she looked up at him, she realized that she had been thinking about him, nearly every day since the last time she'd seen him, that a part of her had been hoping she'd run into him too. "Are your sure your family wants company?"

"Yes," he said. "My dad's coming down and we'd love to have you. Please?"

Sweeney smiled. "Okay, okay," she said. "What time should I come?"

FORTY-TWO

"How about this one? I think it's Pucci," Anna was saying as she held up an orange and red shift that Sweeney vaguely remembered her wearing in old family pictures.

"No. The color's bad on me. And you're much tinier than I am."

"Yeah?" Anna held it up. "Maybe. Let's see what else is here."

They were up in the attic, going through the hanging cedar wardrobes where Anna's discarded dresses and skirts hung alongside those that had belonged to Sweeney's grandmother. Sweeney stood hunched over under the low eaves, snuffling from the dust, and looking at each neglected outfit that Anna took out and held up.

"What do you think everyone else will be wearing?" Sweeney asked.

"How should I know? You know when the last time I went out to dinner was?" Anna considered, and rejected, a Victorian-looking lace dress, with a high neck and puffy sleeves.

"But what do you think?"

"Why are you so nervous?" Anna, who was holding a floor-length madras patchwork skirt, looked up at Sweeney, studying her shrewdly.

"I don't know. Just because it's the Putnams. It's the house and Newport and everything, I think."

"But you went to the wedding and you were okay, right?"

"Yeah, but I had Toby with me. Toby makes everything easier."

"Oh," Anna said heavily.

Sweeney flipped through the clothes and pulled out a navy blue sleeveless dress. "Look at this. It's silk," she said, holding it out to Anna.

"That's pretty. I remember Mother wearing that. Try it on. She was tall, like you."

Sweeney unzipped her sundress and stepped out of it, then stepped into the blue dress, letting Anna zip up the back. The silk rustled against her skin and she smoothed the front. "What do you think?"

"You know what? It actually looks great." Anna led her over to an old oval dressing mirror in one corner of the attic. "Can you see?"

Sweeney stood in front of the mirror. It was forties' day dress, with a little waist that hugged her own and a knee-length skirt. "I like it," she said. "Is it okay to wear it?"

"Of course."

"You don't think I'll be overdressed?"

Anna rolled her eyes. "Sweeney, I really don't know."

Sweeney stood in front of the mirror, inspecting her pores in the low light. "Oh God, why am I going? I don't even want to go. It's going to be awful."

"No, it's not. It'll be fun. You should get out and mix. That's what Mother always said to me. 'You should mix.' I always had this image of a bunch of people in a blender. She didn't know what to do with me. All I wanted to do was paint."

"Poor Grandmother and Grandfather. Ending up with two crazy artists."

"I know. I think it was part of why I was so willing to put my own work aside for Juli's for so long. I always felt as though I was letting them down. And Paul, because he was older, had sort of got first dibs on letting them down. I wasn't allowed." Sweeney could hear the bitterness in Anna's voice. She didn't say anything.

Anna pulled out a large pink dress and held it against her body.

'Oh God, look at this," she said. "This must have been one

of Mother's maternity dresses. Can you imagine. Women had to wear such awful things back then." The dress was a soft, baby pink color and it had a Peter Pan collar with little pink flowers embroidered on it.

Sweeney watched Anna holding the dress up in front of her. "How come you and Uncle Juli never had kids?" she asked.

Anna folded the dress in half and laid it down on an old bed.

"I never really found out why. There was something wrong with one of us, but we never knew who. In those days you didn't go to doctors about it the way you do now.

"I always wondered if it was my fault, if somehow, psychologically I kept myself from getting pregnant, if I was ambivalent about it. You know, it would have been hard with our lifestyle. I don't think Juli would have liked staying home on Saturday night because we couldn't find a baby-sitter, or you know, all the nursery things. He liked the idea of it, but the reality would have been a shock."

"Did he ever . . . with . . . ?"

"With Stella? No. So perhaps it was a problem with him."

Sweeney watched Anna's face. "Do you think about it? Now?"

"Sometimes. Not that often. Still, it was hard. People ask you, you know. It's amazing how rude they can be. 'When are you going to have a baby? Don't you want kids?' Things like that. I remember that it got really hard for a while to be around our friends who had kids. I'd see people on the street pushing strollers and I'd think, 'If any idiot can get pregnant, why can't I?' " Anna closed the wardrobe door and gestured for Sweeney to turn around so she could unzip her.

Sweeney stepped out of the dress and got back into her clothes.

Anna reached up to find the cord for the light. "But it was just as well, in the end, wasn't it?" she said. "The way things worked out?"

Together, they walked down the stairs.

FORTY-THREE

was just dark when she pulled into the Putnams' driveway
nd in the late spring evening light she could better see the
eauty of the house than she had on her last visit. Approach-
g it up the long drive, the rooflines stood out against the blue
nd yellow sky, gesturing toward the crashing waves beyond.
he lawn stretched steeply down toward the water. Sweeney
lt dizzy, as though she'd stood up too fast.

Her knock on the front door sounded pathetically quiet, but
ne tried once again before rapping harder, her knuckles
marting against the wood. In her other hand she held the
lips she and Anna had picked and wrapped in wet paper tow-
s and tin foil. Pressed and smelling of the lavender water
nna had found in a cupboard, the silk dress felt smooth and
ol against her skin.

When there was still no answer, she went around the side of
e house. Like many of the Newport cottages, Cliff House
d more lawn than garden, and she followed the stretch of
osely cut grass around to a wide stone patio at the back of
e house. A set of steps led from the patio down to a kidney-
aped swimming pool lined with dark green tile. Four
aise-longues lazed emptily next to the pool. At one end of
e lawn, looking out over the ocean and flanked by the three
lden retrievers, was the slumped figure of Paddy Sheehan,
s hands dangling over the side of the wheelchair.

Sweeney looked around. There was no one else outside, so
e walked over to the chair and leaned down. "Hello, Mr.
eehan."

He started—he had been asleep, she realized—and the dog jumped to their feet, excitedly wagging around Sweeney's legs. "I'm sorry," she said. "I didn't mean to wake you up, I was just looking for Jack. Do you know where he is?"

Paddy Sheehan's eyes met hers and he said, "What, what" as his hands grasped at the wheels of the chair.

"I'm sorry. I was just looking for Jack. I'm Sweeney St. George."

His arms relaxed over the edges of the chair again and he said accusingly, "You were at the house. Are you a friend of my grandson?"

"I was Brad's professor," Sweeney said.

"He was a good boy," Paddy Sheehan said. "He liked to catch crabs. He'd put the line in the water and sit there for hours. He was patient. Patient, you know."

"Yes," she said. "I liked him very much."

"He was a good boy." Paddy Sheehan stared out over the water, as though he'd forgotten she was there.

"I know." She wasn't sure what to do. "I was very sorry."

Suddenly, Paddy Sheehan looked up at her and said, "They think I can't hear what they're saying, but I do. I hear everything. I hear what they're talking about. I hear the fighting."

"Fighting?"

"Too much yelling. They don't know I can hear them."

Searching fruitlessly for a way out of the conversation, Sweeney was relieved to look up and find Jack, dressed in khakis and another old T-shirt, coming across the lawn to meet them. She was instantly self-conscious. The dress was too much.

"You made it," he called out. "Is Paddy monopolizing you out here?"

Sweeney let him kiss her and then she put on the cardigan she'd tied around her waist.

"Cold?" Jack asked, handing her one of the beers. She shook her head and he said, "Come on inside and say hi to everyone. You ready to come in, Paddy?"

Paddy Sheehan didn't say anything, but Jack took the hanlles of the wheelchair and pushed him across the grass toward he house.

They entered the house through a set of French doors at ne end of the patio. Sweeney had lost her bearings and vasn't sure where in the house they were until Jack led her hrough a huge formal dining room papered in arts and crafts ines and full of dark, mission furniture. A few watercolors of cean scenes hung along the walls, but they hardly competed vith the view of the Atlantic through the large windows gainst the back wall. The room had once been formal, but ow the table was covered with piles of mail and everything)oked slightly worn and battered, the upholstery faded, the rood dull.

They came into a big, old-fashioned kitchen, complete ith a huge butcher block island in the center and bathtub-zed sink against one wall. Sweeney could almost imagine hite-aproned Victorian servants preparing the family's meal. ut the kitchen had been updated with a shining restaurant-ality stove and a giant Subzero fridge, and it was Kitty who ood at the butcher block island rolling out piecrust when ey came into the kitchen. Melissa and Camille were sitting a big round kitchen table, peeling and coring a pile of ranny Smith apples in the center of the table. When Melissa oked up to greet her, Sweeney had to fight to keep her face apassive, to keep from staring at Melissa's bruised and raded face, her forehead a mess of red scratches, one cheek ained with purple.

Sweeney handed the tulips to Kitty as Drew came in. He id hello to Sweeney, got a beer out of the refrigerator, and anced at Melissa with a concerned expression on his face. It is the first time Sweeney had seen him out of a suit and she is struck by how much heavier he looked in khakis and an ford cloth shirt. His suits must have been expertly tailored disguise his girth.

Kitty smiled. "Oh, they're beautiful. My favorite. Jack, can u put them in water?" She handed them to her son. "Jack d that you're down visiting some family."

"Yeah, my aunt."

"What's her name?" The green skin of an apple unwo[u]
expertly from the white flesh under Camille's knife.

"Anna Schniemann."

"Oh, so you're . . ." Kitty looked up. "You must be Pa[ddy's]
daughter."

"Yes."

"Oh . . ." Her eyes darted quickly from Sweeney to [her]
son. "No, use the crystal vase, Jack. Crystal's nice w[ith]
tulips."

"How are you feeling, Melissa?" Sweeney asked her. "[I'm]
so glad you're okay."

"A little sore." She looked up.

Kitty smiled. "We're so grateful that it wasn't more se[ri-]
ous." She gasped. "Oh, Andrew." They all looked up to f[ind]
Andrew Putnam standing in the doorway, holding his o[wn]
bouquet of tulips—white and long-stemmed and far more e[le-]
gant than Sweeney's bunch of multicolored blooms. [He]
smiled shyly at Kitty.

"Hey, Dad," Camille said, getting up and giving him a h[ug.]
She glanced from her mother to her father, who were still s[tar-]
ing at each other.

"How's our next congresswoman?" Andrew asked, turn[ing]
to his daughter.

"Tired," she said. "This is the first relaxing thing I've d[one]
in weeks."

"Don't be so sure," Andrew said. "We may ask you [to]
stump after dinner." He handed the bouquet to Kitty, [but]
didn't touch her. "It looks like someone else knows you l[ike]
tulips."

"Those are from Sweeney," Kitty said nervously, bef[ore]
unwrapping them next to the sink and poking them into [the]
vase alongside Sweeney's tulips.

Andrew shook Sweeney's hand and nodded at Drew a[nd]
Jack and Paddy before kissing Melissa on the cheek. "H[ow]
are you, dear?" he asked. "We were so worried." Meli[ssa]
flinched when his lips touched her forehead.

Kitty set the vase in the middle of the table. "There, [that]
looks nice, doesn't it?" But the effect wasn't right. The flow[ers]

were all different heights and the long-stemmed tulips drooped precariously over the edges of the too-small vase. They all watched as one of them bowed toward the table and the stem snapped in half. The head lolled obscenely, scattering pollen on the table.

They had dinner in the kitchen, everyone sitting around the big round table, the dogs lying on the floor and hoping for pieces of roast chicken. The sky was growing dark and over the water, the clouds were gathering darkly too. A chilled breeze came through the half-open screen, and Sweeney shivered in her thin dress.

"Should we eat in the dining room?" Andrew had asked tentatively, after taking the white tulips out of the vase and finding a taller one for them.

Kitty, clearly uncomfortable, had almost snapped at him. "I hate the dining room. It's better in here." So Sweeney and Camille had made up the table with place mats and now they all sat in silence and watched Drew carve.

There were roasted carrots with the chicken and Camille had made a big green salad.

"This is great, Mom," Jack said. Awkwardly, everyone else murmured that the food was delicious. From across the table, Camille met Sweeney's eyes.

Drew looked across the table at his brother. "How's the show going, Jack?"

"Good. Sold a couple pieces." Jack got up and went to the refrigerator to get another beer for himself and one for Sweeney. Kitty watched him as he returned to the table.

"People buy that crazy stuff?" Camille grinned and Sweeney had the sense that they were acting out some kind of childhood ritual.

"They buy your b.s.," Jack said. "Why not mine?" Everyone laughed, but there was something oddly edgy in his voice.

"I saw the plans you sent over, Drew," Andrew said. "Everything looks good."

"That's right. How are the plans for Yuppieville coming along?" Jack asked. He turned to Sweeney. "Remember how I

told you that we have these other buildings near mine in th
Back Bay? Drew wants to turn them into a yuppie paradise."

Sweeney met Camille's eyes across the table.

"It's on hold," Drew said. "It's going to be too expensive t
repair the buildings so we can go ahead with the construction."

"But you knew those buildings were damaged during th
drilling for the tunnel," Camille said innocently. "And it wa
worth it to you to fix them before, right?"

"Yeah, but when we went in and did the inspections, w
found all kinds of asbestos. I just heard yesterday. It wou
cost a fortune to remove it. We'd be better off tearing th
houses down, but there are historic preservation issue
Maybe some day we'll do it, but not right now.

"As it is," Drew continued, taking a bite of his chicke
"Grandfather Putnam made out like a bandit. If the tunn
drilling hadn't damaged the buildings, he would have had
spend millions on the removal. I doubt whether it would hav
been worth it. But because of the damage, he got the insu
ance and laughed all the way to the bank."

Paddy Sheehan, who had been completely silent during th
meal, said, "I'll say he did."

Everyone looked at him.

"Paddy and my other grandfather served in the Senate t
gether," Jack told Sweeney as he got up to get himself anoth
beer. The refrigerator closed with a loud click.

"Jack," Kitty said. "Haven't you had enough?"

Jack turned to look at her, the beer in his hand, but Pad
was saying, "You know who worked for him back then? Ge
DiFloria. Gerry DiFloria!" He cackled, then took a noisy b
of chicken, his hand shaking.

Camille looked up at her grandfather. "What do y
mean?"

Paddy cackled again. "He was the aide on the transpor
tion committee. Those two were thick as thieves."

"That's right. He was the aide on the . . . ?" Sweeney s
Camille look up as they both had the same realization.

"He was pretty shrewd, my old man," Andrew sa

Sweeney watched as he and Camille exchanged glances across the table.

Camille's face was tight. "Yes," she said. "He was. I'm sorry. I just remembered a call I have to make. Can I be excused?"

Kitty looked confused. "Of course. Is everything okay?"

"Yeah, I just . . . a campaign thing." Camille stood up and she met Sweeney's eyes again before she left the room.

Sweeney watched Kitty's eyes follow her daughter.

"Well, I'm going to get up and clear some of this stuff away." Kitty stood up suddenly.

Andrew jumped to his feet. "I'll help you," he said. "Paddy, you doing okay?"

"I think I'm about ready for bed."

"I'll take him up and then help you in the kitchen," Andrew said. "Why don't you guys all go sit on the patio. We'll come out when we're done."

They took their drinks out on the patio and as soon as they were out of earshot, Drew turned to Jack and raised his eyebrows.

"I know," Jack said. "What's going on there?"

"He came down by himself," Melissa told them. "A week or so ago. She mentioned something about it and then blushed when she realized what she'd said."

Jack said to Sweeney, "It's pretty weird to suspect your own parents of sneaking around behind your back."

"Do you think they're going to get back together?" she asked.

"I don't know. They've seen each other more in the last couple of weeks than they have since they split up."

"They never got divorced," Melissa said. "I always thought that was telling. If they wanted to get divorced, why didn't they just do it?"

Drew looked at her. "You don't know anything about it," he said harshly.

"It's kind of sad, though, isn't it?" Jack said, trying to get them past the awkward moment. "The way he follows her around like a puppy dog. If they're not rekindling the ro-

mance, I hope she lets him down easy." He took Sweene
hand and held it in his lap.

"Do we know your parents, Sweeney?" Melissa ask
brightly. "I didn't realize until Kitty said it that you summe
here too." What she was really saying was that Sweeney did
seem like the kind of person who would summer in Newp
and Sweeney felt a rush of anger.

"Yes, what was the big mystery?" Drew asked. "Did D
have a feud with your father or something?"

"Were they St. George? Like you?" Melissa's express
was cheerful.

Jack looked uncomfortable.

"My father was Paul St. George," Sweeney said, keepi
Drew in her steady gaze. "He was an artist."

Suddenly Drew realized and he looked down at the tab
But Melissa had already started saying, "The one who . . .

"Yeah," Sweeney said. "The one who killed himself. A
my mother's the one who got kicked out of Bailey's Beach
getting drunk and taking off her top."

Melissa gave kind of a strangled laugh. Her mouth wa
round "o."

"Well, God," Drew said, as though there wasn't anythi
else to say. "That's quite a family."

"Yeah," Sweeney said, trying to smile.

"You know who I ran into today?" Jack asked his broth
glancing nervously at Sweeney. "Sam Healy. Rememl
him?" He downed half of the beer he was drinking in a sin
gulp.

"Oh yeah. What's he up to? Didn't he get married to t
woman you went to art school with?"

"Yeah. Trish something."

There was a long silence.

Sweeney excused herself to go to the bathroom and o
she'd found the little powder room off the patio, she splash
cold water on her face and tried to calm down. All she wan
to do was leave, but she felt like it would be rude. So she dr
her face and stepped out into the hallway. Melissa Putnam v

waiting there to use the bathroom. She brushed past Sweeney, looking embarrassed.

"Wait a second. Can I talk to you?" Sweeney asked her.

Melissa looked surprised. "Sure. Of course."

"I never got to talk to you after you left me that message. What was it you wanted to tell me?"

Melissa flushed. "Oh," she said. "I'm sorry about that. It was silly of me. There was something I realized, but I think I was wrong."

"Are you sure?"

Melissa's eyes were wide and she looked from side to side to make sure that no one was listening. "Just forget it," she said. "It's really not a big deal."

"Melissa, I . . . I just feel like you should be careful. If someone did try to hit you on purpose, they might try again."

"Sweeney." She smiled. "That's ridiculous. No one's going to try to kill me."

"Do you remember anything about the accident?"

"I told them. The last thing I remember is that I couldn't sleep and I went for a walk. That's all it was. And thanks, but it isn't any of your business anyways. I have to go to the bathroom. Leave me alone."

In the hallway, Sweeney stood for a moment, shaking with anger again. She was happy to leave Melissa alone. She was happy to leave all the Putnams alone.

When she got back to the table, Drew and Jack were talking about their parents again. "It's so obvious," Jack was saying as he opened another beer. "I don't know why he doesn't just tell her and get it over with."

Sweeney didn't sit down. "I think I'm going to go. It's late and I should be getting back tomorrow morning. Please tell your parents I said thank you." She nodded at Drew. "Good to see you."

"But it's only ten," Jack said, looking up at her. "You don't want to go yet."

"I do actually. Good night." She started walking across the lawn toward the driveway.

"Wait, Sweeney," Jack called out behind her. "Hang on." But she kept walking. She heard the gravel of the driveway crunch under her feet as he caught up and reached for her arm. "Are you okay? What's the matter?"

"Nothing's the matter. I'm just tired and I want to go to bed." She found her keys and got in, starting the car and buckling her seat belt.

But he was still holding the door open. "Is it what Drew said? I don't get why you . . . Have dinner with me. Tomorrow. Just the two of us. Let's just talk and drink and not think about anything, not about my family or your family or anybody's family. Okay?"

"I'm just tired, Jack. I have to go now." She shut the door, eased the Rabbit into reverse, and started backing away. Her heart was pounding, but she kept her eyes fixed on the driveway in her rearview mirror, even when she glanced up and saw him standing there, alone in front of the looming profile of the house.

FORTY-FOUR

❧

When Sweeney came in, Anna was still awake, sitting at the kitchen table and reading the paper. Sweeney nodded at her, went upstairs to change into jeans and a sweatshirt, and came down again, pouring two glasses of white wine and handing one to Anna without a word.

"So what happened tonight?"

"What do you mean?"

"Something must have happened tonight. Otherwise you'd be drinking wine with Jack Putnam instead of me."

Anna watched her.

"I don't know," Sweeney said finally. "I was over there and they figured out who I was . . . I mean, who *we* are. About Paul and Ivy. Besides, it was a really strange evening. There was all this tension."

"Why did you always insist on calling him Paul? It drove him crazy, you know?"

"They found out about the thing at Bailey's Beach and when they figured out about Paul, it was like . . . it was humiliating," Sweeney said, ignoring the question.

Anna sat back in her chair. "I never understood why that thing at Bailey's Beach embarrassed you so much. So she got drunk and took off her bikini top. Hell, it was the most exciting thing that happened there since Doris Duke came out of the water in her see-through bathing suit. Sweeney"—she started laughing—"it's funny. Can't you see that?"

"I don't think it's funny." Sweeney started to get up.

"Sweeney, sit down and look at me."

Sweeney frowned, but did as she was told and when she looked at Anna, her aunt crossed her eyes. Sweeney smiled, then tried to keep herself from laughing, and found she couldn't.

"So what's going on with your mystery?" Anna asked. "You solved Brad Putnam's murder yet?"

"No. I don't think I've solved any mysteries at all." She told Anna about the jewelry and about Belinda Putnam.

"I was sure that I'd figured it out, but the DNA test wouldn't lie. If the baby was a blood relative of Charles Putnam, then how could it have been born more than nine months after his death? Nowadays, I suppose there would be artificial insemination and all that, but in 1863?"

"Doesn't sound possible to me," Anna agreed.

"It isn't. And what it has to do with Brad's murder, or with Melissa Putnam's attempted murder, I don't have any idea. I'm no clearer on any of it than the day the police called me in to tell them about the jewelry, thinking it had been left by a ritual killer."

"I wish I could help you," Anna said. "But I'm afraid all this detective stuff isn't really my forte."

After Anna had gone to bed, Sweeney went out into the garden, sipping her wine and thinking about their conversation. It was almost one and she was feeling restless and antsy, so she decided to take a short walk along the Cliff Walk before going up to read. It technically closed at sundown, but there was a bit of light from the moon and she was able to hop over the fence easily. She strolled along, enjoying the cool breeze and the darkness. She'd be going back to Boston tomorrow and there wouldn't be any more reason for her to be involved with any of the Putnams. She had looked into the jewelry. That was what she had set out to do. There wasn't anything more for her to find out.

Her mind felt clearer out here and she replayed her conversation with Anna. "And what it has to do with Brad's murder, or with Melissa Putnam's attempted murder, I don't have any idea," she'd said to her aunt. Brad's murder. She had a sudden involuntary image of him, lying on the bed, his arms bound, the bag obscuring his handsome face, the jewelry wound around him like strange snakes. Wait. There was something there, something in that image that interested her. She stopped for a moment on the path, thinking. The jewelry. The jewelry. And then she had an image of Melissa Putnam, her bruised and battered face.

"Sweeney," she'd said. "That's ridiculous. No one's going to try to kill me."

But there was something . . . the jewelry. Wait. Oh God. She had to get back to Cliff House.

She stopped and looked up at the bank of earth to her right. She was almost to the Marble House and the first tunnel. If she were to go back to Anna's and get the Rabbit, it would be a good twenty minutes before she was at the house. But she was nearly there, almost to the point in the Cliff Walk where it met up with the Putnams' property. If she could just get over the hedge, she'd be there in a few minutes.

She ran, checking for the house as she went, and when she'd reached it, she stood for a moment, watching the long expanse of lawn. There was no one outside, as far as she could tell, so she hauled herself up over the hedge, scratching her leg, and fell onto the lawn. She lay there for a moment, getting her breath, listening to the pounding of the surf far below.

The house was luminous at night, the pale stone absorbing the moonlight; everything around it seemed darker by comparison. Sweeney looked up at the black windows.

The swimming pool lights were on and they shone green up through the water, casting a strange light up against the house.

FORTY-FIVE

Quinn and Marino had been talking to Drew Putnam's neighbors all afternoon and by the time they had finished with the last one, Quinn was antsy and a little depressed. None of the other neighbors had been able to give them anything. No one had seen Drew Putnam leave or return on the night of the murder. When it came down to it, none of the neighbors they'd talked to even knew the Putnams very well.

"They've been living here for four years and nobody knows who they are," Marino said once they were in the car, heading back to the city. "Does that strike you as weird?"

"Not really. Most of those people were new anyway. That's just how it is in this neighborhood. They're probably used to sticking to themselves.

"So, what's next?" Quinn asked. "Should we start in with colleagues?"

"Not right now," Marino said. "I'm thinking maybe we should go over to the apartment tonight."

"Brad Putnam's apartment?"

"Yeah."

"Didn't we get everything out of it?"

"I told the lieutenant about the kid's friends doing drugs the night he was killed and he said to go back and make sure there isn't any stuff in the apartment, you know? I mean we checked, but checking when you know something and checking when you don't are two different things. Might as well do it tonight."

"All right. Whatever." Quinn shrugged. He'd been in the

apartment about ten times now and it hadn't offered up anything very interesting, but he was willing to indulge Marino.
He headed for Cambridge and they used the key they'd gotten
from Jaybee.

Quinn took the bedroom and methodically checked every
drawer, every shelf in the closet. He lifted the mattress and
looked carefully underneath. Then he checked under the carpet, to make sure there wasn't a loose floorboard that could be
used as a hiding place. When he was done, he moved on to the
other bedroom and did the same thing. Nothing.

When he came out into the living room, Marino was standing over the empty fish tank. "This aquarium, Quinny," he
said finally. "It was full when we came in here, right?"

"Yeah, there were a bunch of fish. The sister put them all in
a plastic bag, said she was going to take them back to the pet
store or something."

Marino picked up one of the little bottles next to the fish
tank and read the writing on the back. "Flakes for tropical
fish. Do not overfeed." He picked up a little green net, waved
it at Quinn, and then picked up the pair of rubber gloves
folded up next to the tank. "They take a look at these for
prints?" he asked Quinn, holding up the gloves.

"I don't know. He must have used them to clean out the
tank, huh?"

Marino looked at them thoughtfully. "My kid's got a fish
tank. Course he begged me for it for Christmas last year and
now he can't be bothered to even feed 'em once a day."

Quinn watched Marino turn the gloves over in his hands.

"Hey," Quinn said, after a minute. "We've been trying to
figure out all along how the killer got the bag over Brad Putnam's head without leaving any prints. Maybe . . ."

Marino looked up at him and nodded.

"That's what I'm thinking, Quinny. I don't think my wife
ever uses gloves when she cleans out the fish tank. She just
takes the fish out, dumps all the water out, washes the little
rocks or whatever . . ."

Quinn walked over to the kitchen. "They're dishwashing
gloves, aren't they? So what if the killer was looking for a pair

of gloves. He finds them by the sink. Uses them and then can't figure out what to do with them. If he washes them out in the sink, someone's going to notice that there aren't any dishes in the drying rack. Besides, a wet pair of gloves next to the sink is going to look awfully suspicious. But a wet pair of gloves next to the fish tank. You'd think that he'd just been doing something with the tank, wouldn't you?" He thought for a moment. "Wait, the girl, Becca, said one of the fish was dead. When they came in."

"Dead?"

"Yeah, floating on its back. Belly up." Quinn remembered Becca Dearborne telling him about it as she sobbed out the details of finding Brad. "I should have known something was wrong," she'd wheezed. "He never would have left it in there."

"The soap!" Marino said. "The gloves must have had soap on them! The killer uses them, dips them into the tank so it'll look like they were used for cleaning up after the fish or whatever, and then folds them up neatly with all the other stuff. When we first got the aquarium, my older kid thought it would be funny to put bubble bath in there. It was like the Valentine's Day massacre." Marino grinned at him. "We got it," he said. "We got it!"

They bagged the gloves and the rest of the aquarium supplies. "Hey," Quinn said as they were about to get into Marino's car. "There's this guy I've been trying to interview, one of the neighbors. He's been away, but since we're here, maybe we could just see if he's in."

"Sure. Sounds good." Marino locked the gloves and other stuff in his trunk and they went around to the back of the building and knocked on the door. They heard a loud, "Yeah, hang on," then footsteps coming toward the door.

"Hi, yeah?" The guy who had opened the door was about Quinn's age, with spiky dark hair and a lopsided grin. "What can I do for ya?" His accent was South Side—upper crust—Dublin, what Quinn's North Sider mother would have called a "Ballsbridge accent" after the tony suburb.

"Hi," Quinn said. "I'm Detective Tim Quinn of the Cambridge Police Department. Are you Lorcan Lyons?"

"Yeah, that's me. I've been expecting you ever since I heard. Come on in."

His apartment was sparsely furnished, a single, hand-me-down–looking couch in the middle of the living room and a bunch of posters on the wall. The posters all featured what looked like fancy writing from a Bible, huge curling letters with little pictures on them. "Illuminated Manuscripts from Europe," one of them said under the picture. A suitcase, still full of clothes, was sitting in the middle of the living room floor.

"So what can you tell us about Brad Putnam?" Quinn asked, once the guy had told them to sit down on the couch and brought a plastic chair in from the kitchen for himself.

"I'm sorry . . . ?" He looked confused.

"Your neighbor, Brad Putnam. Did you know him?"

"Yeah, of course. But I thought you were here about Alison."

"Alison?" Quinn and Marino looked at each other.

"Alison Cope, the girl who was run down. I couldn't believe it when they told me. I was pretty well devastated when I heard. I didn't know her that well, really. Not yet. But she was quite a girl. She . . ."

Marino was sitting up on the couch, staring at Lorcan Lyons. "Wait a second. You knew Alison Cope?"

"Isn't that why you're here?"

"No. We're here about your neighbor, Brad Putnam. But tell me about Alison Cope."

"Well, we'd been out a few times. She stayed over here the night that Putnam kid was killed. I thought that's why you wanted to see me."

"She was here the night Brad Putnam was killed?" Quinn asked.

"Yeah. She was house-sitting for me. Staying here a couple of nights. We hadn't been dating that long so it was kind of an odd thing to ask her to do, I suppose, but I don't know a lot of people and it gave her a chance to get out of the dorm, you know. Stay in a real house."

"None of her friends knew she was staying here. Why is that?"

"I don't know. She was keeping things kind of quiet. Maybe because I'm older or something. I don't know. Anyway, I gave her the keys and said she could stay."

"But how do you know she was here that night?"

"Because I called to check in and she answered the phone."

"Did it bother you? That she answered the phone?"

"Not really. I don't have any other girlfriends at the moment. It wasn't any problem really."

"She must have seen something that night. What could she have seen that night?" Quinn asked Marino. They both looked at Lorcan.

"I don't know. Brad's apartment's up there." He pointed through the window to a window up on the second floor. "The shades are down now, but he and Jaybee used to leave them up most of the time. She might have seen something through the window."

"Did she say anything on the phone?"

"Not about that."

"You're sure? There wasn't anything that struck you as strange?" Marino asked.

Lorcan shook his head. "I don't think so. I mean, she didn't say anything like, 'Hey, someone's killing Brad Putnam through the window.'"

"Ain't that a bitch," Marino said, grinning.

Quinn thought out loud. "Suppose Alison *had* seen something. What would she have done about it? Why wouldn't she have called us?"

"I don't know," Lorcan said. "Maybe she didn't actually see the person killing Brad, so she didn't realize what she'd seen until later. Or didn't realize there was anything wrong with it until later."

"Yeah." But Quinn was still thinking.

Marino got up to go. "Thanks for your help. If you think of anything, please call me." He got a card out of his pocket and handed it to Lyons. "By the way, where did you meet her? At the university?"

"No. We worked together for a while."

"Where?"

"At the Davis Gallery. We both worked there on weekends."

Quinn said, "The Davis Gallery? The one on Newbury Street? What did you do there?"

"I was kind of a glorified receptionist. I sat at the front desk. Answered phones. Ali worked there for a couple of months doing the same stuff. We'd chat when she came on and I had to give her the messages and whatever. But then she got an internship downtown and she quit. That was when I got the nerve to ask her out."

Lorcan looked curiously at Quinn, who was standing stock still in the doorway.

"The Davis Gallery," Quinn said. "Wait. That's where Jack Putnam shows his work. I think that . . ." He looked at Marino. "I think we've got to get down to Newport."

"Why?"

"I'll explain on the way."

FORTY-SIX

❧

It was as she came around the side of the house that Sweene heard the sirens. Shrill and clear, they rose through the nigl air, and she sprinted around the side of the house to find Kitt Putnam standing in the driveway in a long flannel nightgown

"What's going on? Where's Melissa?" Sweeney called o to her.

Kitty looked up, tears streaking her face. "Oh my God! she said. "Oh my God! She's . . ." and Sweeney looked i through the open front door. Melissa was lying at the bottor of the stairs. She wasn't moving, and as Sweeney rushed t her body, an ambulance came screaming up the drive.

"She's in there," Kitty told the EMTs. They swarmed int the house and then there were more sirens and she looked u to find Quinn standing in the doorway. Marino was in th driveway, talking to some other cops.

He didn't seem surprised to see Sweeney. "Where's Jack? he demanded. "Where is he?"

"I don't know. I wasn't with him." Sweeney was confuse What was he doing here? How did he know? But there wasn time to ask.

"We've got the driveway blocked. Is there any other wa off the property?"

"There's the Cliff Walk," Sweeney said. "Down there." Sh pointed toward the bottom of the lawn.

"Show me." Quinn took a flashlight from his belt an switched it on as they ran down the lawn to the hedge, an

tood there, looking over the Cliff Walk. Quinn's flashlight
ast a wide arc of light on the greenery below.

It was then that she saw the figure on the path, leaning out
ver the rocks.

"Freeze!" Quinn called out. "Police." In a fluid motion that
ouldn't have taken more than three seconds, he had his gun
ut and he was holding it on the figure below. The flashlight
lattered to the ground. "Freeze!" he called out again. In the
noonlight, the figure hesitated, then started running.

Sweeney's heart was pounding. She put a hand on
Quinn's arm. "Don't shoot," she said. "I've got to talk to
im."

It was as though she wasn't there. He stood stock still, the
un trained on the path ahead of him. "I'm warning you that I
vill shoot," he called out again. "Freeze."

Sweeney looked down at the stretch of dark and empty
ath. "I'm going down," she told Quinn. "Look, I think he's
oing to jump. I know what happened. I can talk to him."

"No!" He didn't even look at her. "Do not go down there!"

"I have to. He's going to jump." And before she knew what
he was doing, Sweeney was over the hedge and running
long the Cliff Walk. Ahead of her she heard the low slip-slap
f footsteps against the gravel path. In a quarter mile or so, the
ath would get very rocky. Without a flashlight, it would be al-
nost impossible to make her way.

The moon still hung hugely in the purple black sky and the
ir was scented with salt and something else, honeysuckle
naybe. She felt suddenly alert and alive, like an animal. All
f her senses were in overdrive.

Up ahead was the entrance to the second tunnel. The
noonlight was gone once she was inside. Terrified now, she
elt her way along the wall, feeling first the stone and then the
orrugated metal that lined the moist, rounded walls. After
naybe thirty seconds of shuffling, she saw moonlight again
nd made for the end of the passage.

But first she put her hands out to find the tunnel's walls. In-
tead she found human flesh, warm human flesh that moved

and put its arms out and grabbed her, whispering hoarsel
"Be quiet."

She started to scream, but a hand covered her mouth an
she could taste salty skin against her lips. She felt herself be
ing dragged along the gravel floor of the tunnel and fought fo
breath as the close, damp air gave way to the sky and the
were on the path again, heading for the rocks.

"No," she tried to cry out, kicking and twisting. But sh
was being dragged toward the edge of the path, and belo
were the jagged shapes of the boulders. Below that was th
water.

Then they stopped. The voice was unrecognizable in he
ear. She smelled sweat. "Is she dead? Melissa? Is she dead?"

"No," Sweeney gasped. "They took her to the hospital."

"Oh God."

He let her go and as she struggled to sit up and get he
bearings, Drew Putman made his way to the rocks and s
down, head in hands.

"She may be okay, Drew," Sweeney told him. "It may b
just fine. Let's just go up to the house and talk about this. W
can explain everything to them. It's not too late. You still hav
a chance to go back and make this right."

"How do you know?" It came out in a sob. "You don't un
derstand."

"I think I do." She told him about how she had figured
out, about everything she had learned over the last few week
and finally he stopped crying.

"Let's go back up to the house," she said. "Let's just g
back."

But then they saw the flashlights up ahead on the path, ar
heard Quinn's voice calling out. "Sweeney? Where are you?"

"I'm here," she called back. "Don't shoot. It's okay. He
going to come up to the house and explain everything."

But Drew was already up and running toward the edge o
the path. "No!" she screamed, and closed her eyes as she li
tened to the sound of a body falling against earth. She opene
her eyes.

Quinn had Drew on the ground and he was handcuffing his hands behind his back.

"He needs to explain," Sweeney said. "Just let him explain."

Quinn looked at her and she thought she saw anger in his eyes. "You shouldn't have done that," he told her. "Are you okay?"

"Yes," she said. "But what are you doing here? How did you know to come?"

"We found out that Alison Cope was in Brad's building the night he died. I think she looked up and saw someone in the window that night. And we found out that she worked at the Davis Gallery. I thought that . . ."

It was the last piece she needed.

"Can you tell me what's going on?" Quinn asked her. "Do you know who killed Brad?"

"Yes," Sweeney said. "I do."

"I want to know what's going on." Andrew Putnam told Quinn. "I deserve to know what's happening."

They were all sitting in chairs in the living room at Cliff House, Sweeney at one end of the room with Quinn and Marino and Drew. Quinn had taken off Drew's handcuffs but he was sitting next to him, a hand on the arm of Drew's chair. The rest of the family was sitting on the other side of the room and she was conscious of their bewildered eyes on her, especially Jack's.

"I'm going to let Sweeney explain," Quinn said. "I think she's got all the pieces."

She turned to Andrew and Kitty. "This all started with Petey's death. Five years ago, Camille, Jack, Drew, Brad, and Petey were all in a car and the car crashed and Petey was killed. By the time the police got there, no one was saying who had been driving. But one of the people in that car had been driving that night and was responsible for Petey's death.

"As you all know, Brad was one of my students. A couple of months before he died, we had kind of a strange conversation. He was asking me if I thought he should tell someone something. It was kind of a roundabout way of asking and at the time I didn't know what he was talking about. I do now. Brad was wondering if he should reveal the name of the person who was responsible for Petey's death.

"Then he was killed, and although it took me a while, it finally occurred to me that maybe he had been killed because he was going to reveal that name. He was very angry that night. He got extremely drunk, which was uncharacteristic for him, and his friends say that he was going on and on about how he didn't have courage. I think it's pretty fair to say that he was getting up the courage to reveal the name of the person who was responsible for Petey's death. I think what he was asking me was whether I thought it would make his parents feel better, whether it would give them any peace." She looked around at Camille, Jack, and Drew, then back at Kitty and Andrew.

"When you heard about how Brad had been found, you thought that one of your children might be responsible. I did too, and Jack came forward and admitted it. But then we discovered that in fact Camille had tied Brad up. Assuming she was telling the truth, whoever it was that killed Brad must have come along later and put the bag over his head and, for some reason, put the jewelry on him. That was the thing that I couldn't figure out. Why had this person put the jewelry on him?

"So for a while I was very focused on the jewelry—which turns out to have been the right thing to be focused on. I began to think that maybe Brad had been killed because he was going to reveal something he knew about the jewelry, something that turned out not to be very important. But it was good to be looking at the jewelry and I should have stayed on it. I think that once, I almost got to the truth, but I became very confused about it all."

She stood up. "Think about how Brad was found. The bag had been put on his head first, *then* the jewelry had been put on. That, to me anyway, suggests that the jewelry was something of an afterthought, or at least something that occurred to the killer *after* killing Brad. So why put it on? What if the murderer put it on because he or she hoped that it would point the police away from the truth?"

"What do you mean?" Quinn asked. "Point us away from the truth?"

"Try to picture yourself as the killer. You don't want Brad to reveal what he knows about the night his brother was killed. You think that it's a safe bet he's not going to do it, that he's going to abide by the promise he made that night never to tell a soul. But then one night, you get a phone call. He's drunk. He says that he's tired of the deception. He wants to tell the truth. Finally he wants to tell the truth. You go to his apartment to try to talk to him. But by the time you get there, he's passed out and someone has tied him to the bed. He's going to sleep off his hangover and the next day he's going to go to the police and tell them what he knows. You can't let this happen. You're desperate. The scene already suggests something sordid. What can you do?

"You look everywhere for something you can put over his head. That's all you can do. But there aren't any plastic bags in the house. You look everywhere, opening drawers and cupboards. Nothing. Then you go back into the bedroom and there, on Brad's bedside table, or on his desk, is a plastic bag. It has something in it, some pieces of jewelry, but you dump them out and you put the bag over Brad's head and secure it with the tie and it's all over in just a few seconds." Sweeney said it very softly. "Maybe he doesn't even wake up."

Kitty gasped and began to cry.

"But didn't you find fingerprints on the bag? How did this person not leave fingerprints?" Andrew asked.

Quinn said, "There was a pair of dishwashing gloves. The killer was very smart. He or she used the gloves, then rinsed them out in Brad's fish tank to make it look like he had used them to clean the tank."

Sweeney continued. "So Brad was gone. But what to do with the jewelry? The killer gets an idea. Why not put it on him. It will make the police think he's been with a woman, or had dressed up. They'll try to track it to a woman, start look-

ing into whether Brad was a cross-dresser, anything but t[...]
truth about why Brad was killed."

"But no one would think that," Jack said. "We all kne[...]
where the jewelry had come from."

Sweeney saw realization dawn on Andrew's face. "N[...]
everyone," he said. "Not Melissa."

Kitty looked up sharply.

"Yes," Sweeney said. "It was Melissa who killed Brad."

Camille had begun to cry too and now she got up and ca[...]
to stand next to Sweeney. "But Melissa wasn't driving the c[...]
the night Petey died."

Sweeney looked over at Camille and Jack and Drew. "N[...]
that's right. But she couldn't let the truth about who had be[...]
driving that night get out."

"Oh God," Drew cried. "Oh God."

Sweeney continued. "It was Brad. Brad was driving th[...]
night. But it could have been any one of you, and I think th[...]
you all decided that no one was ever going to know. Y[...]
wanted to protect him and you told him that he was never [...]
let anyone know about it, and that none of you would eithe[...]
She looked at Drew. "I think you thought you were doing t[...]
right thing, but it weighed on Brad. He wanted to come clea[...]

"He always seemed so, just so *sad* to me, and I finally rea[...]
ized that what he asked me that day in my office might ha[...]
been about whether he should reveal his own role in l[...]
brother's death. The night he died, he was very angry and [...]
said to some friends that he didn't have any courage. As [...]
said, I thought maybe he meant that he didn't have t[...]
courage to tell which of his siblings had been driving the c[...]
but I think now that what he meant was that he hadn't had t[...]
courage to reveal that it was him, to stand up to Drew and Ja[...]
and Camille, who after all just wanted what was best for hi[...]

"But that night Brad had decided he was going to tell, [...]
nally. It was a strange night. He and some of his friends h[...]
been spending a lot of time in cemeteries, playing with Ou[...]
boards and having what seemed to some of them to be supe[...]
natural experiences. A month or so ago, while they were pla[...]

ing with the Ouija board, Brad got a message from a so-called spirit, saying it was his brother Peter."

Kitty looked shocked. "What do you mean?"

"I think that Brad made the Ouija board spell out his brother's name because he was feeling guilty. It also spelled out the name of an ancestor who Brad had been doing research on. In any case, in the last few weeks of his life, he was grappling with the question of whether he should come clean about having been the driver the night Peter died.

"The night he died, he had been out with these friends and according to them, he got very, very angry, and then very, very sad. He drank more than was normal for him, and I think he had come to the decision that he was finally going to tell his parents, finally going to face the consequences.

"He made three phone calls, one to each of his siblings, to tell them that he was going to confess. The call to Jack wasn't answered. The one to Camille was, but he didn't tell her what he was going to do on the phone and by the time that she and . . . well that she got to his apartment, Brad was already passed out. She had a very good reason for not being able to stay with him." Sweeney looked at Camille. "So she did the best she could and she left him.

"Brad also called Drew that night, except that Drew didn't answer the call." She looked at Quinn. "When you asked him about it, I remember that he looked kind of surprised. But he went along with it. He had to, because he realized that someone at his house had a seven-minute phone conversation with Brad. What I think happened is that Melissa answered the phone. And Melissa heard Brad say that he was finally going to come clean about the night of Petey's death. And she had to stop him. She told him to go to sleep and then she went to his apartment—Drew must have been out—and she killed him in the way I've described."

"But why didn't Melissa want Brad to confess? I don't understand," Quinn asked. "She wasn't in the car. Drew hadn't been driving. Why would she want to stop him?"

Sweeney looked at Drew. "Because knowing that Brad was

responsible for it was all she had. It was the only way she could hang onto you. Isn't that right? Someone told me that you and Melissa had been very off-and-on and then you got married suddenly after Petey's death. You must have told her about what really happened that night. I don't know if it's why you got married or if it's why you've stayed married, but I think that Melissa threatened to tell about Brad, ruin Brad's life, if you left. She could always hold it over you. And Brad was going to take that away from her."

"But who tried to kill Melissa?" Jack asked.

"That," Drew said, "was me." He began to speak. "I knew almost from the beginning of course. Because of the phone call, as Sweeney said. They asked me what time Brad called me the night he died. I hadn't been there—I was out driving, which I do when I can't sleep—but I knew in that moment that he must have talked to Melissa. I wasn't sure yet that she had killed him. I thought maybe she had gone to talk to him or something, but in any case it implicated her in some way. So without thinking about it, I said I had talked to him. I didn't know what to do. I had lied to the police. It didn't seem like it was going to help Brad to have this huge . . . scandal. I didn't ask her. I didn't want to know. But she knew that I had lied for her and she knew she had me. She knew there was no way I could leave her now, because she was holding the whole thing over me.

"But then that night, the night I hit her with the car, she just told me. We were down here and we were arguing and I was so angry that I couldn't hold it in anymore. I referenced the fact that I had lied for her and she said, 'Do you want to know how it happened?' I was afraid someone would hear so I told her we should go for a drive and as I was driving, she told me about how she had done it. And then she told me that she hit the girl too."

"Alison Cope?" Marino asked. "Melissa hit Alison Cope?"

Drew took a deep breath. "Alison Cope saw her in Brad's apartment that night, through the window. She must have lived in one of the other apartments or something. Anyway, she had worked at the Davis Gallery for a while and she recognized

Melissa from Jack's opening and they had one of those moments of recognition, like, I've seen you somewhere before. Melissa told me she wasn't too worried about it. She just thought she was some girl who worked at the gallery. But then Alison came to Dad's house after the memorial service and introduced herself to us. Later, she got Melissa alone and she said something about having seen her. She didn't want anything, Melissa said, she was just hoping that Melissa had some kind of innocent explanation, so she wouldn't have to go to the police. Melissa made something up, but she could see that the girl didn't believe her. So she asked some kids about her, found out where she works now, and followed her home one night. She said she just drove through the intersection. I couldn't believe what she was telling me.

"She was crying. She felt bad about it. She said she was almost in a dream when she killed Brad, that the only reason she was able to do it was that he was unconscious and it didn't seem like killing really. She just put the bag over his head and he was so drunk he never even woke up. It was like a series of lies and once one thing happened, she had to keep going. I was crying. I didn't know what to do. I told her to get out of the car and she got out and I was going to just let her walk home, but then she looked up at me and it was like she knew she had me. She knew there was nothing I could do. And all of a sudden, I saw that there *was* something I could do. I think I understand what it felt like for her when she killed Brad. There was just this one little thing that she could do—that I could do—to make the whole thing go away. But I couldn't go through with it. At the last minute, I put on the brakes. So she wasn't hurt that badly. She knew I didn't have the guts to kill her. She knew she had me.

"When they told me she was going to be okay, I was relieved. It was like I hadn't done what I'd done. But then tonight, she was lording it all over me again, taunting me with the fact that I hadn't been able to kill her when it came down to it. I knew that it was never going to end."

"Is that why you pushed her down the stairs?"

Drew nodded.

Kitty stood up. "I heard them arguing tonight, and I heard her say, 'You can't ever tell about Brad because I'll tell about you hitting me. You didn't have the guts to kill me then and you don't now.' They were screaming at each other. I heard them go out into the hall. Drew was trying to get her to be quiet, but she wouldn't. I didn't know what to do. I was going to try to go out and stop them, and then I heard her scream and when I looked out I found her, and Drew was gone."

They were all silent for some time and then Drew looked at his parents and he said, "Did you know? We never said anything."

"I knew," Kitty said, crying now. "I knew that the only reason you would lie was to protect Brad. You kids had always protected him. When he was six, he broke my mother's Waterford vase and Jack lied and said he'd done it. Because you were always getting in trouble, Jack. You could handle it. But somehow you knew that Brad couldn't. It was what I thought of, when you wouldn't say anything. I knew right away. That's why we never asked you. You must have thought it was strange that we never asked you."

Andrew took Kitty's hand. "I was there that night. The night of the accident. At the bar. You kids never said anything to the police about it and nobody else did either. But you can't imagine how guilty I was. I . . . I never took another drink and it was why I left your mother."

"He was so riddled with guilt. He couldn't even look at me. I reminded him of Petey," Kitty said, wiping the tears from her cheeks. Andrew let her lean into him, circling his arm around her, and it struck Sweeney that together the two of them looked just about right in the house, Andrew's formality tempered by Kitty's casual sloppiness.

FORTY-SEVEN

Marino and a Newport cop took Drew to the police station to get a statement from him about the hit-and-run and Quinn said that they would be getting statements from all of them the next day.

"For now, you can try to get some rest. The hospital will be calling soon."

Jack walked her out to Quinn's car and Quinn, after looking confused at the way Jack looked at Sweeney, figured it out and said, "I'll just . . . I have a phone call to make. I'll wait in the car."

"Where are you staying tonight?" Jack reached for her hand and she let him take it.

"I don't know. Probably at Anna's."

"My dad's coming down here to stay for a couple of weeks," he said. "Isn't that something? They're going to try to put things back together."

"That's great," Sweeney said. "I'm really happy for you."

"Yeah." He smiled and for a moment he looked like a small boy, before his mouth straightened and she could see how tired he was, how sad he was.

"So after this is all over, can I call you?"

Sweeney took a deep breath of the moist, spring air and stood for a moment, watching him.

"I don't know, Jack."

He pulled her toward him and she saw that his eyes were red with drink and wakefulness. She could smell the tangy staleness of his breath. "Look. This wasn't exactly the opti-

mum way to start a relationship but I feel like there might l
something here and I don't want to regret not finding out wh
it is."

Sweeney looked out into the darkness. She could smell tl
sea air.

"Jack, why do you think you're interested in me?"

"Because you're beautiful and smart and because I'm a
tracted to you, which by the way doesn't necessarily follc
beautiful and smart. But in this case it does."

"I'm not fishing for compliments. I really want to know."

"I don't know." He looked confused. "Do I have to be ab
to explain it?"

"I think you're interested in me because I'm a drinker," sl
said, withdrawing her hand from his.

He tried to give a charming smile. "Well, is there anythir
wrong with that?"

She studied him in the dark, but he was a ghost. "I have
go."

"But—" She turned away from him and got into the c
and nodded to Quinn. They were gone before he could st
them and Sweeney imagined him standing in the drive, tl
yard dropping away behind him.

"Do you want me to take you to your aunt's house to get yo
car?" Quinn asked once they were out on Bellevue Avenue.

Sweeney was silent for a moment. "I want to get back
Somerville. I feel like I just want to get out of here, you knov
But I'm too tired to drive." And though she didn't say it, sl
didn't want to be alone.

"Why don't I drive you back to the house and make
some breakfast," he said after a minute. "Then I'll take yo
home. You can get someone to bring you back for your car.'

She smiled up at him gratefully. "Thanks."

They drove for a few minutes in silence before she sai
"Do you want to know about the jewelry?"

Quinn turned to look at her. "What do you mean? V
found out about the jewelry. The brooch must have be
wrong."

"No, the brooch was right."

"But the test is foolproof. My friend said that . . ."

"The test was right too," she said. "It was the hair that was wrong."

"The hair . . . ? What do you mean?"

"I mean the hair in the locket wasn't Charles Putnam's. I assumed that it was because it was the same color as the hair in the necklace. But there was no reason that Belinda Putnam, if she had a sweetheart in those months after her husband died, a secret sweetheart, that she shouldn't have asked him for a lock of his hair. Perhaps they were somewhere where she didn't have any scissors, so he reached up and he pulled some hair from his head and he gave it to her and she put it in her locket. Locks of hair were used for mourning objects, but they were also used for sentimental jewelry. Sweethearts gave each other locks of their hair to remember each other by. And I think that's what that locket was."

"And he was the father of the baby. So of course that would make sense that the test would match," Quinn said. "But who was he?"

"We don't really have any way of knowing. But I have this idea about that. I was trying to think where she could have met someone. In those days it was quite common for widows to visit their husbands' graves. Remember what I was saying about how Mount Auburn represented a switch in the way that people thought about death? It was a lead-in, in many ways, to the Victorian preoccupation with death, the sort of sentimental attitude about the deceased. I was thinking that it was probably the only time in her day that she was alone. And I was thinking that maybe she met someone at the cemetery. A workman, or perhaps a fellow mourner. I don't know. I have no way of proving this, of course. But it's what I think must have happened."

"Are you going to tell them?"

"I don't think we need to," Sweeney said after a moment. "It doesn't matter to them, really. It doesn't matter to anyone."

The sun was coming up, hesitantly, the light gradually changing from purple to blue to gray as they headed north.

He called his wife from the car. Sweeney watched the sky o
the window and listened to him say softly, "Yeah. I'll be home
forty-five minutes or so. I'm going to bring Sweeney for breal
fast. No, no. Don't worry. I'll make something when I get ther
How are you? Yeah? Did she sleep okay? Yeah, love you too."

Sweeney turned to watch his face as he hung up the phon

"She's expecting us," he said, trying to smile.

"How is she?"

"Much better. Her sister went home and she seems muc
more even. The doctors said it was just a matter of time."

The house was perfectly silent when they came in, and
struck Sweeney that it had been cleaned. There was a vase
daisies on the coffee table and someone had been baking. Th
air was filled with a chocolatey sweetness.

"Maura?" Quinn called out, dropping his coat on th
couch. "We're back." There was something false in his voic
Still, the house was eerily, emptily silent.

Sweeney stood there looking around the room. She wasn
sure why, but her heart was thumping. Later, she wasn't su
if she saw the white rectangle first or if he did, but they we
both staring at it.

"Timmy," it said, in clear, black letters.

"Do you want me to . . . ?" she asked, gesturing at the doc
She's left him, she thought. "I can take the T home."

Quinn didn't say anything, he just stepped forward ar
picked up the letter and stared at it for a moment, turning
over in his hands as though he recognized it, as though it we
an object he knew very well.

Wordlessly, he handed it to her.

"Are you sure . . . ?"

"Please." It came out in a sob.

Sweeney opened the envelope.

"Darling Timmy," the note read. "By the time you rea
this, I'll be gone. I'm in the bathroom, but please don't con
up. I don't want you to see me. I have fed Megan and she ha
gone to sleep. I kissed her. I don't know what I feel for her, b
of course you have to lie and tell her that I loved her when sl
is older and can't remember me.

"I can't explain to you why. I'm a danger to you, to you and Megan. I've been having bad thoughts these last few weeks and it is a relief to have made this decision. You can't know what sweet relief it is. 'Easeful Death.' You said that to me once. I don't remember what it's from, but that's how it feels. When you found me in Mrs. M's garden that day, I knew what I was going to do. It will be fine.

"I love you. And I am sorry."

She looked up to find him racing up the stairs.

"Don't!" she called out. "She doesn't want you to . . ." And she followed him up the stairs, dropping the letter on the floor. She felt that she would do anything she could to stop him from seeing her. But when she gained the landing on the second floor, she found him holding Megan, who was bewildered and had begun to whimper.

"She's dead, isn't she?" He held the baby to his chest, almost crushing her and Sweeney couldn't think of anything to do but to rub his arm. He moved away from her as though he couldn't stand the touch, burying his head in the baby's soft, sparse hair, rubbing his lips against her face. Megan looked up at Sweeney and gave an enigmatic smile.

"I don't know. She wrote that she was going to. Should I . . . ?"

"No, no," he said.

Strange things occurred to her. There was a wedding photo of them in the hall, Maura in a too-puffy dress and odd-looking white headband decorated with beads and crystals, and it struck her that Quinn's hair was too short, that he looked nearly bald in the photo.

"I knew," he whispered, still rubbing his face against the baby's. "I knew as soon as we came in."

Sweeney went downstairs to call 911.

It was a couple of days later that she took out her address book and sat at the kitchen table. Toby had brought her a bouquet of peonies and she leaned forward to inhale their sweet, spicy scent.

She thought of Ivy. Ivy had always loved peonies. She

liked to tuck one behind her ear or in the buttonhole of her dress, pink ones or red ones, to set off her hair, the scent of them trailing behind her as she walked.

Sweeney thought too of Ian, of the words that would have to be answered.

The grass is newly green and everywhere there was a sense of life trickling back into things, of that sweet syrup that runs through all living beings. There were daffodils everywhere I looked, daffodils that not so much fluttered and waved at me as bowed. The fruit trees were in full flower, the branches of the cherry trees like lamb's tails with their heavy flowers.

She turned to the "I's," found the number for Ivy at Summerlands, and copied it out onto a slip of paper. Then she turned the B's, where she'd tucked the business card onto which Ian had written his home phone number all those months ago. She hadn't copied it into her book yet. She wrote that number down on another slip of paper and put it next to the other one.

For a long time she sat staring at the numbers. Finally she crumpled one of the pieces of paper and dropped it into an empty sugar bowl in the middle of the table, next to the peonies.

Sweeney picked up the phone and dialed the code for the United Kingdom, then the number, imagining her voice going out across the air, vibrating along some cables—did they even have cables anymore?—below the vast ocean, carrying out her message, irrevocable.

"Hello?" The voice came clear and loud.

"Hi. It's Sweeney," she said. She pictured the sand shifting with the weight of her words, setting to motion the softly undulating seaweed. It rippled and danced. It would never fall back in the same pattern again.

ACKNOWLEDGMENTS

I ask the forgiveness of the residents of the city of Boston for saddling them with a troublesome and fictitious public works project so soon after a real one.

A number of books were very helpful in my research into Mount Auburn Cemetery and the history of Newport, Rhode Island. Among them were *Silent City on a Hill: Landscapes of Memory and Boston's Mount Auburn Cemetery* by Blanche Linden-Ward; *Lord, Please Don't Take Me in August: African Americans in Newport and Saratoga Springs, 1870–1930* by Myra Beth Young Armstead; and *Newport: A Short History* by C. P. B. Jefferys, and *The Collectors Encyclopedia of Hairwork Jewelry* by C. Jeanenne Bell.

For help with information about their areas of expertise, thanks to Christine Ashcroft of Genelex Laboratories and Frank Pasquarello of the Cambridge Police Department.

I can't express how much I appreciate the dedication and friendship of my agent, Lynn Whittaker, and the help of everyone at St. Martin's Press. Kelley Ragland is an author's editor, and I am grateful for the assistance of Benjamin Sevier, Linda McFall, Rachel Ekstrom, and Carly Einstein.

And for support, commiseration, friendship, and for providing fun, I send grateful thanks to my friends: Kara McKeever, for chicken wrangling and many other things; Kathy Burge and Rich Barlow; Margaret Miller; Rachel Gross and James Sturm; Jennifer Hauck; Susan Edsall; Vendela Vida and Ali

Flynn. A huge thanks to Victoria Kuskowski for design a
friendship. And thanks especially to my family, Tom, S
and David Taylor, for all of their support, and to my wonde
ful husband, Matt Dunne, to whom this book quite literal
owes its existence.

Keep reading for an excerpt from
Sarah Stewart Taylor's next
Sweeney St. George Mystery

JUDGMENT OF THE GRAVE

Coming soon in hardcover from St. Martin's Minotaur

April 19, 1775

John Whiting sat in his father's workshop, looking up at the night sky through the open door. It was a clear night, the blue-blackness filled with stars, and he looked for the ones his father had taught him to recognize, the pinpricks of light making out patterns in the night as surely as his father's chisels etched patterns on stone.

His father liked stars, liked carving them on his grave-stones, and one of John's favorite border designs was the one with the little starbursts along the edge. His father used stars in various ways as ornaments and John remembered when he'd realized that his father found inspiration for his work everywhere around him—the leaves he brought back from his walks in the woods, the summer flowers John's mother collected from the fields and placed in pots around the house. Even seashells and the very waves of the ocean. All of these things ended up on the grave markers made in the workshop of Josiah Whiting of Concord.

John knew that his father was one of the best stonecutters in the area. He knew this because of the way people talked about his work, and because his father was always busy. Lately, it seemed he'd hardly had time to complete one order before another came in. He'd joked to John that people must be dying in greater numbers than usual, for he never seemed to have a moment to spare.

"*Once I have you trained, once the sign on the shop re*
'*Josiah Whiting and Son,' then we'll be able to take on e*
more work," *he'd said only a few days before. Josiah had be*
training John, but John knew it was only wishful thinking t
they'd be able to take on much more work. It was true t
there were things he could do in the shop, the fine carv
work and some of the lettering, but stonecutting was ha
back breaking labor, and with his bad leg, there was no w
John could be much help. There were days when the pain w
so bad he could barely stand.

He shifted in his father's chair, feeling the leg groan at h
He'd learned to handle this kind of discomfort. The best th
was to keep moving, so he lifted himself out of the chair, fou
the cane his father had carved for him leaning up against
wall, and hobbled out into the night air.

As he passed the stable, he heard Monteroy whinnying n
vously in his stall, and the anxiety he'd been feeling ever si
the horse had come barreling into the yard that afterno
still wearing his saddle and saddlebags, the reins trailing a
muddy, returned in force.

Where was he? He should be back by now. It must
nearly midnight and his father had been gone since almost
time the night before. The alarm had been raised that the r
coats were on the march and all of the men from the minu
men companies were to meet at the tavern to take orders. Jo
had watched his father as he'd dressed by the fire. By
rights, he should have gone too. He was sixteen, more than
enough, but he wasn't able to fight anymore than his six-ye
old sister was.

"*You take care of things, John. I'm depending on yo*
Josiah had said as he'd slipped out into the night. He'd tal
John's hand and held it for a moment, a strange, sentimen
gesture, and then he had been gone.

They'd heard news of the shooting on the green in Lexi
ton, and then had heard the shots fired at the bridge. Joh
brother Daniel had run down through the woods and s
shots being fired. He said he'd even seen a dead redcoat ly
on the ground and the minutemen chasing the regulars out

town, shooting at them from behind trees and stone walls. But he hadn't seen Josiah, he said.

John tried to calm himself. His father was an excellent marksman, one of the best in Concord, and he was surely with John Baker, his closest friend, who John himself had been named for. Nothing bad could happen to Josiah if John Baker was there. But then where was he?

John heard a rustle in the trees and he hobbled out on to the path. "Father?" he called into the darkness. There was only silence and then a short "yip" as Jack, the family's spaniel came hurrying up, his tail wagging, and his tongue lolling.

Beyond him, there was only the black and empty night.

ONE

Sunday, October 10

Sweeney St. George had just found another example of a gravestone by the elusive round skull carver, when the late afternoon peace of the cemetery was broken by the sound of gunfire.

"Crack! Crack! Crack!"

Without looking to see where it was coming from, she hit the ground, her arms covering her head, her heart slamming against her rib cage, all of her nerves going nuts as she heard another series of shots come quick and fast.

"Crack! Crack! Crack!"

"Don't worry. It's just pretend," said a voice behind her, and Sweeney turned to find herself facing someone who at first appeared to be a short man with a high, girlish voice. His bald head glinted in the sun and he looked up at her with huge eyes in a pale face.

But he wasn't a man. He was a boy, a completely bald boy of about eleven or twelve and as Sweeney looked into his intense brown eyes, which gave him the look of a young Ben Kingsley, the boy flushed and looked away. He reached down quickly for a baseball hat lying on the ground, and put it on his head. "It's a reenactment. Up at the Old North Bridge."

"You mean, like Civil War reenactors and all that?"

"Yeah. Except it's not the Civil War. It's the Revolutionary War." She almost expected him to finish up with a "duh."

"Oh yeah, we're in Concord, aren't we?"

She had come out to Concord in order to find some more examples of the work of the eighteenth century stonecutter Sweeney had come to think of as the round skull carver. Sweeney, who studied gravestones and other funerary art for a living, had been after the round skull carver for months now, ever since she'd seen one of his stones in a Lexington cemetery and been intrigued by his unusual border designs, and his oddly shaped death's heads. They were very human death's heads, she thought. That was the best way to describe them, with their round skulls and almost cheery expressions. She had found five stones she was positive had been made by the same carver and after a doing a bit of asking around, discovered that no one knew who he was. So she had done what she normally did when looking for a carver's identity and checked the Middlesex County probate records for the names of the people buried beneath the round skull carver's stones. The records often stipulated payment to this or that gravestone carver for the deceased's stone, and it was one of the only ways of finding a particularly elusive carver. She hadn't had any luck yet, but now that she had found one of the stones in Concord, she could try again. And Edward Martin's stone boded well because it was large one, with elaborate carving on the side borders. It had cost a nice sum when it had been made in 1740, and since Edward Martin seemed to be a man of means, there was a good likelihood that he would have a probate record stipulating where his worldly possessions would go after death.

And, here, in the South Burying Ground in Concord, i

hadn't taken her long to find another one. It was all there, the distinctive shape of the skull, the delicate wings at its side, the odd, unnaturally twining plants in the border design, the cramped lettering the carver had used to write, "Here Lyes the body of Edward Martin."

The boy looked down at her notes. "What are you doing?"

"I'm taking notes on this gravestone. I'm trying to figure out who made it."

The boy sat down next to her and looked at the stone. "You don't know who made it?"

"No, it's not signed, but I've found a whole bunch of stones around here that I'm almost positive he made, and now that I have Edward Martin's name, I can see if his will lists the name of the person who made his stone. It's kind of like being a detective." Another shot sounded and Sweeney started. "That didn't sound pretend," she said.

"Well, they don't put any bullets in the guns," the boy said. "They're not allowed to. And the ones up at the Old North Bridge, they're not even allowed to point the guns at each other. So it's kind of stupid. They just, like, shoot them up in the air. My grandfather has reenactments up in his field, though, and up there they can pretend they're really fighting because it's not National Park property. They did Battle Road at the last one, which is also stupid because it's not even the right time of year."

Sweeney didn't say anything, but clearly more explanation was needed and he went on.

"Well, you know, the Old North Bridge and the shot heard round the world, that whole thing, that was in April." He looked around at the orange, red and yellow trees and, as though he were breaking something to her, said gently, "This is October."

"That was when we shot back at the British, right? I kind of forget my Revolutionary War history."

He looked up at her, his face swollen and puffy, then said condescendingly, "The British regulars were on their way out to Concord because they were going to take all the guns and stuff from the provincials. So the minutemen and everybody stood on the green in Lexington, and the British shot at them and killed a bunch of them. No one thought they would actually do it. Then they came to Concord and we thought they were burning houses down. So the provincials decided they'd had enough and they went up to the North Bridge. No one really knows who fired the first shot, but we got a bunch of them. The redcoats had to run away back to Charlestown, and the minutemen hid in the fields and behind the walls. They never knew what hit 'em. That was called Battle Road."

Sweeney remembered a bit of Longfellow, something her father used to recite. She quoted, " 'You know the rest. In the books you have read/How the British regulars fired and fled . . . ' Do you know that one?"

The boy picked it up. " 'How the farmers gave them ball for ball/From behind each fence and farmyard wall/Chasing the redcoats down the lane/Then crossing the field to emerge again.' " Here Sweeney remembered the rest and she joined in again. " 'Under the tree at the turn of the road/And only pausing to fire and load.' "

He smiled up at her. "Of course, Longfellow kind of added stuff. You know, like, to make it sound better. But that's how we won the war," the boy said in an authoritative way. "The British liked to fight in the open field, and we knew how to fight guerrilla style."

"So, what, did you write a book or something?" Sweeney sat down on the ground and leaned her back against the gravestone, wrapping her arms around her knees. It was October and, though they'd had a few nice days last week, there was no denying it was getting cold.

"No, I just read a lot. My mom is director of the Minuteman Museum, so she knows about all this stuff. And my dad likes it, too."

"Yeah? What does he do?"

"Oh," he said disinterestedly, reaching up to scratch his scalp under the baseball hat. "He makes gravestones."

Sweeney studied him for a moment. The puffiness of his face made him seem younger than he must be. Studying his eyes she decided he was closer to 12 than 10.

"That's a coincidence," she said. "I study gravestones."

"That why you're here."

"Yeah. I'm an art historian. Do you know what that is?" A nod. "So, I study gravestone carving over time, the different art that was used. That's why I'm out here actually. I'm working on a paper about eighteenth-century gravestones."

"You mean like for school?"

"Kind of. I don't have to hand it in to a teacher, though. It's going to be published in a journal."

He didn't say anything for a moment and she was anticipating the usual bewildered response to her odd livelihood, when he stood up and, gesturing her to follow, led her over to a stone near the back of the cemetery. "That was made by one of our ancestors," he said.

She studied the stone. It was a tall slate headstone with elaborately carved shoulders and a rounded tympanum, giving the stone the "bedboard" shape that had become common among early New England stonecutters.

The strange death's head at the top of the stone was about the size of an actual human face. The skull was shaped like a lightbulb, with wide-set, rounded eyes, complete with pinpoint pupils. The mouth was a crude box, filled with lines that approximated skeletal teeth. But what its creator had carved above the figure's head was the remarkable thing. The skull had a Medusa-like head of hair, thick tendrils that rose above it in an electrified halo. In contrast to his hair, the skeletal face stared out blandly from the stone, seemingly unperturbed. She read the name on the stone, Abner Fall, and the dates of his life and death, 1721 to 1760. In the thin light, it was impossible to make out the very faint epitaph at the bottom.

"So what was this ancestor's name?" Sweeney had seen some similar stones near Plymouth, but the medusa heads were unusual for the Concord area. She was intrigued.

"Josiah Whiting. He was like my great-great-great-great-great-grandfather or something. A lot of greats."

"How much do you know about him?"

"Well, he made gravestones. And he fought in the war." He clarified. "The Revolution. He was some kind of hero or

something. My grandpa's always talking about it. He's a
member of the Concord Minutemen. Josiah was a member of
them, too."

"Is your dad a reenactor, too?"

"No. He was in Vietnam and he says that he doesn't like
war, even pretend ones. He won't even go to them. But I like
the ones where you can see people die, or pretend to die. It's
interesting. It's like a play, kind of, it's like you can see what
it might be like."

"So you said your dad makes gravestones. Does he own a
monument company?"

"Yeah. Well, I guess the family really owns it. My grandfather."

"What's it called?"

"Whiting Monuments."

It was one of the big ones in the Boston area. "I'm
Sweeney St. George by the way." She offered her hand.

"Pres Whiting." He shook her hand seriously, looking up at
her for a minute with those dark, huge eyes and then looking
away. "I never heard of anybody studying gravestones before."

"Well, I spend a lot of time in cemeteries, taking pictures,
tracing the work of different stonecarvers, and sculptors. I
usually teach, too, so, you know, I spend a lot of time with my
students, helping them and stuff, though I'm not teaching
right now." She hoped she didn't sound bitter about it. A lowly
assistant professor, Sweeney hadn't been assigned any classes
for the fall, so she was using the time to work on some of her
own research.

Pres reached up to scratch his head again, then gave up and
took the hat off. Through the thin skin stretched over his skull,
Sweeney could see snaking blue veins, a few burst blood ves-
sels. She saw a vein twitch on his temple and he seemed a
shade or two paler. But maybe it was just the light.

"Yeah, I like cemeteries, too. I like to sit in them and read
the stones. A lot of the kids at school think I'm weird because
of it. But then they pretty much just think I'm weird. Even before this." He pointed to his head. "Now it's even worse. It's

because of chemotherapy," he explained suddenly, as though he was afraid she would think it was something else.

"I'm sorry." She didn't ask why he had to have chemotherapy, even though she wanted to know.

He looked sad for a minute. "Did people ever, like, think you were weird because you liked to go to cemeteries?"

She smiled. "Oh, yeah. I was *so* weird when I was a kid. Weirder than you probably. How old are you?" Sweeney asked him. What she really wanted to ask him was how sick he was and if he was going to be okay.

"Twelve." He pulled a fleece jacket out of his backpack and put it on, zipping it up to his chin. "How old are you?" But she could see he was just asking to be polite. Anyone over twenty probably just seemed old to him.

"I just turned 29, last week."

"Oh. What did you get?"

"Nothing much. It's different when you get older. Too bad, really."

"Yeah." He looked off into the distance, then closed his eyes for a moment and Sweeney felt a flash of concern. He *was* pale. She could see it now. He looked the way people looked before they threw up. When he took a deep breath, she could hear the air in his lungs.

"Are you okay?" she asked him.

"Yeah. I'm just tired. I'm going to walk home."

"Can I give you a ride?"

He looked horrified. "I'm not supposed to get in cars with strangers." He stood up and waited for a minute before hoisting his backpack on to his shoulder.

"How far do you have to go?"

"Just up to my grandparents' house. They live up by the North Bridge." Sweeney had walked past the Old North Bridge yesterday. It was a good three quarters of a mile up Monument Street.

"Do you want me to walk with you?"

"No."

She hesitated, not sure what to do. "Okay, well it was nice to meet you. Maybe I'll see you around."

He studied her for a minute. "Yeah, I like to go to cemeteries."

"Okay then. Bye." She watched him walk off, making his way slowly along Main Street. He walked like an old man, his steps slow and cautious, as though each one hurt him. Sweeney gathered up her notes and slung her bag over her shoulder. And before she knew what she was doing, she was walking along, keeping the top of his head in view. She could follow him for a little bit, just to make sure that he got there okay. She'd be able to stay out of sight and that way, if something happened, if he collapsed or got sick, she could call and get him some help. If he caught her, she could just say she was walking up to the Old North Bridge.

Up ahead of her, Pres Whiting walked slowly along Main Street, then turned left and walked across Monument Square. She thought about how there were certain people who you met in life, people who stuck with you, who you were willing to take care of, and how once you had taken responsibility for them, it was hard to give it up. It was dangerous to take that responsibility at all. You never knew where it was going to lead. I'm just making sure he gets home okay, she told herself. That's all. And Sweeney, who did not pray, found herself saying a prayer for him, a prayer that he would be okay.